UNSECRET IDENTITY

ERIC ICARUS  BOOK ONE

UNSECRET IDENTITY

ERIC ICARUS  BOOK ONE

JON MCBRINE

CONTENTS

UNSECRET IDENTITY

ERIC ICARUS — BOOK ONE

ERIC BOXWORTH
SKETCHBOOK
PRIVATE
Me→

Chapter One: *UP*

DAVID

"**P**OWER!"

David had their attention now They were a small group of high-ranking uniformed officers and money guys in expensive suits who would ordinarily have better places to be. They were all important, and most notably, they were all there, listening to what David had to say.

"We all crave it, but what is it really? Loyalty, trust, love, influence, blah-blah-boring. No, no, no—I mean power."

David moved across the wide stage only a few feet above his audience. A middle-aged man, he wore his graying-brown hair slicked back and allowed some stubble for a sleek but rough-and-tumble look to impress his potential buyers. His clothes blended with the black curtain, and he positioned all the stage lamps to spotlight him; David was the one speaking, after all. Above him, a sizable sign bearing the words "BOXWORTH DREAMINEERING" gleamed in the light. That sign—that name—had to be big so they could all see it and know.

"Is power control?" David said into his microphone

headset. "Yeah, but I think I should rephrase my question to be, 'What powers power?' Dominance, strength, maximum magnanimous might...! Guess what? They don't mean jack without power. You got power over a big pile of nothing if you can't so much as light a light bulb. But it's not all about wattage and joules, gentlemen and ladies. What fuels your fate? Long ago, I asked myself this very question..."

Huddled tightly in the large showroom, David could sense the crowd's patience collectively slipping. For many of them, this wasn't the first time they'd heard David speak, and he was fearful that they'd already made up their minds.

"You need a power source for your force, of course!"

David proudly smiled as the words left his mouth. Then the air left the room. An older military general in the audience leaned over to a woman in uniform next to him.

"We coulda used a bomb like that in the war!" he whispered.

The woman's face remained polite but nodded in approval.

David cleared his throat.

"Without energy, simply put, nothing works."

The general leaned in the opposite direction, this time to a slick businessman.

"If he tries to sell us that ultra-robo-what's-it again, I'm not kidding; I'll put on that suit myself and do the Cha-Cha."

The smirking suit coughed into his hand to cover his grin.

"Why, without power," David said, soldiering on, "not even the premier weapon in modern warfare can be utilized!"

David gestured to his right.

"Not even..."

From behind David, heavy, slow thumps quaked the floor, followed by mechanical whirring sounds.

"...the Ultranaut warsuit!"

The curtain gave way to a hulking suit of armor at least seven feet tall, walking up the stage. The metal beast towered above David with its bulky, geometrically shaped shoulders. Thick-coated green wires covered its robotic frame, snaking in and out of the rectangular arm and leg casings.

"The ultimate in wearable war-tech," David went on, "this near-indestructible suit of armor marries the pinnacle of bionic battlefield weaponry with irreplaceable human ingenuity!"

Thrusters on the hefty boots complemented a wide, smooth jetpack on its back. Sleek cannons mounted on the gauntlets and the thick chest plate made for an imposing figure. White paint coated the armor plating with light blue accents in stripes, plates, and other outlining dots.

David waved at his creation, bursting with pride. He pointed to the side of the helmet where angular steel sheets with blue lights blinked from tiny apparatuses. The helmet itself was made of thick, transparent glass with a greenish tint. What was perhaps most impressive was that it was a fully automated unit with no person inside.

Right on cue, techno music blared from unseen speakers. The hollow armor's exterior lights flickered and beamed, putting on a small light show. From above, rafter-mounted air machines sprayed mists of theatrical smoke engulfing the Ultranaut suit. A woman in the audience coughed.

Ultranaut posed with cannons aimed high, then

swiveled to a fighting stance, targeting the crowd. Fear washed over the general's face as he readied for an attack, but instead of bullets, confetti popped out of the cannons in a glistening display. The audience snickered, but the general was not amused.

The machine flexed its bionic biceps upward, then downward, and bent one arm to pose while the other pointed to the distance. It broke out into a robot dance, hamming it up. Nervous, David softly clapped. The music cut off. The suit's lights stopped blinking. The armored shell saluted and then stood at attention. The general rolled his eyes. David waited a rehearsed moment for them to awe at his invention's mechanical majesty.

It was a moment of silence.

"Ultranaut is, um, an impressive show of, eh, force."

David shuffled across the stage in quiet awkwardness, closing the distance between himself and the suit of armor quicker than he had planned.

This is your last chance, David, he thought. *Time to earn your place in the history books.*

"It is not, however, this morning's focus. No, we are not here today to discuss what is the, er, next wave of battle-wear such as Ultranaut..."

While there was little to no motion in front of him, a blur caught his attention from stage left. Squinting under the stage lamps, David spotted a fourteen-year-old with unkempt brown hair and a drab olive-green short-sleeved shirt worn the day before. The boy scurried along the second-tier promenade lining the large room. In seconds, he disappeared into a hallway just above the stage lights.

Fantastic. Eric is running late—again—and will probably miss the bus—again, David thought. *Driving him to school is all I need. I can't keep these people waiting. People I'm lucky that showed up on such short notice, let alone see me at all.*

The assembly's indifference toward Ultranaut was palpable. A guy with a mustache in a pressed suit surfed his phone. Others joined in as little squares lit up in the crowd.

"...But rather, um," David said, swallowing his pride with a literal gulp.

A disheveled man in the front row whacked the side of his bulky smartphone. The screen's light flickered, and he let out a frustrated grumble. David recognized the device's defective design.

Must be a representative from Slate Technologies, David thought. *If it weren't for me, they'd be the laughingstock of the tech world. Not for long.*

"We're here to talk about what powers this marvel of the modern age."

A single drop of sweat slid down David's well-lit forehead.

"Imagine a clean energy source that could power an army of Ultranaut warsuits!"

David looked down at the bored faces of his uninterested audience.

"Or! Or! Or—an entire city!"

Every head in the audience snapped up, and all eyes locked on David, just as he'd planned. Clean energy had the science world abuzz with possibilities. It was a proverbial goldmine.

"And not just within our lifetime," David continued. "I'm talking about right now. Right here and now!"

The mustache guy in the crowd lowered his phone, letting its screen brighten his face. David couldn't believe he didn't recognize him before.

Baron Maddox, he thought, forming a smug grin. *The head honcho of a multi-billion-dollar tech company, here to see what his little ol' former partner has to show. This is too perfect.*

"Clean energy, folks. And where does this clean energy come from?" David said. "Well, what's cleaner than air? Okay, so I know we have kind of a smog issue here in New St. Cloud City, so, not the best example, but..."

The general looked at his wristwatch.

"Look, I don't know about you," David said. "But I can't wait to live in a world where we have the power to rely on ourselves and not some costumed jerks calling themselves 'superheroes.'"

That got a big sarcastic "oh, really?" smirk from Baron. David ate up how sweet it was going to be, proving Baron and everyone else wrong. Even in the low light, the audience's sour faces reminded David that he stayed in the minority of loathing the Super Society.

"I, uh, that is to say, um, what I am proposing is that we take, well, you see, we basically can suck the molecules and atoms right from the air and—"

David closed his eyes for a moment, trying to find the resolve to hold it together.

"Energy is all around us," David said. "But without a way to properly harness this energy, then it's lost to us, or worse, something tragic could happen."

Ultranaut powered down with a *bwoo* sound that trailed off into nothingness. The helmet and shoulders sunk, and its lights faded.

"Breaks my heart every time I see that."

He wiped his misty eyes. David had achieved the antithesis of crowd work: the audience stood confused, silent, and a little creeped out.

Baron went back to surfing the web again. David's nostrils flared at the disrespect. All words abandoned him, and his thoughts became a garble.

Come on, David, he thought. *If you don't pull yourself together, you might as well kiss any chance at funding goodbye.*

"What if I told you I have developed a device that can convert the air around us into pure, clean, sustainable energy more powerful than anything that has ever come before?"

David knew he had to squeeze the trigger and reveal the hook.

"What if I told you I have that device right here, ready to go now?"

The curtains retracted, unveiling a massive translucent, white-domed structure with four large black metal arms running up the surface, connecting at the center. A grid-like pattern cascaded across the dome's surface. It lit up as it began its activation process, providing additional light so that David could better see the faces of those in the audience.

"I present to you—the MegaCore."

Bluish-pink light radiated from lengthy tubes that encircled the dome's broad base. A heavy hum set the room abuzz as the dome emitted a soft, white light, phasing in and out of dullness. David walked across the stage, pointing at his large invention.

Wires and cords surrounded the dome, attached to it like eels bunched together in a bind, coiling around the floor to different bulkheads. Monitors large and small displayed data tracking information forming a wall behind the dome. Workstations lined up across the wall as automated drones zipped around in the air, each emitting light beams fizzling into holographic projections of the dome's status.

"This amazing feat of technological advancement can sustain massive amounts of energy for months at a time," David said, walking backward across the stage. "The syntho-stasis units are automated and self-repairing, maintaining optimum performance at all times."

Metal arms lowered cranes with repair tools and cameras to inspect the generator's functionality. The drones and cranes maneuvered behind the dome with syncretic ease. David smiled a satisfied grin at the dazzling demonstration of cybernetic development. The Ultranaut suit, however, stood dormant.

The audience's mouths hung ajar in awe of what they witnessed. A woman rubbed her glasses' lenses, seemingly unconvinced she was seeing what was right in front of her. Despite the audience's apparent astonishment, the severe absence of applause queued a tiny heart attack waiting on standby within David's chest. He waited for something, anything, in the form of an audible reaction.

Finally, a sound came.

"I'm sorry, I have to take this," Baron said, sidestepping by other guests to make his exit into the darkness.

It's the V-neck. They hate the V-neck, David thought.

He nervously covered his upper chest, partially exposed from his attitudinal attire. David then stormed to center stage. He tried pushing Ultranaut, but the thing weighed a ton. Finally, David stepped in front of the armor and faced his inactive audience.

"The MegaCore absorbs molecules and atoms from the air through the dome's surface-filtration matrix. It converts the collected particles and other elements from the environment and transmutes all of them into pure energy. I'm through being humble about it; this is going to change the world!"

"So, if I cough on this thing, it'll power up my coffeemaker?" the old general remarked, snickering to the uniformed woman beside him.

"I'm sensing you're more of a show-not-tell kind of crowd," David said. "So, how about a demonstration? That's what you all came here for, right?"

David whipped out his smartphone from his front pants pocket and hovered his finger over the touchscreen.

"When I simply tap this button on my command device, I initiate the action sequence, and the MegaCore will launch the transference process! The power will channel through the generator's engine and expel it throughout this building, turning my headquarters into a brilliant beacon lighting up the city!"

From below the stage, the audience watched as David inched, centimetered, millimetered his fingertip closer to the lit screen of his mobile device.

"Like a vacuum, the MegaCore will absorb enough particles to give you the biggest, best display of next-gen, bleeding-edge tech you've ever seen! Get ready, this is going... to... 'suck!'"

David's fingerprint gently lowered to the screen like a feather's touch.

BOOM!

ERIC

"Next time there's a big explosion, I need to remember not to land right on my butt," Eric whispered while creeping up the hallway.

He winced as his back pressed against the wall. The shiny plastic mallet in his hand rattled. Eric tightened his grip, quick to steady his only means of defense. Its hollow piggybank-like interior carried enough quarters to give it some oomph in case he had to use it—as well as enough noise to attract any unwanted attention from whoever had attacked.

Peeking over the guardrail showed him the dim MegaCore, dull from inactivity.

It's not in a million pieces, Eric thought. *But if that's not what caused the mini-earthquake we just had, then what—or who—did?*

Eric's jaw dropped at the disarray of the first floor. The audience members had gone to whatever hiding spots they must have found, leaving room for colorful figures to occupy the floor. Seeing the Super Society up close felt different than Eric expected. Their unconscious costumed bodies strewn about his home made a freaky first impression.

Whoa! What're they doing here?! he thought, gazing slack-jawed at the KO'd crime-fighters.

Eric pondered if he had summoned them via some cosmic happenstance. He looked at the novelty hammer in his pale hand—a gold-painted replica of the Golden Gavel used by Judge Justice, the leader of the original Super Society, the city's greatest protectors of yesteryear. It even said as much on the engraving on the handle.

What could take them all out like that? The O.G. Society would never go down like this.

One of the teen heroes stirred in the rubble, silhouetted by the sunlight pouring in. Petite and blonde Powerhouse rummaged through where the kitchen used to be—she flipped over the solid steel oven and lifted the fridge with ease. Eric's eyes popped, watching the girl's metallic arms do such heavy lifting. A big yellow guy lay motionless near the stage, which Eric took as an excellent sign. The jaundiced behemoth was a mystery, but he looked like a nasty supervillain type.

Eric gawked at the massive hole in the rear wall.

They crashed right through the building!

The damage would be enough to anger his father, David, but expensive equipment flung everywhere would get him raging.

Add a superhero smackdown interrupting his big presentation, and Dad should be ready to go nuclear.

"BRAIN..." Eric said, placing the gavel on the floor with a shaky, unsure hand.

His phone displayed the words "BRAIN – Boxworth Remote Artificial Intelligence Network."

"Awaiting your command," the robotic voice said from his phone's speaker—loudly.

Eric punched the volume down button.

"Where's Dad?" he said quietly, enunciating each syllable to avoid repeating. "Where's everybody else that's not wearing tights?"

"The building's system is operating at forty-five percent," BRAIN reported. "I will require repairs before I can complete your request—"

"Forget it," he said, sighing as he pocketed his phone. "Can't risk waking up the yellow dude. Gotta make a move, though. Gotta make sure the—"

"Coast is clear!" David said from below.

Eric leaned over the rail to see David poking his head up from the side of the stage.

"I've already lost so much," David said. "I won't let some super-freaks take my sign, too!"

The long Boxworth Dreamineering banner

sagged, in danger of slipping away. The Super Society's crashing entrance loosened the hooks suspending the sign. Gashes, scratches, and frayed edges decorated the green lettering.

"That's what you're worried about? Are you for real?!" Eric said under his breath.

An old army general popped up from the stairs on the opposite end of the walkway.

"Thought I saw somebody up here!" the old-timer whispered. "Better make yourself scarce, boy! No sense in waiting to get your eggs scrambled!"

"Hey!" Eric hissed. "You're an army guy! Shouldn't you be calling, y'know, the army?!"

"Don't need to! The Super Society is already here!" the general said before slinking down the stairs.

Guttural grunts came from below.

"They pass on Ultranaut, scoff at the MegaCore," David grumbled. "I can't let those vultures think David Boxworth is dead to the science world!"

Eric darted his eyes to see David climbing the access ladder attached to a tall girder.

"Dad!" Eric whisper-yelled.

A few broken rafter-mounted lamps darkened the area, but the remaining lights were still difficult to bear. Squinting, David outstretched his arm, but the support beams stood just out of reach.

"Powerhouse!" an unmistakable voice shouted.

Startled, Eric looked over his shoulder to see Truther on the first floor, getting to his knees.

Though his cowl was black with a thick metallic, golden "T" placed over where his eyes and nose would be—as well as extending over his upper lip—Truther's face and chiseled chin made him instantly recognizable. Truther's wavy blonde hair danced in the breeze blowing in from the large hole in the wall.

Eric's fandom of the first Super Society peaked when he was around nine, but he couldn't ignore the grand spectacle.

He's right there! Judge Justice's former sidekick, Sidebar, all grown up as Truther, the adult leader of the new team! Eric thought as a whirlwind of nostalgia jostled in his mind. *Wow... this would be so much more awesome if I wasn't a hundred percent sure I'm going to pee myself.*

Powerhouse ran up to Truther.

"You're okay!" she squealed. "I thought you were, I mean, I was looking for, but—!"

"Go-Go, Extra, and Supercut are down," Truther said. "Check on your teammates, hero!"

A litany of garbled swear words caught Eric's ear. David was at eye-level with him, ten feet away.

"I can't fail the business again!" David muttered.

Eric's father leaned his body over to extend his reach. David's fingertips grazed the banner's border.

"Dad, what are you doing?! It's just a sign!"

"That banner is our family's flag! It stays up no matter what!"

David's hand on the ladder slipped. Eric's heart stopped. David steadied himself, and Eric could breathe again.

"Hang tight, Dad! One of the superheroes will save you!"

Eric waved to the floor below, but the oblivious heroes did not notice.

"Your rampage ends here," Truther announced as he approached the unmoving yellow giant. "It's over, Cybertooth!

He reached into his utility belt and whipped out a pair of silver shackles.

"Good thing you still have feet and that these are

expandable."

Cybertooth spun to face Truther, revealing more of his bizarre features. Below his nose, a flat, metal plate covered his mouth—a vertical line ran down the center of this steel mouthguard, making for an evil robo-beaver appearance. Cybertooth coughed out a glitchy snarl as if regurgitating static.

His metal tooth-plate flipped up—a small metal orb launched from his mouth. Truther raised his arm's T-gauntlet and fired a pulse of energy at the speeding ball. The spherical bomb detonated on the impact of the laser blast, erupting into a white wave of energy.

BWOOSH!

Eric clamped his hands onto the guardrail, riding out the vibrational force. David held onto the buckling ladder for dear life. The girder shrieked with tension. The support beams bent under pressure. The long strut above the stage shook, wiggling the lamps mounted to it. The wavering sign slipped away as the hooks behind it followed suit; one by one, they popped free.

The big banner fell and was about to belong to the air when David stretched his body, grabbing hold of the edge.

"Dad, no!" Eric screamed.

Unable to avoid his fate, David leaped from the teetering ladder, surrendering to the fall.

Eric felt his body lift. His limbs felt hollow. Weightless, he knew just to push. Instinct carried him over the guardrail. He grabbed the collar of David's V-neck, then gripped his armpits. He hoisted his father up, rescuing him from being a heap of broken bones on the stage below. Eric's feet dangled, floating.

Eric's hands trembled like they were going to wriggle off his wrists. He struggled to lift David, who outweighed him by nearly a hundred pounds. They hovered with Eric's arms now wrapped around David's waist. David dropped the sign, staring at his son as if for the first time.

"I've got you, Dad," Eric said softly.

David's breathing grew rapid and heavy. His face tightened as if fighting to hide any emotion. A moment of unbearable silence passed between them.

JAYCEE

Jaycee couldn't believe what she was seeing. She blinked like crazy under the canary-yellow domes over her eyes. Steadying herself on a toppled-over workbench, she raised her head, straightening her blue Powerhouse mask. She saw Eric Boxworth, a slight boy her age, short and lacking muscles, carrying his father, David, as they descended. Eric's body was semi-svelte if someone could be such a way. In all honesty, he had a sort of skinny-fat thing going on. Eric sucked wind as they landed.

Eric looked petrified, but David just stared at him. Finally, David said something, but Jaycee couldn't hear whatever it was that unnerved Eric. He hurried off past the massive domed structure and disappeared out of sight.

Jaycee looked around, but everyone lay still, knocked out or slow to recover. Even Cybertooth appeared out cold. Jaycee returned her attention to the stage to see David walking away in a huff. He may not have looked amazed, but Jaycee tingled in sheer awe of what she had seen David's son do. Jaycee hushed herself as if not wanting to wake up the rest of the

world, but she couldn't hold in her wonderment.
"He can fly!"

SPRING
FORMAL
DANCE

Chapter Two: *TAKEOFF*

JAYCEE

SHACKLES SNAPPED AROUND CYBERTOOTH'S ANKLES. Truther pressed an electronic locking mechanism in the center of the chains. A little red dot lit up.

"Take this piece of cyber-trash to the HQ, Go-Go!" he commanded.

Truther posed while Go-Go swooped in to grab the disoriented Cybertooth. Her psychedelic-patterned tunic materialized as the speedster slowed. Her curly hairdo wiggled into place.

"Sure thing, Truther!" Go-Go said. "This will only take a sec."

Go-Go took the defeated villain by the feet and bolted away. The *whoosh* of air flipped up Jaycee's ponytail. Extra and Supercut stood behind Truther in the middle of the wrecked showroom. Military officers, executives, and financiers had emerged from their scattered hiding spots to bask in the heroes' glory.

The squad cars' red and blue emergency lights flickered in the periphery from outside the damaged building, just beyond the huge hole. Police officers joined the gathering crowd in gushing over the superheroes.

Supercut stretched his hands. Steel, stubby contraptions encased both his right and left index fingers. With a *fikt* sound, two identical blades sprang out. Supercut taunted, hooking his finger-blades and taking mock-jabs at the laughing group of businessmen and women. Supercut's bare arms were hairier than most grown men's—he was like a little round furball everywhere except his boyish face, which always made Jaycee giggle.

Big, bad baby-faced Melvin Medina, she thought, shaking her head while trying not to laugh.

Extra projected a row of duplicates of herself, posing for selfies. Jaycee rolled her eyes at the chain of red spandex, exposed midriffs, orange utility belts, and oversized steel discs wrapped around every shoulder.

Tiffany is on the team for two minutes and gets to redefine tackiness, Jaycee thought. *But when I request one small upgrade for my strength-enhancers, I get a lecture about budgets. So unfair.*

"Citizens, the Super Society appreciates your cooperation," Truther spoke aloud to no one in particular. "And always remember, a life of lies lands you in jail, but the truth shall set you free!"

Truther shook a few hands while Extra and Supercut signed some autographs. Jaycee's head floated in the clouds.

Did I really see what I saw? Did I see Eric fly?

A few yards away, brooding in a shadowed area of the floor, David sat alone on a bulky synthetic humanoid prototype. The motionless robotic endoskeleton erratically spewed purple fluid from vents on its cybernetic face. It popped with electricity sparks.

Mr. Boxworth has been awfully quiet, Jaycee thought. *Is he hiding something about his son?*

The loud engine of their helicopter, the *Pegasus,*

chopped the air outside.

"Okay, team," Truther shouted as he pointed to the distance. "Let's move it. We got a city to save!"

With that, the crime-fighting crew ran through the hole they had created. Jaycee hesitated.

"I'm right behind you," she yelled. "Just gotta, um, do a final perimeter scan!"

Jaycee headed for David, but an old army general blocked her path.

"Mr. Boxworth," the general said, smoothing his dress uniform and wiping the dirt and dust away. "Today's events were unfortunate, but luckily, the fickle finger of fate didn't poke us, and we're here to tell the tale. Listen, your Mighty-Core—"

"MegaCore," David corrected.

"Sure," the general continued. "It's worth a looksie; I'll give you that. But you and your facility are in no condition to demonstrate anything now. We'll give you some time, and maybe another opportunity will arise. In the meantime, you can send us the schematics of your air-sucker engine, and we'll submit it for review."

The general swiveled. Jaycee made her move, but the older man did an about-face.

"Oh, and a piece of advice, son," the old-timer offered. "Cool it with the Ultranaut tin can suit. If we were interested, we would've taken a nibble by now. And besides, we don't need any new-fangled robo-protectors. We got the Super Society."

The general gave Jaycee a nod, then joined the dispersing crowd. David simmered as the synthetic humanoid he sat on spewed purple goo.

A guy on his phone hurried into the building. He slicked back his black hair and patted his well-trimmed mustache. Jaycee greeted her father with a big smile.

"Hi, Da—!" Jaycee blurted.

Don't blow your cover, dummy! she scolded herself.

He gave her a quick wave en route to David.

"If they only knew," she whispered. "My dad is secretly the most awesome superhero ever, Truther!"

He adjusted his ruffled suit over his fit physique. A proud grin stretched across Jaycee's face.

"And his quick-change skills are definitely goals!"

"Hope that was an important call, Barry," David said as Baron approached. "Don't think I didn't see you get up during my presentation. You missed a heck of a show."

"Sorry to miss my crime-fighting clients in action, but business never sleeps, you know that," Baron said back, disconnecting his call. "You got a lot, um, going on here, but the MegaCore, it... it intrigues me. It's been a while; here, this is my updated contact info."

Baron produced a business card that Jaycee had seen a thousand times before. It read "Baron Maddox" as the C.E.O. of "PANTHEON SOLUTIONS" in large, bold letters. Under the text was a holographic overlay of the Pantheon upward-pointing lightning bolt logo.

"Old-fashioned, I know," Baron admitted as he handed the card to David. "But a paper card is something real that people can actually touch. Anyway, scan the card with any reader device, and it'll take you to our holo-communications vista. We'll set something up. We'll discuss."

Baron stepped aside, planting his phone to his ear. With none of the confidence a costumed protector ought to have, Jaycee stepped closer.

"I'm not interested in getting your autograph," David remarked, sneering.

"No, I just, um, I mean, I saw, or at least, I thought I saw you," Jaycee fumbled. "You and, well, you're gonna think I'm nuts, but—"

"Your team is waiting for you, hero," Baron said to Jaycee with a wink.

She gave a nervous salute. Her eyes shifted to David. He shook his head and stood, kicking a downed drone.

Baron surveyed the devastation around them and whistled.

"Wow. Superheroes, huh?" Baron said, walking toward the exit and leaving David Jaycee alone in the dim light.

Jaycee held up a finger, eager to ask David a million crazy questions.

"Yeah," David said, his voice dripping with disdain. "Superheroes."

Jaycee's finger curled like a dying flower.

Guess I'm getting answers on my own.

She shrunk into herself and hurried to her teammates.

ERIC

The door opened to a thunderous echo announcing Eric's arrival.

Was the door always this loud? Eric pondered as he pulled on the shoulder strap of his backpack.

He walked in front of the entire class in silence. Eric considered only a few things more horrible than having his classmates stare at him; he assumed eating fire ants was worse, but not by much.

"What goes up must come down," Valerie proclaimed to a drowsy classroom in front of a

blackboard that read "MS. VALERIE COOPER –
TODAY'S LESSON: FUN WITH PHYSICS." The
deadened gaze of his fellow students chilled Eric,
slowing his already hesitant steps. Contrarily, Valerie's
apparent ignorance of Eric's entrance gave him a
glimmer of delusional hope that maybe he could
somehow slip by undetected.

"Thank you for joining us, Mr. Boxworth."

Eric felt Valerie's judgmental gaze following him
to his seat in the back of the room. Students at their
desks covered yawns and succumbed to heavy eyelids.
Luckily, the other kids reoccupied their indifference to
Eric.

"Sir Isaac Newton's first law of motion states that
objects continue to move in a state of constant velocity
unless acted upon by an external force."

Their instructor droned on like a living, breathing
sleeping pill.

"An object's resistance to a change in motion is
known as inertia. This will be on the test, people..."

Young heads perked up.

"...or will it?" Valerie asked with a devious smile.

Young heads sunk back down.

"As I was saying," she continued, "for those of you
who actually did your homework last week, you'll recall
that—"

"Sorry-sorry-sorry!"

A blur of a blonde rushed in. The door opened, not
nearly as loud this time, which just wasn't fair.

"Miss Maddox," Valerie said while stroking
her straw-colored hair in mock shock. "Here in my
classroom, what a rare sight to behold! Please take a
seat, Jennifer; there's enough of the first period left for
you to learn something useful."

The girl played with her ponytail as she spied

for an open seat. Jaycee found the perfect spot and dropped her pink and blue bookbag next to Eric.

The teacher went on with her verbal sedative. Eric stood his textbook on his desk and hid his face inside it.

My feet are on the ground, he thought, taking a deep breath. *I rode the bus here. I'm not floating. It was just an adrenaline-fueled dream. An extremely realistic dream.*

Something felt odd, but this was already a peculiar day anyway. Even though everyone had ceased staring at him, Eric remained on high alert. He leaned his head back and peaked to see what was occupying his peripheral vision. His new neighbor's big, blue eyes looked right at him. Her excited grin struck him as even stranger. Eric eased his face back into the book's pages.

Her sky-blue shorts and pink top, accompanied by her blonde locks, were too bright of a presence to ignore.

"You're Eric!" she whispered.

"Uh-huh..." he said with his face still lodged inside the book.

"I'm Jaycee! My name is Jennifer, but my initials are J.C. My middle name is Claire. I hate it, so I just go by Jaycee."

"Okay..." he whispered back. "Um, I'm Eric because my name is Eric."

"What do my experts on Isaac Newton back there have to contribute?" Valerie interjected, rattling them both. "Anyway, as I was saying, did an apple really fall on his head? Who knows? The point is..."

Sweat poured from Eric's pores. Pit stains on his shirt were not the bold fashion statement he was trying to make. He slid his fingers through his hair, which fell back into unkempt bangs. The teacher had called him out twice in less than five minutes, but at least the worst was over.

A small sliver of paper poked at his book's cover. He lifted the book and slid the folded note into the little surface area between his face and the pages. He opened it in secret. In pink ink and curvy handwriting, it read, "Jaycee is spelled J-A-Y-C-E-E."

Eric leaned back, furrowing his brow. Valerie had her back turned to the class. With lightning-quick reflexes, Jaycee handed Eric another note which read "C or K?"

While keeping an eye on the back of Valerie's teal cardigan, Eric circled "K." His hands trembled as he passed it back to her.

Jaycee's eyes lit with excitement as she quickly wrote and passed another note: "Erik! Like a Viking! I was a Viking 2 Halloweens ago!"

"What?" Eric's bewilderment got the best of him.

It also caught the ear of Valerie.

"Final warning, Mr. Boxworth," she said with a stern tone.

She went back to writing on the board.

"I thought you meant, like, am I okay?" Eric whispered to Jaycee. "Which I'm not! I don't know why I lied! It's Eric. With a 'C.'"

Jaycee went to work, hurriedly writing out another note. Like a phantom, the message seemed to materialize on his desk.

The note read: "Eric! I 'C' what you did there! What are your known hangouts? Who are your known associates? Have you ever gone by any different names? :)"

"My what?" Eric asked. "What're you talking about?"

"That's it!" Valerie snapped.

Eric realized he was not as quiet as he had thought.

"Principal's office—now," Valerie commanded.

Eric's pulse quickened and sweat beaded on his brow. Valerie pointed at Jaycee.

"You, too, Miss Maddox."

Jaycee's eyelids fluttered.

"But Mom!"

• • •

Eric inspected a piece of thread that had sprouted from the outer seam of his gray shorts. He kicked up an old, worn-in sneaker to examine his foot. He focused on anything to distract him from having to talk to Jaycee. Avoiding her proved to be not an easy task since Jaycee was, of course, sitting right next to him in the small lobby.

Eric rested his face in his palm, contemplating his fate. The receptionist sat behind three large monitors. Eric could only see her wiggling beehive hairdo. She tapped at her keyboard with fervor. In Eric's mind, there was no doubt that she wrote criminalizing entries in his permanent record, or his obituary. This marked Eric's maiden voyage to the principal's office; return trips were not on his bucket list. He pulled out his phone from his backpack on the floor and stared at his reflection in the black glass.

"First-timer, huh?" Jaycee said, breaking the quietness. "Principal Garza is a kitten. You'll be fine. My mom, er, Ms. Cooper, does this whole zero-tolerance thing to try and scare kids. Totally doesn't work."

"They won't, you know, call parents or anything, will they?" he asked, unable to hide the fear in his voice. "I really don't need my dad knowing about this."

"Not sure," she said, shrugging. "My dad's always too busy at work, and my mom practically lives here, so I just get stuck at school anyway. Pretty flushed, but nothing really happens, so I deal."

"Really? I've seen you in, like, three classes all year," Eric said.

Despite her sporadic scholastic appearances, something about her stood out as familiar. Perhaps she lived in his neighborhood.

"Okay, so I skip sometimes," she confessed. "But everybody does. It's, like, a known thing."

A news alert notification blipped up on Eric's phone. The headline read, "Super Society Saves the City Again! Next article: Truther, eligible bachelor – True or False?" The accompanying picture depicted the destruction of the Boxworth Building. Eric turned it facedown. His stomach knotted.

"You spend a lot of time with your dad?" she asked.

"I guess. Not really. What's with the weird questions?"

"Uh, ya know, we're friends, right?"

"This is literally the first time we've ever spoken."

"We're, um, getting to know each other," she said. She looked away from Eric.

"Don't blow this," Jaycee whispered to herself. "Be chill, say something subtle. Act cool and say something natural."

Before Eric could react, she whipped her head back.

"If you could have any superpower, what would it be?"

She lowered her head to congratulate herself.

"Perfect," she murmured.

His head shot up. A wave of panic tremored throughout his body.

"Eh... Right now?" Eric acted fast. "Invisibility."

"Waste of a pick; you pretty much already are!" Jaycee said, chuckling. "Strategic in a battle, though! I'd have super strength, but that's obvious. I mean, it's super not obvious. I mean, there's nothing super about it!"

Eric looked at her as if she had just landed on this planet.

"Well, maybe we should start talking more," she said, appearing to go into damage control mode—something very familiar to Eric.

"Talking got me here," Eric chided as he slumped in his chair. "Talking to you."

"What're you gonna do? Take a vow of silence?" Jaycee quipped back. "That'd be a pretty flushed way to live. Listen, Eric, you can't hide forever."

"Mr. Garza will see you two now," the beehive-haired receptionist said from behind her wall of monitors.

"You're just shy," Jaycee said, grabbing her bookbag as they stood. "I'm sure you got plenty to say; just gotta get you to start talking more."

Jaycee squatted, looking intensely at his eyes.

"Listen up," she whispered as if giving top-secret orders. "When we get inside, let me do all the talking."

She marched through the door to the principal's office.

"Is 'flushed' a thing people started saying, or—" Eric said.

"C'mon!"

He grabbed his backpack, pocketed his phone, and hustled out of his seat. Stepping into the cramped office, he saw that Jaycee was already sitting in front of the principal's desk. Eric looked down at the name on the desk plaque, which read, "Hilario Garza, Curator of Future Minds."

"Don't let the fancy title fool you," Principal Garza said. "I'm just a friendly tour guide for future minds. Please, sit down."

Eric lowered his bag and took a seat next to Jaycee. Garza stood. His pupils bounced up and down from behind his headset's thin glass visor—streams of holographic data sprawled up in front of his eyes.

"Jennifer," he began.

"It's Jaycee; everybody knows that."

"My apologies, Miss Maddox!"

He stroked at his bristly soul patch under his lower lip.

"I'll keep it one-hundred with you—you've missed a lot of classes this year."

To Eric's surprise, she crossed her arms and had nothing to say. Principal Garza skimmed more lines of information from his visor. He stuck his fingers in the little pockets on his silky brown vest. Eric thought those little slits were decorative, but it wasn't stopping this guy from giving his fingertips a rest.

"We've been pretty chillaxed about you missing days," he revealed. "But I'm afraid today's tardiness was counted as another absence. One more and, well, there's no dope way to say this, but you'll be suspended. The next step after that is expulsion."

She arched an unimpressed eyebrow. Principal Garza read more of his holo-info.

"And Mr. Eric," he drawled out, still taking in Eric's file, which, for whatever reason, seemingly took forever.

How much on me is there to read?

The pause wrought havoc on Eric's nerves. He gripped the arms of his seat. The beehive lady outside was calling his dad; he just knew it. The thought of his father having to come to pick him up made his skin crawl. Eric couldn't bring himself to look away from the man in front of him, the tormentor who would surely seal his doom.

Eric floated in his seat. It felt like maybe two inches, but he was hovering all the same. Principal Garza was too distracted to notice, but Eric dared not take his eyes off him. Eric couldn't be sure if Jaycee witnessed him floating in his chair.

What is happening to me?!

"Well, good news, Eric; I can't find anything on you," Principal Garza finally said.

The sudden revelation sent Eric dropping into his seat. The principal looked puzzled as Eric crossed his legs, (badly) acting like he merely needed to adjust himself. Jaycee did a poorer job of masking her amazement—he noticed those wide eyes of hers getting even bigger.

Sweat dripped from Eric's forehead. He told himself it only looked like he leaned in his chair, but relaxation did not belong on the day's itinerary.

She didn't see anything, nobody saw you, nothing happened.

"Nothing to be alarmed about," Garza assured. "All your basics are here. It's just there are zero comments about you anywhere."

He removed his headset.

"Real talk, buddy. I know you're a good student. Not a troublemaker, maybe a little quiet, but a good kid. I want to see those test scores get a boost, though. Hey, I remember my ninth-grade year being totally not crunk, but, trust me, high school gets better, home-dog."

The principal sat a leg on the edge of his desk, letting his sandal hang on his toes. Motivational posters adorned the wall behind him.

"I can relate to where you are now, Eric. Man, I remember how tough it was being a, well, nerd. No friends—and the kids I did talk to were just a bunch of B-words. That's right, 'bullies.' But I focused on what's trill, believed in myself, and now I'm the principal, and I'm home-dogs with all the students!"

Eric's mouth cracked open, and he squinted one eye.

Does that headset of his come with a translator?

"Anyway, the point is, Eric," Garza continued. "I get to make up for a lot of lost time—time I didn't spend being the world's coolest principal like I am now. I don't want you to have to wait until you're grown up to be the real you. You feel me, dawg?"

Jaycee stood abruptly.

"We're not in real trouble, so we'll be leaving now."

She walked to the door. Eric sat, trying to be as still as a statue. Visibly annoyed, Jaycee grabbed him by the arm.

"My door is open any time you want to have a rap sesh, kids!" Principal Garza said to their backs.

Jaycee hoisted her bookbag with one hand and pulled Eric with the other. They exited with Eric barely grabbing his backpack on the way up and out. They whisked past the receptionist's monitor barricade and into the empty hallway.

The locker and classroom doors were closed, but the red, white, and gold-painted school spirit blasted out in the open. Bulletin boards displayed Golden Eagle pride, as did banners hanging from the ceiling and even in an empty trophy case. Jaycee released Eric's arm and stood in front of a "Stay in school!" poster.

"It's Friday. We're not in class. Where're we going?" she asked with an eager smile.

"Uh, to get my Social Studies book from my

locker," Eric said, looking at the hand-drawn Spring Formal Dance sign behind her instead of making eye contact. "We're already late for second period."

"You got a lot to learn about playing hooky, Eric," she remarked as they walked by a mural of a triumphant eagle spreading its wings. "That class is so boring. Is it boring? Must be a real snooze-fest!"

"You're not in my class," Eric pointed out. "I don't think you are, anyway. It's possible you're supposed to show up, but don't."

He retrieved his phone from his pants pocket and saw the time.

"Man, I'm so late. Do we get a principal pass or something? I'm gonna be marked absent for sure!"

"All the more reason to ditch!" Jaycee surmised, adding a cheerful clap.

They halted in the middle of adjoining hallways, standing over a large logo of their school. "North NSC High School, Home of the Golden Eagles" stretched underneath their feet.

Eric stared at the painting, too distracted to stop Jaycee from nabbing his phone.

"Hey!"

"Here," Jaycee said as she tapped away at his screen. "This is me."

She handed it back to him. A text message popped up from "Jaycee (^o^)/." Eric inspected the little picture in the word balloon.

"It's, um, a zombie emoji?" he asked, unsure of what just happened.

"A female zombie!" she specified. "You have my number, so when you change your mind about class, you can hit me up!"

He studied the message as if there was some hidden meaning. His eyes alternated between the screen and the bubbly blonde before him.

"I'm probably messing this up somehow, but... this is a Spring Formal thing, right?"

Eric raised his head.

"I mean, like, I wasn't even gonna go, and if I did, I dunno, I guess I just expected that I'd ask the girl to the dance, not the other way around."

She smiled that perpetually positive grin of hers. "What dance?"

Humiliation stung so hard that he couldn't breathe. Eric knew that words like "What? Sorry! Huh? I was kidding! I have to go!" dribbled out of his mouth, but he had gone numb from embarrassment. He sped past the lockers, forgoing his textbook requirements, and fled the scene.

JAYCEE

Baffled, Jaycee stood watching Eric scurry away. Her instincts kicked back in, and she was just about to go after him when she saw him do it: as Eric speed-walked farther away from her, Jaycee spotted his feet lift from the ground. It would have gone unnoticed by unassuming eyes, but Jaycee saw his shoes floating a few centimeters above the floor. She knew what she had to do.

Jaycee rushed to the opposite end of the hallway to her locker. She dialed the lock combination in the blink of an eye and opened the red-painted metal door. After ensuring that the coast was clear, she withdrew her phone from her pocket, pink case and all, and positioned it inside the locker with the front camera facing her. She dug inside her bookbag and found her mask. After shimmying the cowl on, she became the superhero Powerhouse. From the neck up, at least.

Jaycee tapped open an app with a white double-S logo on her phone, then stuck her head inside the locker. She pressed her thumbprint on a scanning button. A connectivity status icon flashed over a Super Society logo. In an instant, the face of Truther stared back at her through the small screen.

"Situation report, Powerhouse!" he ordered.

His image reflected on the yellow-tinted domes covering Jaycee's eyes.

"You got my intel about the flying boy, right?"

"Yes," Truther said. "And next time you have highly sensitive information, be sure to send it through secure channels and don't text it. And we tend not to use smiley face emojis in our communiqués."

She spoke cautiously, struggling to suppress her eagerness.

"Two more instances of aerial events, sir!"

"You can just say whether or not he floated," Truther said, sighing. "Any documentation? Record any evidence?"

"Negative," she admitted. "Might be hard to get a pic or a video. Eric, uh, might think I'm a creepy stalker."

"Stay on him!" Truther demanded. "Do what you must to gather as much intel as possible. Buddy up, study up! If this boy can really fly, as you say, he may be a potential threat to the Super Society. It's our job to monitor all so-called 'powered people,' so if there are any 'P.P.'s' around, we'll get 'em!"

"I'll go above and beyond, sir!"

She saluted, holding back a giggle.

"Notify me once you have something," he

commanded. "See that he stays on campus. It's the easiest way to keep an eye on him."

His voice lightened, sounding more natural like her dad, Baron Maddox.

"I know I'm a tad overprotective of you, but you proved yourself this morning. Good job, Powerhouse!"

He lowered back to his super-serious leader voice.

"Due to the delicacy of the situation, I'm entrusting only you with this assignment—because I believe in you! Make sure that kid is the real deal, hero! Truther: out!"

His image vanished. Jaycee grabbed her phone and bookbag, slammed her locker shut, and strode with purpose through the hall.

"Okay, flyboy," she said. "Let's dance!"

She paused.

"Dance... Eric..."

She felt she was onto something but didn't know what it was.

"Mask! Duh!"

She slid the mask off and resumed her mission.

Chapter Three: *CLIMB*

ERIC

DESPITE THE HUGE NUMBERS THAT pizza day drew, Eric sat alone at a round table in the cafeteria. Even the older teenagers with cars stayed on campus to pack the mess hall, lengthening lines and contributing to the ocean of chatter surrounding Eric's lonely little island. He smirked at the ironic posters of healthy snacks and nutritional information spread throughout the place. It made his thin slice of sauce, cheese, and tiny cubes of pepperoni that much more delicious. The aroma of oven-baked pies was an appetizing way to end the school week.

Eric wiped the grease from his hands and pushed in small earbuds to drown out the murmuring masses. He tapped his phone, and heavy metal music blared in his ears. He munched on his side salad while composing a text message:

"Dad, I can't explain what I did. It was the first time I ever did that. Idk what is going on. I hope ur not mad. Pls don't tell anyone."

His thumb wavered over the send button.

Once you send this, there's no going back. For

all you know, with what happened, Dad might have thought he was hallucinating.

As quickly as he wrote the draft, he backspaced it into oblivion.

The guitar solo bursting in Eric's eardrums reached an intense high note. He raised his head to see Jaycee grinning back at him. Jolted, he yanked his earbuds out.

"Jaycee!" he blurted. "Uh, what's up?"

She placed her tray down across from him, taking the seat without it being offered.

"The sky, dummy!" Jaycee joked.

Awkward alarms sounded off inside his brain.

She can't know... Can she?

"Um, anything interesting happen in your 'How to Be Boring' class?" she asked. "What do you do in Social Studies anyway?"

"I studied how to be social, but I don't think it's working," Eric answered with dry sarcasm to mask his internal freak-out.

"That's a joke you've been saving, and it totally worked!" she said with delight. "That's the best feeling, isn't it? To finally have the right opportunity to say this awesome thing you've been holding in."

"Yeah, well, it's not like I have anyone to tell it to."

He nodded to the horde of fellow kids encompassing them.

"Hey, I'm sorry for, you know, being weird this morning."

"Jeez, such a drama queen," she mocked. "I get it, though; you were running late. Your dad's, like, this inventor guy, right? So, he must always be on you to get to class. I bet if you bring home anything less than an A-plus-plus, it's a huge disappointment, and he goes to work building your robot replacement."

Jaycee scarfed down her first of three slices of pizza in the blink of an eye. Eric's eyes enlarged at such a slender girl chowing down.

"Skip breakfast?"

"Rude," she retorted. "You don't talk to many girls, do you?"

Eric's face puckered as if he was trying to escape inside himself.

"What? No! That's not what I meant, I—"

She laughed.

"Relax, I was just playing!"

She took another bite.

"I work out a lot. My, uh, athletic program keeps me carbing. I don't talk to a lot of boys, and the ones I do, I usually end up hitting."

"Oh," Eric said before taking a nervous sip of soda. "Well, I'm not sure I'm the strait-laced student you think I am. I might take your advice and bail."

"You can't leave! You gotta, you know, stay in school! Children are the future! Say no to drugs!"

"I'm starting to think you're on drugs," Eric said.

He lifted his tray, sliding his emptied plate and paper bowl of half-eaten salad onto the tabletop.

"Something pretty major happened with my dad earlier, and I dunno, doesn't feel right being here instead of at home taking care of it."

"Forget what I said about skipping," Jaycee said. "You got issues at home, so—"

She drank a big gulp of water.

"—a call from the principal isn't gonna make things any smoother."

"Today already sucks," Eric lamented.

He held up his tray and hid his face behind it.

"Things can't get much worse. You may want to duck."

A balled-up barrage of trash hurdled toward them. Eric felt the vibrations of each crumpled cannonball pelting his plastic shield. Jaycee dodged a speeding plastic bottle that bounced on their table.

She looked over to their would-be bombardiers: a cadre of jocks in letterman jackets sneering from a few tables over.

Jaycee's hands balled into fists.

"Those jerks! What's their problem? I thought you were invisible."

"I'm not who they were shooting at. Trust me," Eric explained. "This happens a lot."

He gathered the garbage that landed on the floor and collected it with his own.

"They were aiming for those guys."

Eric pointed his thumb at their neighbors, a squad of bespectacled nerds. A hairy-armed, rotund dork led their in-progress fantasy card game, oblivious to the jocks' weak wrath. The lead nerd's shorts exposed thick leg hair, but it looked like puberty hadn't reached his baby face yet.

"Melvin, the Dungeon Master, and his band of adventurers," Eric said. "Natural enemies of jocks."

Jaycee gazed upon the geeks' dragon-themed t-shirts and blemished skin. Her jaw dropped at their game leader.

"O-M-G, Super—I mean, Melvin?"

"You know him?"

"I'm, uh, on a team with him," Jaycee said. "Er, a math team!"

Eric raised his eyebrows in confusion. She looked over, taking a skeptical glance at the angry athletes. A tall skinny one looked the most ticked off.

"Those are our school's sports guys?"

"There's a reason the trophy case is empty," Eric

said.

He shoved his earbuds into his backpack.

"Anyway, I'm not sure anyone would notice if I left."

Eric grabbed his bag and tray and walked to the trash can. Jaycee followed with a half-eaten pizza crust hanging from her mouth as she shouldered her bookbag.

"At least let me show you the proper way to ghost this joint—consider it a parting gift," she offered. "But I got some calories to burn, and I happen to know that we have P.E. together."

"Would it surprise you that gym is my least favorite subject?

He slid his trash into the receptacle.

"Okay, I'll stick around," Eric said. "But only for one more class, then you can show me your stealth-ninja way of abandoning my education."

"Sweet! I like you, Eric. I hope I don't end up hitting you."

• • •

A whistle chirped, signaling that gym class was in session. Eric happily lost himself in the herd of a dozen boys taking to the basketball court. They stepped past the empty metal bleachers to meet their hard-as-nails instructor at the half-court mark.

Elderly Coach Gorman stood at attention, watching the adolescents gathered around him. The coach's shorts went way north of his knees, exposing his spider veins—an unbearable sight, yet Eric couldn't look away. The whistle dropped from Coach Gorman's wrinkled lips with a thin string of drool that hung like a spider's web trail.

The girls sprang out of their locker room from the opposite end of the gym. They wore matching gym attire and assembled next to the boys. Slower to exit, Jaycee double-timed it to catch up to them.

"Lissen up, boys and girls," Coach Gorman shouted. "No hoops today, no dodgeball. We're gonna do something you'll actually use in the real world—climbing ropes!"

Coach Gorman pointed a shaky finger at a row of knotted cords hanging over padded cushions near the girls' locker room. Eric craned his neck, looking in horror at how high up they went.

"Single file, one at a time! Line 'em up!" the coach ordered.

Even with a hoarse voice that sounded like he gargled with gravel, the coach's commands still sparked discipline into the kids, each obeying without pause. Eric dragged his feet to the rear of a coed line. Jaycee hung back to be last in her row so she could stand next to Eric.

"We finally get to do something cool in P.E.!" she said, beaming with excitement. "Glad you didn't ditch."

"Leave? And miss rope burn day?"

Coach Gorman's feeble legs carried him to the front of the group.

"This exercise requires peak upper body strength!"

"I have the strength of a mosquito," Eric whispered to Jaycee. "You picked a good day to come to class—you and everybody will get to see me die from humiliation."

"Hey, you were able to lift your da—!" Jaycee said before cutting herself off.

She formed an awkward smile. Eric side-eyed her while Gorman continued his breathy spiel. The coach's skeletal hand grabbed a rope. It wiggled in his frail hand like a worm.

"Iss simple! Pull! One hand over the other! If you need motivation, just recall a time when you had to escape up a tree from a pack of rabid apes! Or, if necessary, make something up! Lemme show you how it's done!"

Eric winced at the sight of the octogenarian wrapping another unsteady hand around the braided stretch of nylon.

"If he passes out, then class is canceled, right?" Eric whispered to Jaycee. "There's no way Coach Gorman can make this—"

Coach Gorman speeding up the rope derailed Eric's sentence. The kids froze, awestruck as the senior citizen slithered down with ease.

"You waitin' for a gran' invitation?" Coach Gorman yelled. "Elbows up, people! Climb, climb, climb!"

One after the other, students attacked their respective ropes, hoisting themselves knot by knot. As the line got shorter, Eric grew more anxious.

Ropes are used to hang people, he thought. *So why are they forcing kids to play with tools of execution?*

There had to be a way out of this. Eric scanned the gymnasium for possible escape routes. Instead, he saw Melvin relaxing in the bleachers. Melvin proudly displayed what looked like some kind of doctor's note to anyone who would look his way.

Wish I thought of that.

Eric lost himself in thoughts of fleeing while Jaycee took her turn. She scurried up her rope, then shimmied down in quick, efficient succession.

"Outstanding, Maddox!" Coach Gorman praised.

He directed his crinkled eyes at Eric.

"You're up, boy; go get it!"

All the kids' attention focused on Eric as he

approached the rope. The thick braid felt smoother than he anticipated, but he could not bring himself to form a firm hold. He gave the rope a gentle tug and inspected it as if checking to see if it was up to regulation.

"We don't got all day, Boxworth!" Coach Gorman barked. "In my case, I might literally not have all day, so get climbin'!"

Eric exhaled a long breath and wrapped both hands around the rope. He closed his eyes to concentrate on his breathing, anything to distract himself from the embarrassment of barely being able to lift himself two inches.

Focus, he told himself. *Just... do what you know you can do.*

Eric held a loose grip, moving one hand over the other repeatedly, and he felt his body lift. His legs hugged the rope, and he grunted to sell the struggle.

This is for sure not a dream! Eric thought.

He feared ascending too quickly, but he remained confident that the façade worked. He pretended to pull, one hand over the other, while secretly flying.

Whatever's going on with me has its advantages.

Eric's momentum halted once his head touched the circular stopper. The thin, wide disc held its place, secured roughly twenty feet in the air at the halfway mark between the rope and the rafters.

Eric peered to see the other kids and Coach Gorman looking back at him. They seemed so insignificant from up there. Eric permitted himself to linger a few seconds, letting a wave of calmness wash over his body. Then, he spotted Jaycee pointing her phone at him. Her device's camera flashed a vivid spark that stayed behind Eric's eyelids.

"Stalker alert!" a red-haired girl named Tiffany

snickered, pointing at Jaycee.

An upsurge of giggling swept throughout the other girls. Jaycee stuffed her phone into her shorts pocket and gave death stares to her contemporaries while Tiffany smirked. Tiffany rose to Queen Mean Girl status in her first week despite being a new student.

Great, I'm gonna hear about this from Tiffany in Spanish class next period, Eric thought. *Definitely no bueno. Unless...*

Eric maintained his climbing charade, sliding down his lifeline, then releasing his grasp to submit to gravity once again. He rubbed the fading flash flare from his eyes. As the sparkles dissipated, Eric saw Tiffany and her small gang of girls surrounding Jaycee. He didn't consider himself lucky, but he knew an opportunity when he saw it.

Chapter Four: *FLY*

JAYCEE

"WHAT A CREEPER!" TIFFANY TEASED. "Can I borrow your phone so I can post about this on literally the entire Internet?"

Jaycee openly wore her fury, curling her lip. She got in Tiffany's face.

"Listen, Extra," Jaycee said, careful to keep her voice down. "I know you're new around here and to the team, but if you wanna go toe-to-toe, we do it in costume."

"Two words," Tiffany said. "Breath mint."

"Like I even care what you think!" Jaycee snapped at her.

"You like Eric!" Tiffany mocked.

"What? No!" Jaycee insisted.

She held up a fist.

"You know what I like? I like punching stupid girls in the face—!"

Coach Gorman's screeching whistle cut through the ears of the crowd.

"Knock it off!" the coach ordered.

He marched up to Jaycee, parting the cluster of female students.

"No phones allowed in gym class! Rules are rules! Maddox, you think I don't know you were already in the principal's office today?"

The coach stuck his furrowed face in front of Jaycee's, but she stood her ground.

"I get it, Coach," she said. "Technology confuses you. I bet when you and your caveman buddies first discovered fire, it really freaked you out."

Coach Gorman backed off. His apparent retreat raised the eyebrows of the other kids.

"Nice try," the coach said with a quivering smile. "Seein' Principal Garza is too easy on you. You think sassin' me will get ya outta more drills? Let's see what a jury of your peers thinks about you after y'all run some laps."

Groans and whines erupted from the class.

"That's right. You can thank Maddox here for the bonus cardio for today. Now, get to lappin'!"

Jaycee's classmates glared as they rushed past, one furious frown after another. She sighed and joined the others in sprinting around the court. Jaycee made a few strides when she noticed something missing—that someone was missing. Jaycee slowed to a brisk walk and perused the bleachers but saw no sign of life. She eyed the jogging group ahead of her, but a teenager of interest was not among them.

Where's Eric?

Jaycee picked up the pace, outrunning the flock, leaving them in her dust. Her head bobbled while directing her eyes to the ceiling, but still, Eric was out of sight. She spotted Melvin lounging in the bleachers.

"Is this really what you do at school, Supercut?" she whispered, slowing to a crawl as she neared him. "I must've missed more days than I realized."

"Just keepin' up appearances as my dweeb alter

ego," Melvin said back, matching her hushed tone. "And after this mornin', I could use a break."

"Is that doctor's note even real?" Jaycee asked, pointing to his paper. "Does my dad know about this?"

"Yer dad don't know squat, and neither do any of the other airhead babysitters at Pantheon. And I'd like to keep it that way, so zip it, P.H."

Unlike herself, the other teen members of the Super Society were foster kids before being recruited, so Jaycee sympathized enough to let certain attitudes slide.

Dad may be their legal guardian, Jaycee thought, *but teammates or not, no way I'm calling him brother. I don't even wanna think about how Tiffany is technically my sister. Ew!*

Melvin may not have been a blood relative, but he pushed buttons the way only a real family member could.

"Speakin' of yer dad," Melvin said. "Tell 'im excellent job adding Tiffany to the Super Society! She is smokin'!"

Ugh, the sibling thing just got so much grosser!

"Miss Maddox!" Coach Gorman yelled from across the gym. "That don't look like runnin' to me!"

Jaycee shook her head as she jogged away.

"Can ya put in a good word fer me?"

She ignored Melvin while sprinting at a careful pace to resume her search for Eric.

"There's a reason Truther chose only me for this assignment," Jaycee muttered.

An idea sparked in her mind. She halted, allowing the other kids to speed past her.

"Lose your boyfriend?" Tiffany said, sneering while turning a corner.

"Yes! I mean, no!" Jaycee yelled back.

She slowed to a walk and then whipped out her phone. Jaycee swiped through the pictures she took of Eric climbing.

"I'm onto you, Eric."

Spreading her fingers, she enlarged a blurry still frame of Eric's hands cupping but not touching the rope.

"I'll get ironclad proof that you can fly. A superhero always completes her mission!"

The group of runners lapped back around toward her.

"I always get my man!" Jaycee declared.

"So, Eric is your man, huh?" Tiffany jeered as she dashed by Jaycee.

"Omigod—shut up!" Jaycee grumbled before bolting after them.

• • •

Jaycee pushed through the metal doors leading to the roof, the hinges screaming as she let the door slam shut. It took her half a second to find him, sitting by himself next to a boxy metal storage unit, hanging his head between his knees.

"Shoulda known you'd be up here," Jaycee spoke over the strong gusts of air. "You made it pretty clear you aren't afraid of heights."

Eric looked up with red-rimmed eyes, clearly not expecting her.

"I suck at ditching," Eric confessed. "I didn't even leave school property. How'd you know I'd be here?"

"Hiding on the roof is Skipping School One-Oh-One, duh," Jaycee said, scoffing. "Rookie move, Eric. It takes dedication and hard work if you're going to slack off."

Eric smoothed some crumpled creases along the bottom of his green shirt. Like her, he seemed to have found time to change out of gym clothes while sneaking away.

"I hope you didn't get into too much trouble in P.E., but—"

"But suddenly, you care about what happens to me, is that it?" Jaycee finished for him. "It was pretty flushed for you to bail on me. You could've at least texted me back."

She swept her hair back, maintaining a man-eater expression as she awaited his response.

"I saw an opportunity, and I guess I took it," he said, his shaggy hair flowing in the breeze. "You really weirded me out, taking those pictures."

She crossed her arms.

"Ego much? Who said I wanted pics of you? Maybe you just got in the way of my shot; you think of that?"

She did not lie technically, but Eric's half-frown indicated he wasn't buying it.

"I'm sorry," he said.

Eric stuck his hands in his pockets.

"Look, it's not exactly private info," he said. "No use in trying to hide it, but, well, my dad's facility, my house pretty much, it, uh, blew up this morning."

Jaycee's stiff upper lip loosened as she relived flashbacks from earlier in the day when, as Powerhouse, she fought Cybertooth alongside the Super Society and the subsequent explosion that decimated the already damaged Boxworth building.

Eric looked at the skyscrapers on the horizon. In the distance, the towers' glass shined in the sun, and the various drones whizzing past one another twinkled in the natural light's reflection. The unmanned devices zipped as far as the Kell Bridge that led to the bay on the city's far-east side.

"Last thing my dad told me, in not so many words," Eric said. "Well, he sorta demanded that I go to school today, but I don't know. School feels like the last place I should be, yet I can't even bring myself to leave."

The discernible sadness in Eric's eyes was more than simple social awkwardness. Jaycee was at a loss, unsure how to engage Eric, so she sat beside him in a wordless disquiet.

The silence between them felt like a heavy shroud as the minutes passed. Jaycee never put much thought into her words, but she realized she must find the right thing to say.

"So, are you, like, homeless now or something?" she asked, finally.

"No, but I haven't heard anything from my dad or anyone."

"You could stay at my house!"

"Thanks, but, um, I seriously need to go home first before I do anything, so I can, you know, face the music."

Like a thunderbolt, a revelation struck Jaycee.

"Music... Dance!" she uttered so suddenly she surprised even herself.

She popped up.

"Let's not wait for some dumb formal. Just show me what we were gonna do."

Eric took her hand as she helped him up. It was the first time Jaycee noticed he was about an inch taller than her.

"I've been meaning to ask you this all day," Eric admitted. "What in the world are you talking about?"

"You mentioned asking me to go to this school dance," she recounted. "Well, we should prolly practice.

So, you can't go until you let me see your moves."

"I'm not so sure. What if someone catches us?" Eric pointed out.

Despite the worried look on his face, Eric did not resist Jaycee placing his hand on her side. She followed his lead, moving like wooden mannequins as they waltzed in a clumsy box formation.

Their sloppy slow dance guided the pair in a jagged zig-zag path across the roof. Eric directed to rotate, which caused him to have another near-stomping situation for Jaycee's hapless feet as they lumbered closer to their original spot.

"It's a good thing we're practicing; you're pretty horrible," she said. "And it's okay if you want to at least pretend you're having a good time, Cardboard Boxworth—I've been saving that joke!"

She tilted her head, anticipating a response.

"I've actually never heard that one before," he said. "You should feel honored."

"Whatever," Jaycee said. "Spin me."

Eric's minimal effort to extend his arm kickstarted Jaycee's twirl. With her eyes closed, she accelerated with every turn. Jaycee tripped over a concrete parapet, tumbling over the short barrier that aligned the roof's edge. In an instant, she set on a crash course with the pavement. As she hurtled downward, Jaycee's instincts commanded her to open her mouth to scream in terror, but a force knocked into her, propelling her to the sky.

Eric held her in his arms, flying her back to the roof. Jaycee's jaw dropped while seeing the world whip past her. She looked up at Eric—his face was pale and determined. After a shaky landing, he lowered her down haphazardly. Jaycee dropped to her feet, smiling at a disjointed Eric.

"You're heavy," he said, gasping.

Eric's eyebrows darted up to his forehead, knowing he'd placed his foot firmly in his mouth.

"I'm sorry! I'm sorry!"

"For saving my life?" Jaycee said in awe. "That was, that was, I mean, that was so cool! Do it again!"

"Aw, man, aw, man..."

Eric paced with his hands on his head.

"You don't think anyone saw that, do you?"

Jaycee's giddiness faded as she noticed Eric's distress. Eric bent over, head down, and planted his hands on his thighs.

"Who else knows that you can...?" Jaycee asked. She hesitated.

"Who else knows?"

"My dad, I mean, he'd have to, I think. I don't know."

He looked up at her.

"You have to promise not to tell anyone."

She saluted.

"I, Jaycee Maddox, solemnly swear not to tell anybody that you can fly even though it is incredibly awesome!"

Eric brushed past her and sat with his back up against the storage unit. She turned and retrieved her phone, opened the Super Society app, and readied for a video call with Truther. She paused, observing how pathetic the boy looked.

"Eric," Jaycee said, sighing. "You have to talk to your dad."

Chapter Five: *WINGS*

ERIC HAD HIS CHOICE: GO in through the main entrance of the Boxworth Building or step a few feet to the right and walk in through the large hole in the wall.

A cleanup crew picked up the remaining rubble from the morning's super-brawl. Yellow hazard lights blinked from the dump trucks and excavators parked near landfills where the servicemen and women worked. Debris and other chunks of wreckage filled each bulky vehicle to the brim.

Eric entered through the gigantic gap leading into the first floor of his home, strolling unnoticed under the workers' chatter and the banging and clanging of the heavy machinery. Eric's backpack slid down his shoulder a bit as he paused by the threshold, such as it was, to soak in the damage the blasts had dished out. Before rushing off to school, Eric was too concerned with fleeing than analyzing the details of the destruction. He felt as if he stood inside a massive, serrated mouth that had puked up a messy construction site.

Beyond the workers salvaging what they could from the devastation, the neighboring trees, shrubbery, and other greenery maintained their beauty, unchanged by the chaos. Eric always enjoyed the lushness of the foliage, thinking it a cozy hiding spot deep in the city's heart, outside the colossal science laboratory he called home.

At least there was still something of a view, Eric thought, kicking at a chunk of concrete.

Sounds of traffic and passersby commingled with the laborers' breaking down of blocks. Eric took notice of the casual commuters as they passed. This type of havoc presented nothing new to them, a byproduct of being a citizen of a city under the protection of costumed heroes.

"What do you mean it's not considered an Act of God? All superheroes have god complexes, don't they?" Eric overheard his father bicker into a headset microphone.

David wore a harness wrapped around his torso connected to pulleys suspending him roughly fifteen feet high. Pitch-black safety goggles shielded David's eyes from his sparking laser device that sealed a crack in the metal wall. He repaired the crack, deactivated the welding tool, and lifted his dark eyewear.

"Well, how was I supposed to know superhero insurance was a real thing?!" David shouted into his headset.

Eric's head curved to follow David's swoop from one makeshift perch to another. Eric almost tripped over a thick bundle of wires that lay exposed. He took more careful steps deeper inside the facility while multi-armed robots whooshed above his head. The football-sized, insect-like units flapped their wings in a frenzy, boosted by little thrusters. They tended to numerous areas of the wrecked workshop with different tools protruding from their steel appendages.

Swaying from his suspension cables, David monitored a small hovering drone while welding shut a tiny tear in the wall.

"Yes, it's my home. Yes, it's also my place of business. Yes, it got blown to smithereens!" David said, continuing his call. "I don't know, file two claims, then! Send a bill to the Super Society if you have to! Hold on."

David smacked the drone, and the welding ceased. He turned the metal bug to face him.

"What do you think you're doing? You're just scratching up my wall! I built you better than this!"

David snatched a roll of duct tape from his toolbelt, ripped off a shred with his teeth, and slapped it over the gash.

"You're lucky money's tight, or it'd be the scrapyard for you. Now, beat it."

David plucked the drone, and it buzzed off. Eric positioned himself below his father.

"Da—"

Burrrrr! The booming sound of a drill burrowing into a hunk of concrete came from outside.

"Hey, Dad!" Eric started only to be once cut off by the raucous drilling.

David swung to the rafter by the left side of the stage. Multifarious machines and other gizmos lay sprawled out by the untouched MegaCore. Annoyed, Eric raced over to him, bidding his father's attention.

"Dad," Eric shouted.

"I can't hear you."

"Dad!" Eric yelled louder this time.

"Can you hear me?"

"Yes, Dad, I need to talk to—"

"Someone's yelling; sorry, there've been people in and out of here all day," David said as he pushed the microphone closer to his lips. "Anyway, the bottom line is that I know I'm insured, and someone has gotta pay to clean this up, and it ain't coming out of my pocket! Yes, I know what out-of-pocket means!"

"Dad!"

David spun to see his son hovering in front of him.

He blinked, once, twice, three times, as though he had dust in his eyes. Eric didn't know what to expect from David's reaction, but silence hadn't occurred to him.

"Did Maddox put you up to this?" David finally said, tugging the microphone away from his face.

"Jaycee?" Eric asked with a furrowed brow.

"Barry stole my anti-gravity belt design. That's what this is, right? I knew it!"

David laughed.

"A big, fat lawsuit against Pantheon should get me the cash I need to get back on my feet! Sure, Barry actually got it to work, but theft is theft!"

David gripped a metal support pylon within the rafter's grated structure and secured his footing. He gazed at the massive engine on the stage below.

"Ah, but my real fortune is with the MegaCore. If I could just get another chance to prove what it's capable of—hey, is this call being recorded?"

David held the earpiece closer. Eric frowned; he simmered, beyond frustrated. Eric circled his father, swirling up a few feet, then back to David's eye-level. Eric's adept flying surprised even himself. On the other end of David's call, a faint, tiny voice asked if he was still there. Speechless, David gave his son a quizzical look.

"I'm not wearing any tech-thing," Eric spurted out.

"I can really fly, and I don't know how or why, and it's freaking me the heck out!"

He heaved up and down, grasping for the breath he had just expelled.

"I'm gonna have to call you back," David said, staring at Eric with a steely gaze.

David pressed a button, and his earpiece *blipped* as it powered off. He carefully removed the headset.

"Go to your room."

"Huh?"

David rappelled to the floor, wasting no time unbuckling himself from the harness.

"I don't remember asking, Eric," David said as he manned a mobile computer station. "Your room. Now."

"Is that all you have to say?" Eric asked, drifting high above.

"Keep it up, and you'll be grounded," David warned.

Eric looked at his dangling legs and waved his arms.

"Not sure if grounding me is gonna work, Dad."

His father pushed the computer cart away.

"I. Am. Serious! Now, get down from there and go up to your room!"

"Fine, I was going there anyway!"

Dodging a couple of drones, Eric flew past the stage toward the promenade lining the facility's second-tier level. He tiptoed the railing and then landed on the mounted iron walkway. Eric punched in a code on the panel by a set of doors, and they slid open. He stormed through the corridor, passing unmarked, windowless doors as he made his way to his bedroom. Eric tossed his backpack onto his unmade bed and kicked off his shoes.

"BRAIN, turn on 'Eric's Bedroom's Lights,'"

he commanded, and the automated system lit the overhead lamps.

"I have turned on the lights as you requested, Eric," BRAIN's robotic, omniscient voice projected via the speaker panel by the door.

"Really? I didn't notice," Eric said.

"I can activate the lights once more if you like," BRAIN offered, not registering Eric's sarcasm.

Avoiding the surrounding clutter, Eric pushed aside the dark blue curtains above his bed and peeped through the lone window.

"Forget it," Eric said.

The laborers piled into trucks and finally drove away.

"I have forgotten it based on your request," BRAIN said.

Eric kicked away some shirts on the floor and slumped into a chair, ignoring the scent of body spray hanging in the air. He rolled it over to his television mounted on the wall by the door. A loose stack of comic books, pens, and notepads sat near a gaming console on the dresser beneath the TV. Muscle memory guided him to swipe up a controller, and with a tap of a small button, both the wide monitor and the game system came to life.

Eric watched with glassy eyes, lost in thought, as production company logos and disclaimer graphics appeared on the monitor. The bright title screen flashed, accompanied by up-tempo music. Eric, on autopilot, coursed his way through the menu.

He snapped out of his zombie-like trance, if only for a moment. Something felt off.

What just happened?

This is what he did every Friday evening, but it didn't feel right for some reason.

I told Dad that I have this strange ability, and I'm being punished for it. My life is officially a freak show. Oh well, it's not like I was gonna be normal anyway.

Sighing, Eric put on his headset and adjusted the microphone piece. Voices of fellow gamers streamed into Eric's ears, already in progress with their digital missions. Instead of joining an online crusade to vanquish alien enemies, Eric launched the custom character creator feature.

A buff ninja materialized in the center of an armada of menu choices. The character name "Katana Dragon" hovered over the rotating masked figure. Eric scrolled through color choices for his fighter's serpent tattoos, but repeated notifications interrupted him. Online users called for Eric to join the action.

"I'll enter the arena later," Eric said. "I'm not strong enough yet."

He selected the disconnect option on the screen, and the online notifications disappeared. Muting the sound, Eric flipped through the various enhancements he could alter his ninja with claws, fire-eyes, spiky shoulder pads—all boring.

What's this?

Eric's stomach twisted, but it wasn't with dread for once. Excited, Eric clicked on a set of wings that attached to his ninja. He spun the avatar, nodding in approval.

"Eric, we need to talk," David's voice came through the speaker.

"BRAIN, lock 'Eric's Bedroom Door,'" Eric ordered, and he heard the gears inside the door make a quick turn and then *click*.

"You know I can override that," David's voice rattled through the speaker. "The 'B' in BRAIN stands for 'Boxworth' after all—and that's patent-pending in case we're somehow being monitored!"

Eric rolled his eyes and browsed through varying colors for his ninja's fluttering wings.

"The workers have all left, and I've secured the building," his dad said. "I... I just want to make sure you are safe."

"Look, Dad, I get it," Eric said, still engrossed in his game. "I mean, we were straight-up attacked today. That Cyber guy could have other supervillain friends. He could come back."

"I'm not worried about that," David's disembodied voice said. "With the upgrades I'm installing as part of the remodeling, this place will be a certified fortress. I want you to be safe from..."

"From who, Dad?"

"Me," David revealed. "Specifically, the people who associate with me. The people I attract."

Eric put the controller down.

"You mean those army guys. Like the ones you were trying to sell to this morning?"

"Eric, if any of those people saw you or knew that you can, you know, do what you do, they'd stop at nothing to take you away from here. And, I'll be honest with you, buddy, I'm still trying to process this, and, well, I'm scared. Not of you! No, I mean..."

Leaning back in his chair, Eric exhaled a deep sigh.

"I don't even understand what I can do or how I can do it. I just, sorta am able to, I guess."

"We can figure that out," David said. "But in the meantime, I don't know what else to do besides hiding you. Go to school, act like everything's normal."

Eric shut his eyes.

Why couldn't I get teleportation powers instead? Or anything to escape without making a scene.

"If those military people, those businesspeople, if

they catch you, then they'd poke and prod you," David said. "They'd study you... I know because it's what I would do."

Eric got up and stood by the door without a sound, resting his head on the cool metal.

"I don't want to be some experiment. Not yours, not anyone's."

It sounded less like a defiant declaration from Eric and more like a fearful plea.

"Look, man, I'm not gonna pretend I know what in the world is happening," David admitted. "I can't focus on that, but protecting you from being a government lab rat, that's my job right now. It's what your mom would've wanted."

DAVID

Eric and David ate their reheated pasta in silence. The noodles sat in a plastic container near the middle of a long metal table, next to a few power tools. The aroma of tomato sauce mingled with the smell of motor oil. Automated machines repaired other machines a mere handful of yards away in the large workshop/showroom serving as a dining area and dimly lit kitchen.

Instead of a conversation, drilling, mechanical churning, and chunky whirring noises filled the room. Earlier in the day, David personally oversaw that the refrigerator and other appliances were repositioned to be as closely as they were prior to the attack.

The fact they still work is proof that I'm not completely cursed, David thought.

"Leftovers night is a real party, huh, pal?" David said after the awkwardness had reached its boiling point.

"Every night is leftovers night," Eric pointed out.

"Well, we're real wild men then. Party every night, right?" David commented, hoping to get a reaction from his son.

He, of course, received more quietness. David pulled out his phone and tapped.

Clank clank clank. A clunky, dark gray steel-plated robot bulldog walked up to Eric's feet. The artificial animal struggled with every *chrrt* sound its gears made.

"Would you look at who decided to join us?" David said, bursting with fake enthusiasm. "It's Responsi-Bulldog!"

The faux canine raised its head and rotated it to an unnatural degree.

"Woof. Woof," Responsi-Bulldog barked in a flat human voice that sounded suspiciously like David. "I have been programmed to teach Eric responsibility. You have not taken me for a walk in—"

Its voice crackled into a loud, overdubbed yell.

"—three-point seven years. Woof. Woof."

Eric lifted his leg away from the small robotic pet.

"Dad, why is this thing out here? It's falling apart."

"It'd be in much better condition if you gave him some repairs," David suggested.

The robo-dog walked headfirst into the table leg, repeatedly hitting its face, metal on metal.

"Woof. Woof. Working hard builds character. Woof. Woof," it said between *clangs.*

"I'll, uh, get around to it later," Eric said.

Responsi-Bulldog stopped and lowered to sit. It lifted its back paw to simulate scratching itself in jarring, sudden spurts of movement.

"Get to it later, okay," David said, scoffing as he downed a forkful of spaghetti. "What if I looked at the big hole in the wall and decided to 'get it to it later?'"

David lectured with his mouth full.

"Boxworth Dreamineering is going down the commode, but I'll just 'get to it later.' My son can fly for crying out loud, but I'll just get to that later, too!"

The air hung heavy between them. Eric twirled his noodles around his fork, spinning in a slow cycle. David put his fork down and wiped his face with a napkin.

"Hey, listen, I didn't mean what I said—Boxworth Dreamineering will be fine. I just need to sell the MegaCore. We'll be okay."

Eric sat back, still and quiet. David knew this move. Eric did this while waiting for the right moment to excuse himself. Responsi-Bulldog sat near him, jolting with sparse erratic malfunctions but otherwise motionless.

"It's just a lot to take in, alright?" David admitted.

"I won't do anything," Eric said, speaking in a low tone with his chin lowered onto his chest. "I won't use my power. No one else will know. I don't want your company to go under because of me."

David stared back at his son from across the table. Their distorted funhouse reflections on the steel tabletop mirrored their discomfort.

"You're not my burden, Eric," he assured in a softer voice, betraying the scowl he wore. "Is that what you think?"

Across from them, automatons worked on machinery. Sparks shot out from the mechanical tools.

"When did this start?" David asked, rubbing his eyes.

Eric put his fork down, slow and steady, trying not to make a sound.

"Today was the first time," he said. "Like, I jumped up to reach for you, and I just kinda stayed in the air."

"What do you mean you stayed there?"

"I don't know," Eric went on. "I jumped, and everything seemed like it was in slow motion, but it was just me. I was floating. It's been gradually getting worse since this morning."

"Worse?"

Perplexed, David sipped his iced tea while his eyes darted back and forth.

"Nanites, maybe. It's possible you emit some kind of gravity manipulation field. Can't be the anti-grav belt; I could never get that thing to work. Could be an extra-dimensional force—"

Eric downcasted his eyes.

"Come on," Eric said. "This is getting weird."

"Weird? Yeah, we're only at the tip of the weirdberg, buddy," David remarked. "One day, you're my normal teenage kid, and boom, the next day, you're flying around like Peter Pan. Yeah, I'd say this classifies as weird."

"I meant this." Eric corrected, pushing his plate away from him. "Eating dinner out here. We never do this. I just wanna go watch TV in my room."

"Hey, man, your mom always wanted us to, you know, eat like a family, so why not—"

"Stop talking about her!" Eric shouted.

David shut up and rested his elbows on the table, lacing his fingers together. Even the machines ceased. The silence loomed like an overcast sky.

"I want to understand," David said. "You have to realize, though... It's impossible not to study you."

Eric pushed himself from the table and stormed off to the stairs. In a rush, he propelled himself over the stairwell. David watched the tips of Eric's sneakers slide across the walkway. David sat alone, frowning as he stared at the plastic dish of noodles.

He swiped his phone's screen until he reached an image of a woman in a lab coat. It was his favorite picture of his wife, with her strawberry blonde hair tied back, working at her desk (David couldn't remember what job it was; he guessed it was self-replicating data research project). She had protested modeling for such a mundane backdrop lacking glamor. She wore her most natural smile, though, immersed in her element.

"You got out before he became a teenager," he said to the screen. "You always were the smart one, Eliza."

He lingered on the image a moment before swiping it away. He rested his chin on his clasped hands and stared into nothingness.

"Ah, Eric," David said. "I'm just trying to help."

"Woof. Woof. I have to—poo and pee—let me out to do my business," the robot mutt played from its voice box. "Responsibility stinks, doesn't it? Ha. Ha. Woof. Woof

"You said it, Responsi-Bulldog," David muttered.

ERIC

Eric fell back onto his bed. His eyes fixated on the plain, tiled ceiling. The ambient noises of the city soothed him only for a few breaths. His room had served for so long as a refuge from the anxiety ambush that was the outside world.

Now, this may as well be my prison cell.

"Reminder," BRAIN said, speaking up from Eric's pocket. "A parent-signed permission slip is required to attend next week's field trip to the Comic-Convention Superhero Celebration."

"That's not gonna be easy to get, BRAIN," Eric said. "Dad hated the Super Society even before they tore up our house."

He pulled his phone out and opened his messages from Jaycee. He sent a simple text of a male zombie emoji. With his phone face down on his chest, Eric stared into nothingness. Lost in his thoughts, Eric levitated, hovering a foot or so above his mattress. His consciousness slipped, casting him into a lucid numbness.

Eric didn't know how much time had passed—his phone's vibration startled him, sending him crashing to his bed. A message notification from Jaycee displayed: a female vampire emoji.

He responded with a male vampire emoji and "there should be a werewolf emoji."

Less than a minute later, she texted: "ikr!!"

Eric smiled for the first time in what seemed like a very, very long time.

Chapter Six: *UPGRADED*

JAYCEE

O F ALL THE WONDROUS SPECTACLES within the Pantheon Solutions Tower, taking the main elevator was Jaycee's absolute favorite thing to do. She pressed her forehead on the thick glass, ogling the enormity of the building with a wide grin.

As she rode up the extensive wall, Jaycee soaked in the view. Buzzing drones and mobile workstation platforms flourished with kinetic liveliness. The Pantheon skyscraper devoted its first five stories to open-concept transparency. Jaycee loved seeing the hollowed interior's outer rims alive with dressed-to-the-nines-managers presenting three-dimensional graphics. The massive windows encasing the building's base let the world see the statuesque employees tending to various communications in their wall-mounted cubicles.

A pleasant-sounding woman's voice pumped through the overhead speakers: "Welcome to Pantheon Tower. Please enjoy your visit and remember—think infinitely!"

Melvin and Tiffany seriously take this place for granted, Jaycee thought. *Yvette is the only one who sees how stupidly, crazily awesome it is here, and she's gone half the time.*

A large, dense pipe stretched down the center of the cylindrical tower. Lush organic green leaves covered the tube along with tropical flowers that looked like a speckled rainbow. A series of large, flat lamps lined the circumference, projecting light onto the leaves.

"The 'Plant Pipeline,' as it is lovingly referred to, provides natural air for all Pantheon Solutions family members," the woman on the recording continued. "It is a living ecosystem in the center of our headquarters!"

Even the lift itself smelled of lilacs, which failed to cover the bleached sterility completely, but Jaycee didn't care. Her mother and schoolteacher, Valerie Cooper, chose not to gaze upon the impressive rotating promenades encircling the high-rise. Instead, she zeroed in on the chipper young blonde woman in a formal pink dress accompanying them on their trip up.

"Barry is very excited to see you two," Chelsea, their cheery concierge, said.

She leaned down to Jaycee.

"Especially you, Jennifer!"

"It's Jaycee; everybody knows that," she corrected, tugging at her bookbag hanging on her shoulder.

The woman smiled and nodded to be polite. Jaycee sensed the lights were on, but no one was home.

"I'm sure 'Barry' is very excited," Valerie said, donning an obviously fake smile.

A slick, white drone, the size of a basketball, propelled itself, with blue-white energy emitting from its underbelly. It moved concurrently with their elevator. The drone's robotic arm waved to Jaycee from outside of the glass. She giggled and waved back, noticing the small variety of iced bottles it carried in its indented back. It whisked itself away to a floating podium near a bullpen of well-dressed workers.

"Wow, floating bottle service! That's new!" Jaycee said.

"As you surely know, employee morale is of the utmost importance here," Chelsea chirped. "Mobile refreshments units, or M.R.U.s for short, are just one of the many joy incentives we provide to our Pantheon family members who work on Saturdays."

"Mr. Maddox at least knows how to keep some people happy," Valerie jabbed.

Jaycee rolled her eyes.

Ding!

"Oh! We're here!" Chelsea said.

The transparent doors slid open, and they exited onto a shiny hardwood floor. Like the spacious levels below them, Jaycee's father's office was an expansive suite unto itself. There were no doors other than the elevator—huge windows circled the enclosed room. Every angle provided a jaw-dropping view of the daylight-kissed city. Baron stood by his broad desk in the center of the room.

"There she is!"

Baron welcomed with outstretched arms. His white slacks and blazer matched his ivory-colored desk.

"Hi, Dad!"

Jaycee ran at least twenty feet across the airy area to embrace her waiting father. Valerie was in no such hurry. Once she sat in a cushy chair at the end of the desk, Valerie placed her bag down, not looking at her daughter.

Jaycee noticed the desk's surface displaying an old image of Judge Justice and his kid sidekick, Sidebar, both posing—the Judge in his robe holding his Golden Gavel and the teen dressed in red and white spandex and mask. Pictures of the original Super Society members always brought a smile to Jaycee's face, but she especially loved seeing Sidebar.

Dad looks so young; it's freaky! Jaycee thought, covering her grin.

"You'll have to pardon me," Baron said, tapping the desk.

The image vanished.

"You caught me being nostalgic for simpler times for our beloved Super Society."

"Jennifer, go wait outside," her mother instructed.

Jaycee looked around.

"Uh, Mom, I literally can't."

"Jennifer Claire. Now," Valerie insisted.

Baron nodded at the concierge, and she gestured for Jaycee to follow her. Jaycee's eyes fluttered in protest, but it was no use. She followed Chelsea into the elevator. Bored beyond belief within picoseconds, Jaycee leaned against the door and pulled out her phone.

Her breath fogged the glass. Jaycee wiped it away and saw Baron taking his seat across from Valerie. He mouthed a few silent pleasantries.

"While we wait, I can tell you some fun facts about Pantheon Solutions," Chelsea said. "Pantheon Solutions doesn't just pave the way to the future with next-gen technology; Pantheon Tower's top floor serves as headquarters of the next generation of superheroes, the Super—"

"I know you're new here, Chelsea," Jaycee said, "but you can save the tour guide bit. Big boss man in there? I'm his daughter. That really was a fun fact, though!"

"Yes, and we are thrilled you are visiting us today!"

"Right..." Jaycee said. "This is a great convo we're

having, but I won't let soundproof glass keep me out of the parent loop."

She tapped at the Super Society app on her phone. After entering a series of passwords, she toggled through various audio settings.

"Being the non-newbie I am, I know a few tricks to hack the speaker system."

"Oh, how interesting!' Chelsea said.

Baron's voice entered the elevator.

"You know, we can say anything in front of our daughter."

Jaycee pretended to scroll through her phone while keeping an eye on her parents. Baron waved his hand over an area of his white desk. A flat, round piece of the surface slid back, and a chilled bottle of sparkling water popped up through the hole. He took the bottle, and the desk sealed itself as it was before. He twisted the lid off.

"Care for any?"

"No, thank you," Valerie said. "But I'll tell you what I'd really like, Baron."

She crossed her legs and pulled down her black and blue checkered skirt over her knees.

"Please, do tell," he urged, blatantly staring at Valerie.

Ew, Dad, you may not be aware I can hear you, but you gotta know I can see you, right?

"I'd adore it if you greeted us yourself instead of sending your latest ditzy bimbo," Valerie said.

"Imaginative as ever, I see," Baron said before taking a sip of water. "Pantheon Solutions is strictly a professional environment."

Valerie gripped her armrests. Jaycee followed Baron's eyes right to Valerie's ringless finger.

"I will not mince words with you," Valerie said.

"Jennifer is failing in all of her classes."

"What a snitch!" Jaycee muttered.

"I find that difficult to believe," Baron said. "She's such a bright girl—"

"She skips school. With great frequency," Valerie stated. "The fact that you—despite living in the evolved age of mass communication—aren't aware of this is, to be blunt, alarming. You alarm me, Baron."

Baron twisted the cap back onto his bottle.

"And you, Valerie, astound me."

He sat so still that Jaycee could see the condensation of the bottle dripping over his hands.

"I am not telling you how to take that," Baron said. "But please be assured it is intended for complementariness."

He waved his hand over a bare area of his desk, and it opened once more, this time producing a clear coaster. The desk resealed itself, and Baron set his bottle down.

Valerie cocked an eyebrow.

"I wouldn't lose sleep over wondering whether or not I'll inform you of what I intend on taking and how I'm going to take it."

"With all due mutual respect," Baron resumed, "our daughter could attend any prestigious higher learning institution in the world. She only goes to your school to be close to you. I do not question your skills as an educator. Please understand me, but the school itself is... lacking."

Valerie smirked but was quick to stiffen her lips.

"I want you to know how serious this visit is. It's just that you have a wealth of resplendent resources and..."

Valerie withheld a laugh.

"You blame it on the school," she said as her smirk

faded. "That is just so fascinating and revealing to me. Not at all surprising, though."

Baron leaned back in his chair, sizing her up.

Maybe I don't want to be hearing this, after all, Jaycee thought.

"The principal has stated that one more instance of 'playing hooky,' as it were, will result in Jennifer getting expelled," Valerie cautioned.

Angry, Jaycee pressed her thumb on her phone's screen so hard she thought it might crack.

"Oh, come on!" Jaycee blurted. "Like Principal Garza would even go through with it."

Baron and Valerie turned to look at her, both sharing unamused expressions. Horrified, Jaycee realized her thumb was firmly pressing the "microphone" icon on her screen.

"Jennifer, how are you even talking through the—"

"We'll discuss this later," Baron said, cutting off Valerie.

Her mother's squinted eye let them both know how irritated she was. Her parents resumed their conversation, but Jaycee felt little relief.

Gotta be more careful when I use the app!

"Pantheon offers academic sponsorships for underprivileged children—"

"That's awesome, Chelsea." Jaycee nodded back to her parents, keeping her thumb a safe distance over her phone.

"As I said, I will not mince words with you, Baron," Valerie said. "This may be one of your weekends, but I know about all the times she sneaks off to go see you."

Oh, Mom, she thought. *You think you're so smart, but you don't even realize your own daughter is Powerhouse.*

As Valerie spoke, Baron looked at Jaycee. She

smiled. He smiled back.

"If Jennifer has one more unexcused absence, I will fight for full custody," Valerie warned.

Both Jaycee and Baron's crystal-blue eyes shot back at Valerie.

"She's a teenage girl skipping school," Baron countered. "One sign of trouble, and you're off to see the lawyers?"

Valerie stood.

"You have grown Pantheon Solutions into an unprecedented conglomerate of software and hardware enhancements that has revolutionized our quality of life. Look, I still wear my Pantheon Zeta Watch."

She slid back the sleeve of her silky turquoise blouse to show a thin, pale gray band clasped around her wrist. The blank, rectangular watch face projected high-definition holographic photos in front of her. Jaycee reminisced while watching the device's two-dimensional slideshow of pictures of herself, Valerie, and Baron when they were younger and happier. The last still frame showed a more recent awkward family snapshot of Jaycee bearing a wide grin while her parents wore miserable scowls.

The pictures disappeared.

"Even with all the upgraded creature comforts, this place is not a well-suited home for Jennifer," Valerie said. "You being the benefactor to the Super Society only puts her in harm's way, and there's not a judge alive who would disagree with me."

Baron stood to match her and tapped his desk; small squares lit up where he pressed his fingertips.

"Dahlia," Baron requested. "Print out the documents I just sent to you and bring them here, please."

Roughly five feet behind Valerie, a wide circle cut

through the polished floor. The disc retracted with a motorized *whssk* sound. A thick glass tube slid up from the hole. Inside the transparent chute, a fit woman stood wearing an outfit like Chelsea's.

That's not all that's similar...

The clear door spun open, stopping behind the petite blonde assistant who could've passed as Chelsea's twin. Both Jaycee and Valerie's jaws unhinged as they watched Dahlia walk toward the desk with a short stack of papers in her hand.

"Are you two, um, related?" Jaycee asked Chelsea.

"Oh, we're all family here at Pantheon!" she cheerfully replied.

Baron accepted the sheets and gestured for Dahlia to stand by the desk.

"Thank you, Dahlia," Baron said.

He reviewed the pages, then handed them to Valerie.

"What is this? A 'double your pleasure' fantasy?" she said, giving a fake courtesy smile to Dahlia.

The other woman answered with a bright, toothy grin.

"What you hold in your hands are legal documents that will start your journey of sole custodianship of our daughter," Baron explained. "I have not signed anything. Me delivering your first steps does not imply I won't contest this. You'll do it anyway, so this is just one more thing I can help you out with."

Valerie read over the documents with the same stern face Jaycee had seen her grade papers with a thousand times. She placed the documents flat on the desk and leaned over. Her brow scrunched as she aimed her face at Baron.

"I hope you know how much I don't buy into this little powerplay of yours. You endanger our daughter by providing a superhero team their base of operations from the building you call both work and home—which is another red flag, not separating the two. You also keep your robo-assistants below a trapdoor!"

"There's no trapdoor!" Baron said. "And I most certainly do not 'keep' my assistants down in some dungeon like you're implying. Right, Dahlia?"

The woman smiled, seemingly focused on the nothing in front of her. Baron rubbed his eyes.

"Dahlia, it really doesn't help sell the whole 'I don't have trapdoors and dungeons' thing if you don't talk."

She didn't blink.

"Do they not drug test employees anymore?" Jaycee asked Chelsea.

"Oh, you should never do drugs!" Chelsea said.

Jaycee was careful not to make eye contact as she looked back at her parents.

I have my blonde moments, sure, Jaycee thought. *But these ladies are beyond clueless.*

"Remaining connected after our estrangement has been a lengthy, arduous process," Baron said. "Having been deprived of a traditional, nuclear family myself, it pains me to think of what Jaycee may endure."

Swiping up her bag, Valerie turned from Baron.

"I'm aware of your familial embitterment," she said. "But you forget, I know the, shall we say, less publicized version of your saga after you ran away from the foster home."

"Oh, by all means, recite back to me the things I merely allowed you to know."

"Please do!" Jaycee whispered from behind the glass. "I love hearing about Dad's glory days as Sidebar!"

"Okay, so I never prodded you for insight on your time spent as a young ward for Patrick Gilroy," Valerie said. "You want to keep your years with that strange recluse a secret; that's fine with me. But don't pretend the Gilroy mansion wasn't a cozy way to spend your days as a blossoming youth. The latchkey kid routine won't work on me."

If Mom hasn't figured out by now that Mr. Gilroy was Judge Justice, she never will!

Baron sat, relaxing in his cushioned chair. Valerie leaned her weight onto her free hand on her side.

"Look, I don't mean to disregard your contributions to helping underprivileged foster children. That's commendable, but honestly, at this point, all I want is for us to coordinate as much as possible for Jennifer's sake, okay?"

"Family means everything," Baron said. "I try so hard to keep us together, yet you tear us apart."

"You make sure the outside world sees your 'model employees,'" Valerie taunted. "But underneath all this extravagance, you turn a blind eye to the minors you endanger in your crime-fighting group. And they're led by this adult stranger we're supposed to love? Who is Truther, anyway? Honestly, Baron, you have children living here—my students!"

"Yes, I provide a home for a few deserving orphans. Every day they can see what I have made of myself. I can show them what they could never get on their own. I motivate them. And what fine companions they are for Jaycee."

"I wouldn't call Melvin and Tiffany BFFs," Jaycee said under her breath.

"You seem to enjoy surrounding yourself with 'fine' companions, eh, Baron?" Valerie said with a spiked brow.

"Again, they are strictly my valued employees, but nice try," Baron shot back.

I don't miss these fights, Jaycee thought.

"Your interest in my social life is very flattering, though," Baron said with a smirk.

"If my interests were of any concern to you, perhaps we'd still be married."

Right on cue, Mom and Dad are spiraling out of control and seeing who can dish out the sickest burn.

"You know, sometimes I wish you still worked for me," Baron said, resting his elbow on the desk while placing his chin in his palm. "You were the only one around here who wasn't afraid to hurt my feelings with the truth. These days I can't even build a robot that'll do that."

"I suppose life is a breeze with your embarrassment of riches," Valerie said. "And I'm very much enjoying my chosen career path, thank you."

"It remains a mystery why you didn't take me to the cleaners during the divorce. Have teachers' salaries changed that dramatically?"

"Enough is enough," Jaycee whispered.

She scrunched her lips, mentally fitting the gears of an idea in place.

"Hey, wait a sec—Chelsea, that's your voice on the recording when you enter the tower, right?"

"It was a hoot recording all of those!"

"A hoot and a half," Jaycee said, tapping away at her phone. "Mom and Dad may not listen to me, but I know a way around that. Hey, Chels, can you say something for me?"

"Welcome to Pantheon Tower," she recited with glee. "Please enjoy your visit and remember—think infinitely!"

"Ooookay," Jaycee said, mouth agape.

Relying on her to say anything other than what she already knows isn't a good idea.

"Gonna have to do this the techie-way. Good thing I inherited uber-geek genes from Mom and Dad."

A slew of passcodes got her deeper into the network, fluctuating in and out of pages, settings menus, and firewalls.

"Too easy," Jaycee said with a self-satisfied grin.

"Save your stunts for court days, Baron," Valerie said, crossing her arms. "I may not have the top-dollar attorneys you have, but—"

"Reminder for Mr. Maddox," Chelsea's voice blared through the sound system—the actual Chelsea's smiling lips did not move, however.

It worked! Jaycee thought.

"Your massage therapy appointment begins in five minutes," Jaycee said into her phone's mic, producing Chelsea's voice.

"Strictly professional, sure," Valerie said in a huff. She walked to the elevator.

"In the meantime," Valerie said, "I hope your years as a superhero team manager maintain their prosperity. If you'll excuse me, I have to go say goodbye to my daughter."

As Valerie approached the elevator door, Jaycee's thumb tapped with a speed that would rival Go-Go's.

"And de-hacking the sound system is... complete!" Jaycee whispered.

The door opened, and Jaycee and Valerie switched places in the chute. Her mother gave her an extra-long hug goodbye. She watched Valerie look back at her from the other side of the glass as Chelsea pressed a button sending the elevator down. Jaycee dwelled on how remorseful her mother looked, but only for a moment.

Jaycee skipped past the clear tube near the desk. She waved at Dahlia inside the rounded elevator car just before it was sucked into the floor.

Baron sat on the edge of his desk.

"Cute trick with the elevator audio," Baron said. "That's my genius girl!"

Jaycee responded with a smug, closed-eyed smile.

"What do you say we get down to business?" he asked with delighted anticipation.

Jaycee nodded in excitement. Baron tapped a space on his desk, and in an instant, large metal plates lowered, covering the massive windows around them. The automated process took less than a minute, providing more than enough time for Baron to take his seat. Jaycee hurried and sat at the other end of the desk.

Baron waited for the office's visibility to be completely blocked off. He leaned over to speak candidly.

"You ready?" he asked.

"Affirmative!"

He nodded.

"Masks on!" Baron said.

Jaycee swung her bookbag around and reached in. After a moment of rummaging, she pulled out her Powerhouse mask. Donning the cowl, she became a full-fledged superhero. However, the rainbow unicorn on the center of her powder blue shirt and white shorts didn't match the crime-fighter vibes.

Baron waved his hand over a clean part of his desk's surface. A rectangular slat of the tabletop withdrew into itself, and from the cavity, it propped up Truther's mask. He slid it over his head. The big gold "T" on his face extended low enough to cover his mustache. The sewn-in blonde wig fell into place with a convincing wave atop his head. Jaycee positively loved watching her father put on that mask—and she loved that she was the only member of the Super Society that knew the truth about Truther.

Yvette being out with Melvin and Tiffany makes this even sweeter. No one to butt in.

"What news do you have on the boy, hero?" Baron said in his lowered superhero voice.

"Yesterday, I noted a total of five instances of the subject displaying his ability, sir."

She pulled her phone from her pocket, readying it to show the video evidence of Eric floating up the gym ropes.

"Documentation attempts were..."

Something stopped her. She inserted the device back into her pocket, mentally cursing her disloyalty.

"...inconclusive."

"Keep on him, Powerhouse. He'll be more likely to trust someone his own age. It may take some time, but I'm confident you can wear him down. If you can acquire irrefutable proof that this kid is legit, we may have a huge crisis on our hands."

"Permission to speak freely, sir," she stated rather than requested.

"You don't have to ask if you can—"

He exhaled and dropped the issue.

"Of course, Powerhouse."

"It's just that, um, maybe he's not a threat," she fumbled out, keeping her head low.

Baron stood. She looked up at him, expecting the worst. Her father remained silent for a moment that felt like it had taken a geologic age to pass. Mercifully, he finally spoke up.

"Meet me in my lab. I want to show you something."

• • •

The long trip up in the concealed elevator gave Jaycee time to get into full costume as Powerhouse. The hatch opened, and she walked inside a small, dim chamber, smaller than the broad elevator doors would suggest. The red bulb above doused the space in a crimson glow. She entered a code onto an access panel beside a featureless door.

"What is the secret password?" an automated voice requested.

"Justice!" Jaycee proclaimed with enthusiasm.

"Error," the voice said. "The password changes every thirty minutes. You just missed it. Additional identification is required. Request retinal scan."

The right side of her mouth struck upward in an aggravated half-grin. She twisted the yellow-tinted dome over her right eye, popped it off, and leaned forward, letting the panel's green laser swipe over her pupil.

"Powerhouse identity confirmed," the automated voice said.

Relieved, she pushed the eye-cover back onto her mask.

"However," the voice continued, "retinal scans can be faked. Request thumbprint scan."

Jaycee rolled her eyes and removed her metallic glove by tapping a button on the underside of her wrist. She pressed her thumb onto the screen.

"Thumbprint recognized," the voice said. "However, how do I know you did not just chop off the correct thumb and use it to get in? I cannot take that chance."

Jaycee slumped in disbelief.

"Request bodily fluid sample."

"Um, excuse me?!"

The door suddenly opened.

"I saw you on the camera. Come on in," Baron said from beyond a series of diamond-shaped workstations. "Sorry, after the first security scans fail, the system is programmed to ask for increasingly annoying forms of I.D. until the person eventually just goes away."

Jaycee walked through the maze of black and white computer terminals, listening to the low hum of the translucent cylindrical power generators lining the walls. She searched past a long chrome table with shiny robot arms operating on the innards of a golden T-shaped gauntlet. The *fzzz* noises coming from the assemblage of tools working around her made it difficult to zero in on anything else. She passed transparent boards covered in notes and equations handwritten in several different marker colors. She sifted through the surrounding sounds to trace where her team leader was hiding.

Jaycee found Baron in full uniform as Truther, sitting at a console behind a wall with monitors of varying sizes spread across it. Each screen showed different news feeds and surveillance footage from around the city. She approached him from behind, marveling at his dedication to overseeing the city's safety.

"Powerhouse reporting for duty, sir!"

She saluted.

"No saluting," he reminded without looking.

Jaycee drew back her hand in a flash. He turned to face her. He kept himself in shape but would never admit to his super-suit padding out some additional muscles. A golden arm brace lay on his lap, like the cybernetic attachments Jaycee wore, but this new piece was slick and glossy.

Standing, he presented it to her.

"Try this on."

She accepted with shaking hands.

"Is this...?"

He nodded. With a touch of a button underneath a tiny panel by her shoulder, Jaycee detached the metal brace that encased her right arm. She handed the old apparatus to her father and snapped on the new, shimmering attachment. It linked with her suit's system, and the new brace lit up with activation. Jaycee felt a surge of energy flowing throughout her body.

"I already feel so much stronger!" she said, beaming and flexing the coils around her fingers.

"This charging meter will turn green when it's fully powered," Baron advised, pointing to the small panels below her knuckles.

Jaycee clenched her fist and watched with glee as the little panels lit up. First, they glowed blue, flashed a few times, then radiated with green light. She couldn't take her eyes off the sleek way the brace outlined her bicep and encased her forearm. She admired the gear's circles and oval-shaped intricacies around her wrist. Unlike the equipment Jaycee was used to operating, this armor piece felt much more organic.

Embarrassed that she had lost herself in adulation, Jaycee toughened up and stood at attention.

"It is very impressive, sir!"

"It is pretty cool, right?" Baron said with a mischievous grin under the lower part of the T-emblem of his mask.

"Yes, it's so awesome!" she squealed, unable to contain her excitement. "You finally built it! I didn't want to ask about it because I didn't want to seem pushy, but you made it finally, and I'm so happy that it's finally here, O-M-G finally!"

"Upgraded battle-tech is essential for optimum

crime-fighting, and you may need it if this flying boy proves to be an enemy."

A wave of uncertainty crushed her joy.

"I dunno," Jaycee mumbled. "He seems, y'know, pretty good to me."

"We can't afford to take any chances," Baron warned. "Him being the son and heir to David Boxworth's, well, not fortune, but his Dreamineering company and all of its technological assets makes the boy a person of interest we simply can't ignore."

"What happens if he, you know, can really fly?" she asked, afraid of the answer.

"That would depend on our evaluation of him and, frankly, whether or not he chooses to cooperate," Baron explained.

He held up a fist.

"Trust me, for his sake, he better play ball."

He relaxed his fist and put his hand on her shoulder.

"Don't worry, hero. We'll find out the truth behind Eric Boxworth. Dismissed!"

"Yes, sir!"

She raised her hand to salute but caught herself.

"Oh, and, uh…"

Bad idea, Jaycee… she thought. They didn't want you to hear. So, I shouldn't ask. Yep, bad idea… that I'm totally doing anyway.

"What were you and Mom talking about?"

"Not with the masks on."

She nodded as her eyes fluttered.

FLOATER

Chapter Seven: *FLIGHT*

ERIC

"TEST FLIGHT ONE, RECORDING. MARK date and time. Subject codename: 'Floater' is ready for takeoff!"

"'Floater?!'"

Eric's disgusted expression told his father all he needed to know.

"We'll workshop the name," David assured while holding up his phone.

The screen displayed a timer and an audio graph that bounced with each syllable he spoke.

"Bon voyage!"

Eric felt the force of David's push on his back through the thick cushion of his padded coat. Feeling even that slight impact didn't bolster Eric's confidence in his puffy head-to-toe safety suit as he dropped from the fourth-story platform. The interior of the Boxworth Building's showroom blurred as Eric rapidly descended. The big, blue crash-pads below grew closer with each passing millisecond.

I'm gonna die! I'm gonna die! I'm gonna—

"Fly!" David shouted from above.

As if on command, Eric soared upward. The thrill

of not perishing intermixed with the panic of not being able to stop himself. His momentum rushed him straight for the steel wall. Closing his eyes, Eric braced for the impact, but when that didn't come, he realized he wasn't moving.

Hovering nearly fifty feet in the air, Eric peeked over at the enormous, barricaded hole in the wall. He looked below at the under-reconstruction work area with the crash-pads in the center. His grinning father leaned on a guardrail on the promenade.

"Okay, so I'm not dead, but I still should've never agreed to this!" Eric conceded.

He waded his arms in the air. Eric resisted the urge to steady himself, letting himself float haphazardly. A small drone buzzed up next to him. A cylindrical camera protruded from its face like an extended black nose.

"The sooner we understand your powers," David said, "the sooner we can figure out what the heck we're gonna do about them."

Eric watched David pull his phone to his lips.

"Note," David said into the microphone. "Floater's abilities appear to be instinctive; literally fight or flight."

Eric looked over, seeing his face pop up on David's screen.

"I have some ideas for names that don't sound like I live in a toilet," Eric said.

Eric pushed the drone-camera out of his way, then flew along the mounted walkway that lined the vast room's wall. A long, skinny rectangular drone followed him. Eric stopped when he reached David's perch. The thin drone split, then expanded itself and unfurled an orange mesh net. The net connected at either end of the drone's two halves, positioning itself below Eric's feet.

"Little overkill, Dad," Eric said, pointing down at the floating net.

He pressed into the padding of his oversized top. It resembled a puffy beige winter jacket with matching pants.

"And I'm sweating like crazy in this sumo wrestler suit."

"Alert! Visitor at the main entrance! Alert!" BRAIN projected throughout the room.

The announcement startled Eric, shaking his concentration. Panic seized his mind, and he fell. His flailing hands grabbed David and pulled him over the guardrail. They plunged into the net below—their combined weight proved too much for the drone, sending them crashing again. They twisted as they plummeted, tangling in the net.

Fly or die, Floater, Eric thought to himself. *Rise above or smash the concrete.*

Eric concentrated, thinking of birds, balloons, and airplanes, how one might think of running water when they need to pee.

"Alert! Visitor at the main entrance! Alert!" BRAIN repeated.

Eric set them down gently. Grunting and grumbling, they struggled to free themselves from entanglement to no avail. David fought to move them to the entrance doors, dragging the heavy drone sections behind them.

"Dad, hold still!" Eric pleaded. "Whoever it is can wait!"

"It could be a potential MegaCore investor! Or an insurance agent!" his father reasoned, struggling in the mesh. "BRAIN, open main entrance!"

The smooth metal doors retracted into the wall. Eric felt a mixture of relief and horror when he saw Jaycee standing there, smiling only the way she could. He watched her look them up and down. There was nowhere to run or hide; Eric suffered the embarrassment intertwined with his dad.

"Uh..." she said.

Her smile transformed into a confused but courteous grin.

"Eric, are you, um, available?"

While stuck in a cumbersome position in the net in his padded suit, Eric could hardly turn his head to face his father, despite him being so uncomfortably close.

"Don't do it—" Eric begged.

"He's a little tied up at the moment," David said with glee.

JAYCEE

The tangy mustard blending with the chili soaking the bun was euphoric. Jaycee gobbled up the hotdog but carefully held a napkin under it so she wouldn't risk spilling chili sauce on her unicorn shirt. As a bonus, the hotdog cart's delicious smell helped cover up Eric's body odor.

Jaycee pretended not to notice the boy's pit stains while he dispensed ketchup on his otherwise plain hotdog.

"I think 'safety first' is super cool and everything, but you're gonna have to get a protective suit that breathes a little more," she suggested.

The afternoon sun beat down the city street, unusually warm for an early spring day. Fortunately, Eric had changed into short-sleeves and shorts.

"Y'know, at least for the summer."

That was subtle, right? she thought.

"Hey, not so loud," Eric said.

He led them farther up the sidewalk by a swanky hotel.

"It's one thing to make sure my dad doesn't know that you know, but I can't keep up with the whole neighborhood knowing that you know what I know, you know?"

"I don't know," she said with cheerful obliviousness.

Fashionable tenants blew in and out of the revolving glass doors of the complex's entrance. They seemed far too concerned with their phones to notice Jaycee and Eric's attempts at sneakiness. Jaycee chowed down the last bit of her chilidog, tossing the wrapper in a nearby waste bin. Even this snobby building's trash cans were gold and shiny.

She placed her thumbs under her bookbag's shoulder straps.

"I'm surprised your dad let you loose upon the world. How does he know you won't go up, up, and away?"

Eric looked annoyed and continued scarfing down a hotdog.

"It helps that he's busy doing a gazillion other things, like fixing ground zero, a.k.a. our home," he said. "Your folks let you roam free a lot?"

"Oh, my dad knows where I'm at."

She noticed a billboard mounted on the top story of the building across the street. It displayed a team picture with the words "THANK YOU, SUPER SOCIETY FOR KEEPING NEW ST. CLOUD CITY SAFE." Powerhouse stood front and center, posing next to Truther.

Jaycee caught Eric glancing up at the sign, so she acted fast.

Hello, secret identity gods? It's me, Jaycee. Maybe a little heads-up next time?

"If my mom knew I was out by myself, she'd freak," Jaycee said while sidestepping in front of Eric in a desperate attempt to block the billboard somehow. "She'd really lose it if she knew I was hanging out with a boy, like, as if I'm, like, a child."

"Well, I do have a reputation as a heartbreaker," Eric said.

He crumpled the hotdog wrapper and tossed it toward the golden waste bin. The ball bounced off the rim and pelted to the ground. A slender woman in a silky dark blue blouse with sheer black sleeves lowered her oversized sunglasses as she exited the building. The haughty lady's sneer pressured Eric into picking up his crinkled ball and properly disposed of it.

"You're the personification of smooth, Eric," Jaycee quipped. "Did you get the dork gene from your dad, or did your mom pass down some spaz DNA, too?"

Eric looked down with a sudden interest in his shoes.

Mom! Duh! Good going, you idiot! Jaycee cursed herself.

"So, is your Saturday so dull that you decided to come visit me?" he asked, not selling the sullenness he wore mere seconds ago. "Not that I'm complaining."

"Are you kidding me?" she asked. "I find out my new best friend has a legit superpower, but I can't tell anybody, so who else am I gonna talk to about it?"

"Again, my, um, skills aren't exactly something I want to advertise!"

Eric rolled his eyes. A second later, his pupils darted up.

"How long has that been there?"

Jaycee swiveled her head to look up behind her. He had spotted the billboard.

Well, that's just flushed.

"They blow up my house, and they get a big sign right on the same street?" he asked, placing his hands on his hips.

Jaycee was one to laugh in the face of danger, but Eric eyeing that stupid sign made her sweat bullets.

"Hey, you thirsty? I'm thirsty. Let's go not be thirsty," she said, grabbing Eric's arm and leading him to the high-rise's entrance.

They crammed into the building's revolving door, spilling out on the opposite side. Eric regained his balance as Jaycee used the momentum to skip to a big, comfy green chair next to a big stone fountain. Cherub statues stood in the clamshell-shaped structure. Soft jazz music played behind the gushing sound of babbling water.

Eric's jaw dropped at the sight of the shiny white tiles on the floor, each with an intricate diamond in the center. It became Jaycee's turn to roll her eyes as she watched Eric gawk at the crystalline chandelier suspended above them. The smallest details floored Eric—his eyes trailed the smooth wooden finish of the reception area's countertops across from them.

"Well, at least now it'll be the scent of 'poor' that people smell instead of your B.O.," Jaycee teased.

Duncan, the hotel's concierge, approached.

"Miss Maddox, what a pleasant surprise," he said, adjusting a pocket on his perfectly pressed uniform.

She had never seen him in anything less than formal attire, never a wrinkle on his suit, his slicked-back hair always perfectly set.

"Hey, Duncan," she said with a lazy head nod.

"Will you and your father be staying with us today?" he asked, adjusting his tie. "We can prepare the usual suite."

Bored, Jaycee whipped out her phone and reviewed her notifications.

"Nah, just popped in for some water."

"Sparkling or still?"

"Surprise me, Duncan," Jaycee said while fixated on her phone.

"Will your, ahem, friend be staying as well?"

She snuck a peek at Duncan, looking down his nose at Eric, who was too absorbed by a mural to notice his condescending stare.

"Yep," she answered.

"Right away," Duncan said, and off he went.

"Earth to Eric," Jaycee said, waving at him. "You gonna sit, or what?"

Eric took a seat on a matching chair next to Jaycee's.

"You come here a lot?"

"You don't? You live down the street," she reminded. "I'm just jay-kaying, of course, you wouldn't! Unless you need to stay here while your house gets rebuilt. The rooftop pool is super awesome. You'll love it!"

"My dad can't afford this place," he admitted. "Not unless you plan on buying a robot suit or a big engine thing anytime soon."

Duncan returned with two glasses of bubbly water.

"Thanks," Jaycee said, accepting the drinks.

Eric took his water without saying a word. Duncan raised his eyebrow at the boy.

"If there is anything else at all, Miss Maddox, please let me know."

Jaycee gave him a nonchalant thumbs-up, and the

man left to attend to the hustle and bustle of the lobby.

Eric sipped and scrunched his face. He placed the glass down on a table between them.

"So, why is it this place seems to love you, but the feeling isn't mutual? I mean, the water sucks, but everything else is amazing."

She put her phone down in her lap.

"Rich people are so phony. They just care about my last name. If they know you don't have any money, then they treat you like—"

"Like me," Eric finished for her. "My dad thinks you're a spy, by the way."

Jaycee almost spat out her water. Her cheeks puffed up as she choked it down.

"That's cray," she said with a nervous twinge.

"The daughter of his biggest business rival decides to drop by unexpectedly? Yeah, totally not suspicious. I bet you're wearing a wire."

He leaned over to her, keeping an eye out for any eavesdroppers.

"My dad is developing a top-secret USB-butt device," he whispered. "Just stick a thumb drive up your—"

She pushed him away, laughing.

"Cardboard Boxworth is making a joke! What'd they put in that water?"

Jaycee's smile dissolved as she peered out the clear entrance doors. Their drinks quaked, rippling the liquid inside.

That can't be good, she thought.

"I, uh, have to go to the bathroom; all that water, y'know?" Jaycee lied.

Suddenly, the windows shattered, raining shards of glass. The hotel patrons scrambled for safety.

"Please, everyone, remain calm!" Duncan cried.

People ignored his plea and rushed to the room's far side, distancing themselves from the entrance. Their fear escalated to terror as glass bits pelted the floor.

Jaycee gasped when she saw an enormous blob of a man take heavy steps toward the wrecked entrance frame. A bulky metal apparatus encased his upper torso. The huge, round stunted cannon clamped onto his face was a dead giveaway that this was the monstrous villain known as—

"Blowhard!" Jaycee whispered in shock.

Chapter Eight: *AIR*

JAYCEE

H AVING ONLY READ CASE FILES about the brute, Jaycee was blown away by how big he was in real life.

"I gotta message for all youse greedy, rich snobs!" bellowed Blowhard. "The Guerrillas are rising!"

"What? Like, a-apes?" a terrified bellhop stuttered from behind a stack of luggage crates.

"Naw!" Blowhard said, annoyed. "Like guerrilla warfare! We's a group of what you'd call 'menaces to society.' And our first act of war is takin' out 'high society!'"

"Eric, go find cover!" Jaycee ordered, but he had already crawled under his chair.

Blowhard's face-mounted weapon unloaded, launching a concentrated wave of air pressure. Hotel staff and guests toppled over, flailing like boneless dolls.

Pushing through a swarm of people, Jaycee ran to a utility closet at the end of the reception area. She slipped through the cracked door, squeezing between mops and shelves stacked with cleaning supplies.

Not exactly glamorous, but at least it's empty! she thought while closing the door.

She threw down her bag and began her transformation into Powerhouse. She shimmied into the form-fitting costume.

Thump! Thump! Reverberating footsteps quaked the floor.

"Well, I won't have to worry about Blowhard sneaking up on me," Jaycee said.

After zipping up her uniform, Jaycee pulled out two metal discs: silver and gold. She slapped the silver one onto her belt and the gold one onto her shoulder. The silver disc initiated a linking sequence, and small half-circle shapes ejected from the buckle and spread across the strap. The gold disc sent metallic loops spiraling down her right arm, linking with a panel over her knuckles and lighting up once the activation was complete.

She slung her bookbag over her shoulders and ran out of the cramped closet. Panicked pedestrians spilled out of hallways and huddled by the elevators lining the rear wall. Blowhard slogged through the emptying lobby.

The villain's flabby thighs and big belly stretched the tight, black unitard he wore. The hunk of blocky metal hung on his shoulders like a cyber-trash linebacker's football pads. Exhaust gushed from the large metal howitzer protruding from his upper body. Blowhard's angry vermilion eyes narrowed behind the steel helmet connected to his massive head.

"Run, lil' scared elitists!" he said, laughing. "Flee while I take ova your fancy palace!"

Eric darted by, making a beeline for the revolving doors at the front—or what was left of them.

"Oh, no!" Jaycee said, screeching to a halt. "Eric! Er, I mean, citizen!"

She dashed over, taking the frightened boy's hand.

"You should find cover!"

"I don't live far away," Eric said. "I'd rather take my chances at home!"

"Look, there's no time. You'll just have to come with me!"

"No offense, but I've had some bad luck with superheroes recently, and—"

Jaycee hoisted him up and hauled off with Eric like she was carrying luggage.

Great, now I gotta escort him, or he'll run straight into danger, she thought. *For this, I better get a photo, video, artist's rendering—every kind of documentation of your flying abilities, Eric!*

Careful not to max out her strength-enhancing armor, Jaycee placed Eric behind the receptionist's desk.

"Stay out of sight!" she ordered.

"Powahouse!" Blowhard said. "We ain't neva got to dance, have we?"

His hearty laughter jiggled the cellulite on his bare arms. The morbidly obese man pressed a raised button near the base of his odd ordnance, causing it to expand. This signaled the truncated chrome barrel's readiness, but Jaycee was prepared for the airy attack this time. She marched up to the towering man.

"When youse gets to kingdom come, tell 'em Blowhard sent ya!" the lethal lummox's voice boomed via hidden speakers within his armor.

POW!

Jaycee landed on her feet with her fist still outstretched. Her jumping uppercut knocked Blowhard loose from his head-cannon, obliterating the exhaling executor's hulking artillery attachment. The force toppled the fatty foe, rippling his exposed chins on the way down.

Jaycee held her hands at her hips, donning a satisfied grin.

"When you get to super-loser prison, tell 'em Powerhouse sent ya!"

Police sirens wailed in the background as people slowly emerged from their scattered hiding places.

"Is the gorilla man gone?" Eric said, unseen from behind the receptionist's desk.

"The who?" Jaycee said. "Oh! The Guerrilla guy! He's dunzo! Everyone is safe now!"

Jaycee glanced down, noticing the nylon strap over her shoulder. She leaned her head back, facing the sky.

"Ugh," Jaycee groaned. "Was I really wearing my backpack the entire time? Like, where am I even supposed to put this when I change? For serious!"

ERIC

Jaycee inspected his room, scrunching her nose at a pile of dirty laundry. It was, in a word, uncomfortable.

As if I wasn't on edge enough already, thanks to the 'air show.'

"Cool doll!" she said, picking up a miniature replica of a superhero from Eric's nightstand.

"It's actually a figurine; it doesn't move or anything," he explained, embarrassed. "It was a gift from a long time ago, not a big deal."

"My dad would love this. He's a total fanboy of Judge Justice."

Jaycee held it in front of her face to get a closer look at the detailed mini-statue's cape and mask. She touched the gold-painted gavel molded into the little hero's hand. Her commenting on how quaint his belongings were was not the way Eric had imagined having a girl in his room.

"Superheroes aren't really popular around our house, but that one's cool," Eric said, wincing at Jaycee casually placing the figurine down. "Just, ah, be careful with some of this stuff."

She opened the nightstand's drawer, rummaging through what was inside.

"Please don't—"

"Student of the year?"

She pulled out a small bronze plaque bearing Eric's name and academic achievement.

"Nerd alert!"

"That was back in elementary school, so—"

"Boring, boring, boring," she scoffed while digging through pens and rubber bands in the drawer.

"You draw these?"

Jaycee held up some drawings from atop his dresser. She perused through the sheets of various fantasy characters: a wizard, a half man-half dragon, and an armored titan.

"They aren't finished, just works in progress," Eric said, trying to grab them from her as she whipped them away.

"Not bad at all!" she complimented. "I really like the dragon guy! Wouldn't that be so awesome to be part animal? I'd be half-armadillo so that I could armor myself up! Kinda like a turtle but being a turtle would be way too slow!"

"They're just sketches. Designs and stuff."

Eric acted humble, but he could feel his face reddening, giving him away.

"Who's the babe?" Jaycee asked, looking at a framed picture of a woman on the wall across from his bed.

She was smiling, lovely, and young. Jaycee said the name "Eliza" under her breath as she read aloud the handwritten notation on the bottom of the photo. Eric stepped in front of her, blocking Jaycee's view.

"Secret crush? O-M-G, Eric!" she spouted. "I mean, looks a little old for you, but shoot your shot, dude!"

"That's my mom."

Her teeth clenched, and her eyes squinted into a mask of mortification.

"Sorry..."

He sat on the bed, looking down.

"S'okay. It's a pic from when she and my dad first got together."

"She's very pretty," Jaycee said. "Your dad totally punched above his weight."

"Heh, yeah, it was her hair. Strawberry blonde hair—Dad said it made her look like an angel—typically followed by some inappropriate remarks, which Mom would elbow him in the ribs for. I clearly didn't get the good hair gene."

He ran his fingers through his hair, messing it further.

"Do you mind if I ask what happened?" Jaycee asked. "I mean, you don't have to tell me! It's sooo none of my business! Sure, I'm curious, and I know you've never talked about her at school, but, um... I'll tell you something I've never told anyone about me if you do, like, I guess—"

"It's been four years," Eric said with a heavy sigh.

He felt the urge to shut down, but there is only so much deflecting a person can do before it becomes exhausting. He was tired of dodging, yet the words still had trouble finding his mouth.

"My mom... She... worked with my dad on this

military weapons program—it was a Pantheon-sponsored project. They were building a robot-soldier suit of armor. Your dad was there. I dunno how much, if anything, he's told you."

The genuine concern on Jaycee's face made it tougher for Eric to go on.

"Mom and Dad fought a lot about the direction. They just plain fought a lot. She quit the program so she could be home with me and..."

He looked away from her and slowed his breathing, trying to keep the tears at bay.

"So, my dad arranged it so she could be there for when they debuted Dreadnaught, this robot-soldier thing they'd been developing. My mom didn't want to go, but I begged, begged, and pleaded for her to go just so..."

He hated how his voice lightened as it trailed off. Jaycee sat next to him.

"They'd been letting me stay by myself without a sitter," he continued. "And I just... I just wanted the place to myself. I convinced her to go. There was an accident, and that stupid robot malfunctioned. It started going haywire, shooting at people and..."

Look at her, he told himself. *Face her. Do. Not. Cry. Be strong.*

"I sent her away just so I could goof off and play video games, and she... I know, it's stupid; I mean, I was a kid, but..."

He faced her with misty eyes.

"She would've been okay if she stayed."

He looked down and wiped away his tears. He resisted ugly-crying himself into an inconsolable mess. Still, his mouth hurt from the strain of withholding an all-out weeping fest. He could feel Jaycee stir beside him. Finally, he ground his palms into his eyes, abating the tears. Then he looked over at Jaycee.

She wore the mask of Powerhouse. Eric burst into a fit of laughter. She did not look anywhere close to being amused.

"Um, hello? I'm revealing my alter ego! What's so funny?"

"It was super obvious!" Eric said between chuckles.

"Hey, we're trading secrets, aren't we?" she pointed out.

Her eyes fluttered.

"I thought, y'know, we were being vulnerable, and, I dunno, you just confided in me, so I returned the favor!"

Eric leaned back on the bed, catching his breath.

"It's cool, it's just, I mean, there's this villain guy attacking people, you sneak off, and, like, a minute later this Jaycee-shaped superhero shows up? And before even that, you could pretty much tell. It explains a lot."

She stood up, crossing her arms.

"Well, you're not exactly all that stealthy either, hover-boy!"

"And looking like a superhero who's late for school is stealthy?"

He pointed below her chin. Jaycee glanced down, noticing the nylon strap over her shoulder. She leaned her head back, facing the ceiling.

"Ugh," she groaned. "Don't remind me."

He sat up.

"I have a million questions about being on a legit superhero team!"

"So, uh, this means you aren't mad at me and my team for blasting a giant hole in your wall?"

"This totally makes up for that!" Eric said. "My dad'll hold a grudge forever, but I gotta say—and I'm being for real—you dropping everything to go face this psycho villain? I'm not sure I could do that. Well, I had my chance, I guess, and, uh, yeah, that wasn't my proudest moment."

Jaycee paced a bit as if pondering her response. She picked up the Judge Justice figurine.

"You saved your dad, right?"

She spoke as if she was talking to the figurine.

"Y'know, yesterday? And don't lie, I saw you. But, anyway, there was plenty of chaos—er, chaos that was caused by both sides—and you flew in despite how dangerous it was."

He shifted on the bed, nervously watching how she handled the tiny Judge.

"Uh-huh..."

"Imagine if the whole world was your dad," she resumed, lowering the small statuette.

"Me and my dad haven't exactly been close ever since... you know. The insane robot thing."

"Even better!" she said. "Imagine caring about each and every person just as much so that you'd risk everything to save them, even if you aren't BFFs. Being a superhero is pretty much like that, plus you get to wear a cool mask!"

"A mask that exposes the lower half of your face, your hair, and you can clearly see your eyes—"

"Laugh it up. You know you want an autograph."

Chapter Nine: *GROUNDED*

JAYCEE

TO: TRUTHER

FROM: POWERHOUSE

SUBJECT: SUPERHERO LOG ENTRY - MONDAY

Saturday was a major breakthrough
but got zilch yesterday - I was
unable to observe. His father has
become increasingly restrictive, but,
little by little, I am gaining Mr.
Boxworth's trust. Now that I've been
granted access to their home, I have
to continue to do a remarkably amazing
job at not blowing my cover and
hiding my secret identity, so no video
reports. It's email only for now.
Properly documenting Eric's flying
abilities has been difficult since
he's afraid of his own shadow. I'm
going to try a more direct approach,
so don't worry, I'll get this kid

high. That sounds bad, but you know
what I mean.

- Powerhouse

"Jaycee, are you even listening to me?" Eric said from what seemed like a few planets away. "My dad pretty much had me on lockdown all day yesterday because of that, ya know, Blowhard attack. So, I've got a full day's worth of mundane nothingness I'm dying to dish about."

Jaycee hit send on her phone and darted her eyes to Eric.

"Sorry-sorry-sorry," she said, stuffing her phone into her jeans pocket. "Had to email my dad; he likes for me to check-in. And I'm, like, um, you're my father, not my parole officer, for serious."

"I'm lucky my dad even let me go to school today—which is something I never thought I'd be happy about," Eric said, navigating between fellow students as they meandered their way to class.

High-schoolers packed the hallway, wall-to-wall, locker-to-locker, filling their precious time between bells with as much chatter as possible. A few kids wore Pantheon Solutions-brand holo-face filters masking themselves with three-dimensional digital images—a puppy replaced a girl's head with its long tongue hanging out. Another was a laughing emoji come to life as if by magic.

"You gotta admit," she said. "My dad creates some cool stuff."

Eric rolled his eyes, making a "pfft" noise. Jaycee smirked because she knew she was right. They passed the teacher's lounge, where Jaycee caught a glimpse of middle-aged educators in short-sleeve button-collar shirts and khakis utilizing their treasurable free time to chug coffee, eager to get on with the morning. The teachers grinned like excited children—summer break was so close everyone could smell it.

Jaycee sniffed the dense chemical odor of body spray as they brushed past a small group of boys.

"Ugh, Eric, do guys ever stop being gross?" she asked, waving away the cologne cloud.

"What?" he asked, taking a whiff. "You don't like the smell of a phoenix's swagger?"

"I'm sure you're very familiar with it," Jaycee quipped. "Hey, what d'ya say we sneak away at lunch and film you using your powers?"

His arm grabbed her forearm. She relented to being pulled to a nook between lockers, his body shielding her from the river of students.

"Would you please stop?" he hissed. "I—"

He paused, waiting for a bearded math teacher to pass.

"The comic-con is tomorrow!" the teacher announced to the kids in the hall. "You must have your permission slips ready if you want to attend! If not, you're stuck here with me all day, taking math quizzes!"

Once the teacher walked out of sight, Eric resumed.

"I can't risk being seen at school!"

"You know what? Just for a second, I thought you had a backbone."

Jaycee slid around him, hoisting her bookbag over her shoulders.

"I thought maybe, just maybe, I might've inspired you with my super-heroics."

"You got no computer to hide behind now, punk!" a voice shouted.

Jaycee and Eric spun their heads and saw a

lanky jock in a letterman jacket leaning over Melvin: Dungeon Master by day, Supercut by night.

What is it now, Melvin? Jaycee thought.

Jaycee recognized the jock from when she and Eric had been caught in the cafeteria crossfire. The jock crossed his arms while Melvin cowered in fear. Melvin darted his head to the side, trying to avoid eye contact with his tormentor.

"Not so chatty now, are you?" the bully accosted as he pushed Melvin up against a locker.

The metal door rattled from the impact.

If this jock only knew he was dealing with a Super Society member, Jaycee thought.

Jaycee moved forward, ready to swoop in, but stopped once Eric placed his hand on the sleeve of her pink shirt. He had this look about him—if Jaycee didn't know any better, she would have taken him for being brave. It didn't look bad on him, but it didn't look normal either.

"Tell me how my backbone looks," Eric said before launching into action.

Jaycee stood stunned as she witnessed Eric barge between Melvin and the skinny jock, pushing the two apart.

"Leave him alone!" Eric warned the bully, which only appeared to intensify the taller jock's aggression.

A crowd of students emerged around them, chanting and egging on the combatants.

Don't do anything stupid, Eric! Jaycee thought.

"Hey, loser, how about you mind your own business?!" the jock said, grinding a fist into his palm.

A barricade of kids fenced in closer around them. Melvin hid behind Eric.

"Oh, yeah? W-well, uh," Eric stammered. "How about you pick on someone your own size? Oh wait, since there are no other giant freaks around here, I guess you can't, can you?"

Pretty stupid, Eric! Not the worst witty banter, but still pretty stupid!

Eric received a few cheers, but Jaycee knew he was in over his head. Jaycee weaved through the mass of students, preparing to dive in for the rescue.

"Hey!" the jock yelled, pointing at the hairy Dungeon Master.

Melvin ducked as if Eric's modest frame could conceal him.

"That coward has been posting garbage about me on the Internet! Making fun of me for not making first string on the basketball team this year. Roasting me for throwing up in biology class even though that was only once, and it was back in fifth grade! He's a total cyberbully!"

Eric looked back at the cringing nerd.

"Is that true?" Eric asked Melvin.

"I got over a hundred likes for that," Melvin explained with a shrug.

"Are you kidding me?"

Eric sighed and looked back at the jock.

"Okay, um, well, it's just some trolling, so I think we can all calm down—"

"Tell that to my fist!"

The jock cocked his fist back, readying for the final blow. The kids pressed closer, aiming their phones and cameras at the skirmish, anxious to record the pummeling.

Not the top-secret video of Eric's powers I wanted, but I'll take it!

Jaycee aimed her phone at the squabble.

Might as well get a clearer shot of Eric flying, and besides, orders are orders!

Jaycee noticed Melvin backstepping into the pack while everyone focused on the brawl-to-be.

"Smart move, Supercut," she whispered to herself. "Remove yourself from the situation. Protect your secret identity!"

Melvin winked at her as he disappeared into the crowd.

"Starting to wonder how much of this cowardly nerd stuff is an act," Jaycee muttered.

"Whoa, whoa, whoa," Eric said, outstretching his hands. "This has just been a misunderstanding. I don't think it's a problem that we need to—"

"You're my problem now, douchenozzle!" the jock warned.

He swung. Eric nearly fell over, dodging the hit. Eric adjusted the shoulder straps of his backpack and straightened his navy-blue t-shirt. They circled each other as the raucous audience clapped for their student gladiators. Jaycee followed Eric with her phone, zooming in to capture the growing frustration on his face.

"That's it, then!" Eric shouted. "You wanna know what I can do? Then, let's see how you like this!"

Eric's clenched his fists and squatted, readying for a leap. Jaycee widened her camera lens to get a better shot of the display. Eric's face tightened, and his body trembled. The jock's rage dissolved into confusion as everyone waited for something, anything, to happen. Eric grunted and began to sweat. Jaycee put the phone down. She knew something was wrong.

Eric yelped and collapsed onto the ground. Jaycee hurried over, trying to tend to him, but laughing kids blocked her.

The bell rang.

"What's going on here?" the bearded math teacher

said, struggling to reach them.

Jaycee burrowed through as kids fled the scene. In a race against the teachers, Jaycee slid to her knees and stopped by Eric's keeled-over body. He wrapped his arms over his stomach, writhing in agony.

"Eric, what's going on? Talk to me!" she pleaded while gently grabbing his arm.

"Let's get a look at him," the math teacher said, hunching over Eric.

"Back off!" Jaycee barked. "Give him some space! Eric, what happened?"

"I don't know. I don't know. I don't know," he said between quick breaths.

Jaycee noticed her phone was still set in camera mode.

Orders are orders—but what do I do now?

Truther's suspicions of Eric replayed in her mind but seeing him balled up on the floor confirmed that this boy posed a threat to no one. No one except himself.

• • •

```
TO: TRUTHER

FROM: POWERHOUSE

SUBJECT: SUPERHERO LOG ENTRY - MONDAY
(CON'T)

You may be getting a call from mom
about how I left school today because
I was sick—go with it! I couldn't
risk skipping but faking like I was
going to puke all over Principal
```

Garza has been so worth it! I hitched
a ride with Mr. Boxworth, and he took
me and Eric back to their HQ. Eric's
sudden pain has gone away for now,
but I'll keep you up to date as this
situation develops. In the meantime,
I must remain a ninja-like spy, so
Mr. Boxworth doesn't suspect that I
know Eric's secret!

- Powerhouse

"Eric, who else have you told?!" David yelled.

Scrunched up in the shaft above him, Jaycee
forced a smile from behind an air vent. Eric's dad stood
in the middle of computer terminals and stacks of
equipment crates. His arms folded over his chest; there
was no mistaking his fury.

Eric lowered down, facing the vent.

Whrrr!

"Calm down, Dad," Eric said. "No—"

Whrrr!

"—one—"

Whrrr!

"—else—"

Whrrr!

"—knows but Jaycee."

Eric removed the vent plate and tossed it down
to David, who batted it away. It *clanged* on the floor.
Floating, Eric pocketed screws with one hand and held
a power drill in the other. Jaycee silently acknowledged
that the weirdest part of this whole scenario was Eric
operating a tool of any kind.

Eric extended his arm.

"Need a lift?" he asked with a sheepish smile.

Jaycee curled her fingers over the thin borders of the square opening and heaved herself forward, so her head poked out.

"Eric, be careful," David cautioned. "And don't drop my drill!"

"You sure about this?" Jaycee asked.

"Don't worry, I'm feeling way better," Eric assured.

"It's not that. It's the ankle weights you're wearing."

"They're not even heavy!"

He grabbed her arm, and she slid through, gripping her tightly with his free arm. Gravity yanked them down, and they sank through the air.

Uh oh! Jaycee thought.

Jaycee's stomach dropped to her feet as she braced for impact.

They fell ten feet in the blink of an eye, collapsing onto the hard floor. Jaycee felt the familiar rush of adrenaline swirled with ache like her body knew it took damage but was having too much fun to admit it.

Catching her breath, she detected a stale odor, like old paper, but as she gazed around the room at metal and gears, she could not pinpoint the source. Eric groaned as his dad hurried over to them. Eric lifted his wobbly arm to hand the drill to him.

"Thank you," David said, accepting the tool.

Jaycee sat up as David put the drill onto a table covered with other random parts and robot innards.

"Miss Maddox," he started, putting on work gloves. "When I say wait in the other room so I can speak to my son, that doesn't mean hide in the air vents. I'm also going to assume you haven't told anyone else, especially not your father."

Jaycee got to her feet while Eric sat up slowly.

"I'm also going to assume," David went on, "that

you know what would happen if other people found out about Eric."

He grabbed a white lab coat hanging behind him.

"Oh, yeah!" she said.

She regretted saying that with as much confidence as she did. David gave her a funny look, then donned the white coat to look even more like a mad scientist.

"So, I have my options," David said while sifting through some of the junk by the drill. "I can get really angry that Eric blabbed, which not only endangered himself, but me, you, and, frankly, it's a one-way ticket to Bad Time's-ville."

He picked up a janky-looking thick belt.

"My other option is to put you to work. Catch."

He hurled the belt at her. She caught it, and its heaviness caught her by surprise as its momentum twisted her around.

"It's a weighted belt," David explained. "Give it to Eric."

"I'm totally fine, by the way," Eric said, oozing with sarcasm. "I slowed my descent at the last second, softening the landing, but I still took most of the impact. It feels like lightning is shooting through my entire body, but, yeah, other than that, it's all good."

Jaycee helped raise him, but Eric kept going up until his sneakers floated next to her head.

"As I'm sure you've seen, Miss Maddox—"

"It's Jaycee."

"Okay, Jay See—"

"No, like, it's like all one word," she said, pushing Eric's foot away from her face.

"Isn't that what I said?"

"It's just Jaycee, Dad," Eric chimed in.

David sighed and rubbed between his eyes.

"When you work for me, you're 'Miss Maddox.'

Like I was saying, I'm certain you've seen Eric fly around as the boy gravity forgot, but for reasons I haven't solved yet, he's having a hard time staying down. My current hypothesis is that it is involuntary, and... it could be permanent."

Jaycee pulled the heavy belt up to Eric. The boy smirked and shook his head, dismissing David's theory.

"I can program a prosthetic appendage to respond to mental commands, but a geneticist I am not," David said as he pulled out a tray of small tools, some of which looked a little too pointy for comfort. "I can tell you this, though—whatever power you have, Eric, it's definitely a naturally occurring, organic, biological force that is continuously pulling you up instead of keeping you still. That, or it's just ADHD."

Jaycee craned her neck to see Eric float even higher.

"You think strapping on more weights is going to hold me down?" Eric asked, drifting toward the open-air shaft near the ceiling.

David held up a gun-like device with a thin, sharp end.

"It's a temporary fix until we find a more permanent solution."

The sharp end sparked. Jaycee walked into a slow twirl while watching Eric.

"Hey, Eric, you didn't fly at all yesterday, did you?"

"Um, no, I, uh, didn't," he said, hyper-focused on his dad.

"Well, okay," Jaycee continued. "So, like, you gotta be up, but you were down all day, which makes me think, like, the longer you're grounded, the more it gets all hurt-y. Like, you physically must be airborne. Gravity is totally your superhero weakness!"

Eric stared at her from above, and David stared

at her from across the lab. Their silence was deafening and not at all comfortable.

David set down his pointed instrument, and Eric descended. Eric took the weighted belt from Jaycee and strapped it on. Eric struggled a bit, but his body crept upward. David returned to folding his arms, looking at Jaycee from behind the table as if he was speculating about what species she was.

Clank clank clank. Jaycee's eyes widened at seeing a mechanical dog crawling out from between David's legs.

"Greetings, human, I am Responsi-Bulldog!"

A robotic dog appeared out of nowhere. Its voice sounded like David talking into a tin can.

"Woof. Woof. I achieve a sense of fulfillment by meeting new friends. More people to clean up my poop. Ha. Ha. Woof. Woof."

Jaycee tilted her head up at Eric. He nervously shrugged.

"Um, cool toy?" she complimented in a feeble attempt not to freak out.

The room fell silent save for the whirring of the junky robo-dog's gears struggling to move.

• • •

TO: TRUTHER

FROM: POWERHOUSE

SUBJECT: SUPERHERO LOG ENTRY – MONDAY (CON'T EVEN MORE)

Eric's condition has worsened, and he feels intense pain if he stays grounded too long. Mr. Boxworth theorized that Eric will eventually have to be constantly afloat. We are doing more tests, but it's safe to say his flying abilities are for real! Working on documentation. Say hi to the rest of the team for me! Tell Supercut that items in the Super Society breakroom fridge are labeled for a reason, and I'll know who to blame if my yogurt goes missing again!

- Powerhouse

Jaycee held up her phone as she cheered on Eric. He stood still in a cleared area of the showroom.

"How much longer do I have to stand here?" Eric asked, sticking his hands in his pockets.

"Until you are inexplicably overwhelmed with pain," David said, eyeing the screen pointed at his son.

"It's been, what, five minutes?" Eric assumed. "I don't think anything is gonna happen—"

Eric's knees buckled, and he clutched his gut. His body fell forward, unable to stand through the torment. He rolled onto his stomach and pushed himself up, bouncing into the air. Suspended above Jaycee and David, Eric shook his head and shoved his hands in quick downward waves. He wiggled his feet like he was attempting to fling the pain off his body literally.

"Longest time yet between fits of ground-based owwies," David reported while tapping his phone. "Since we started recording them, of course."

"A personal best!" Jaycee enthused.

Eric curled his lip and brushed away at dust on his

shirt.

• • •

```
TO: TRUTHER

FROM: POWERHOUSE

SUBJECT: SUPERHERO LOG ENTRY - MONDAY
(CON'T AGAIN)

Attempts to normalize Eric's
floatiness have been… unsuccessful.
I'll be sending you videos of him
flying soon. He still hasn't shown
any signs of being a diabolical evil
genius, but at least we somewhat know
what we're dealing with!

- Powerhouse
```

Jaycee breathed through her teeth as she watched Eric roll into the lab in an old wheelchair, strapped in by thick, weighted belts. Eric's face mirrored her discomfort. David trailed Eric, tapping on his phone until they stopped at a lifeless skeletal prototype hanging in front of a vertical row of computer servers. The creepy, blank-eyed humanoid android resembled something found in a Halloween store.

Jaycee walked up to the wheelchair, hesitant to touch it but curious to inspect the straps wrapped around Eric's legs and chest. Eric's crinkled brow indicated that it not only looked like he was trapped in a medieval torture device but also felt like one.

"No aerial activity, no signs of distress," David

noted. "I think we're onto something here!"

Jaycee and Eric shook their heads at him in unison.

"Okay, I can kind of see how this idea could maybe come off as insensitive," David admitted.

Jaycee crossed her arms, glaring.

"Fine," David said with a sigh. "Back to the drawing board!"

• • •

```
TO: TRUTHER

FROM: POWERHOUSE

SUBJECT: SUPERHERO LOG ENTRY - MONDAY
(CON'T CON'T)

Eric's abilities and weakness have
been confirmed, but I recommend
delaying taking any further action.
There is as much to learn about Mr.
Boxworth as there is about Eric.
Their whole building is full of
rinky-dink failed experiments. It's
totally the Island of Misfit Robots!
I'm gathering more intel on this
place, though I don't think anything
here poses any kind of threat other
than potentially being a killer
techno-haunted house one day. To be
honest, I kinda feel bad for Eric.

- Powerhouse
```

"You fire the maid?" Jaycee asked with an unabashed level of snark.

Crates of synthetic eyeballs covered the pool table. Plastic sheathes stuffed with cords and wires draped over the inactive pinball machine. Line after line of code filled the old-school arcade game screens. Jaycee surmised that this was once a fun rec room that has since been mutated into a hoarder's palace.

"We had a maid; it was a robot," Eric said from the couch. "I know I'm usually a pretty positive person who doesn't get all moody or morbid, but I'm fairly sure the robot maid killed itself, and its body is hidden in here somewhere."

Jaycee stepped over what appeared to be the plastic casing for a drone and sat next to her forlorn friend on the light gray sofa. Eric stared ahead at the large black mirror of a television monitor.

"I know this whole sitch sucks," Jaycee said. "But still, being able to fly is pretty awesome! And this is coming from me, a bona fide costumed crime-fighter!"

She put her feet up on the coffee table in front of them.

"I mean, you have real superpowers. How cool is that?!"

Eric carefully shifted his legs to the side and swept them up, slowly lowering his red knee-high leather boots next to hers. Jaycee's eyelids fluttered as she gazed upon the lengthy lifts attached to the bottom of his feet. The white laces lined down the front of the elongated footwear.

"I don't feel very cool," Eric admitted. "And I don't even want to ask why my dad had these boots in his closet."

"Your feet aren't technically touching the ground when you walk, right?" Jaycee pointed out. "You get to be taller and look like a rock star, so it's a win-win!"

"I don't think it matters if I'm walking on stilts or pretending the floor is lava," Eric said.

He reached between the couch cushion and the armrest and dug out a remote control.

"It's more like... More like my dad is right. I'm eventually gonna be a forever-floating ghost person. I'll get my meals delivered to me, and as the delivery guy is walking up to the house, I'll creepily float in the window staring at him. Neighborhood kids will dare each other to go see the Window Man. That's pretty much my future in a nutshell."

He pressed a button on the remote, and the large TV flickered on. Eric flipped through black-and-white surveillance footage of different rooms throughout the building.

"Your all-Boxworth Building channel package is pretty flushed, Eric."

"Sorry, this is pretty much the security footage TV."

"Is there a camera in here?" Jaycee asked, making sure to sound innocuous while scanning the room.

"Yeah, up there. It's blocked, though."

She looked up to the corner behind them, where he pointed. A stack of crated parts, casings, and metal appendages touched the ceiling, obstructing the view of any camera that may have been behind it. Next to it stood a pile of prototypes of various mechanical animals. One looked like the lifeless, incomplete cousin of Responsi-Bulldog. It was beyond unnerving.

Eric pressed random raised buttons on the remote.

"I think if I toggle through different modes, I can get some real stations, or—"

He stopped at the high-angle view of David, hunched over a desk, lazily scrolling the little wheel on his mouse. The man looked like he hadn't slept in days. Eric sighed.

"Jaycee," Eric said. "You have to leave."

She leaned forward, raising her eyebrow. "Um, excuse me?"

"I mean it," he said.

He sounded sincere but seemed scared to look at Jaycee.

"Our dads being who they are, you being a member of the Super Society... I mean, you, Jaycee Maddox, are a member of a real-life superhero team!"

With some effort, he faced her.

"If you get out now, maybe you can escape before it gets too big..."

The exertion proved to be short-lived, and Eric's head went back down.

"I don't have to be your problem."

Jaycee stood and pointed up.

"One: I'm your best friend!"

She raised a second finger.

"Two: I'm a superhero!" she said, lifting another. "Third: I'm a compassionate human being, duh! Like, maybe the most compassionate, but I don't like to brag."

Eric leaned forward, studying the live video of his dad.

"If you think I'm backing down from a challenge, you are cray," she said. "Double-cray."

Eric tossed the remote onto the wooden table by his feet.

"You know what..." he started, entranced by the TV screen. "I'm the cray one. I'm flushing triple, quadruple-cray if I'm gonna stick around here waiting to be some flying monkey test subject."

"Eric, I love these rando outbursts of yours,"

Jaycee said. "But let's have some chill for a sec—"

She stopped when he abruptly pointed at the TV. Jaycee walked closer to the screen. The monitor David stared at showed a movie clip of Eric flying in the showroom. Images of bills with the words "PAST DUE" stamped on them floated next to the video window. A new browser popped up. Jaycee's brain melted a little when she recognized the numbers it presented. Above those familiar digits displayed the words "CALL BARON MADDOX." The enlarged resolution pixelated the details, but Jaycee knew how this looked.

Uh oh, she thought.

The hum of a dial tone purred behind her.

There's audio?

She closed her eyes and gritted her teeth. She couldn't help but listen.

"Thank you for calling Pantheon Solutions, the offices of Baron Maddox. How may I improve your world today?"

The voice of the chipper blonde assistant Chelsea was unmistakable.

"It's David Boxworth," Eric's dad said through the room's speakers.

He sounded like he looked: exhausted.

"Tell Barry I'm ready to talk business."

Jaycee peeked at the screen. David expanded the video of Eric flying on his monitor.

"Tell him I'm prepared to make an offer that he'll find very 'intriguing,'" David said.

"BRAIN, turn TV off," Eric commanded.

An unseen source softly chirped, signaling the TV's deactivation. Eric seethed. He simmered in a quiet, slow, heavy-breathed rage—the exact amount of subdued fury Jaycee would expect from him.

"He's gonna sell me off to your dad?!" Eric

exclaimed.

Damage control!

Jaycee turned and pushed out her hands, wiping away negative vibes.

"Okay, it does kinda-sorta appear that your dad might be considering exploiting you to pay some bills. Or maybe he's turning you into an Internet celebrity. Who's to say? Now, I don't want to jump to conclusions, but—"

"Of course, he's doing this!"

Eric folded his arms.

"All my dad cares about is his stupid company that's failing, and it's really his fault that it's going under, but he blames me, and now he's just gonna use me to help himself, and all he does is lie!"

"Don't worry," Jaycee reassured. "No one'll poke or prod you on my watch! I got my dad wrapped around my pinky-winky finger. It'll be an N.B.D.D.; no big dad deal."

The phalanx of half-truths and weak promises welled up behind her eyes. She didn't like withholding so much from him, but... but...

Jaycee's face stiffened as she thought of Truther; she thought of the mission.

"...I have an idea," Jaycee revealed. "How'd you like to totally bail on your dad right now?"

Eric lifted a leg, then the other. Jaycee met him by the table as he slid his protracted platform shoes off the surface. He got to his feet, standing a full head taller than Jaycee.

"I was born to bail!" Eric declared.

Jaycee contorted her lips at the lame comment.

"Even if that was true," she said, "it wouldn't have sounded cool."

"It's the boots, right?"

"They don't help."
"Good call; I'll take them off."

. . .

```
TO: TRUTHER

FROM: POWERHOUSE

SUBJECT: SUPERHERO LOG ENTRY - MONDAY
(LAST ONE, I SWEAR)

Forget proper documentation! The
direct approach is best! I'm bringing
Eric to you!

- Powerhouse
```

Chapter Ten: *ASCENT*

ERIC

JAYCEE'S FACE FILLED THE FRAME.
"Going to my mom's, Mr. Boxworth! She's a teacher, so it's totally legit and safe! Eric will be fine, don't wait up! I'll text you! Well, that'd be weird if I texted you, plus I don't have your number, so I guess Eric will text you! 'Kay, bye!"

Eric slivered into the picture.

"Uh, um, uh," he sputtered. "Yes, I am unharmed, and I trust Jaycee; we will not do anything bad. We are leaving now, okay and bye."

"Jeez," Jaycee said with a sneer. "Could you sound more like I'm kidnapping you? Might as well blink twice if you want your dad to call the cops—"

The video stopped. Eric's reflection on the surface of the screen stared back at him.

"We coulda tried another take of that, Jaycee."

He lowered his phone. Jaycee lounged in a cozy chair with her legs propped up on a big, featureless white desk in the center of the circular office. The fading afternoon sunlight glistened on the metal and glass towers surrounding them. Eric stood motionless, gawking at the scenery through the vast, clear panes encircling them. Jaycee being so nonchalant in the presence of such a fantastic view was perhaps the most impressive thing about this entire building.

This is her dad's office? Eric thought, awestruck. *How does he get any work done?*

"It's been, like, two hours," Jaycee said. "Your dad's lack of any communication whatsoever means he bought it. So, relax already."

Eric paced around on the slick hardwood floors, not knowing which direction to go. The spacious office smelled like a doctor's office—clean, safe, yet unsettling.

"Maybe he hasn't responded because he knows we made things so much easier for him by coming here," Eric theorized. "'It's cool, Dad. I wanted to deliver my body to the highest bidder personally. I hope they keep the receipt in case I'm defective.'"

Bored, Jaycee randomly tapped at the blank surface in front of her. A small portion of the desk slid open. A chilled glass bottle of orange soda pushed itself up. She took it, and the desk resealed itself. She popped the cap off and took a sip. Eric resisted the urge to clap as if he had just seen a magic trick.

"We're getting out in front of whatever's going on, that's all," Jaycee explained. "Taking the initiative! Being proactive! Waiting for my dad to get out of a meeting... Waiting, waiting, waiting..."

She guzzled the orange pop. After downing half the bottle, she let the glass linger in her hand, hanging off the armrest. Eric approached the ivory-colored desk.

"On the way here, you were so hyped about showing me all the cool things at Pantheon, but now you're fighting sleep," Eric observed. "Does living in a superhero base of operations get boring that quickly? I'm still getting over the talking mirrors in the bathroom! Super creepy and weird, but I want one!"

"I mean, like, I don't stay here all the time, but, yeah, when I do, there are so many crazy-cool features and attractions, like the giant plant-pipeline in the middle of the building," she said. "And you haven't even seen the Super Society stuff yet. But I dunno; I only really get to talk to Dad's, well, I suppose you'd call them co-workers, and even then, that's not all the time."

"Didn't you say Melvin lives here?" Eric asked. "And Tiffany, too, right? They're part of the Pantheon foster kid program thing, right? Do they get to see the Super Society, too? Do they know about you? Are the, er, assistants, like their legal guardians—?"

"Whoa, slow down there!" Jaycee said. "I see Melvin sometimes; Tiffany is new, but the less I see of her, the better. I've probably told you too much already, but I'll say this: you're the only person I've unmasked for, ya know, outside of the team. So, feel free to feel special."

Leaning forward, she lowered the soda onto the desktop. A thin, translucent-blue coaster spat out from a slit in the desk and landed flat just in time for her to place the bottle onto it.

"The assistants are nice, but they're not much for conversation," Jaycee continued, whisking her legs down. "I don't know what their whole deal is, but they and all the other underlings seem happy."

She shrugged, then rolled her chair closer to the edge of the desk. Eric sat on a rounded corner of the surface, letting his feet dangle over the side. He caught Jaycee, glancing over to see his feet hover in their unnatural way.

"Your family visits, though, right? Cousins? Grandparents? Twice-removed uncles?"

"We're not close on my mom's side, and my dad was given up as a baby," she confessed.

Putting an elbow down, Jaycee rested her chin on her palm.

"And Dad's always so busy-busy-busy."

She looked down. With her other hand, Jaycee grazed her fingers over the smooth surface. Small bright squares lit up as she touched the desk, leaving a little trail of white light that faded as quickly as it appeared.

"I dunno, I guess, to be honest, even with all the next-level tech here, it gets kinda lonely."

Jaycee looked weird. She looked... vulnerable. Eric always had to fight to keep his misery from spewing out, like trying to cover leaking holes in a wall, but the holes keep multiplying, causing more and more water to spill through. For Jaycee, though, any uncovered shred of sadness seemed so unfamiliar. Her blonde hair fell in front of her face, and the light washed over her golden locks, making it look like a halo graced the top of her head. She didn't bother stroking the strands back. Seeing Jaycee like this stirred confusing emotions within Eric.

How? Eric wondered. *How could a girl so tough, so brave, so radiant, be so... so oblivious?!*

Eric thrust his body upward into the air. The high ceiling gave him room to spin, flying circles above her. He momentarily didn't think of the open-air audience from neighboring skyscrapers.

"Are you nuts? This place is amazing!" Eric said while twirling his body like a soaring cyclone. "You've seen my building. Everything there is old rebuilt junk my dad thinks will sell one day."

He flew concurrently to the windows, mere inches from the curving glass.

"How you're not constantly social media-ing the mess out of this place is a total mystery. Prolly some non-disclosure thing, right?"

Eric floated upright, staring at the outside world.

"I'd trade the scrap heap that is my house for this any day!"

Eric peeked over his shoulder. From roughly fifteen feet below, he saw Jaycee standing next to who must have been Baron Maddox. Jaycee beamed next to her father, but Eric sensed a shielded uneasiness from her. Baron did not hide his astonishment.

Eric descended slowly, touching down with practiced ease. His chose not to show emotion, though he couldn't help but feel his insecurities seeping from his pores.

Baron's eyes trained on Eric, following his every move.

"You're real..." Baron whispered.

"Eric," Jaycee said. "This is my dad, although you know who he is. I guess you've never been introduced, but then again, my dad used to work with your dad, so you've prolly already met—"

"Jaycee," Baron said, quieting her without looking away from Eric.

Her face flushed with embarrassment.

"So, I have to go to superhero practice."

"Training," Baron corrected, rolling his eyes.

"Right! Training! I'll let you two get at it! Eric, my dad is a total ge-ni-us! He'll know exactly what to do! Have fun!"

Jaycee shrunk into herself a bit, unable to contain her giddiness. Such idolization of one's father was an alien concept to Eric. She made her way to the glass elevator across the room. Her ponytail whipped behind her as she looked back at Eric. She raised her eyebrows, acknowledging the nerve-racking yet exhilarating excitement of this meeting, a feeling he couldn't return.

Seeing Jaycee go so easily disappointed Eric and being alone with her dad creeped him out. Baron was so tall. His pinstriped gray suit was as slick as the floor. His hair and mustache were so... dark. Baron was nothing more than a fuzzy memory to Eric, a phantom in his mind appearing in the background. Yet he loomed over Eric, tangible and intimidating.

"My, uh, my, um," Eric stuttered. "My dad..."

"I received your father's message," Baron said with a smile. "I have not issued a response if that is what you are enquiring about. I admire David's devotion to being your protective parent and simply trying to do what he thinks is best. Can I be candid with you, young Mr. Eric? I do not wish to discuss your father. It is you who is the focus here. You are a gift to the world."

Before Eric could process the words, Baron walked to his desk.

"I know, I know, I come on too strong. It's what I always do," he revealed, hands up, surrendering to his foibles. "Please, take a seat. No, correction, don't sit. Jump. Spin. Float. Fly!"

Eric's hands found themselves retreating into his pockets.

"So, I guess this answers any questions about what you know about me."

Baron hopped up onto his desk to sit.

"I step into my office, and there's this kid Zip-A-Dee-Doo-Dah-ing in the air with no strings attached. I put two and two together."

He slid himself to the center of the smooth surface.

"Forgive my daughter for her brashness. I know being brought here isn't an ideal situation, but I want you to feel completely at ease. I want to give you room to breathe.”

Eric looked around. The vast office offered nothing but space. Eric peered over to the elevator. Jaycee stood close to the glass, giving a thumbs up. Baron waved at Jaycee and then tapped on the desk. The elevator propelled upward and out of sight.

“She has better things to occupy her time instead of just rubbernecking our encounter,” Baron said. “She has her training. Or homework, I assume. What matters is you, Eric.”

He clapped his hands.

“How remarkable is it that I’m talking to young Eric Boxworth like this? I recall you being such a little guy, and now here you are. So big, so special!”

A tingle spread throughout Eric’s legs, like tiny pins and needles pecking at his muscle tissue. Those little spikes snapped like minuscule electric shocks, and Eric knew the pain was coming.

“So, this is gonna sound weird, but I kinda have this condition,” Eric said, levitating. “I don’t know why, but I can only be on the ground for a while before it hurts, and I have to...”

Baron scooted off the desk and walked up to Eric. He placed his hands on Eric’s rising shoulders. Eric caught himself ogling the man’s big, fancy silver smartwatch.

“You have to be free from the shackles of gravity,” Baron said.

Baron lifted his arms and spread them like wings as Eric floated higher and higher. Baron laughed with sheer joy.

“I am witnessing not a miracle but a veil being lifted from all that we thought was possible!”

Unlike mere minutes ago, this ascendancy did not share the same freewheeling reverie. The unbearable anguish of standing still tugged at Eric's body. He hovered just under the ceiling, sacrificing what little remaining chance there was at anonymity.

A soft mechanical whirring emanated a few feet above Eric. A disc formed in one of the black-and-white speckled tiles on the ceiling. The round, flat lid slid into itself like the desk's wizardry. A spherical white drone, approximately fifteen inches in circumference, dropped through a gap in the tile. Like a space-age bowling ball, the floating orb emitted a bluish-white light from holes on its rear. Its "face" lit up with tiny bright blue dots. The spots swam across the drone's smooth shell.

Eric drifted closer to it, inspecting the drone's lights.

"I don't get it," Eric said. "People make incredible things all the time. This drone can fly. What makes me so special? What sets me apart, other than my involuntary handicap?"

The moving blue dots mesmerized him.

"Eric," he heard Baron say from below. "I want you to know something. I operate a company that develops a bewildering number of unprecedented advancements in technology. I design and build unbelievable things every day. I know implausible, staggering, mind-boggling extraordinariness when I see it."

Eric turned his attention to Baron, who craned his neck, utterly in awe.

"I hope you can see past the drone's scanning of you," Baron said. "I don't think you are faking, but I must detect foreign devices, if any are present, for security."

Eric flew to a window, placing his hands on the glass. The warmth felt good.

"Ya know," Eric said, "I used to love the Super Society when I was a kid. Then the new generation destroys my home."

His eyes followed a commercial airliner flying off in the distance beyond the buildings.

"I don't know what to believe anymore."

Baron's face appeared on the glass in front of Eric. He didn't understand how, but Eric watched a real-time video of Baron speaking to him, eye-to-eye.

"Your biology is protecting you from slumming it out with the rest of us doomed to walk the Earth instead of soar above it," Baron's projection said. "Yet you see your talent as a hindrance."

Eric floated to the center of the ceiling. Baron trailed him underneath.

"So, what's your deal?" Eric said, crossing his arms. "I, like, barely remember you. Are you just another really smart guy who thinks there isn't anything they can't figure out? I've been around smart guys all my life, and the only mystery of the universe they wanna solve is how to get paid."

"From what I can see," Baron said, "I am a mere student eager to learn all that you can teach."

His tie shimmered in the afternoon light. Eric sat in mid-air, crisscrossing his legs.

"You know what? Just do whatever it is you're gonna do. I can't hide this. I can't pretend to be normal. I let myself walk right into a big super lab that'll prolly experiment on me or clone me, or whatever, just because a girl told me to."

Eric watched the deceptive stillness of the cityscape.

"Jaycee likes you very much," Baron revealed.

Eric remained sitting in his quasi-lotus position while descending to face Baron.

"She say something? I mean, yeah, stupid, of course, she would've, but... she say something?"

"You're all she can talk about," Baron confirmed. "How could she not? Everything seems so trivial after meeting a person with the remarkable ability to fly."

Eric spun, turning his attention to the large window behind him. The more he stared at the shiny towers surrounding them, the less impressive they became.

"I dunno how mad at her I should be. I mean, she obviously told you about me before now, but... I guess I'm not used to people being amazed by my... power."

Referring to his ability as a power grossed him out.

"That'll wear off sooner or later, and then she'll see the regular me. She'll realize I'm just another boring loser."

"Marketability, my young friend," Baron said from behind him. "It's all about presentation—regular means stable, responsible. Replace 'boring loser' with 'mild-mannered.' You're describing your alter ego. Now tell me about the flying dynamo who's taken over my office."

Twisting his lips in perplexity, Eric looked over his shoulder.

"Huh?"

Baron tapped at his gaudy smartwatch. Holographic images of Eric zipping around the vast perimeter of the office appeared before Eric.

"This is..." Eric said. "This is from, like, only a few minutes ago!"

"That free-spirited flyer you see? I want to know more about him," Baron said, gesturing to the room's vast openness. "The truth is very important to me. However, I recognize the importance of how people perceive what's real. The first thing that has to go is the name. 'Eric Boxworth.' No offense to you or your father, but that's not a name you put on a poster."

He strolled ahead of Eric.

"Let's see, you can fly, so I'm thinking Sky-Man? No. Flyboy? I'm not hating it..."

Eric rushed through the air to catch up with him.

"I'm not sure what's going on here, but I can tell you one thing, I'm not gonna be called 'Floater!'"

Baron cocked up an eyebrow.

"Our marketing department will come up with a much better codename than that, trust me."

Baron paused. He looked confused, which didn't appear to be something he experienced often.

"I manage superheroes—you're here to join the Super Society. This is why Jaycee brought you to me, is it not?"

Eric bolted back up to the ceiling. He lay flat against the tiles. Eric pushed out a fearful thought, imagining a hole opening and swallowing him to take him to wherever the drones lived.

"Whoa, whoa, whoa. The Super Society uses your building as their headquarters. Everybody knows that," Eric said. "But just because I'm here doesn't mean I'm gonna start wearing some lame mask. And I'm not putting on a padded suit, and I definitely don't need any safety nets!"

Baron looked up at him.

"Do you see anything holding you back?" Baron asked.

He scrunched his forehead.

"We need to negotiate on the mask, though."

"To do what? Hide my unsecret identity?"

Eric scoffed, putting up a knee to make his upside-down lounging more leisurely

"There's no hiding for me. Nature or whatever cruel twist of fate saw to that."

Baron pointed up in agreement.

"Yes!" he shouted. "Spectacular! And they say I'm one of the smartest men in living history! No mask, just you! Except with a better name, of course!"

Baron gazed around him, searching for inspiration. He squinted in the sunlight. It appeared as if a designated sunbeam struck him right between the eyes.

"Eric Icarus."

"So, I'm gonna fly too close to the sun?" Eric asked. His uneasiness escalated.

"Wearing a fake set of wings sounds exhausting," Eric said. "So, I'll pass on whatever it is you're thinking up."

"Memorability is the name of the game, my young friend," Baron explained. "Agreed, though, wings would be a little much. I'm considering more of a backpack attachment thing. We'll workshop that."

He scrolled and tapped at his watch with lightning-fast fingers. Eric rolled onto his side.

"Put a cone around my neck like a sick dog while you're at it."

He poked at the perforated ceiling tile, curious to see if he would activate something.

"Maybe I should've just gone with my dad's idea and be strapped down to a wheelchair."

"Your father cannot protect you as I can."

"Is this your brilliant plan to do something about my 'gift?'" Eric jeered.

Replacing anxiety with aggravation proved oddly liberating.

"Rebrand me so it'll be even easier for more rich dudes with corporations like you to come hunt me down? I'm such an idiot for coming here—"

"Yes, you will be hunted down!" Baron yelled.

The jolt yanked the breath from Eric's body.

"Government agencies, corporations, everyday

people will never, ever let you be! And if you somehow escape them, then it's only a matter of time before a deranged supervillain captures you, tortures you—or does much worse—simply because you exist!"

Rattled, Eric closed his eyes as tightly as he could.

"You think I don't know that?"

"Life is about choices, young Mr. Eric," Baron went on, doing nothing to conceal his anger. "I permit you to leave of your own accord, back to your father or elsewhere, so you can gamble on what the inner circle of those that know about you will do with your secret."

Eric cracked open an eyelid to see Baron walking toward the elevator.

"What am I supposed to do?" Eric asked in a quiet, little voice.

"No one has made any decisions for you thus far," Baron said without looking back. "You may have allowed people to influence you, but you seem to know everything now. You've been granted the sensational ability to be anti-gravity, and I do very much mean rebelling against the forces of nature. But you're the boy who deems flying an ailment."

Baron stopped by the elevator's rounded glass door.

"You found your way here easily enough; you can find your way out."

Eric sat up, and blood rushed down to his head.

"But-but! I can just leave? What about Jaycee?"

The door slid open.

"I'm sure you'll see her at school," Baron said. "Assuming your 'condition' allows you to go out in public again."

"You won't help me?"

"You don't want assistance," Baron said. "I shall mourn the wasted opportunity to explore the boundaries of humanity with you, but you've made your choice. It's an eventuality that I'll figure out how to make a better version of you anyway. I'm an intensely busy man, Mr. Boxworth, so if you will, please."

Eric looked at the upside-down world around him.

"What..." Eric said, catching the trembling in his voice, hoping Baron didn't notice.

He cleared his throat and feigned enough confidence to form words again.

"What happens if I stay here?"

"Destiny happens," Baron said. "You join the Super Society. You take our mission of defending truth and justice to the next level. Your mere presence on the team will strike fear into the hearts of criminals, for they will know that even the sky itself is under our protection."

Flipping downward, Eric barreled toward Baron's desk. His body's rotation mildly dizzied him. Absent-minded, Eric's shoes brushed against the desk's bare surface, creating a wild spasm of lit-up squares.

"You're serious, aren't you? Me? A superhero?"

With his head lost in the clouds, Eric's inadvertent commands shot up three glass tubes from random spots on the floor. A young blonde woman occupied one, her twin stood in the other, and the third encased a floating row of sphere-droids connected like a ball-bearing centipede.

His periphery sensed Baron rushing to follow his forward momentum. Eric heard the man tap away at his lavish watch.

"Fist-fighting bad guys?"

Doubt coated Eric's voice.

"I couldn't hurt a fly. Not for lack of trying, my hand-eye coordination isn't the best. I'm not good with a flyswatter."

"You'd train with Jaycee, of course!" Baron said.

Eric glanced behind him. More small tubes popped up from their holes on the desk like moles. With overlapping hands, Baron pushed them down in a fit.

Eric floated off the table and then did an about-face. Aloof, he grazed the tips of sneakers once more across the desk, lighting up a track of bright squares. Coasters and glass bottles full of colorful liquids jumped out of various circles on the desk. Baron nearly fell over, trying to catch them all. He fumbled with a couple of bottles that shattered on the floor. Sticky, syrupy fluids splashed all over the man's slick jacket and tie.

"I don't have a lot of options, but this seems a bit extreme, doncha think?" Eric reckoned. "Isn't the whole idea for me to hide?"

The drone with the iridescent blue dots on its face swooped in, extending a trio of robotic arms that unfolded a thick, silver mesh net. Baron dumped the glass remains into the netting, and the drone zipped away. Dark grape and cherry-smelling cola dripped from Baron's expensive suit as disdain dripped from his face.

"It's called hiding in plain sight," Baron said, curling his upper lip.

Baron uttered a throaty grunt, sounding like he was holding back a snarl.

"It is my hope that one day you won't need to rely on such theatrics. The world isn't quite ready for you yet."

He retrieved a small blue silk handkerchief from his breast pocket and patted down the sugary soda.

"By publicizing your predicament, you eliminate the need for subterfuge."

"Yeah, but the hiding part?"

"Okay, maybe a little subterfuge," Baron clarified. "If what I said about the hounds of society and the underworld alike prowling after you was frightening, then good. It's a very appropriate fear. You don't need good intentions. You need this."

Eric hovered, watching as Baron waved his hand by the smooth-edged surface of the desk. A tablet ejected into his waiting hand. Baron presented the smart device's screen to Eric, displaying a digitized mock-up of Eric in a green bodysuit. The tablet's speedy creation of his digital rendition displeased Eric.

It did make my physique more flattering, though, he thought.

"This was rendered as we were conversing, so we'll have to add detail later," Baron said. "In the meantime, your induction into the fraternity of costumed do-gooders will deter any unwanted suspicions. Not even your teammates will know of your real power."

The image of Eric turned. The similarity between this and Eric's video game character's design mode was uncanny.

"What's that on my back?"

Eric pointed at the screen as he floated closer to Baron.

"The main reason we aren't putting a cape on you," Baron remarked. "Also, it's the source of your power. According to the world at large, anyway."

Eric reached out, and Baron released the tablet. Eric lowered, swiping a finger over the screen, slowly spinning his computerized image.

"So... I'd be lying, but not lying?"

"You'd be shielding yourself from the world's curious claws," Baron said. "All while being afforded the freedoms that come along with being a beloved protector of the innocent and avenger of justice."

"And Jaycee would be on the team with me?"

A reassuring smile formed on Baron's lips as he nodded. Eric turned away from him, spellbound by the tablet's image.

"You can have your cake and eat it, too," Baron said from behind him. "Hmm. Are you sure I can't talk you into wings?"

Eric spotted a stylus pen lodged into the base of the device. He pressed in the top, and it slid out. Eric marked, crossed out, erased, redrew, and colored using the on-screen editing tools.

"Assuming I go along with this crazy plan," Eric said while scribbling over the tablet's glass surface. "I have a few of my own ideas about the costume."

Eric felt Baron step closer to peek at what he was drawing.

"We can have that made in an hour," Baron confirmed.

"Can my name be Katana Dragon?"

"That is..." Baron said.

He seemed unsure where to land on that—he wiggled his fingers as if playing an invisible piano.

"That is something we will consider..." Baron finally said. "But I think we'll go with Eric Icarus for now."

Eric curled his lip at the dismissal, but only for a moment. Excitement reverberated across his skin.

QUALITY TIME WITH DAD

Chapter Eleven: *HOVER*

ERIC

T HE FLORAL PIPELINE STRETCHING UP the first five floors of Pantheon Tower stood as a truly remarkable feat—marrying nature with science. Eric gazed like a slack-jawed tourist, but David didn't look impressed. The padded cart propelling them upward provided a clear view. They stared at the intertwining foliage covering the massive botanic beam.

Being this close to the cylindrical bionetwork was way cooler than seeing it from the elevator like the previous day's visit.

I think I preferred yesterday's company, though, Eric thought.

David's fingers tapped the white armrest, muttering something. Eric's reflection bent along the curve of the smooth yellow metal of the oval-shaped shuttle. A day before, Eric was designing a legitimate superhero costume. As if awoken from a dream, he found himself back in a plain orange shirt and cargo shorts.

He spotted David gawking at the large leaves and flowers stemming from the core of the tropical tube.

"Unbelievable. Un-f—"

David's grumbling disappeared under the blaring of prerecorded audio-guide announcements.

"—ing-believable!"

He finished his outburst amidst the buzzing ambiance of the workstation rings surrounding them in the tower's otherwise hollow interior.

"The 'Plant Pipeline,' as it is lovingly referred to, provides natural air for all Pantheon Solutions family members," the woman on the recording said. "It is a living ecosystem in the center of our headquarters!"

Morning light spilled in through the enormous surrounding windows. Little white orbs floated in the distance. David let out a mocking whistle, causing Eric to slide in his seat, trying his best to hide.

"He has his drones carrying drinks?" David said. "Unbelievable. Un-f—"

Eric couldn't hear him finish over the *fwoosh* sound of the airflow. Like a nauseating amusement park ride, their car spun to face the rows upon rows of gorgeous employees. The centrifugal shift made Eric's stomach lurch.

I knew I should've flown up here myself!

"The elevator would've been fine," Eric caught himself saying while gesturing over to the glass chute lining up the massive wall across from them.

"Barry enjoys showing off," David commented. "Any advancement of humanity is a great opportunity to rub his wealth in your face."

They shared a chuckle, something uncommon for them. Eric and David's laughter faded as they both seemed to realize the strangeness simultaneously. They looked away from each other, making for an even more awkward trip in the two-seater transport pod flying them up via patented Pantheon propulsion technology.

With their legs hidden in a cramped space

under the bright yellow hull of their flying car, they resigned to the roofless seating. The smooth dashboard presented welcome messages and factoids about Pantheon's founding.

The hovercraft docked onto a large platform, leading to the rounded glass doors of a separate, smaller chute.

"Dad, I know you got a lot to talk about with Mr. Maddox, but please don't take too long. The Super Society is scheduled to make an appearance at the comic-con, and I haven't even officially met the team yet!"

"I know what's going on here."

"You do?" Eric asked, his nerves jostled.

Eric turbocharged his mental memory bank, desperate to dig up if he'd said anything weirder than what he had already told his dad.

"Getting your friend to convince her father to 'recruit' you into the Super Society?" David said, smirking. "It's an elaborate stunt to get into the convention because you didn't think I'd allow you to go."

Eric gulped.

"Well, it's a bit more—"

"It's clever, is what it is!" David said, beaming. "I'm pretty proud of you. I'm gonna pick Barry's brain about how he got the anti-grav belt working, but this all makes sense!"

David stepped onto the short bridge connecting to the platform. He steadied himself on the transparent handrails while walking onto the orange walkway.

"Wait," Eric said. "I can go?"

"Oh, heck no. But I love the effort you put in!"

Eric hopped onto the walkway, trailing his dad. Protests formulated in Eric's mind. His thought train derailed when Baron stepped out of the elevator car at the end of the path. His silver suit and tie glistened in the light.

"Welcome, Boxworths!"

"I appreciate you taking time to indulge the kids' scheme," David said as he approached him. "You got me; you did. I even believed the whole flying bit. That took finesse. It almost makes up for you deciding to go all in on a prank instead of immediately notifying me where my son was."

"Am I to understand you're here only to accuse me of something other than recognizing your son's marvelous talent?"

Baron flashed a big smile.

"I hope you are well, young Eric."

"Oh, you know," Eric said. "Same existential crisis, different day."

That got a laugh out of Baron, but David was not in a cheerful mood.

"It's been quite a while since you and I worked on anything together, Barry," David said, exchanging a quick handshake with the other man. "You've obviously done well for yourself, and, hey, I'm happy for your success, I really am. But I prefer to be more of my own boss, ya know?"

Eric rolled his eyes.

"Boxworth Dreamineering is my baby," David went on. "I don't have to share it with a board of bean counters or some Ivy League school grads who don't know the first thing about running a real business."

"And what an exciting venture it has become, wouldn't you say...?"

Baron continued his canned courtesy response, and Eric's attention drifted. He held onto the guardrail to ensure he didn't float away along with his thoughts.

Business talk bored Eric to tears, but this was especially excruciating since the clock was ticking.

He couldn't help but look back to absorb the scope of the place. The layered rungs surrounding the massive pipe were alive with activity. Further down, little flying robots sprayed mists of replenishing water onto the flora.

A vibration led Eric to check a text from "Jaycee (^o^)/":

"Dude! Where r u?!"

Before he could compose a response, David patted him on the shoulder, jolting Eric back to reality.

"I assure you, David, my intentions are purely for Eric to realize his true potential," Baron said, ushering Eric and David into the elevator. "Perhaps a visit to the Super Society headquarters will be more convincing."

Like a quick-drawing gunslinger, Eric shot off his reply to Jaycee:

"We're on our way to the HQ. My dad thinks this is all a big joke! Tell me again why I don't just run away from home?"

The glass doors shut, and they began their automated ascent. Baron tapped at the panel.

"I'm sure once you see Eric and the Super Society together, you'll realize there is no ruse. No doubt, you will freely provide your parental blessing on this bold new alliance."

Eric studied his reflection in the glass, but his focus shifted to David straightening his black V-neck shirt. David adjusted the pointy tip of his collar, aligning it just right. They would have arrived earlier if David had been swifter about settling on charcoal slacks—which Eric admitted did add some flare to his father's typically all-black attire.

"It is crucial to maintain consistency," he says,

Eric thought, recalling the morning's lecture. *"Being a Boxworth means being a brand." Did he even listen when I told him about the Icarus name?*

Muted whites and grays of concrete and metal replaced the workstation rings' lavish views.

"Barry, we're both busy guys, so I'll do us all a favor and cut to the chase," David said. "I'm sure Eric going to Willy Wonka's chocolate factory for the first time got him excited, and he jumped at the chance to go on a ride-along with the big boys."

"Um, I'm right here," Eric said, unnoticed.

"Listen, I've been an unreal, miraculous, once-in-a-lifetime-level of cool about this," David said. "About you, Barry. Now, I got my options. I can drop the 'it's all good' act, cuss you out, alert the media, contact lawyers, call the cops—or you can match my level of chill and just do what you know's gotta be done."

"I will acquiesce that we are both busy men," Baron said. "So, for the sake of time, please clarify. What is it that I am to do?"

"Jeez, I get snubbed on the yearly genius ranking list, but you're the tippy-top smarty-pants?"

"Dad, please," Eric whispered.

"The anti-gravity belt. I may've abandoned it years ago, but it's still my design."

After a *ding,* the clear doors opened, and Baron guided them into a white hallway. The lamps lining the floor along the winding path beamed soft light onto their feet.

"Right this way, please," Baron said, picking up the pace. "Forgive me, but I am not at all familiar with what you are referring to."

"You stole my invention!" David exclaimed. "And you're using Eric to test it! Which I can overlook as long as you're in a check-cutting mood."

Mouth agape, Eric fell behind.

"Are you for real?"

He shook his head, watching the two adults approach a pair of ruby-colored doors. Eric would've deemed the absence of knobs, handles, or buttons peculiar if they weren't in Pantheon Tower. Another Jaycee text rattled his phone:

"Don't come in yet! We aren't in costume yet! Stall!" A series of frightened emoji faces followed.

Eric executed a well-practiced hover-walk to catch up to them.

"I have no interest in that particular device," Baron said to David, placing a hand on the crimson door. "Come now, the team awaits."

"Hold up!" Eric blurted.

He wedged himself between them.

"Barry, you can try and distract me with your rainforest pipe-thing—"

"Dad, you can't go in there!"

"Eric, not now!" David said. "Anyway, you can try to sidetrack me by showing off your child army of superheroes, but I know what you're really—"

"I want the MegaCore," Baron said, removing his hand from the door.

David snickered.

"Man, that was a Hail Mary. Look, I was half-kinda-sorta-almost joking when I sent you that message. I mean, I'm not the desperate type, but..."

"This sounds like a big deal," Eric interjected. "You should probably discuss this in a conference room or something."

His attempt to gently push them felt like nudging a brick wall.

"I have a project that will require an immense power source to function," Baron said. "If you demonstrate to me that your engine can truly produce the amount of energy I need, then we shall initialize a developmental partnership."

"It's kinda big..." David said.

"I'm devoting an entire floor to it. I may go as far as reconfiguring the rooftop HQ just to show how imperative the project's success is."

"The MegaCore isn't something you can throw in the trunk of a car," David said.

"You keep your prototype. Based on my specifications, I'd provide you with all the materials needed to construct the new, much larger size. Think bigger, David."

David rubbed his temple, grinning in disbelief. Baron remained as serious as a judge.

"So, what, I just give you my life's work, eh, Barry?"

"A contract is being worked up as we speak. We really must not keep the team waiting any longer. The Super Society has a scheduled appearance—"

Baron placed his palm back on the red surface. This time, it lit up where his fingers were. Eric's heart pounded in panic.

"At the comic-con!" Eric said. "I like where your head's at, Mr. Maddox! We should get going!"

The door slid open, revealing Jaycee—not in a flashy costume, but a powder blue top and casual shorts instead.

"Hi, Dad! 'Sup, Mr. B!" Jaycee said with a huge grin. "Can I call you 'Mr. B?' I think you got a Mr. B vibe, for sure. Unless it's Dr. B?"

"Mr. Boxworth is fine, Miss Maddox."

Eric flashed her an "I'm sorry!" look, grimacing with gritted teeth. She answered with a "what the heck?" look.

"Ahem, Jaycee," Baron said. "I trust you are merely visiting the Super Society while on your way to the comic convention."

"Er, yep!" she said, her eyes bouncing back and forth like ping-pong balls. "Got the permission slip and everything!"

She led them inside a spacious rooftop enclosure. It looked more like a giant swanky apartment than a superhero headquarters. The thick, enormous windows encasing them provided an incredible view of the city from their sprawling one-hundredth-floor suite.

Assembled in the center—between two cushy couches—stood Extra, Supercut, Go-Go, and Powerhouse posing in all their costumed glory: hands-on-hips and all smiles. Eric's eyes enlarged to wide saucers staring at the crime-fighting crew. Beside him, he noticed Jaycee's childlike smile, just as ecstatic.

There they are, Eric thought. *This is actually happening! I'm joining the team!*

Eric's forehead wrinkled when he realized Powerhouse stood with her teammates, yet Jaycee stood next to him. Baffled, he leaned over to her.

"You have a twin sister I don't know about?" Eric whispered.

She shushed him. Baron addressed them a few steps up from the central lounge area near the espresso machine.

"Here before you are none other than New St. Cloud City's phenomenal teen heroes."

"We've met," David said with a frown.

David curled his lip. Eric followed his father's squinted eyes to see the sleek silver helicopter on the landing pad, not too far behind the glass. The *Pegasus'* landing struts sat atop a big double-S Super Society logo sprawled across the platform.

"Today marks a special day! We are welcoming the newest member of the Super Society!" Baron said, gesturing to Eric. "Team, I'm excited for you to meet—"

"Eric Icarus!" Eric said, stepping on Baron's big line.

A *clink* sent Eric's attention over Melvin, who racked a thick set of dumbbells in the far-left corner. Despite wearing workout clothes, he still looked out of place among exercise equipment.

Nearby, a slightly older, athletic African American girl Eric didn't recognize ran on a treadmill. She wore a Golden Eagles t-shirt, so he assumed she went to his school.

"Eric Boxworth?" he heard Melvin whisper to her. "What's he doing here?"

I could ask you the same question, Melvin.

"Hi, uh, other superheroes," Eric mumbled.

His mouth fell open while taking in the airy scenery of their see-through suite.

"Wow, you guys keep things... transparent."

Utterly unamused, David tapped on the phone in his pocket, making little *tup tup tup* sounds—weirdly matching the rhythm of the *pat pat pat* sounds of Tiffany pounding on a punching bag. Her red tracksuit matched her boxing gloves.

Eric cupped his hand, whispering to Jaycee.

"I thought this was Super Society members only."

She ignored him.

"Truther is on monitor duty," Baron said. "But allow me to properly introduce your new teammates."

He motioned to each costumed Society member.

"Extra, Go-Go, Supercut, and Powerhouse."

Eerily quiet, they each gave a quick head nod to Eric.

Okay, that's a little creepy.

"Ah, yes, well, as you can see," Baron said, "in addition to managing the Society, I provide housing for a small group of teenagers here in the tower. All classmates of Eric and Jaycee."

The kids waved while the superheroes held their poses like living mannequins.

"I have a partiality for wayward youths, as my charitable foundations will attest. I never knew my parents..."

While Baron ambled into a story of his orphaned youth, Eric raised his eyebrows at Jaycee. She made a quick shushing motion, silently telling him to keep his curiosity to himself.

"...These are no mere sidekicks," Baron said. "They are the city's premiere protectors!"

"Yeah, and you're the premiere profiteer," David said. "Lemme guess, as their legal guardian, you get the kids' cut of the licensing and merchandise?"

"Dad! They're right here!" Eric said through the side of his mouth.

Why did I think my first official day as Eric Icarus would be any less sucky than usual?

"The Super Society is a legitimate force dedicated to justice, nothing else," Baron said.

"I'm sure being above the law has its perks," David said, followed by a mocking chuckle.

"We operate in the only city that permits superheroes," Baron corrected. "Not like those backwoods vigilantes in DeSalvo County."

The Super Society's motionless gaze turned beyond unnerving at this point.

"This squad, like Eric, represents the future," Baron continued. "Much like the MegaCore."

"Just a second," David said, patting the air like he was putting out an imaginary fire. "Aren't we forgetting to talk to, I dunno, lawyers and accountants? The MegaCore is my masterpiece. I won't agree to just anything."

"It goes without saying that your proposed compensation shall be an unreal, miraculous, once-in-a-lifetime level of cool. And by cool, I mean payment—"

"Yep, got it, loud and clear," David said, grinning ear to ear. "I'll sign whatever Eric needs to go play superhero. We have work to do!"

David made a beeline for the exit. Baron joined, quick to follow.

"Any Super Society members looking to upgrade to exo-armor?" David asked while the red door slid open. "The Ultranaut warsuit would look great on Truther, just sayin'."

"Don't press your luck."

Baron gave Eric and Jaycee a wiggly wave as he followed David into the hallway. Eric walked up to the Society, extending a hand to Supercut.

"Hey, so I guess we're officially teammates now, huh?"

His fingers phased through Supercut's fist.

"Hands off the virtual merchandise!" Melvin shouted from the workout bench.

Recoiling his arm, Eric watched in amazement as the photons dispersed.

"Never accept cheap imitations," Tiffany remarked, unstrapping a bright red boxing glove. "As if any of you could handle having hard light copies like myself."

The rest of the holographic heroes dissolved into thin air, spooking Eric.

"Heck the what?! I mean, what the heck? What were those?"

"Holograms," Jaycee said, stepping up to him. "It's not perfect, but they help hide our identities from nosy parents. Oooo! The emitters should be called 'Protector Projectors!'"

"So, that means...?"

"Eric, you were gonna find out eventually anyway."

Jaycee pointed to each kid.

"Melvin Medina, a.k.a Supercut. Of course, you know Tiffany Sneeder, a.k.a. Extra. Meet our field commander, Yvette Wallace, a.k.a. the fastest high school senior alive, Go-Go."

Yvette hopped off the treadmill.

"Welcome to the team!" she said, wiping sweat from her brow.

"With Yvette going to college next year, there's an opening for field commander," Jaycee said, winking at her.

"To remain eligible for my Pantheon scholarship, I'm away a lot with my extracurricular activity," Yvette said to Eric.

She side-eyed Jaycee.

"But I'm for real with this hero thing. You won't get my job that easily."

"Sure, sure..." Jaycee said, nudging Eric. "Hey, Go-Go, since you'll be 'gone-gone,' can only five super-people make up a 'society?'"

Melvin threw himself onto one of the wide couches in the center of the room.

"I can't believe Mr. Maddox just sprang a new member on us! And of all people!" he said. "No offense, Eric, but I've seen you in action. Ya don't got what it takes to hang with this squad."

"As if anyone would believe the Dungeon Master is a superhero," Tiffany chided while sitting on a barstool in the lounge area.

She reached over the marble bar top to pick out a bottle of sparkling water from a tray of ice.

Melvin shot her a mocking grin before collapsing on a fluffy pillow.

"Hey, let's focus," Yvette said. "We're already behind schedule. Masks on, people!"

"We all know why Eric is really on the team anyway," Tiffany added. "This is the only way Jaycee knows how to get a guy to go out with her."

Tiffany strutted to the lockers on the sidewall where Yvette waited. The vaults outsized anything at their school. They connected to what appeared to be a storage facility only a handful of yards from the helicopter.

Jaycee stayed behind with Eric. She grumbled. He gulped.

"Don't sweat them," she assured. "They just don't like sharing the spotlight."

The others pulled out their colorful uniforms.

"I'm more worried about changing in front of everyone," Eric admitted.

"Relax already. My dad is all about public accessibility, but not when it comes to getting dressed."

The large, reinforced glass doors dimmed, blocking out the morning light. In mere seconds, giant pitch-black squares hid the room.

"Well, that's a start..." Eric said, scanning the room for a stall, a curtain, a partition, or anything that would provide a semblance of privacy.

"We have less than an hour until our con appearance," Yvette said, swinging her wide locker door open. "Let's make this quick!"

She stepped inside and closed the door—a glossy plaque labeled "GO-GO" adorned its otherwise featureless metal face. Eric spotted the large unit at the end of the row. Sure enough, it bore the name "ERIC ICARUS."

"Your private dressing room awaits," Jaycee said, pointing her thumb at his locker.

Hers happened to be next to Eric's. She stepped inside and shut the door, leaving him standing alone.

"Um, how do I open it?" he asked, inspecting the smooth chrome door.

Eric pressed his palm to the cool surface.

"Worked for Mr. Maddox..."

Eric heard a *click* sound, followed by the door swinging itself open. Easily the coolest changing room he'd ever seen awaited inside. On his right sat a minifridge, stocked with water bottles, sports drinks, and sealed protein shakes behind its glass door. On his left sat a cushioned bench with a TV monitor on the white wall. A tall, clear cabinet beside it contained three top-of-the-line gaming consoles and controllers. Eric's eyes bugged out when he spotted the VR headset on the bottom shelf. Toward the back housed a small shower and toilet space.

"Why would you ever leave this locker?!"

He held his breath when he saw it: against the wall by the sink, a steel wireframe held a sleek blue jumpsuit. Small neon blue lamps shined upon it like a shrine. It stood showcased against a backdrop of an iridescent Super Society logo.

Eric approached the uniform, astounded to see his design come to life—leather straps wrapped around the upper thighs with matching gloves and boots. Thin pockets stretched down the sides of the pant legs. It bore a lighter blue from mid-chest up, layered in protective rows that lined up the collar.

His regular clothes couldn't come off fast enough. Eric almost tripped over his shorts, mesmerized by the shiny new outfit. With gentle ease, he took the costume down. He stuck an arm through a slick sleeve, then slid into the pant legs. The insulated material warmed his skin.

"This is the most comfortable thing he'd ever felt," he said, zipping up the shirt. "I'm never taking this off!"

He slipped his feet into the boots and put on the gloves. They felt thin, but the textured lining on the fingers hinted at their durability. One final item rested on a hook. He grabbed the metallic blue backpack as if he was handling a precious treasure.

"Way better than wings."

Its aerodynamic tip had rounded edges that reflected the overhead lamps. The center was wide and flat. A sleek silver stripe ran across it, like an S-shape connecting to its inverted counterpart. Sky blue rectangles striped down the middle. Eric held it from the fins on its sides.

"Way lighter than I expected," he observed, tapping at its hull. "It really is just a prop, huh?"

He put it on, connecting the straps—the central buckle over his chest was a glossy emblem in the form of a light blue arrow pointing up. Three thin, dark blue bars with sharp, winged tips were aligned behind the shiny arrow—the angular stripes resembled an "E." With every excited breath, Eric's feet hovered higher.

He turned to the mirror across from him.

"Hey, there, Eric Icarus," he said, smug as can be while checking out his reflection. "Looking pretty 'fly,' Eric Icarus, haha!"

He held the same arrogant grin despite his furrowed brow.

"And I'm never saying that again, haha!"

Knock! Knock!

"Get caught in a zipper, flyboy?" Jaycee said from outside. "I can send in Melvin to help..."

"No way!' the other boy yelled.

Eric returned to the floor. As he neared the door, it opened itself. His new teammates waited on the other side, all in costume. Even under the yellow domes of her Powerhouse mask, he could see Jaycee's eyes widen at the sight of him.

He gave her a nervous smile.

"Forgetting something, sweetie?" Tiffany said.

Despite the same red hair flowing out of her mask, it floored Eric that she was Extra.

"W-what? Am I supposed to wear a cup? That makes sense; I can get mine from gym class. I haven't used it yet—"

"Where's yer mask, babyface?!" Melvin cut in.

His Supercut cowl pointed up like the ears of some animal, but Eric couldn't tell which one.

"I don't really do the whole mask thing."

"Real smart," Melvin mocked. "'Gee, I wonder who that unmasked kid is? Pretty sure he goes to school with that handsome Hispanic lad, Melvin Medina!' Even the dumbest bad guy could piece it together. Then we'd have some real trouble on our hands!"

"Hey, when has Mr. Maddox let us down?" Yvette said, stepping in. "Y'all better not act this way when we see Truther."

Her silver wraparound Go-Go visor hid her eyes, but Yvette still held a welcoming smile.

"Nice threads, Eric Icarus. What's your hustle?"

"My what?"

"Your ability," she said. "Your unique tech? Ya know, what special equipment do you bring to the squad?"

Eric froze. Jaycee marched up next to him.

"Let me handle this," she said to Eric, winking.

She faced the team.

"Eric Icarus is the evolution of crime-fighting! His

amazing abilities will usher in the next generation of heroes! Like his namesake, he'll soar to new heights while protecting this great city as an unmasked champion of virtue! You won't believe your eyes when you see this teenage phenomenon fly through the air like an avenging angel! That's right, with his astonishing and natural gift of flight, Eric Icarus will put the 'super' in Super Society!"

Catching her breath from her ringmaster spiel, she whipped her head over to Eric and gave him two thumbs up with an ear-to-ear smile.

Eric felt the blood leave his face like someone painted him with the pale brush of fear. He leaned behind Jaycee, quickly whispering into her ear.

"My powers are supposed to be a secret!"

He heard her breath exit her body. The rest of the team shared confused expressions.

"I, well, can fly, but, uh," he said, facing them. "It's because of my anti-gravity device backpack."

Jaycee's grin faded as she slowly withdrew her upward thumbs.

Chapter Twelve: *LIFT*

ERIC

WILD TORRENTS OF WIND SWEPT through Eric's hair as he looked down at the Super Society's helicopter—the whirlwind of its blades cut through the air in a frenzy. A multicolored mass of costumed people filled the sprawling parking lot.

As he trailed the *Pegasus'* careful descent, Eric noticed each person looking up at the silver aircraft. The intense gusts of air stung his eyes, and the 'copter's roaring engine assaulted his ears. Eric moved his body away from the vehicle. After a few blinks, he saw that the vast crowd wasn't following the superheroes' famous transport. They stared up at him.

An electronic sign above the convention center's main entrance welcomed fans to this year's comic book convention. In truth, it served as more of an annual honoring of the city's colorful guardians. Many considered it to be an unofficial holiday.

"That used to be me, just another fan paying homage to superheroes," Eric said. "And now they're here to see me!"

Eric waved at the people, lowering to only a few feet

above their heads. They shouted their greetings:

"Who are you?"

"Where's the Super Society?"

"That looks so fake! He's not really flying!"

Eric maintained a nervous grin and kept waving.

"Well, I still get to go to the con," Eric said.

He planted his boots on the pavement safely from the landing *Pegasus*. Police officers held the crowd back in a circle surrounding them. The blades spun in a blur, pushing the air around Eric. The thunderous engine collided with the eager audience's cheering. Eric covered his ears but quickly withdrew his hands—it didn't seem heroic to cower at all the loud noises.

How do superheroes not go deaf? he thought.

Costumed fans engulfed the lot, leaving little room for cars. Homemade Truthers, Extras, Powerhouses, and Supercuts flocked to greet the 'copter. A woman dressed as Go-Go pushed herself in front of a Judge Justice near the front of the crowd. She jumped up and down, screaming in excitement. The Judge looked as scared as Eric felt.

Brave crime-fighters probably don't run and hide from crazed cosplayers, right?

He gave "Go-Go" a thumbs up. The woman wore what looked like a silver-painted hairband around her face. Despite not seeing her pupils, Eric avoided making eye contact.

The uproar surged when the vessel's mirror-like hatch slid open. Truther stepped down a small set of steps, extending a gloved hand to the applauding audience. His epic white cape flowed in the unruly breeze. Jaycee popped out behind him, decked out in her uniform.

"I'm never gonna get used to calling her Powerhouse," Eric said to himself, shooting her a big grin.

She didn't see, too busy to notice Eric while doing a double-handed wave to the raucous crowd. In their uniforms, Yvette, Melvin, and Tiffany exited as Go-Go, Supercut, and Extra. Each received the royal rock star reception. The Super Society ducked under the blades and rushed to get closer to the adoring public. Eric stood alone and off to the side. He fidgeted with his matching dark blue gloves and adjusted his elbow pads.

Flattering as the new outfit was, Eric assumed he wouldn't have looked more dumbstruck if he'd stepped off a bus with a hayseed in his teeth. A policeman approached him.

"Hey, no fans beyond this point!"

"No! No! I'm with them!" Eric shouted.

The officer gave him a puzzled look.

"Oh, uh, okay…" the policeman said, backing away.

Further bewildered, Eric glanced over to see Truther giving him a quick nod.

"Thanks, um, Truther!" Eric yelled, but he was already looking away.

The automated 'copter ascended, floating into the bright sky. It left behind forceful winds, causing numerous people in the crowd to clutch onto their loose costume pieces. One of the frontline fans wore a convincing replica Truther costume. Eric did a double take to ensure his mind wasn't playing tricks.

"This is unbelievable!" Eric yelled.

"I know, right?!" Tiffany—the real Extra—said, pulling him closer to the group. "All this earning potential around us, and we're not allowed to franchise! We can't even have a superhero social media account!"

She bore a toothy smile and shook her hand at the masses.

"Wave goodbye to all the money flying out of the

window!"

While approaching the excited crowd, Tiffany placed her palm on her chest in faux humility. Jaycee grabbed Eric's arm and led him nearer to the audience. Truther walked alongside them. Eric couldn't stop staring at the man's white leather uniform and the golden T's decorating his arms and shoulders. Eric got a kick out of the fact that they shared the same Super Society logo double-S belt buckle.

"You want me to tell all these people to leave you two alone?" Powerhouse said, snickering into his ear.

"I've never seen him up this close," Eric said back as candidly as he could under the noise. "I didn't get a chance to introduce myself. He knows who I am, right?"

"He does, and soon everyone else will!"

The sea of people chanted, "Su-per Society! Su-per Society!" Despite the multistory convention center's stout frame, Eric felt unsure it could hold the staggering number of fans. Rabid fans of all ages far beyond outnumbered the security personnel. Eric puffed his cheeks in a big, anxious sigh.

"So, what am I supposed to do exactly?"

"Just float around and look pretty," Jaycee said. "On the ride over, Truther told me all about how you don't have to really do anything."

"There's a lot of people here who will depend on me if a disaster strikes..."

"Chill. The con is just a big debut party for you. Posing for selfies, flying around, and waving to fans, that's all. It's not like you'll have to fight anybody."

Yvette and Melvin joined them as they formed a line facing the crowd.

"There are way more fans than last year!" Yvette said.

"Special event or no, it's still a Tuesday morning," Truther grumbled. "So many businesses are unattended; it's open season for criminals."

"You're just mad 'cause you can't stay long enough to sign autographs," Powerhouse said.

A trio of cosplayers dressed in replica Sidebar outfits burrowed their way to the front. Cops threw up warning hands, so they kept their distance. Eric raised an eyebrow at their skintight red and white zip-up jumpsuits and deep-pocketed utility belts.

"Fans dressed as Sidebar?" Truther said. "I'm not sure if I should be honored or disturbed that my sidekick days are getting the nostalgia treatment—that spandex costume wasn't even flattering on me."

"I keep telling you," Jaycee said. "The people are ready for a Sidebar comeback!"

Ignoring her, Truther stepped forward. He pointed at a group of fans dressed as Aqua Queen, Sureshot, and Laser Lass. Seeing the original Society lineup getting some love made Eric happy.

Truther tapped at the side of the T-shaped emblem on his mask.

"The Super Society welcomes you all to this year's superhero celebration!"

Whatever Truther activated amplified his voice.

"The main attraction is a showcase honoring the Golden Gavel, the legendary weapon used by none other than my former mentor, Judge Justice!"

The booming applause made Eric reconsider covering his ears.

"But first," Truther said, "it is with great pride that I introduce the newest member—"

"I love you, Truther!" a fake Judge Justice screamed.

Next to the wannabe Judge, a girl cosplaying as

Go-Go cringed.

"Thank you, citizen!" Truther said. "Anyway, as I was saying—"

"Can you sign something for me, Truther?!" the Judge shouted.

Under the eyeholes of his baby-blue Judge Justice mask, the feverish fan's maniacal eyes bulged. He ran forward, immediately chased by a policewoman.

Panic squeezed Eric's muscles, but his new leader remained unfazed.

"They get crazier every year," Truther muttered.

The Judge wrestled free from the officer.

"I got something you can sign right here!" the Judge yelled, reaching inside his flowy black robe.

He whipped out a strange-looking pistol—instead of a barrel, it had a metal, arrow-shaped clock hand aimed at Truther.

"Okay, I can definitely take this guy!" Powerhouse said before charging after the "Judge."

"No, Powerhouse!" Truther yelled.

"Stand aside, citizens—"

A lightning-quick squeeze of the trigger stopped the girl mid-sentence and froze her in place. Nothing discharged from the pistol, yet its shot created mass chaos. People scrambled in every direction.

Truther hot-footed over to Powerhouse as she teetered only a handful of feet across from him. His black-gloved hands caught her stiff body before she could slam against the street. With gentle ease, he laid her statue-like body onto the pavement. Eric couldn't bear to look at her locked in a running position with her facial features unnaturally stuck in an eerie wide-eyed smile.

Bang! Bang! Bang!

Shrieks of terror sliced Eric's ears. Melvin, Tiffany,

and Yvette took well-trained positions around him. Everyone saw them as Supercut, Extra, and Go-Go assisting the cops in crowd control. Eric, however, stalled as confusion slowed reality around him.

"Don't just stand there, Icarus!" Melvin yelled from somewhere.

Bodies bolted all around Eric. In the eye of the storm, he spotted the mock Judge.

"Outta my way!" the fiendish gunman sniveled.

Hurrying through the frightened mob, the pretender pulled the loose-fitting Judge mask off, revealing another cowl. His forehead bore a semi-circular design of clock hands while the exposed lower half of his face showcased a long, thick black mustache. Eric had followed the Super Society's adventures long enough to recognize him.

"Time Thief!"

The villain flung his Judge costume off, revealing his skinny frame. Plowing through a couple of colorful masqueraders, Time Thief raced toward the building's front doors. With his feet floating above the street, Eric willed himself after him but lost the evildoer in the fracas.

"Eric Icarus!" Truther shouted. "We got a hero down!"

"Is she dead?!" Eric asked, hovering next to Truther.

He dreaded the answer.

"Time Thief's nanites only mimic 'freezing' by reducing her heart rate to resemble... She'll be fine. It'll wear off."

Truther's familiarity with Time Thief's gadgetry assured that the way he "stole" time is just part of an elaborate illusion.

"I read about him!" Eric said. "His swarm

of microscopic cyber-mites causes his victims to essentially blackout!"

"Powerhouse is down! Repeat: Powerhouse is down!" Truther reported into an unseen microphone. "Drone Alpha, extraction, my location."

The *Pegasus* flew overhead, popping out a white orb. The helicopter veered out of sight while the drone descended to where Truther and Eric waited. The smooth spherical drone spanned three feet in circumference and emitted blue light from its rear propulsion unit. Automated arms popped out of the floating machine, collected Powerhouse, and ferried her away to safety.

"I'm reviewing drone footage on my visor. Time Thief is in the building!"

"What can't you see in that visor?" Eric asked.

The frantic herd of fans blocked the way into the center. Sounds of panicking people swirled around them.

"Too much potential collateral damage to go in guns blazing."

"What do we do, Truther?!"

"Go-Go!" he said, pressing his temple. "Get the others and help evacuate the area!"

Eric dodged a running pair of mismatched gangly cosplayers in poorly fitting copies of Extra and Supercut's uniforms.

"There's a supervillain with a raygun or something in there!" the Supercut impostor warned.

"Run, man!" the "Extra" said. "Let the real Super Society take care of this!"

"But I'm..." Eric began to say, but they fled without looking back.

"The team can handle crowd control," Truther said. "We need to get inside!"

"Maybe I should just go wait in the helicopter."

Truther placed a firm hand on Eric's shoulder.

"I understand what your 'position' on the team is," he said in a fatherly way, an unfamiliar tone to Eric. "But right now, I need you to be the hero I know you can be!"

"Easy for you to say! You're Truther! I mean, come on, you've been doing this your whole life! And you've got a power suit!"

Truther glanced over his shoulder, then tapped a button on his gauntlet. In a flash, a neon-blue orb of cascading light spread around them. The soundless energy rippled like a curved lighting storm.

"See?" Eric said. "You can even make cool holograms with your wrist!"

"Honesty above all is part of the Super Society hero code."

"It is?" Eric asked. "But we're hiding?"

"This holo-sphere conceals us..."

Truther pressed on his temples. *Whizz* sounds emitted from his face emblem's inner mechanisms indicating an unlocking sequence.

"Because only one person needs the truth right now."

Eric's bulging eyes matched his dropped jaw when Truther unmasked, revealing Baron Maddox underneath. Removing the cowl ruffled Baron's black hair, yet it and his mustache still somehow oozed with class. The mask's sewn-in blonde toupée wiggled like a lifeless, albeit full-bodied, glossy animal.

"Mr. Maddox!" Eric yelled, quickly covering his mouth.

He spoke through his fingers.

"You're going undercover as Truther?! Does the rest of the team know?"

"Eric, I am Truther. The whole 'I love the truth' stuff should've clued you in by now."

"The wig, the way the big 'T' covers your face," Eric said. "I always thought Truther was this clean-cut blonde guy. Maybe I shoulda went with a mask after all, huh? Yours sure had me fooled!"

He gave Eric a friendly grin.

"Yes, I have a special suit that I invented, but I'm just a man," Baron said. "What you have is pure, natural power."

"This is incredible, Mr. Maddox!"

"No one else on the team knows my true identity, not even Jaycee."

He shimmied the cowl back on.

"I'm entrusting you with this information because I believe in you, Eric!" he said.

"Mr. Maddox, I-I-I will, I mean, I won't—!"

"You won't let me down," he answered for him, straightening the big "T" over his face. "And it's codenames only while the mask is on."

He tapped at his wrist, dissipating the bright blue globe.

"What can I do, though?" Eric asked. "I can't fire lasers or anything! The only thing I can do is fly!"

"Eric, how much can you lift?"

"Huh? Like, in pounds?"

One look at the cluster of people congesting the way to the building entrance told Eric what he had in mind.

"I'm not gonna like this, am I?"

"Catch me!" Truther ordered before sprinting toward the huddled mass.

The heels of his boots sprang out, catapulting him into the air. His running start boosted him up and over the stampeding fans. Eric launched himself on a crash course with Truther. He stretched his arms, bracing for the worst.

"You're so flushing heavy!" Eric screamed, struggling to hoist Truther's thick frame.

He could barely wrap his arms around the broad man's waist. Eric could hardly see over Truther's white cape sticking up in his face.

"Faster, Icarus!" his leader demanded.

Eric carried him over the bedlam below—the tips of his boots just narrowly avoiding scraping a few scalps. Eric aimed low enough to glide through the open entrance doors. He navigated them down the massive lobby, dodging scared civilians, wide support columns, and deserted food vendor booths.

"Take me to Time Thief!" Truther yelled.

"Oh, sure, because he told me exactly where he is!" Eric shouted back, thick with nervous sarcasm. "Did he not text you, too?"

CHOOM!

The seismic shockwave erupted from a higher floor, hurtling Eric and Truther to the quaking ground. They stumbled as the place rattled, raining debris all around them. The surrounding windows shattered— tiny glass daggers found exposed flesh, delivering needling pain. Eric covered his eyes with his forearm.

Eric dodged a chunk of drywall, unsure of how to even breathe in this situation. Meanwhile, Truther dove into a pedestrian, knocking the man out of the path of a falling food cart.

The man looked at him in shock.

"I-I-I—"

"Get yourself to safety," Truther said as a bowling ball-sized piece of concrete landed mere inches away from him.

Eric took cautious steps around shredded posters,

abandoned collectibles, and plastic prop weapons. He paused in the center of the littered entry hall, scanning the kiosks, escalators, and discarded luggage.

Truther tapped at his temple, then pointed up.

"My system detects that the quake came from the sixth floor!"

Eric gazed at the tiered walkways curving around the building—each story had an extended balcony that could look out at the open lobby. In the center of the top floor was a wide open entry to the main showroom.

"Lemme guess, no time to take the stairs?" Eric said. "Truther, my arms are jelly!"

"Catch me!"

Truther bent his knees, activating the spring-loaded lifts in his boots. After a running start, his high-tech heels gave him a boost, propelling him upward—reaching soaring heights of maybe five feet in the air. Truther landed on a jutting metal ledge hanging over a t-shirt booth. He jumped, pushing his body higher once more off a broad windowsill.

"Super-suit-enhanced parkour," Eric commented. "If I weren't so freaked out, I'd be impressed!"

Eric shot himself up, targeting Truther. He curled his arms, hooking the armpits of the heavier man. Eric strained, but their combined momentum carried them to the edge of the sixth-floor guard wall. Truther released himself and landed with grace just outside the entrance. Eric hovered above, hesitant to get close.

Reverberating murmurs of the captive crowd echoed from inside. A few escapees stumbled out, nearly tripping over their loose-fitting costume boots while lanyards flipped around their necks. The hysterical VIPs rejoiced at seeing the black, white, and gold defender coming to rescue them. Truther brushed past them, bulldozing his way to the main event. The fans hightailed it.

"We can cover more ground if we split up!" Truther said as he dashed inside. "Take the back of the room!"

"We should probably wait for the others, right?" Eric asked while lowering to his feet but received no answer.

Truther's presence garnered some "oohs" and "ahhs" from the awestruck audience, but they quickly quieted themselves back down to a nervous mutter.

Eric took a breath and crossed the threshold, navigating his way through a mass of scared people. Fortunately, it appeared that no one else had been "frozen." This fact tipped Eric off that Time Thief needed them cognizant, ensuring their safety, at least for the moment. They had backed themselves to the walls, leaving the middle of the expansive showroom clear, save for the costumed villain standing on top of an autograph table.

"I know one of you geeks has it somewhere!" Time Thief screeched.

He raised his black-sleeved arm, presenting a chunk of metal in his red-gloved hand.

"I'm serious! Anybody tries to make a break for it, and I'll bomb every last one of you!"

Eric hunched behind the sea of distracted conventioners. He scurried past knocked-over tables, piles of loose action figures, and rows of long boxes full of comic books. He stopped by a pair of garbage bins by the back wall. A tall duo of "Truthers" stood in front of Eric, blocking his view. Eric stood on his tippy-toes and stretched his neck but could only go so far.

I've already flown around, so why don't I just...?

He cut the notion short. He dared not levitate, fearing what further chaos the distraction could bring.

I can't see a thing! he thought. *Why couldn't I get stretchy powers instead?*

"Who are you dressed as?" one of the Truther twins whispered to him.

"Uh," Eric said, stalling, realizing his big superhero debut wasn't going as planned. "I'm, er, a new character. He's super-cool. You'll love him."

"Oh, okay. No offense, but I hope the real version has a better-quality costume."

The guy turned away to face the craziness. Irked, Eric scrunched his lips. The line of fans in front of him paid no attention, so Eric felt free to float.

This is more like it!

Raising just above the crowd's heads, Eric witnessed Truther emerging from the other end of the room, approaching Time Thief. The lanky lunatic's smooth black leggings shined under the overhanging lights. No one could ignore this guy if they tried.

Okay, I'm not as fake of a superhero as I thought I was gonna be, Eric thought. *But superheroes probably do more than just watch, right?*

"Why don't you tell these people the truth, Time Thief?" Truther demanded.

"Truther!"

Time Thief spat as if saying the name tasted foul. The cutout holes in his mask exposed his beady eyes.

"How's your junior partner? Bored stiff?!"

Eric winced at the man's sinister laughter. Surrounding the two enemies, the horde of people bumped into each other, trying to get some distance from the standoff. Eric moved farther along the rear of the fearful audience.

"What do I do?!" Eric asked below the crowd's ambient chatter.

Marching past a cardboard cutout of himself,

Truther pointed an accusing finger at Time Thief.

"You're a coward and a fraud!" he declared. "You and all the pathetic villains in this city rely on bootlegged technology to commit your petty crimes!"

Truther stopped to let the barrels of his gauntlets flash; they warned of the punishment due.

"That vibrational shockwave detonator you're holding? It's just a knockoff from last year's Pantheon science expo. You're nothing but a marauder. Absolutely pitiful."

That got a few chuckles from the crowd. Infuriated, Time Thief shook the device as if the shuddering motion would intensify its menace.

"You laugh, but I am merely an ambassador of anti-Society rebels! There are more of us, you'll see! Once we're united, those you label 'supervillains' will be collectively known as the Guerrillas!"

"You mean, like, apes?" a fan asked.

"Isn't that a rock group or something?" another chimed in.

"No!" Time Thief grumbled. "Like, you know, guerrilla warfare! And attacking your celebration of the banal has been the first strike!"

"All Super Society members report to my location," Truther ordered, making a bit of a show of holding his earpiece for dramatic effect. "It's over, Time Thief. Your 'monkey business' ends now."

"For crying out loud! It's Guerrillas! Like 'guerrilla tactics!'"

"These bad guys need to stop trying to make 'guerrilla' happen," Eric said under his breath.

"We've beaten you, and we'll beat any other scavenger friends you have," Truther said.

We have? Eric thought. *We will?*

"Hand over the bomb and go quietly," Truther

said. "These people get to walk out of here. That's the only way this ends."

"One more step, and I press this button, and everybody's bones and organs get all shook up!"

Time Thief's thumb caressed a pill-shaped trigger on the explosive.

"I'm not going anywhere until I'm holding Judge Justice's Golden Gavel!"

"No!" Eric blurted.

A shaking woman shushed him. Instincts dropped Eric to his feet. He spotted a crumpled banner peeking out from under a nearby booth advertising the exhibition of Judge Justice's coveted mallet.

"I can't let him take it!" Eric whispered.

"So, that's what your game is, huh?" Truther said. "Let me guess—this is your last big score? Sell a piece of superhero history on the black market and call it a career?"

"This is a declaration of war!" Time Thief yelled. "With the prized possession of this city's woefully lauded legend, I will have proven that I—we—are a force to be reckoned with!"

Readying for an explosion, Eric crouched. He spotted an unlabeled wooden crate behind a short Powerhouse cosplayer. Beside the girl's blue boots, the lid cracked open just enough...

"No way," Eric said.

"I know it's here!" Time Thief screamed in the background.

Eric snuck closer to the crate. Something golden inside twinkled.

Using his gloved fingertips, Eric slid the lid off the crate.

"Give it to me now! Now-now-now!" Time Thief shouted, stomping his foot on the table in a fit.

Eric clasped the heavy handle of what waited inside the crate. It felt right. He removed the object, carefully crouching so he could conceal it as best as he could. He had fantasized about this moment for so long—but with puberty in full swing, Eric's fantasies were becoming more and more one-tracked. This dream, though, had endured and was coming true.

Eric marveled at the Golden Gavel in his hands. His novelty piggybank was an accurate replica, but this was so much larger. The light streaked across its brassy finish. His wide eyes gazed back at himself in the reflection.

"I know what Judge Justice would do."

Peering through gaps between the grouped fans, Eric saw Truther hold his hands up to the villain as if approaching a feral beast. Time Thief punched the air, halting Truther in his tracks.

"You're running out of time in more ways than one!" Time Thief warned. "Give me the Golden Gavel!"

Clutching the hammer of justice, Eric lifted himself above the droves. He speared through the air like a heat-seeking torpedo.

"You mean this?" Eric shouted.

Time Thief turned to answer the voice behind him and—

WHACK!

The impact flung Time Thief from the table. He twisted and flopped face-up onto the floor, sporting a fresh, new bruise and a swelling eye.

Eric hovered with the Judge's shiny mallet in his grip. Gasps and hollering spread around him. The fans knew this oversized gavel was no mere novelty item. The people pushed forward to steal a glance at Eric carrying it, becoming a tangle of limbs and chaos. Eric downcast his wide eyes, amazed at how large the gilded gavel looked in his meager grip. The adrenaline pumping in his veins made it so he could even lift the hefty weapon.

Flummoxed, Eric spotted his leader before him. The steel-toed end of Truther's black boot nudged the downed Time Thief, but the villain was clocked out.

Eric buoyed without a word as the onlookers gawked. Truther gestured toward Eric, which the crowd took as a cue to descend upon the idly bobbling boy. Like an elated gaggle of football fans storming the field to celebrate a victorious quarterback, the liberated fans flocked around Eric. The crowd clapped in thunderous applause. Eric's humble smile caused the uproar of praise to get even louder.

This was not how he expected Melvin, Tiffany, and Yvette to see him when they entered, but there they were. Yvette's Go-Go costume blurred as a dashing distortion, seemingly inspecting the area for any more trouble. Despite being the real deal Supercut and Extra, Melvin and Tiffany walked unnoticed. They parted the sea of men, women, and children, then joined Truther in the middle of the floor. Melvin threw out his hands— finger-claws extended—mouthing an unintelligible gripe unheard under the noise. Tiffany's curled lip made it clear what she was thinking. The jealousy was palpable.

"We escort everyone to safety, but, sure, everybody cheers for the new guy," Tiffany said, scoffing—loudly yet ignored.

The drone cradling Jaycee squeezed in through the showroom doors. The flying sphere found its administrator and presented the cocooned hero to him.

"I did say for all members to come here, didn't I?" Truther said, sighing.

Eric rotated in the air, taking in the scope of the

convention floor. Fans, costumes, and merchandise filled the vast space—with him in the epicenter.

"Ladies and gentlemen," Truther's amplified voice boomed throughout the room. "It is with great pride to introduce the newest member of the Super Society, Eric Icarus!"

Chants of "E-ric Ic-arus! E-ric Ic-arus" erupted.

"Wow," Eric said in a little voice.

"I spent years as Judge Justice's sidekick," he overheard Truther say to Yvette as she materialized next to him. "And not once did I get to even touch the thing, but Eric wields the Golden Gavel on his first day."

Eric came full circle to see the drone tenderly placing its charge on the floor. The mechanical arms retracted, releasing Jaycee. Unscathed as she was, Jaycee remained in her immobile running stance. Truther kneeled to evaluate her as the boisterous adulation raged on behind him. Eric flinched when she instantaneously popped back to life.

"—Powerhouse is here!" Jaycee resumed, smiling as if nothing had happened.

Her body didn't appear to catch up to her brain—she almost crashed into the wall of adoring fans in front of her. The situation's bewilderment found Jaycee. Her mouth contorted. Her eyes squinted under those big yellow translucent domes.

Behind her, Truther placed his hands on his hips and shook his head, acknowledging that she was hearing them cheer on Eric. Eric held up the Golden Gavel in triumph. He felt a big, dopey smile stretch across his face.

Jaycee looked at him in utter confusion.

"Um, have I missed something?"

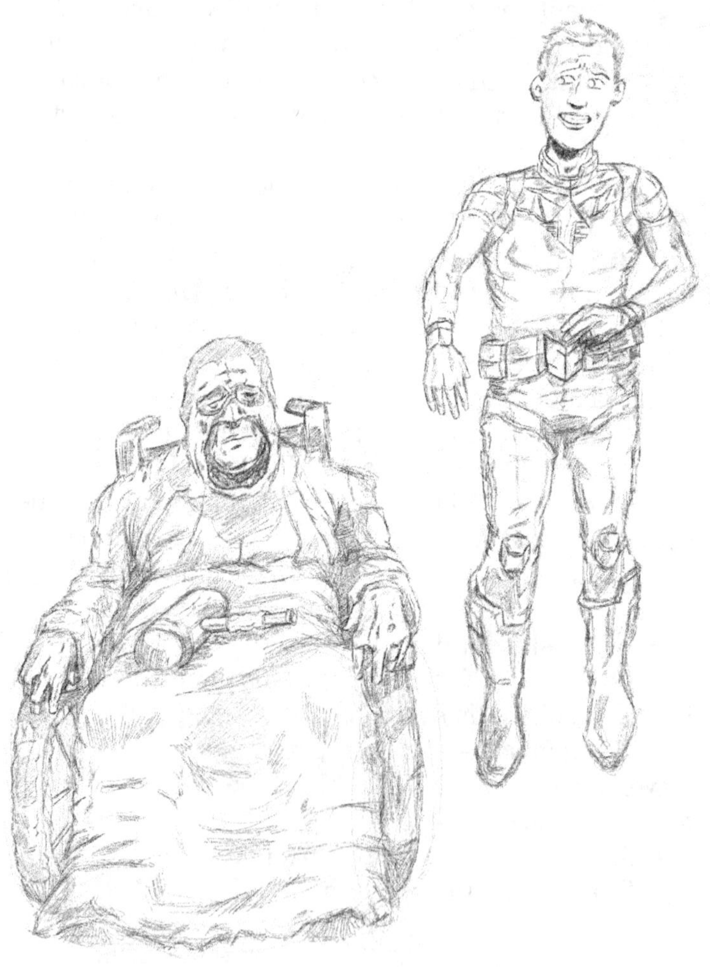

Chapter Thirteen: *ABOVE*

ERIC

ERIC TASTED THE CLEANING SUPPLY cocktail in the air. Bleach stung his nostrils, and he smelled an inordinate assortment of various sprays and soapy liquids. Under the thin veil of chemicals, the foul stench of bodily fluids and soiled laundry firmly held its place. Eric studied the nurses' and orderlies' jaded faces as they trudged around the old folks' home. They looked as near to death as the elderly residents were. Eric felt older just being there.

"Remember, young Mr. Icarus," Baron said. "Float for the cameras—big smile. Never, ever remove your anti-grav backpack. And keep your gloves on while you're at it. You'll be shaking a lot of hands—germs have dominion over this place."

Orderlies wheeled in old-timers into a small common area with tannish-orange wallpaper. Eric's lingering pupils caught up with his body as he turned to face the white linoleum curtain in front of him. The bottoms of his boots floated mere centimeters above the speckled light-brown tiled floor. His superhero costume made him stick out, leaving him uncomfortable. For the first time in his short crime-fighting career, being publicly seen embarrassed Eric. Standing next to Baron made it doubly humiliating—his light-gray suit and shiny silver tie that made Baron look like he owned the building and the entire block.

The murmur of their expectant audience grew from the other side of the curtain. The ambient chatter and clunky grunts of chairs sliding into place became louder as more people fi lled the room.

"Why aren't you dressed as Truther?" Eric asked. "Are any other Society members coming?"

Quick to press his finger on his lips, Baron shushed him.

"Voices down, please," he whispered. "The Super Society remains vigilant in their dedication to protecting the city. They are otherwise engaged in patrolling for criminal activity. Besides, today is about you."

He coulda saved the corporate spiel and just said the other kids are in school, Eric thought.

A nurse pushed a shrouded cart behind Eric and Baron. They peeked at it. Baron beamed with pride.

"And today is also about that, of course."

The curtain rolled away, revealing a roomful of videographers, journalists, and excited civilians packing the modest lobby. Cheers erupted; Eric froze. The overhead lights that had seemed so dim just a moment before shined glaringly sharp.

Eric hovered at the mouth of the hallway, questioning if his flying abilities would help him in the event of a trampling. Baron stepped in front of Eric and addressed the eager crowd.

"Ladies and gentlemen, thank you for being here for this momentous occasion!"

Eric's eyes struggled to adjust to the change in

light. A few heavy blinks later, his vision normalized. A cluster of old men huddled by a window at the other end of the corridor. They each wore the standard curmudgeon uniform of high-waisted khakis with suspenders over plaid shirts. Elderly Coach Gorman sat motionless as the midday sunlight cast deep shadows on his wrinkly face.

How long have I been out of school?

As Eric returned his gaze to the wide-eyed onlookers, Baron's voice faded into his ears.

"...continuing the legacy of this city's costumed crusaders and joining the Pantheon Solutions family of superheroes, Eric Icarus represents the future!"

More clapping. The pageantry was something that would take getting used to, but Eric felt the rekindling spark of exhilaration revisiting him. Meet-and-greets, ribbon cuttings, appearances at charity functions, etc. He'd be checking off all the celebrity boxes just as his early childhood idols did before him. He supposed a nursing home was as good as any place for an autograph signing.

"And we've gathered here today to pay tribute to the past—to a man who has personally meant so much to me," Baron continued.

He motioned for the cloth-covered cart to be brought over to him.

"Yesterday's attack during the annual celebration of our myths and legends was a vile act of cowardice and an attempt at petty theft. But thanks to the Super Society and, most importantly, the amazing new member, Eric Icarus, I am thrilled to be bringing home the gold."

Baron slipped the black sheet from the cart, revealing a glass case containing the Golden Gavel resting on a purple cushion.

The audience boomed with thunderous applause. Eric resisted covering his ears. He decided placing his hands on his hips was the proud thing to do. It's what he'd seen so many other heroic figures do, so it was good enough for him. With an unintentional goober-ish smile, Eric floated a bit higher. He puffed his chest with a deep breath. Baron snuck a wink over to Eric.

"We are proud to be returning the Golden Gavel to where it belongs," Baron said. "And back to its proper owner."

The applause blared even louder. Eric's face grew sore from all the smiling, but it was an easy gig to hover and not say anything. He looked at Baron for some cue, but he stared right through Eric.

Still stretching his cheeks, Eric peered over to see a frail, ancient-looking man pushed in a wheelchair by a large nurse. A loose-fitting Judge Justice costume draped over the nonagenarian patient's pale, thin skin and sagging shoulder pads. A burgundy blanket covered his lap.

The hefty woman parked the chair next to Eric. The old man's eyes sagged as half-closed slits under the eyeholes of his baby-blue mask, surely in the thick of a pill-induced stupor. The abundance of praise for the super senior citizen amazed Eric. He looked pathetic with his black robe/cape combination flowing over the crumpled zipper line of his matching blue tunic, tucked under his fuzzy blanket.

Baron nodded at Eric. He nodded back, retaining his oblivious grin. Baron nodded again with a bit more vigor. Eric took that to mean he needed to wave, so he wiggled his fingers at the happy crowd.

"Give him the gavel," Baron ordered through his teeth.

The nurse lifted the glass casing easily, leaving

the sacred tool open for Eric's reach. Eric gripped the polished handle, evoking a big reaction from the fans.

"We love you, Eric!" a shrill female voice shouted from the mass, which Eric found confusing yet exciting.

Unlike the Time Thief encounter, no adrenaline-assisted boost of strength aided him, but Eric managed to lug the weighty mallet up and out of the case.

He saw Baron keeping a watchful eye on him the whole time, making Eric incredibly self-conscious. Journalists lobbed muffled questions, which got lost under the wave of intermingled chatter. Microphones and recorders of varying sizes lurched closer and closer. The mob grew restless and advanced little by little.

I can't believe I'm holding the real Gavel! Again! Eric thought.

"Hand it over to the man, please," Baron quietly commanded with a frustrated twinge to his politeness.

"Who? The fake Judge over here?" Eric scoffed.

Baron leaned over to him.

"That's the genuine Judge Justice."

"Are you for real?!" Eric asked in a quick whisper.

Some fan I am! Eric scolded himself. *He looks so different from all the old posters. He looks so... real.*

With his smile even more forced, Eric lowered the gavel to the geriatric Judge. The nurse tied her hair into a tight, all-business blonde ponytail. She pulled up her red cardigan's sleeves and easily grabbed the gavel from Eric's trembling hands. She focused on the old man as if there wasn't a horde of people flooding the entryway.

A feeble voice found Eric's ear.

"I failed you, Sidebar."

"Huh?"

Camera flashes burst in a disorientating flurry. Eric knew he ruined the photo-op by blinking. He strained his face to sift past the afterimages left behind by the flares.

"I pressured you into the hero game, my boy," the frail voice rasped. "Just as much as you pressured us, eh?"

Eric glanced over to see the Judge rambling, but a quick look around informed him that no one else seemed to notice.

"I should've just let you be a kid," Judge Justice continued, his eyes in a far-off place and time. "To blazes with secret identities. We should've taken our medicine instead of hiding behind masks."

The nurse lowered the oversized gavel handle closer to the Judge's ivory-colored glove. The latex drooped off his hand as the Judge raised a brittle finger and curled it around the metal rod.

"The Golden Gavel has been properly returned to Judge Justice, ladies and gentlemen!" Baron enthused.

The audience clapped, and cameras flashed once more.

"The other members of the original Super Society retired, right, Mr. Maddox?" Eric whispered. "Where are they"

"Dead. And keep your voice down!" Baron hissed.

Eric gulped. Reporters shouted questions over the ovation.

"Will there be any other new superheroes?"

"Does Eric live in Pantheon Tower with the other members?"

"Will the rest of the Super Society unmask?"

"Please, one question at a time..." Baron said.

"We thought we were protecting a lost child," the oblivious Judge went on. "We were only saving our own skins."

"Um, are you talking to me?" Eric asked through

his teeth while faking a smile for the crowd.

Eric let out a quick sigh of relief, knowing the people focused on Baron. Everyone was too preoccupied to listen to the Judge's soft confessional.

"Eric Icarus is a brand new breed of hero," Baron said, which triggered another slew of comments and queries.

"We made you strong," the Judge said quietly. "Too strong for your own good."

Eric barely heard him over the chatter. Baron stepped in front of Eric, shielding him from the glare of camera flashes.

"There is order in the court once again!" Baron boomed, though it seemed like he was miles away.

The nurse placed the gavel back into its case while the Judge spewed a tiny bit of drool. Lost in a haze of perplexity, Eric found himself with both feet on the floor. His senses alerted him that Baron gave out closing statements and thanked everyone for showing up to their P.R. stunt, but it melted into garbled noise.

A tiny bite of pain spiked up Eric's leg, warning him not to stand for too long. Eric levitated back to reality, and the nurse wheeled the old Judge away.

• • •

Hovering—hiding—up in a corner, Eric spied on the nurse inspecting the life-giving machines next to Judge Justice's bed. The frail man lay snug under his white blanket, his mouth agape. The former hero's face was all wrinkles and lines with his mask removed, like cracked plates of a hard-boiled eggshell. Eric noticed the wisps of white hair sprouting from his liver-spotted scalp. He knew his eye-catching blue super suit wouldn't grant him invisibility, but Eric felt safer huddled up next to the air vent.

Baron nodded to the woman as she exited the small room. Unfamiliar with superhero retirement options, Eric relied on his hunch that these tiny quarters weren't worthy of the protector's legacy. Outside of a novelty figurine in his possession, Eric's fandom of Judge Justice had waned in the shadow of his father's disapproval of costumed heroes. As a result, Eric didn't consider himself an expert on elder hero care. Taking careful steps to the Judge's bedside, Baron glowed with proper due reverence.

Baron dusted off a row of awards lining a wall and repositioned a plant into a better spot of sunlight by the lone window. It seemed much like a child coming to care for an elderly parent.

Huddled in his corner of the wall, Eric knew better than to think Baron wasn't aware of his awkward floating. Finally, when Baron finished tending to the room, he spoke in a low tone.

"I know my visits have been rare; a consequence of my occupation. Your appearance today bolstered my agenda more than you could possibly know. You have my gratitude. And my sympathy."

Eric grimaced, afraid to move or even breathe. One minute, he'd been wrangled to wait in the Judge's chambers, and the next, his new boss was having a heart-to-heart with the most famous superhero of all time.

Boss? Manager? Mentor?

Eric felt unsure of what to call Baron. He didn't know what to make of this whole situation.

"I apologize for not taking swifter action to relocate you to a larger living space," Baron said. "Time is an uncommon luxury. This is not how I imagined you would spend your final days on this plane of existence."

Eric stiffened, petrified by fear.

Am I supposed to be hearing this?

"I have one final request of you, Your Honor," Baron said. "Stay alive long enough to see the great truth that will strike down upon this world. Live just long enough to bear witness to the great becoming of real power."

Okay, super weird thing to say.

Baron leaned closer to the sleeping man's time-creased face.

"How I adored you and your squadron when I was a troubled boy. I was a small child desperately in need of control, enamored with the gods among men that could bend evil to their will."

Baron rose again.

"Oh, how your lie inspired many other pretenders in fraudulent suits, brandishing the new-fangled gadgets and rayguns of the day. Cyborg fakery and prosthetic perversions."

He shrunk his voice to a whisper.

"I was a child, and I loved you."

Baron peeked up. A jittering spasm rattled Eric.

"It wasn't until the waning days of the original Society's career did anyone think to ask if their superpowers were legitimate. The Judge and company never claimed to possess such godlike abilities but never denied them either. I knew. Years before anyone else admitted it to themselves, I knew."

Eric kept his eyes and ears wide open.

"I was around your age, Eric, when I first ran away from a tumultuous foster home and to the city where I saw them up close," Baron revealed. "I dreamed of breathing the same air as superior humans—to ensure that our species wasn't just... this."

Despite himself, Eric lowered centimeter by

centimeter down the wall.

"Trickery. It was all a colorful deception. And superheroes and villains alike all still do it. It's how you're able to fly around unbothered. Do you see this, Eric?"

Eric nodded a nervous nod. Baron turned back to Judge Justice.

"One day, you won't need the backpack, young Mr. Icarus," Baron said. "There will be a time when you can shed away the disguises and special effects and safely reveal to everyone that you exist. One day, very soon, the world as we know it will be forced to accept that the achievements based on our present limitations are meaningless."

Eric floated closer to the unconscious old man, wondering if maybe he slept or if he heard them—and if that mattered.

"We owe a debt to their deceit," Baron explained. "I was taken in as the Judge's ward. I had the unique fortune of living among my champions."

Eric's eyes darted as if expecting something to interrupt them or someone would barge in. Instead, they remained undisturbed.

"The real man before you is named Patrick Gilroy," Baron explained. "When I was wayward, he... saw potential in me then took me in."

He looked at Eric.

"Without them, without him, I would've never realized my true self."

"He mentioned Sidebar to me," Eric said. "I know—or at least thought I knew—about the original members. You used to be Sidebar—the sidekick. They weren't all kids like the current team, right? Except for you as Truther now, I guess—anyway, nobody else had a junior partner except for Judge, er, Gilroy?"

Baron sighed a sad sigh.

"As Truther, I inherited the team, and with it, the responsibility to preserve its legacy. But when I started, I was a sidekick... Sidebar. Just a kid. A child at play."

Eric looked aimlessly at the wall, unsure of how to react.

"The first Super Society paved the way for the freedoms you enjoy now. Do you understand, Eric?"

Eric joined him, staring at the elderly man—the Judge's eyes shut tight in an uncomfortable slumber. Judge Justice served as a spoiler warning for how mortality ends. Even the best succumbed to time.

"Privileged as I was to live with the Judge for a time," he said, glancing at Eric. "I still found myself disappointed at the lack of magic in their adventures."

Baron returned his gaze to the Judge.

"My disillusionment motivated me to course-correct the hollow foundations you established, Your Honor. Your reward for changing the world is ushering in the new age of heroes."

Baron turned and headed for the door, stopping to ooze out a generous amount of hand sanitizer from the wall-mounted dispenser.

"Okay. Enough of that. Respects have been paid. Come now, you still have superhero orientation to attend to."

"I can't believe I never realized who Judge Justice really was," Eric said. "I think my dad mentioned Mr. Gilroy once. Wasn't he super-rich?"

"Wealth and obsession do not mix," Baron stated. "Even with heroics, a singular investment can lead to ruin. You no doubt see the similarities in your father."

"Does he have kids or something? I mean, other than you, I guess, but... Should we wait?"

"The Judge would tell you he chose a life that

would not warrant a family. If he were an honest man, he'd tell you he simply chose poorly."

Eric knew he needed to drift off to the next stop in his crash course on becoming a costumed crime-fighter. Looking down on the older man filled his head with more thoughts than he could handle.

"Take it for the lesson that it is, Eric."

He listened to Baron leave but could not bring himself to follow.

Will this be me one day? After a life of serving the city, will I be left in a small room to die?

Eric imagined himself, years later, a lingering old fool in a young man's costume, wobbling in the air like an abandoned attraction in some low-rent comic-con. Questions about revelations and exposure swam through his head. Even the most impressive, jaw-dropping, amazing people could become yesterday's news, forgotten celebrities overlooked by the next big thing. Eric had only just entered what he reckoned was his fourth or fifth of fifteen minutes of superhero fame, but he believed he understood what Baron was trying to teach him.

"I won't end up like you," Eric said to the Judge. "I'll be better."

Chapter Fourteen: *CEILING*

ERIC

"**. . . U**NITED BY A COMMON ENEMY, Sureshot, Aqua Queen, and Laser Lass were founding members of the Super Society, with Avenging Eagle joining during the later years. They were led by Judge Justice, whose sidekick, Sidebar, grew up to become Truther, linking a new generation of heroes."

Eric awed at the plaque below the large painting hanging on the wall. The illustration depicted the original Super Society members on one side, with the new group on the other. Truther stood in the center. Eric silently read the plaque beneath the painting:

"We fight for justice and the pursuit of truth."

He felt like a little kid again, marveling at the heroes' epicness.

"I hope I earn a spot on the team portrait one day."

His phone vibrated within his pocket. Sliding it out, Eric saw a new schedule notification from the Super Society app.

"'Pose for portrait—tomorrow afternoon,'" he read aloud. "Huh. That was fast."

A spherical drone whizzed through the room. Its smooth white surface's reflection skipped across a wide glass case enshrining oversized golden keys to the city, as well as various rayguns, shiny helmets, and pointy scepters.

I used to only read about these relics from the Super Society's past supervillain battles, Eric thought, gawking at the display of crime-fighting memorabilia. *And now I'm standing in the presence of Professor Malice's bionic blaster! Demono's devil staff!*

Mechanical arms popped out of the drone, holding a small golden plank in its clamps. It positioned itself in a blank space next to the portrait. A tiny drill popped out from each appendage, screwing in the little plaque. As it buzzed off, Eric's eyebrows raised at the inscription.

"'Reserved for Eric Icarus portrait.' So, I get my own?"

Humiliation poured over him.

"Oh, that seems like a bit much, I-I-I mean, that's probably unnecessary..."

The others are jealous enough that I'm getting all the comic-con credit, not to mention the solo Judge Justice visit.

As Eric backed away, a steel door slid shut—the words "TROPHY ROOM" shined, embossed on the smooth surface. Eric walked down the white corridor, his mind spinning from the slew of tutorial videos he had been shown. Ceiling-mounted surveillance cameras followed his every step, so Eric knew he wasn't truly alone, which explained why he was left unattended. Something else puzzled him—why even step at all?

His boots lifted as he willed himself into the air. Flying horizontally at a careful pace, Eric pushed against one wall of the hallway and then the other, plinking along carefree. Feeling bold, Eric twirled himself, waving at the cameras with each spin, then returned to an upright position. He floated closer to the door at the opposite end of the corridor.

The entryway slid open, and he floated through. As a public figure, Eric had no reason to hide anymore. He was free to fly about the world if he had the backpack prop on. He was simply free.

Outside the corridor waited a large walkway lining around the center of the vast tower. Pantheon lightning bolt logos decorated the backs of computer monitors, curving wall spaces, and even patterned the painted flooring. The curvature of the massive windows provided panoramic views of the late afternoon light, calming the spread of surrounding skyscrapers. Eric felt like he transported to a different world filled with peaceful atmospheric sounds of buzzing drones—and the clicks and clacks of keyboards.

Everything was brown, orange, or some dull shade of red from the massive support structures to the floor he hovered above. Eric inhaled the crisp and clear air.

He smiled back at the comely woman operating in open cubicles arranged along the giant rung. He shot finger guns at every high-cheekboned and chiseled-jaw dude manning a standing terminal throughout the promenade's perimeter. Eric wasn't positive about popular people's behavior or how they acted.

Pretty sure I'm killing it so far.

He wanted Jaycee to see him this way. Returning to the Pantheon headquarters after the con had been such a blur—they'd been separated when she was rushed to the tower's medical bay.

She'd think this is pretty flushing cool.

His irregular confidence boosted him upward. Eric paid no mind to the odd, soundless gasps of the model employees and levitated over the guard railing. He flew thirty or so feet toward the wide plant pipeline in the center of the building's lower section in an adrenaline-fueled dash. He peeked down. It didn't look like there was a bottom floor, just an endless flower-tube that went on forever.

His subconscious, or some other mysterious protective force, yanked him back to reality and refocused his eyes on the beauty in front of him. Seeing the lushness of the large leaves up close amazed him. Slews of vivid green vines stretched up and down the wide beam, with tiny colorful flowers sprouting in and around the foliage mesh.

Eric removed a glove and grazed his fingers over the florets and soft petals. Being watched didn't bother him, but something hinted that his supervised exploration was more like a child on his birthday being allowed to eat ice cream for breakfast, just this once.

The smooth leaves dripped, wet from a recent spraying. Eric pushed his flesh deeper into the thicket.

"Neat..." Eric whispered. "...But why?"

He turned to face the multi-tiered workstation rings.

"Um, excuse me, uh..."

He rode the esteem wave and let his voice rise.

"Anybody else think about how this whole place doesn't make any sense?"

No response from a drone, living or otherwise. Eric considered yelling louder, but a solidified thought squirmed out of his scattered brain.

"I guess I don't make any sense, either."

Eric smiled. He understood Baron a bit more.

Eric soared like a speeding bullet, heading straight for the vast network of lamps attached to the circular ceiling. Flickering light emitted from a couple of floors above him, and he wanted to see their source. Slowing, Eric saw an enormous window spanning what must have been forty feet along the bend, just below the ceiling. Unlike the open rings below, golden-orange thick metal plates covered this level, walling it off. The lone window frame presented the activity like a museum displaying an under-construction exhibit. Workers in silver jumpsuits carried loads of heavy equipment in and out of various doors. Eric strapped his glove back on, flying nearer to get a better look. He recognized a lab when he saw one.

Staring beyond his reflection in the glass, Eric watched a man in a dark helmet cut into a steel coil, igniting sparks. In futuristic suits, men and women crowded the area, set to work taking measurements and scanning things with tablets. The workers carried big, black wires and cords into view from the deeper end of the other side of the suite. More of them delivered chunks of metal, plastic casings, and handheld tools into the worksite. They all looked the same—strong, sturdy, utterly capable of inciting change within the world, but one stood out.

"Dad?"

David barged through a cluster of workers, mouthing orders and pointing at the corners of the enclosure. Eric couldn't hear anything beyond the soundproof window, but his father appeared to be the one making the decisions. A goggled worker presented a tablet projecting a holographic schematic of a domed machine. Eric recognized it as the MegaCore's blueprint. David made curlicues with his fingers, then pointed his thumb up, up, up, indicating something needed more of something.

There was his dad, in plain view, in charge of a Pantheon project of all things. It had been a very long time since Eric had seen his father be so sure of himself, reveling in his element. Eric placed his padded knuckles on the pane but couldn't bring himself to knock or even wave. He was flying right outside the window, yet no one, not his dad, could even look up.

"Look, I..." Eric started, but uncertainty derailed his sentence. "I think I understand. It wasn't by design or anything, but I guess I helped you out by ending up with Mr. Maddox. Worked out for me, too. I'm a superhero, Dad."

Oblivious, David tapped on the tablet.

"Everything is still so new, but I would never go back to how it used to be," Eric said. "How it was with you."

David barked inaudible orders at an underling.

"I just needed to say this out loud, even if you can't hear me. Or even bother to look at me. I get to be me, or at least a version everyone seems to like. People like this better than the old me, anyway. And you get to build all your stuff and be important."

David mimed pulling something apart, and the three-dimensional projection of the new MegaCore got bigger. David's eyes lit up.

"We'll both be in the same building, so it's not like we'll never see each other. We'll just both be, ya know, doing our own thing."

Eric turned to leave, but he stopped.

"I can get to a place where I understand why you would've wanted to sell me out to Mr. Maddox. You want to make money, that's all fine. Even focusing on a new project rather than trying to see me, I mean, the feeling is mutual, so it's whatever. What I don't get is..."

Eric pressed his forehead onto the thick, cool glass.

"Why Dreadnaught?"

David gave a thumbs up to his subordinates. He

shook the hand of the one closest to him.

"Why keep it, why show it off, why..."

The air wasn't so crisp anymore. Eric found his breath to be short.

"Was renaming it 'Ultranaut' supposed to help somehow? You had it propped up like a shrine. It murdered mom! It killed her and you..."

He frowned at how blissful David acted, knee-deep in work.

"And you just kept it around," Eric continued. "You were trying to sell it, profiting off the worst thing that ever happened to us! I'm figuring it out—you don't forgive me."

Eric's eyes misted with angry tears.

"I get to be special even though I don't deserve it, and that, that—you just can't deal with it!"

Eric yelled, but the surrounding employees did not react. He freely unfurled his fury.

"Mom died 'cause of me, and you kept your killer robot out just to remind me! Well, you know what, Dad? I can fly! I know you hate the Super Society, but I'm one of them! You don't love me? That's fine. I got an entire city that loves me!"

Dejected, Eric distanced himself from the glass, retreating to the leafy foliage of the vertical garden. He looked down at his costume, swelling with pride. Eric stretched his fists out in front of him and flew back down, grinning from ear to ear.

JAYCEE

"You can't do this!" Jaycee yelled.

"I am your mother," Valerie said, arms crossed. "That grants me authority by the laws of nature and man."

"What does that even mean?!"

Jaycee's foot tapped the hardwood floor. Her ordinarily thin patience for her mother was getting downright anorexic.

"Block the door all you want," Jaycee said. "There are other ways of escaping this house."

"You aren't going anywhere until you've completed your homework—homework I assigned!"

Their standoff turned into a stalemate. Jaycee spotted her bookbag she'd thrown under the coat rack when she first got home.

"Okay, got my school stuff," she said, swinging the bag over her shoulder. "I'm glad we could reach an amicable compromise. I'll be leaving now."

Valerie's rose-colored blouse and sensible slacks didn't make her look like an intimidating bouncer, but she stood just as immovable.

"Jennifer, I won't have you traipsing all over the city. Not after that stunt you pulled with Eric Boxworth."

Jaycee shifted her eyes.

"Mr. Boxworth may have been nice enough to look after you while you were 'sick,'" Valerie said. "But taking his son to see your father without permission? We still haven't fully discussed that, young lady."

"I'm just going to Dad's house, that's all."

"His one-hundred story skyscraper 'house,' you mean?"

"Hey, that was actually kind of funny!" Jaycee said with a genuine smile.

"You can't go to Pantheon Tower."

"Getting less funny," Jaycee said, her grin gone.

Dark burgundy drapes covered the window by the door. A sliver of the outside world peeked through—the afternoon light started to fade.

A Super Society trouble alert could come at any minute! Jaycee thought. *I won't get stuck with monitor duty again. I absolutely have to be there for tonight's patrol!*

"Mom, I need to get going—"

"You can't see your father anymore."

Memories flashed of Jaycee eavesdropping on her parents: Valerie's threat of full custody, Baron handing over some legal documents, and ditzy Chelsea and Dahlia's overall weirdness. Jaycee took a deep breath as she approached the stairwell by the coat rack. She climbed to the fourth step before she sank, succumbing to the weight of reality.

"I know we've kept much from you," Valerie said. "I was hoping there wouldn't be a need even to bring it up, but... I just wanted to protect you."

No, me lying about being Powerhouse is for your protection, Jaycee thought. *You were just putting off having to tell the truth to my face.*

Valerie sat on the bottom step. Jaycee caught her glancing past her, looking at the family photos decorating the ascending hallway. Each picture had Jaycee and Valerie—none featured Baron.

"Look, Mom," Jaycee said before sighing. "How you feel about Dad isn't exactly a secret. Is this just about me spending more time over here? With you? 'Cause, that's an easy-peasy fix!"

"I'm afraid it's a bit more complicated than that. Legally complicated."

"What, like, lawyers?"

Jaycee rolled her eyes as she leaned against the beige wall.

"Been there, done that with the divorce."

"We can discuss the legal intricacies later," Valerie said, focusing her eyes on Jaycee. "The main thing I want to keep you abreast of is that the process of me gaining sole custodianship of you has been put into motion."

"Mom, you know I love ya, but even my hoity-toity translator has trouble picking up what you're talking about sometimes."

"I am coordinating the relocation of your possessions from Pantheon Tower to—"

"Wait-wait-wait," Jaycee said, holding up a hand. "You're moving my stuff? Do we even have room here?"

"Effective immediately, you will no longer retain two residences," Valerie said as if reciting a tax form. "You will stay here with me. Visitation with your father is prohibited at this point, but I'm sure we can work something out for you to see him. With a court-appointed monitor, of course."

"I can't believe you!" Jaycee shouted as she stood. "You hate Dad that much?!"

Jaycee stormed up the stairs, making a point to stomp as loud as she could.

"You're jealous you're not part of his success, is that it?!"

Jaycee turned a corner, fuming as she headed to her bedroom door.

"It was your father's idea."

Her mother's words froze Jaycee's sneakers. Jaycee's mind felt like gelatin. The only image coming through was the "Jaycee's Room" sign taped to her door. The squiggly letters' paint had faded with time. She recalled making it with Baron when she was a little girl.

I could write on the sign as long as he could pick

the glitter color.

The frame's sparkly pink glitter cascaded in her teary eye like a kaleidoscope.

"Your father's direct involvement is how all this has been expedited to the point it has," Valerie said from behind her. "Someone with his influence can bypass many obstacles."

"Obstacles?" Jaycee whispered. "Is that what I am?"

She turned. Jaycee's quivering frown met her mother's stone face.

"Me having sole custody may have been an eventuality," Valerie said. "But it is not something I desired."

"O-M-G, you're such a robot!" Jaycee snapped. "You're like one of the Pantheon drones! I'm starting to think Dad built you!"

"I merely want to be as concise as possible. This is a delicate situation, but I will not sugarcoat it. I won't disrespect you like that."

"Disrespect?!" Jaycee yelled. "You hate Dad, and you're taking it out on me!"

Jaycee charged to her room.

"I'm the one thing you can take away from him!"

Jaycee barged through the door.

"I'm just a bargaining chip to you! You don't care about—!"

The door swung open, revealing a bright pink dress laid out on her bed. The flowy overskirt and glittery lace of the fit halter top came straight out of a fairytale. The subtle bejeweled embroidery design looked tasteful and modern. The loud colors would stand out in any ballroom. The size and style fit Jaycee perfectly.

"I'm serving as a chaperone for the spring formal

dance," Valerie said. "I was hoping you'd attend, so I got this for you."

Jaycee grazed her fingers across the silky fabric.

"I hope it meets your liking."

"It's beautiful," Jaycee said, breathless.

"You can hate me all you want, but this is what's best for you. With all of its superhero activity, Pantheon Tower is simply too dangerous of a place for you."

"I think I just wanna be alone, Mom."

"That's fine," Valerie said. "I'll be in the office if you want to discuss—"

"But not here."

Valerie lowered her hands from her hips.

"You do need to study for finals..." Valerie said in a softened voice. "It just so happens I've made tutoring arrangements for you at the library."

"Oh, uh, sounds awesome..." Jaycee said, forcing a weak smile.

"Don't be out too late."

Valerie walked to the stairwell.

"Mom?"

"Yes, Jennifer?"

Fatigue pulled at the bags under her mother's eyes. Perhaps Valerie always appeared this exhausted, but Jaycee had only seen the ironfisted schoolteacher. For the first time in a long time, Jaycee saw Valerie as just a person and not as her tyrannical warden.

"Thanks," Jaycee said.

Valerie cracked a flat smile and then disappeared down the steps.

Jaycee lingered on the dress.

No way Dad would give Mom everything like this.

"Jaycee Maddox has to follow the rules," she whispered.

Jaycee slid the bookbag onto the mattress by the

dress. Unzipping the main pouch provided a sneak peek of her silver and gold steel strength-enhancing power braces.

"But nothing's gonna stop Powerhouse!"

ERIC

Eric floated down a long corridor, leaving a trail of water droplets. He tightened his grip on the white towel around his waist, desperate to cover himself—he was just plain desperate.

"I am so lost," he whispered, nearing a featureless door.

Overdue for a shower, Eric had been allowed a drone to lead him to the bathroom. Luxurious as the washroom was, it lacked privacy from robotic peeping toms. As Eric looked behind him to make sure no one was peeking, he regretted ordering the automaton to float away.

"Little guide drone, you can come back now..."

Shirtless, dripping wet, and lacking navigational assistance, he told himself that the doorway he approached led to a private changing area.

The door slid open, and he stepped inside.

"Hey, 'roomie!'" Tiffany said, followed by a whistle.

The shock sent Eric to his feet. The jolt shot his hands up—the towel threatened to slip. He pulled on it, almost sending his body back up in the process. He froze when he noticed Melvin joining Tiffany at a dining table in the center of the room.

"Aw, man, was there a pool party?" Melvin asked between bites of his candy bar. "I never get invited to anything!"

Still as a statue, Eric's eyes darted across the room: bookbags under the table, a small kitchen to his right, a cushy couch to his left, and, worst of all, large windows at the back of the room with a gorgeous view of the city—which meant the outside world had a clear view of his bare chest. The others wore casual attire, nothing too glamorous, but still, Eric envied them for wearing anything other than a towel.

"Please tell me this is just another weirdly designed locker room," Eric said.

"Don't sweat it," Yvette said from behind the fridge door. "This is just the break room. We're the only ones who use it. I don't think the employees ever take breaks, come to think of it..."

She closed the door, popping her head out.

"Anyway, when I first got here, I was too scared to ask anyone where anything was—I didn't shower my first two days."

"Melvin still hasn't showered," Tiffany said.

Melvin gave her a mocking grin. Yvette brought a bowl of fruit to the table.

"You gonna stand there drippin' or join the 'Pantheon Pals' for an after-school snack?"

"We're so not called that," Tiffany said, scoffing.

Eric left wet footprints on his way to a seat next to Melvin.

"Um, hey," he said, not sitting. "Uh, well, this is probably the most awkward thing that's ever happened to me—and that's saying something. So, how about an icebreaker? You guys are orphans, right?"

His eyes widened to the size of pale moons as he realized what had come from his mouth.

"Sorry!"

"Oh, please, Eric," Tiffany said after grabbing

a cherry from Yvette's plate. "I'm so over the Little Orphan Annie routine. Though living with Daddy Warbucks is pretty posh."

"Kids have come and gone through here," Yvette explained. "Most of them find new homes pretty quickly or were going through a tough time, and Mr. Maddox gave them a helping hand. Some stay a little longer."

She nodded at Melvin.

"I'll be outta here in no time," Melvin said, cupping his smooth chin. "What parent couldn't love this adorable mug?"

"Is it true you were raised by wolves?" Tiffany asked. "But they gave you up for adoption because you weren't hairy enough?"

"Hey, Tiffany, the spring formal dance is comin' up, and I'll surely be leavin' soon, so you better ask me out now while you got the chance."

"What about you, Yvette?" Eric asked. "How long have you been here?"

The abrupt question killed the room. The others gave each other awkward glances. Eric wondered what he said this time that was so wrong.

"A long time," Yvette said, staring at her bowl. "I'm eighteen, so I'm technically an adult now anyway—"

Beep! Beep!

They took synchronous looks at their phones.

"It's that time, y'all. We got patrol duty!" Yvette announced. "Masks on!"

The windows tinted at the sound of the apparent verbal command. They reached under the table and nabbed their respective cowls from their bookbags. The rehearsed swiftness of them donning their masks took Eric by surprise.

"O-M-G! Are you going out on patrol? Let's go!"

They looked over to see Jaycee stepping into the room, reaching into her bookbag.

"You got a different gig," Yvette said to her, straightening her Go-Go mask. "Orders come straight from Truther."

"Truther, huh?" she asked as if she didn't believe it. "A mission with just Powerhouse and Truther?"

"Nope."

Yvette pointed to Eric.

"Oh…!" Jaycee said. "Um, Eric, why are you in a towel?"

Chapter Fifteen: *WEIGHTLESS*

ERIC

WRAPPING HIS ARMS AROUND JAYCEE'S waist while flying at top speed high above the city's traffic-laden streets proved to be more panicky than fun for Eric. She didn't appear to share his fears—Jaycee looked over her shoulder with those big eyes beaming underneath her Powerhouse mask's tinted domes.

"Don't get me wrong, Eric," Jaycee yelled as they took an unexpected dip only to bounce back up. "Flying is super-awesome, but—"

Her voice sounded like a distant echo distorted by fierce winds growling overtop roaring engines and honking. Within a breath, Eric heaved them above a crosswalk bridge.

"—your powers didn't come with instructions and—" Jaycee continued, only to be cut off by Eric's sudden straining to lift them even higher, zipping up along the nearest skyscraper.

"—Pantheon Tower has some primo practice facilities—"

Eric twisted them away, narrowly avoiding colliding

headfirst into a flagpole.

"—I'm all for living for the moment, but I like the living part—" Jaycee shouted.

Out of nowhere, two window washers appeared directly in front of them, forcing Eric to roll.

"—maybe we should do a few trial runs before we go all Top Gun!" Jaycee shouted.

Eric flew as pure impulse and speed, narrowly avoiding crashing into the cleaners' hanging scaffolding. The dodge left him aimless, though, darting along a building at a dangerous speed. He couldn't tell if Jaycee still shouted—the sensory overload preoccupied his every thought, his every movement, in addition to his unexplained chaotic drive to head for the sun.

The sun is precisely what Eric Icarus got in the form of a blinding glare streaking from the building's freshly shined glass. He grunted, spinning out. Protecting Jaycee replaced his primal priority—he clutched onto her like he was performing the Heimlich maneuver.

Eric led a blind nosedive down the tower, blinking to fight off sunspots as he and Jaycee blurred their way back closer to the ground. With his back facing the building's exterior, Eric felt an abrupt impact from behind. The force skipped him off a large windowpane and forwarded them into the air.

Eric's vision cleared, only to see and feel Jaycee's ponytail whipping at his face. In milliseconds, Eric processed that his rapid downward wavering had scraped his back against the thick glass. If it weren't for his anti-grav backpack, there was no telling if his spine would be—

The backpack!

Eric's worried thoughts boomed over whatever

obscenities Jaycee yelled as they propelled horizontally over the busy streets below. Eric glanced at his shoulders where the dark blue leather straps should be, but they must have been stripped away during the drag. Darting his eyes in every direction, Eric spotted the free-falling pack hurtling alongside the tower.

"Maybe we oughta give terra firma another go, huh, Eric?!"

"You read my mind!"

He heard her yelp as he burrowed down in a race against time to snatch the falling prop.

"Whoooooaaaaa!" she screamed. "Whhhhhat're you dooooing, Eric?!"

"Keeping up appearances!"

Their arching descent's speed increased with each second. He calculated every move.

Gotta get the backpack! People can't know! Gotta look like I'm falling! I'm so screwed without it! Gotta get the backpack!

Eric reached out with his left, leaving his right arm to curl around Jaycee's midsection. His vision tunneled, zeroing in on the blue-hued chrome pack. Everything beyond their careening slope down blurred as a hyper haze of shapes and sounds.

"Eric!" Jaycee shrieked somewhere amidst the reality-warping plunge.

The parked cars directly below grew closer. His fingertips reached inches away from the anti-grav backpack.

Fly! Faster! Eric commanded himself.

The details of the pavement, sidewalk, and parking meters became too clear for comfort. Eric's forearm dug deep into Jaycee's stomach. Her protective Powerhouse uniform would be working overtime, but it would all be for nothing if Eric failed to pull up soon.

Stretching his fingers inside his dark blue glove, Eric extended his limb to an extreme bordering on inhumanity. The backpack's matching blue straps wiggled just an eyelash distance away from his index finger. Physics was his enemy now—Eric's ability to do a vertical U-turn was in serious doubt. His hand was so close. It was almost...

Got it!

Eric swooped upward, spiraling above the pedestrians and the numerous other comers and goers clogging up the busy streetways. In that fleeting instant, Eric came to terms with the fact that he and physics would be lifelong adversaries.

With momentum pulling him, adrenaline electrified his body; Jaycee felt weightless in his arm. Eric squeezed harder on the backpack strap to convince himself that it and his own body had remained corporeal. He saw only streams of tinted glass as he soared back up the building. Eric surmised that this must have been like what an out-of-body experience was like while effortlessly jetting to the building's midpoint.

He slowed, floating them away, drifting down and over downtown's early evening hustle and bustle. In actuality, they hovered for only a handful of seconds. To Eric, though, holding Jaycee while they gazed upon the real world, this was a feeling that could stay in slow motion forever. Unusually wordless, Jaycee breathed, presumably taking in the angel-eye view just like Eric.

Their brief respite dispelled, and Eric came down both figuratively and literally. He targeted the perch of a close-by electronic billboard attached roughly halfway up a large hotel. It was a giant lit-up square, similar to the many digital ads surrounding the cluster of buildings, shops, and street vendors. The quick-changing virtual videos flared with exuberant colors, reflecting like bouncing little flickers across the smooth curved canopies of bus stops sporadically lining the streets.

Eric stumbled a bit before securing his footing on the narrow platform that extended outward, giving them about three feet of standing room. Jaycee hopped off. Her boots *clanged* onto the thin steel platform between protruding rectangular lamps. An advertisement for some new brand of augmented reality headsets populated the pixels directly behind them. The enormous screen's hypnotic waves of bright reds and blues splashed over Jaycee's form, making her look otherworldly.

The ambiance returned to its normal volume, and Eric heard the crossway's chatter below them. The lack of uproar from the preoccupied citizens indicated that Eric Icarus and Powerhouse's flying flirtation with disaster was even briefer than he realized. The competing aromas of the different food trucks and restaurants filled his nostrils. He strapped his backpack on, relieved that his cover was back in place.

"S-sorry, I, uh, I dunno," Eric found himself trying to say.

Out of breath, Eric rode a brief wave of wooziness. Jaycee was all smiles.

"Wow! So cool! I wish I were filming that! Holy—! O-M-G! Okay, so, like, yeah, I was freaked out, but it was awesome, and I was, like, basically flying and holy O-M-G!"

She laughed with her fists balled.

"You're not mad?"

He immediately regretted asking this question.

"Just that, no, what I mean is, I guess I got carried away and stuff."

"Are you kidding? My dad would've been so proud!"

This statement was something she, too, appeared to regret instantly. The huge screen dimmed between ads.

"So, it was cool of Truther to let me fly around for a bit to test my powers. And, hey, I can't think of a better chaperone than you, y'know?"

Why do you like to ruin things? Eric scolded himself for the cringey comment. *What is it about things that you think always have to be ruined?*

She propped a foot onto a thin support beam, stretching a lamp outward. The lamp's additional light softened, most likely set on a timer to fully brighten after dark.

"Babysitting Eric Icarus while the rest of the team goes on patrol," Jaycee said. "I won't lie; it's pretty flushed."

Jaycee waved at a few passersby underneath who must have noticed that two costumed crime-fighters stood above like a pair of gargoyles. While still strange, Eric welcomed his newfound visibility. He joined Jaycee in giving a lazy wave to the people below.

"How weird is it that I'm the one who got stuck in school all day, and you're..." Jaycee said, trailing off.

He held his breath. Eric knew she knew he had been hanging out with her father all day in and out of Pantheon labs. Eric had not been forthcoming with the details of his appearance at the old folks' home earlier in the day.

He exhaled, sounding even more out of shape than he was.

"It's actually pretty boring," Eric said, not entirely lying. "Most of the time, I waited around for your dad in a room full of computers. Or watched your dad work on one of the computers. Now, I can't look you in the eye and truthfully say I'd rather be at school, but it still isn't that great."

Her eyes didn't leave the street.

"Chilling with my dad all day, sure, super not jealous."

For a moment, Eric allowed himself the mesmerizing distraction of staring down at the sheer volume of activity from the various automobiles speeding up and down the lanes. Eric marveled at the rows of stores, sprawling clubs, and the concert venue with its bright marquee. Droves of people crowded the sidewalks.

It was a perspective of his hometown he'd never seen before, not like this. Eric knew only busy city life, but he'd seldom been allowed to venture to the downtown business district, especially not without adult supervision.

"Two teenage superheroes out by themselves, that's pretty cool, though," Eric said as a way to control the damage of his awkward avalanche.

"We've been tailed by a drone this whole time," Jaycee revealed, pointing her thumb above her. "Sorry to burst your bubble there, flyboy."

A white orb, smaller than the ones Eric had previously seen, peeked out from behind the large flat billboard, just above the upper-right corner. Eric looked up at it, but it quickly hid behind the sign as if it had been caught. The automated monitors had been so innocuous that Eric typically forgot about his constant surveillance.

Alone with Jaycee, Eric felt the electric eye's presence wrapping around his body. He figured if the drone meant to linger around, it might as well help him out in decoding the mystery of how to talk to girls. It remained hidden, leaving Eric out of ideas.

"I'm sure this attention from your dad is just because I'm a rookie. I'll be old news in no time."

A wider digital billboard mounted to an office building across them displayed a news ticker scrolling the headline "PASSING THE TORCH: ERIC ICARUS MEETS JUDGE JUSTICE." Following that, it showed a picture of Eric and Baron posing with big grins with the old Judge sitting between them. Eric shook his head.

She's jealous enough as it is, he thought. *I don't even want to think about if she ever finds out that I know her dad is really Truther and she doesn't!*

Slow to sit, Eric fought the inborn fear of slipping and falling to his demise. He sat high enough so that the pain of going too long without floating wouldn't affect him. Eric stared at his dangling feet. He'd been looking forward to spending time with Jaycee one-on-one but found himself with nothing to say.

"I'll be around a lot more," Eric said, a little afraid to look up at her. "My dad apparently works for your dad now. Last night I crashed on a couch in the Super Society's HQ level, and, like, it was the most comfortable thing I've ever felt. It was like floating on a cloud, and I can literally do that. Not that I've ever tried, but, anyway, I'm pretty sure we live there now."

"No one told you about the guest suites?" Jaycee asked. "You do know that the team stays there, right?"

"Yeah, sure, but... Wait."

She sat next to him. Eric narrowed his brow.

"Are you jay-kaying me about there being guest beds?"

"You can probably just have my room," Jaycee said. "I won't be using it."

She leaned back, resting on the illuminated sign. Eric fidgeted for a half-second before freezing. He didn't know if he should join her or keep hunching forward. He peered over his shoulder to see the little drone ball spying. Once spotted, a circle of blue dots flashed on its "face" before hiding itself behind the sign once more.

Eric let out a short breath and mustered up the courage to lean back slightly on the sign's hard surface, touching her shoulder to shoulder. Even though armor encased hers, he still considered it a big win in the physical contact department.

"I think I'll miss the food plaza the most," Jaycee said, forlorn.

"Pantheon Tower has a cafeteria, too?!" Eric blurted. "I didn't even know about the break room! I've had to eat these nutrient-shake-whatevers a robo-butler-thing brings to your dad. He's hooked on the sludge—wait! Go back to the 'missing' part."

"My mom found out about our sneaking off escapade and pretty much has me on lockdown at her place," she explained. "She was cool with us leaving school 'sick' and even going to the Boxworth Building. Taking you to see my dad, though... Well, my mom had zero chill about that."

"I'm guessing the Time Thief attack is being kept on the D.L.?"

Bringing it up made Eric's stomach curdle.

"Sorry I didn't visit you in the medical bay back at the tower. Not that I know where it is."

"Pfft, I was in and out like a hiccup."

She flicked her hand and shook her head with a sharp smirk, dismissing the notion.

"It was easy enough to go to the comic-con as Powerhouse," she said. "It's basically a big field trip anyway. So as far my mom knows, I was there as just another student."

"Hold up. If your mom doesn't know you're Powerhouse—"

"Then I'm lucky even to be here right now," she finished for him. "She's fallen for the hologram trick so many times. Some crazy-smart science teacher she is, huh? Anyway, right now, she thinks I'm studying for finals at the library."

She gazed up at the clear skies above. The transparent yellow cups over her eyes reflected the sparkling light spattering from the LED sign. Her metal arm casings glistened.

"Sooooo, like," Jaycee started. "I'm pretty sure I won't be, y'know, allowed to see my dad anymore. I didn't get my ninja-like sneakiness from my parents, that's for sure. They think I don't hear them talk about..."

She didn't need to finish. Her parents' divorce was fairly common knowledge since Baron was such a public figure, but Eric didn't realize the situation had gotten this dire.

Mr. Maddox didn't mention anything about this.

He braved an unnoticed peek at her face.

"Doing anything superhero-y is going to take some next-level finesse now," Jaycee said. "Worst part is my dad is going along with this whole thing!"

Jaycee's been going through this, and I was too busy living it up. I feel like such a tool.

"Truther has a secret identity, right?" Eric said.

Gotta be careful not to slip the truth about Baron being Truther.

"I bet he has trouble with this, too."

"Truther is an adult," she reminded, still looking up. "The others gotta go to school, but even then, they can go out and play any time Truther gives the go-ahead."

"Have you talked to Melvin or Tiffany? I mean, you're—we're—all under the same roof, so-to-speak, so maybe they heard something?"

"They wouldn't know anything about this," she said, sighing. "I know it's uncool to think this, but in some ways, the other kids are lucky they don't have somebody like my mom constantly on their case. Not everyone gets to go public, Eric."

Clueless about how to react, Eric noticed a nearby billboard displaying the time and date. The school year was coming to an end.

"Um," he began. "So, the spring formal is this week—"

"What's it feel like to fly?"

"Amazing!" Eric said, surprising himself at how ready he was to answer.

"Does it feel like you're weightless?" Jaycee asked.

He parted the seas of his flooding jumble of thoughts and carefully considered his response.

"It's kind of..."

Eric stared down at his hand.

"It's kinda like knowing gravity is there but ignoring it. It's basically swimming, but with no resistance, I guess. I dunno. It's hard to describe. I just do it. As easy as it is to fall, it's just as easy to fly."

She looked over her fingers encased under coils of gold-plated steel.

"W-what's it like to be able to beat literally anyone at arm wrestling?" Eric said.

Talking about himself suddenly seemed so unattractive.

"Invincible, incredible, totally mind-blowing!" Jaycee listed with a smile. "Until I power down and take off my attachments."

Her smile faded.

"You don't have an off-switch, huh?"

"As long as I wear this, I won't need one."

Eric tugged at the shoulder strap of his backpack.

"Y'know, even without the strength enhancers, you could still take me in a fight," Eric said. "Most girls can beat me up, so don't get a big head about it."

"Anytime, anyplace, Boxworth."

She eyed him up and down.

"If there's a fight, like, a real one, you know to keep out of sight, right? The deal with the Gavel and Time Thief was one thing..."

She leaned away, evaluating him the same way the school nurse would. She no longer touched his shoulder. Eric entered the danger zone.

"All I mean is..."

She picked her words out of a minefield.

"Just because you have superpowers doesn't mean you have any combat training. I know my dad is excited about all of this, but I just don't want to see you get hurt."

Hi, I'm your forever just-a-friend, Eric. Nice to meet you, he thought. *If being a true-blue superhero isn't doing anything for me, then nothing will!*

Emasculation felt nearly as bad as being earthbound for too long.

"So, I suppose that settles it," Eric said. "I was only recruited for my looks."

Did that work?

Eric grabbed for miracles to get rid of the little brother vibe he emitted. He wondered how she saw him. He liked her, and she liked him—

That's what this is, right?

Eric wasn't even sure how he felt about her. He buried that uncertainty in favor of the bigger goal. The moment grew quiet again, bordering on insufferable.

"I wish I could fly," Jaycee admitted.

Eric recanted his dismissal of silence and longed for its return. She hit him with too many conversational conundrums all at once.

"I wish—" she said, stopping abruptly.

Jaycee pressed the dome covering her ear. Muffled audio burbled from it.

"There's a guy trapped on top of the Kell Bridge!" Jaycee said. "We're the closest. We gotta go!"

"Say what?"

"They didn't give you a comm?" Jaycee asked, grunting in frustration. "We got superhero business—come on!"

Chapter Sixteen: *DOWN*

JAYCEE

JAYCEE FELT A SUDDEN JOLT as her feet left the ground. Her metal shoulder casings scrunched up by her ears. Eric hoisted her by her armpits, lifting her with their combined momentum to speed through the air. Jostled, Jaycee looked down to see the earth drop beneath her blue boots. Cars looked tiny on the street over the vast body of water so far under them. The Horton River sat deceptively calm and clear from Jaycee's steadily rising vantage point. Every native of the city knew of its waters' abyssal depths—a fact that made a drop into it that much more fatal.

Every organ felt like it was going to be sucked out of Jaycee's body. No rollercoaster could ever equal Jaycee and Eric's adrenaline-charged ascent. They plowed through angry gusts of air; the currents ignored the warm season and grew windier the farther up they went. Jaycee's teeth clenched, and her muscles tensed as they flew over a grid-like platform on the Kell Bridge. The trip lost excitement and speared into a frightening hysteria. She shut her eyes tight.

Don't pass out, Jaycee commanded herself. *Don't*

puke!

"Eric, the trouble alert notified of a male, Asian, early-twenties," she yelled. "He's in danger of taking an unintentional swan dive off the bridge!"

"Looks like we weren't the only ones who got the call!" Eric shouted.

Jaycee's eyelids reopened to see a large, oval-shaped drone hovering just above the thick suspension cable. Red and blue lights flashed from its shiny hull.

"An emergency response unit!" Jaycee said as Eric slowed their ascent. "The city just launched these; I didn't think we'd see one so soon!"

Across from the automaton, a man dangled, connected by a single strap of his safety gear. His harness hung from the base of the guardrail, eight hundred feet above the gridlocked lanes.

"Does this mean we don't have to do anything?" Eric asked, gulping. "I mean, that thing has it covered from here, right?"

"I know this is scary, Eric," Jaycee said. "But the Super Society doesn't wait around for things to work out on their own."

Eric lowered them to touchdown upon the suspension cable. The weathered surface was faded with a dull maroon, only partially painted over with shiny silver. The bridge's round barrel sloped down, stretching a mile long. Eric's jaw dropped, and his eyebrows raised. Jaycee grabbed him by the shoulders.

"We do get scared," Jaycee said, looking at him eye-to-eye. "But we don't look down."

The two heroes' aerial entrance did nothing to soothe the frantic bridge painters who bunched up in a tight workspace behind them. They looked on from the middle of the massive connecting support beam between twin pillars. The workers were clad in bright yellow safety vests, and each wore two sets of harnesses. Paint buckets and rollers with elongated handles sat at the crew's feet.

Jaycee upped her strength level to ensure a firm hold on the rail with a quick tap of a knuckle button. Punishing winds struck the unmasked portion of Jaycee's skin, making her wonder how the workers dealt with it. She worried about how Eric's fully exposed head fared.

Steel met steel as Jaycee's armored hands clamped onto the security railing running down the huge suspension cable. Her eyelids fluttered at the long walkway's curved edges. Jaycee took controlled steps forward. The huddled servicemen shouted warnings, but she ignored them.

Beyond the dangling man was an otherwise picturesque scene of the wide river. Distant ferries and boats sailed along its placid waters, sandwiched between concrete shores. Jaycee considered herself fearless and lacking a phobia of heights, but at this moment, she had an exceptional awareness of how elevated she was. One careless slip was all it would take to spell the end.

"It's just a giant steel tube," Jaycee told herself, feeling a trembling tremor through her bones. "Just a bridge over a bridge, that's really all it is, no sweat."

The huddled workers called out in excitement, seeing Eric soar to the floating, egg-like drone. Its sleek, chrome shell slid into itself, revealing an opening just big enough to fit a person inside. Metallic cords slithered out of its inner chamber. Tentacle-like ropes constricted around the hanging man's waist. Eric flinched as the drone tugged at the frightened man. The man's harness stuck, lodged in a crevice on the security rail.

"Powerhouse?" the hanging man said, puffing out a shocked breath. "And, whoa, it's Eric Icarus! I'm a huge fan!"

"What's your name?" Eric asked.

"H-henry!" he answered, terrified. "I slipped and then—!"

Henry screamed as the steel cords pulled at this midsection, tightening around his safety straps. His harness yanked his shoulders, fighting a deadly game of tug of war. Jaycee bolted down while Eric swooped behind the pod-like unit. Eric wrapped his arms around the machine's circumference, hugging its back. The drone reared with Henry in tow, but Eric pushed against it.

Jaycee slammed onto her kneepads, securing herself on the railing. She stretched her free arm toward Henry. Her armor-clad fingers clenched the neon-yellow safety strap stuck in the railing. With a quick jerk, the tether severed, releasing the man. Henry shrieked as the mechanical limbs hauled him toward the drone.

"Imminent danger detected," the thing's robotic voice announced. "Initiating rescue sequence."

A ribbed metal coil snaked around Jaycee's outstretched wrist. Her Powerhouse armor shielded her from pain, but she sensed the intense pressure.

"It's got me!" Jaycee cried out.

Jaycee's arm felt warm inside the metal casing as the strength enhancers fought to resist the drone's pull. The lights on her knuckles went green as the power levels maxed out. Jaycee held the drone in place for the moment, with Henry suspended in the middle. The drone pushed itself backward, but Eric dug in his shoulder to force it still.

The cybernetic tendrils retracted, luring Henry

to the drone's open hatch. He sunk into the cramped rectangular compartment, covered to his neck with shiny electric eels.

"Citizen secure," the drone stated. "Transport to hospital initiated."

"Well, don't let me stop you!" Jaycee said before yanking down.

The steel cord would not rip, but the sudden jolt caused sparks to shoot from the drone.

"Uh, whoops," Jaycee uttered, contorting her lips in a mortified grimace.

Mummified with chrome cords, Henry yelped, immobile within the tight confines of the shell. Crackling electricity burst in Eric's face. He spiraled away, covering his head.

Jaycee's lungs froze as the vertical drone shook and leaned forward. Tilted, the hovering pod faced the earth, hundreds of feet below. The shiny cables holding Henry in place were the only things preventing his plunge. Henry aimed his exposed, bulging eyes down—a fall meant a splat on the pavement.

Or he'd miss the asphalt and be dunked in the water, becoming fish food, Jaycee thought.

With her arm entwined, Jaycee wrenched the metal vine still connected to the drone. Ten feet separated them horizontally, and it was becoming an airborne stalemate. Eric positioned himself in front of Henry, then shoved at the open hatch's rounded frame. Skinny slots at the drone's base lit up with a radiant blue. An abrupt force pushed Eric off.

The propulsion jets propelled the drone back, taking Jaycee with it. Her boots skidded down the curve of the suspension cable, nearly slipping. The iron guardrail deformed as Jaycee's supercharged armored grip secured herself.

"What's wrong with this thing?!" Henry yelled through a slit in the cords over his face.

"Don't worry! I won't let go!" Jaycee shouted.

She pulled at the cord wrapped around her forearm. The pointy tip of the steel rope crawled up to her bicep, constricting tighter.

"Not that I could let go even if I wanted to," Jaycee said under her breath.

The drone's blinking emergency lights flickered in a chaotic pattern. Jaycee fought to wrangle the machine's erratic bucking.

"Gahhh!" Henry wailed.

An arc of electrical energy surged just above Henry's frazzled black hair.

"This drone is malfunctioning like crazy!" Henry yelled.

"I think I know why!" Eric said over the winds.

As he floated nearer, Eric pointed to a series of markings on the side of the drone's surface.

"'Manufactured by Slate Technologies!'" Eric said. "My dad says all they make is defective garbage!"

"The city must've gotten them for cheap!" Jaycee said, scoffing. "My dad says there's a reason their drones are shaped like coffins!"

"Not helping, guys!" Henry shouted.

A long cord whipped out from the drone, targeting Jaycee. It joined its counterpart, ensnaring Jaycee's wrist. Twin steel snakes twisted around her upper arm. Jayce grunted in frustration—the pull got harder to resist. The security railing screeched as it bent in her vice-like grip.

"I dunno how much longer I can hold on!" Jaycee shouted.

The spiked tips of the metal cables slid over her circular shoulder casings, creeping to her neck.

"Citizen is un-r-r-responsive," the drone blared between spurts of static. "Initiate 'jaws of life' seeeeequence."

Four chrome tendrils sprang from the drone's back. The cords lashed at Eric, batting him away. The sharp ends of the cables spun like amped-up drills. Like a spider waiting to strike, the cords flared, spreading out. The spinning spikes snapped at Jaycee, inches away from puncturing her flesh. Eric grabbed a rattling line, but its strength buckled him like a rag doll.

"Get me outta this thing!" Henry cried out.

A trio of tentacles intertwined, forming a thick, grooved javelin. The combined cords speared at Jaycee—she dodged, but the drill-heads struck the metal suspension cable beneath her boots. The impact knocked Jaycee off her feet, plummeting her toward the ground.

"Powerhouse, no!" she heard Eric scream.

The cords wound around her arm stopped her descent in a sudden jolt. Nearly hyperventilating, Jaycee willed her eyes to keep from peering below. Above her, Eric wrestled the drone's flailing cables. Stricken with panic, Henry's face paled.

Skreeeeeeeench!

The squeal of metal pierced the audio receptors in Jaycee's cowl. The cords held but loosened at their base, a small opening behind Henry's knee. Straining to support the weight of Jaycee's armor, her lifelines sparked with flashing volts. Jaycee's stomach looped as the cord slipped, halting a second later.

Suspended like a broken yo-yo, Jaycee swayed under Henry and Eric. Jaycee swiped for the immense barrel—the suspension cable was less than ten feet away, but the bridge may as well have been in another country. A pair of workers edged up the bridgeway, taking uneasy steps on the huge rod's rounded surface. A bespectacled worker led while his bearded compatriot kept a cautious distance. The drone juddered in place, and the workers ducked.

Eric choked a cable; it squirmed like an angry cobra. Jaycee's cords struggled more, firing off bigger electric embers from their root.

"Nyahhhhh!" Henry screamed.

"System failuuuure," the drone drawled in a hiss of static.

The cables wrapped over Henry's body slackened, sliding as they lost power. They retreated from his chest and arms like loose noodles. Henry dropped from his cramped cage. A tangled nest of flaccid cords saved him from a fatal fall.

Holding back a snapping cord, Eric swooped in front of Henry. Eric's back blocked the view, but Jaycee could see Henry clamping onto a bundle of wires for dear life.

"Henry, this drone is busted!" Eric told him. "The cords are loose; you can make it out—you gotta let go! I'll catch you!"

"I can't! I'll fall!" he shouted.

Chrrrzt!

A thin jet flickered at the drone's bottom, then coughed exhaust in a rapid spasm.

"Emergency! Emergen-gen-gen—!" the drone sputtered. "Emergency-cy-cy-cy!"

Its hull quivered, wobbling Henry from inside. Dangling from the cords took its toll on Jaycee's arm. Tension pulsated through her armor, throbbing her shoulder.

Come on, Eric, Jaycee thought. *Whatever you're gonna do, do it quick!*

"I'm gonna die!"

"No, Henry, you're gonna jump!" Eric said. "Look, I'm not saying don't be scared—just don't look down."

Henry released the wires, then slipped through the lifeless cords. Eric rolled in the air with Henry's body.

"I got ya!" Eric said to him, zipping down toward Jaycee.

KA-BOOM!

Fiery debris scattered as the drone exploded. The shockwave tackled Eric, colliding him and Henry into Jaycee. The leathery texture of Eric's blue tunic pressed against Jaycee's face, obscuring her vision. Jaycee felt their sharp descent and the rippling heat from the blast. She wriggled her arm, sensing the cords still wrapped around her, but the detonation detached them from the drone.

"Eric!" she cried out.

Jaycee's equilibrium shattered, and her muscles clutched her bones. Her only comprehension was seasick motion—she felt herself going up. Jaycee squeezed a peek from the corner of her eye. The smoky shimmer of the destroyed drone dissipated below. Its husk fell to the river, leaving a billowing trail of flames and fumes.

"You okay?!" Eric yelled.

Jaycee noticed the pressure on her side. Eric held her tight.

"Whoooooaaaa-myyy-gooooddd!" Henry screamed from under Eric's other arm.

They landed in a skitter, steadying themselves on the guardrails of the suspension cable. Two bridge workers rushed over, huddling over Henry.

"That just happened!" Eric blurted, hunched over the rail. "That did just happen, right?!"

"Yes, and it was incredible!" Jaycee exclaimed.

She started a little excited jump but stopped

herself. Jaycee tore the loose cords from her arm, curling her lip at the sight of the deadened tendrils in her hand.

"That thing was a total piece of junk, right?!" Eric said, catching his breath.

"For serious!" Jaycee agreed.

Their chests heaved with the exhilaration that comes with cheating death. Their grins hung slack-jawed, amazed at one another. Jaycee tapped the dome covering her ear.

"Hold on," she said. "I'm getting a message from the team—like, finally, right?"

Her head lowered, keeping eye contact with Eric as Yvette's voice chattered through the earpiece.

"Do we need backup?" Jaycee repeated.

Eric and the ecstatic workers exchanged high-fives.

"Situation under control," Jaycee reported. "Eric Icarus saved the day."

Eric turned to her, closing his mouth to form a thin, sheepish smile.

"You don't need the Super Society helicopter to pick you up?"

"Nah," Jaycee said. "I think I'll hitch a ride with you."

Eric blushed so hard that Jaycee thought it must have hurt his cheeks. Eric's bashful grin suggested otherwise.

"Eric Icarus and Powerhouse!" Henry shouted from behind Eric.

Henry held the arm of his crewmate for leverage.

"This is the scariest and coolest thing that's ever happened to me!"

"Glad we could help," Eric said without looking away from Jaycee.

"I didn't move to New St. Cloud City to work on a

bridge, ya know!" Henry went on. "I have a dream of being a superhero just like you guys!"

His fellow bridge workers rolled their eyes.

"That's awesome," Jaycee said, spiking her eyebrows. "But the Super Society wants you to stay safe, Henry."

She grabbed Eric's hand and leaned in close.

"We should probably get out of here," Jaycee whispered.

"I'm gonna call myself the Phantom Phaser!" Henry yelled with a big smile. "I'm gonna attend engineering school next year! I plan to develop a device to let me walk through walls!"

Eric lifted Jaycee's hand in his.

"Guess I have to save the day twice, huh?" he said, just loud enough for her to hear.

Jaycee hid a chuckle.

"Ugh, that so wasn't even that funny," she said, squinting from holding in laughter.

The air blew through Eric's messy hair, and his smile went from sheepish to beaming with a knowing warmth. The sunlight bathed his skin with much-needed color, balancing his reddened flush. His brown eyes looked at her, deep and disarming.

"Eric Boxworth," she said to him. "You might be getting the hang of this whole superhero stuff after all."

"Unless Pantheon Solutions sponsors you, you're just another outlaw!" Henry shouted.

Eric looked over his shoulder at him.

"We're kinda having a moment here, man," Eric said as politely as possible.

"Can you put in a word for me with Baron Maddox?" Henry asked.

"Aaaand the moment's gone," Eric said. "Uh, Powerhouse, we should get going, huh?"

"Now that was funny," she said.

ERIC

Tucked away where the anchorage met rocks and river water, Eric watched the shrubbery fizzle and flicker into pixelated particles. The realism of the unseen drone's holographic projection looked incredible, even if the leaves' shade of green appeared a little too bright to blend with the natural foliage properly. The consummate quick-change artist, Jaycee, stepped through the digital dispersing in her casual civilian attire. She even held her pink and blue bookbag courtesy of a separate Pantheon-made automated drone courier.

"You didn't peek, did you?"

Eric's face reddened, and his skin felt hot.

"No, I would never!" he said, quivering. "I mean, I would, but, ah, um—"

She chuckled.

"Calm down and comb your hair, flyboy."

Eric ran a gloved hand through his ruffled hair, still a mess from soaring to new heights. The noisy wave of traffic had since returned to its regular rush hour rate. The bridge was alive with automotive activity as if nothing had happened. Eric and Jaycee stood a few yards below on the small stony ridge beneath the bridge's entrance. Eric figured he was still so new to the Super Society that few people would recognize him.

Not everyone is a megafan like Henry, right? he thought.

Eric reckoned he was simply a costumed kid

speaking with a regular teenage girl, nothing out of the ordinary. He hoped it didn't look odd anyway.

"So, I thought Henry was having a 'goodbye cruel world' moment for sure!" Jaycee said.

She hiked back up to the upper entrance area where the concrete met the river.

"But you got him to jump! I mean, to safety, that is!" she said. "Important thing is the dude was saved, so, score, but still—hall of fame risky move."

"I was just doing what I thought you would do."

Eric floated up to her. The skyline behind Jaycee lit up with little windows as dusk's darkening descended.

"You stepped up your game in a big way today, Eric," she conceded. "Color me impressed. Powerhouse and Eric Icarus might make for a dynamic duo after all."

"'Eric Icarus and Powerhouse' rolls off the tongue better."

"In your dreams."

She laughed. The evening settled in, and the air felt balmy. Eric let the moment linger, and she smiled at him as her blonde hair fell in front of her face. Eric was confident in how he felt now. He smiled back.

Honk! Honk!

Jaycee whipped her head back to see a convertible pull up to a visitors' space a few yards behind them. The top was down so Eric could see the athletic young black man behind the wheel. Jaycee waved to him—she knew him.

"My ride's here!"

"I thought I was your..."

Awkward much, Eric? he told himself.

"Wouldn't your mom drive you around now?"

"Don't be lame, Eric. And she makes me take the bus now anyway. How flushed is that?!"

She hustled over to the honey-colored four-seater parked in a rest area. Eric drifted after her but kept his distance, hanging behind in a small, grassy park area by the lot.

After some brief greetings to the wheelman, Jaycee looked back at Eric.

"Hey, so, my mom hired a tutor," she said. "Sucks, but I actually do have to study for finals. And she'd do it herself, but she doesn't have time. Plus, my mom being my teacher is bad enough, but also having her as my tutor? That's pretty much my worst nightmare."

Her eyes fluttered, and she shook her face. The realization that she was casually talking to a floating superhero must have occurred to her.

"Uh, Eric Icarus, this is, um, Kevin. Kevin, say hi to Eric Icarus."

"What's up?" the driver said.

His voice had a lightness to it but with masculine confidence. Eric immediately hated it.

"Wow, I've never seen a Super Society member up this close before. This is so awesome! Oh, and you can just call me Kev."

Kev? Eric thought. *No way is this guy cool enough to be a Kev. He can't even fly!*

"Kev goes to a different school... Different from me, that is," Jaycee prattled. "But I guess people would know where you go, right, Eric? Do you still go to school? Anyway, Kev's got a track scholarship—total full ride to college, isn't that fantastic?!"

Kev looked away with a bashful smile. Eric noticed the guy just happened to wear his tightest orange polo.

The guy is sixteen going on thirty, apparently lives in a gym, can pick any future he wants, and, oh yeah, he has a car.

Eric's mouth was a flat line, opening just enough

for a curt pleasantry.

"'Sup."

Jaycee, excited as could be, then got into the smooth ride and waved as they backed up.

"Later, Eric Icarus!"

Kev added a peace sign, and they merged with the traffic venturing into the city.

"Hello, cruel world," Eric muttered.

NORTH NEW
ST. CLOUD
HIGH PRIDE
SPRING FORMAL
CONGRATS GRADS!

Chapter Seventeen: *CRASH*

ERIC

THE ENTIRE STUDENT BODY OF North New St. Cloud High School stood between Eric and first period. They clamored, eager for a look, a word, or a smile. The loud hollering, whistling, and catcalling pulverized Eric's poor eardrums.

He scanned the crowd, trying to find the path of least resistance. Bringing his anti-grav pack was an unavoidable nuisance—the extra attention it provoked was annoying, but a small price to pay to abate his gravity-induced pain.

With so many people eyeing him, Eric told himself that Baron would love the attention. He wore navy-blue shorts and gray with green stitching t-shirt—a halfhearted effort to coincide with his alter-ego's outfit's color scheme, but none of that seemed to matter to the other kids.

Eric smiled and waved as naturally as an undead mannequin, but his new 'fan club' ate it up. Smartphones, smartwatches, and even a couple of augmented-reality visors orbited him, documenting every regular step he took.

Too many people—I can hardly move, Eric thought. *The perils of mega-popularity, I guess.*

Fame also brought on unsolicited high-five invitations. A few pats on the backpack rattled Eric. Under a forced grin, Eric silently begged for no one to notice how hollow the anti-grav prop really was.

"Eric Icarus! Do you have a date for the formal yet?!" an excited girl yelled over the crowd.

Eric whipped his head around, his curiosity piqued. The mystery voice disappeared into the noisy human herd. Eric laughed it off, but that question had been nagging him.

"I can't believe Eric Icarus goes to our school!" a boy said from behind him before an onslaught of new voices rained down.

"Can I get an autograph?"

"You saved my cousin's life!"

"You're so hot!"

Does being famous ever not feel weird? he thought.

The droves parted enough for him to access his locker.

"Mr. Icarus," a girl in pigtails addressed him.

"Can I get a quote for the yearbook?"

She held a recognizable Pantheon Zeta watch, projecting a holographic representation of the year's student spotlight profile page. Eric squinted at the little three-dimensional photograph. It showed an image of him in his costume.

I don't remember taking this pic. But at least it captured my likeness.

The little pixelated Eric gave a thumbs up.

"Uh, oh, okay, um…" Eric fumbled out. "Stay in school! I mean, I haven't been the greatest example lately, but…"

He flashed a nervous smile over both shoulders at the crammed crowd. Peering past the mobile devices outstretched before him, Eric looked for any of the chaperone drones that had been tailing him but detected none.

"Eric! Yo, Eric!" a deeper voice shouted for his attention. "Hey, man, doesn't Tiffany Sneeder and the Dungeon Master live with you? Aren't y'all the 'Pantheon Pals?'"

"Uh, sorta."

"Why're they riding the bus when you could fly them to school?"

"The backpack has a weight limit."

Eric gave a short shrug, which got a few chuckles.

That, and I don't even know where their rooms are, he thought while spinning the combination to unlock his locker.

Looking inside the plain compartment felt like peeking inside a former life. Most other high schoolers decorated their lockers with stickers, posters, or graffiti, but Eric's was a solitary confinement cell for his seldom-touched course materials. Not even this locked-up vault that no one else would bother to see was allowed to have any personality.

Science textbook in hand, Eric shut the locker door. A blockade halted Eric: jocks in jerseys, nerds in button-ups, and kids in makeup—both the mean girl and weird outsider goth variety. Their collective wave of remarks blended into jumbled noise as Eric carved a narrow path through the throng.

When did everyone get so tall? Did standing always feel so heavy?

He couldn't see past the entourage enclosing around him. Body spray and body odor warred within his nostrils. A tug on his shoulder strap yanked

Eric back a half-step. Someone strong pulled on the contours of his blue-steel backpack.

"Gotta get me one of these!"

"Wow, this thing is lighter than air! Oh! That's the point, right? Air, like flying?"

"Bet I can sell this!"

Eric tried pushing his way out, but hands from every side jostled him back and forth. Panic bubbled up to his eyeballs. What originated as a hero's welcome morphed into an all-out riot. Eric knew he could burst his way up in a surge of flying rage.

The newest member of the city's famed squad of protectors attacking teens isn't a good look, he thought.

Eric's left shoulder strap loosened—this spelled trouble. Instincts welled up from his belly. The intensity of the hullabaloo burned his ears. Push. Shove. He couldn't move. Eric felt clawing at the other strap of his precious accessory.

This is unsafe! This is ridiculous! How is this being allowed?

Fretting thoughts of dread stabbed his brain.

I need to get out of here.

Energy radiated from his blood. An invisible power emanated from Eric's heart. A groundswell of force tightened his skin, and, with closed eyes, he clenched his fists.

Leave. Me. Alone!

"Okay, guys, let's back it up, okay?"

The fanatical flock separated, and Eric's breathing slowed back to normal. He opened his eyes to see Principal Garza hold up his gentle hands. The bohemian educator eased into the manic fray with a warm smile.

"We all appreciate what Eric Icarus has done for

this community, but let's all just chillax, huh?"

He wrapped a hover-hand around Eric's shoulder, careful not to touch him. The students made a begrudging trek to their morning subjects. The principal escorted Eric to his classroom, where the open door waited for his grand arrival.

"Dudes and dudettes, let's spread some good vibes to none other than Eric Icarus!"

Principal Garza clapped, and the roomful of classmates joined in the applause.

As he found his seat at the back of the room, Eric's humbleness lifted, and bolstering self-esteem took its place. Dropping his textbook down onto his desk, he gazed around at his peers, making his best "cool guy" face: squinted eyes, pursed lips, flared nostrils.

"'Sup?"

"Okay, dawgs," Principal Garza said from the front. "Let's take a cue from our flying friend and 'raise' those test scores, yeah? This school is the lowest in the county; gotta pump up those numbers! I have an evaluation coming up, and the Board of Education guys have zero chill. Anyway, have a funky-fresh day, everyone!"

Principal Garza clapped on his way out, wiggling his twill sweater's loose sleeves. He gave a little wave to the teacher across from the doorway. Sitting at her desk in the corner by a window, Valerie's hands remained noticeably stationary.

"I assume we'll discuss Mr. Boxworth's absences—?" Valerie started, but the principal had already slinked away.

"Eric Icarus sat next to me?! Wait until my dad hears about this!"

Eric looked to his left to see Jaycee's feigned fangirl act. Eric smirked and gave a courteous head nod. With the added cargo strapped to his back, it was a tight squeeze into his chair and desk combo.

"Having trouble 'fitting in?'" Jaycee asked with a big grin. "That joke just came to me! Like, totally out of the blue!"

Eric squirmed until he found a sweet spot where he could at least breathe.

"I've already sat down. It'll be weird if I take off the backpack now," Eric whispered to her.

"Jeez, you sleep with that thing on?"

"No, but I do need restraints or something! This morning I woke up on the ceiling!"

Valerie pressed a button on a small remote, and a large square screen unrolled down the chalkboard.

"Movie day!" Melvin yelled from a middle aisle desk.

"I did not expect such enthusiasm for a documentary on air pollutants, but I am pleased by this unexpected turn of events," Valerie said over a few groans. "It'd behoove you to pay close attention, for this will appear on the final."

The ceiling-mounted projector shot light onto the unfurled canvas as a student flicked the switch by the door. The room dimmed, and the film's dated soundtrack played. The monotone narrator drawled out facts about particles, sending already drooping heads onto folded arms.

Eric bounced his knee like a nervous woodpecker onto the underside of his desk. This yielded a concerned look from Jaycee. He couldn't help the rapid knee-jerking. His fingertips rubbed up and down the wooden desk's surface. He knew she stared at him, but he didn't want to let on that his condition was acting up.

"How long has it been since you, ya know,

floated?" Jaycee asked in a hushed tone.

Her rightful worry embarrassed Eric. What hurt more than Eric's irresponsibility (when it came to superpowers) was the growing tingling in his feet. The sharp flares of his tendons and muscle tissue burning from prolonged exposure to gravity were becoming way too familiar.

Come on, not now! he silently pleaded. *Can't I at least sit through one class?*

The mysterious stinging spiked up his legs and sliced up to his stomach. Eric blew an uncomfortable breath, making an audible *hooo* sound. He tried to move, but the backpack held him in place, pressing his ribs against his desk.

I'm stuck!

The desk sunk a bit but retained its firmness as Eric rose, taking the seat with him. Beyond the wooden platform where his textbook slid slightly, he saw his classmates pop their heads up to witness the spectacle. In a sitting position, Gripping the desk, Eric peeked down to see Jaycee's big eyes bugging out. Gasps, cheers, and laughter filled the surrounding air. Eric ceased his ascension right as his hair grazed the ceiling tile. The back of the projector hung in front of him.

Still seated, Eric hovered above the class, stuck in his desk.

At roughly twelve feet high, Eric saw every knick-knack, globe, and chemistry set laid on the windowsills. Eric grimaced at the unobstructed view of the oft-ignored periodic table tacked onto the wall. He raised his eyebrows at the plethora of phone screens poorly hidden behind books or students' forearms.

"Should we contact the custodial staff, or is your desk necessary for a supervillain brawl?" Valerie chided.

The kids laughed and exploded into chatter. They unveiled their phones for what was surely some live streaming.

"I..." Eric began—the predicament was humiliating, but he sighed, unable to deny the relief. "... wanted a better view of the movie?"

• • •

Eric floated down the stairwell to the common area near the cafeteria. He received kudos from classmates who had witnessed his Olympic-level shimmying that had freed him from his desk. He had performed the feat hours ago, but Eric was happy to let its luster linger. Exchanging "What's ups?" and fist bumps with other ninth-graders, Eric hooked a thumb over an anti-grav shoulder strap and glided around and under the staircase. A small collection of chairs and wide, round tables awaited him. The hideaway was a happening spot.

A cluster of kids congregated in the corner, ignoring the wall-mounted monitor that played nothing but school-related content, so it may as well have not existed. Behind Eric, a few students studied by an art display. The oblivious boys and girls sat on tall chairs at a high-top table covered with homework materials, all wearing wireless earbuds and shutting out reality—so much so that they didn't notice a real-life superhero in their midst. Eric ambled around a brick pillar and spotted a blonde ponytail hanging from the back of a cozy red chair. Jaycee sat in the middle of the group, talking with someone hidden from view.

A lanky jock ran up to Eric.

"Mr. Icarus!" he said while catching his breath.

Eric remembered him from their ill-fated almost-fight, which involved Melvin.

"Hey, bro, can you do me a solid?"

"Uh, sure," Eric replied, unsure if the jock had any recollection of him.

"So, I'm known as, like, a tough guy rebel, but I lost—well, didn't win—a fight against some nerd, and now my reputation's sort of in the toilet."

He leaned in to whisper.

"Can you, like, help that out and stuff?"

Bemused by which nerd he was referring to—himself or Melvin—Eric opted to comply.

"Better watch out, everybody," Eric shouted to a group of passing kids. "This guy's a killer. Better not mess with him!"

This elated the skinny jock. He replaced his dopey grin with a scowl, but winked at Eric as he stomped off. Fortunately for Eric, Jaycee hadn't left her place, so he floated up to the huddled-up horde. The few facing his way were all smiles and open arms. He got a "Thank you for your service," which he found strange but appreciated the sentiment.

"What's going on, guys? Mind if I hover with you?" Eric said, satisfied with how smooth that came out. "Hey, Jaycee."

A pair of musician-types and an artsy kid gave him room and pulled up a chair so that he could get closer to her.

"Eric!" she said, turning in her seat and smiling. "So cool you're here!"

He bent to sit in the open seat on her right, but made a conscious effort to keep his butt from touching the cushion. His mild buoyancy probably looked bizarre, but Eric surfed the confidence wave, so he didn't care.

"So, uh, you hang out here? When you're here, I

mean," Eric said.

His bravado pulled a Houdini on him. Since he decided he liked Jaycee, Eric forgot how to talk to her. This presented a giant complication if he was going to ask her to the dance. He contemplated if saying she looked nice in her blue tank top would sound stupid, but knew enough not to mention her denim shorts or legs. Best not to wade into creeper-territory.

It shouldn't be this hard to get some kind of confirmation that she likes me back. I mean, I saved Jaycee's life on the roof that one time, so what else does a guy gotta do?

"Hey," she said in a softened voice. "You need to fill that backpack with rocks or something. It's way too light! You can't lose it, understand?"

"Don't worry," Eric said, matching her clandestine tone. "I put my science book in there. Hey, you going to the formal?"

"You put your book in there?" she asked, louder than expected apparently.

She brought the volume back down.

"What happens when you have to get it out?"

"Doesn't matter; class is over!" Eric said. "But, for real, are you going to the dance?"

"What was my dad thinking? At least put some spare parts in there—"

"Jaycee, do you want to go with me—"

Their whispering stopped when Jaycee whipped her head around to see:

"Kev!"

She stood and hugged him, a sight that twisted Eric's esophagus. Coughing on his breath, Eric noticed that Kev wore a yellow polo, which infuriatingly showcased his muscular physique. He sat on the other side of Jaycee.

"Kevin, what're you doing here?" Eric asked.

"He only does half-days at his school since he's already got so many credits!" Jaycee explained for him. "He was awesome enough to come visit!"

"So wild seeing you again, man! Oh, and it's just Kev."

"Hey, Eric, you were talking about the spring formal, right?" she asked.

Eric had a bad feeling about this.

"Kev, could you make it? It's tonight. We could all go. It'll be uh-mazing!"

"I don't see why not," Kev said. "Sounds like fun."

"Yeah, but, oh, man," Eric said. "I don't think it's allowed for students from other schools to go. That sucks, but rules are rules."

"Whatevs, Eric," Jaycee said. "Kev, do you also do dance tutoring? Eric needs a crash course in rhythm."

Kev shook his head and smiled. His white and perfectly aligned teeth offended Eric personally.

"Ha, well, I do more of an air-dancing thing anyway," Eric said. "Which Jaycee knows about since we already practiced. 'Cause we were already going, it was a planned thing. You weren't there, Kev."

"Apparently, neither was I. We agreed to what exactly?"

Kev hid his pearly whites under a confused frown. Eric levitated out of his chair.

"Uh oh! Bad guys are attacking the city! I gotta go join the rest of the Super Society!"

Jaycee and Kev shared shocked expressions.

"Uh, you sure about that?" she asked with a furrowed brow.

Eric backed away with the tips of his sneakers brushed against the floor.

"Yeah, got the message from Truther himself via

a secret communicator. It's a superhero thing. You wouldn't understand."

The last thing he saw before turning away was Jaycee scrambling to check her phone, but she'd find nothing. Mortified, Eric sped off and considered flying into the sun.

Chapter Eighteen: *GRAVITY*

ERIC

THE SCHOOL DAY CAME AND went. Each period had been a blur of glad-handing, which left Eric too preoccupied with posing for selfies than paying attention to the teachers' lessons. Lunch was a question-and-answer session about the Super Society: if Extra was single, what Truther was really like, and how cool it must have been to live in Pantheon Tower. Eric wasn't sure how anyone would know he'd been residing there lately, but he had opted for a not-so-secret identity. The recurring topic was the spring formal dance happening later that evening.

The Pantheon Tower guest room had been more than serviceable, especially considering it was in an office building. The Super Society had been living in Pantheon Tower anyway, so Eric reasoned he was a team player, if nothing else.

I figured having superhero roommates would be more fun, but nooo... he thought. *They're avoiding me on purpose. I know it.*

With the caramel-colored curtains closed, Eric hid the thirtieth-floor view from the tower's east-facing side.

He sat on the foot of the king-sized bed, feeling the silky sheets with his fingers. Jaycee's room had been presented to him as an option, but that felt weird. Plus, he knew she'd be back here. Someday.

The closet, which could've been its own apartment, was open in front of him. The folded mirrored doors on either side showed a different angle of his anxious reflection. His initial request for new clothes had exceeded his meager expectations: t-shirts and shorts from brands he'd never heard of hung in pristine order. His actual wardrobe was still balled-up on the floor of his room back at the Boxworth Dreamineering building, but he couldn't bring himself to go back there. That felt even weirder.

Before today, he hadn't needed anything formal. It was his first dance, and he had nothing fancy to wear despite the closetful of outfits.

"Welp, when you ask the for casual, that's exactly what you get here. Guess I should be more specific next time."

Eric didn't know if he was even supposed to dress up for the event, but every movie he'd seen with a dance or a prom featured dolled-up teens, so he decided he'd follow the formula. Unfortunately, seeking experienced wisdom had been a non-starter. He couldn't catch Yvette before she left early to volunteer as a student chaperone.

Even I think that's nerdy, Eric thought. *Still, no such luck there for advice.*

He couldn't ask Melvin and Tiffany since they had already left for the night—but not together; Eric knew that much. He would need something more dapper than the plain-orange tee and gray shorts-and-sneakers ensemble he wore.

His blue superhero costume lay sprawled out

on his oversized bed. Eric snatched up the anti-grav backpack, leaving the rest of the uniform. He strapped on the pack as he flew through the door and into the hall. He turned a corner to find the elevator. Pressing the "down" button opened the golden doors. He zigzagged his finger over the grid of floor selections until he landed on the right one.

"It's a long shot, but I don't have much time left to find something not terrible to wear tonight."

A text notification sounded off from his phone. Eric slid it out of his shorts pocket just enough to see a message from Jaycee. The words "group" and "Kev" appeared.

"Plus, I need help with getting rid of third wheels," he said.

He pushed the phone back down into his pocket.

"Did I mention I'm desperate?"

Floating inside the car, Eric avoided the familiar stomach upheaval of a typical elevator ride. Instead, the elevator went down, shooting his buoyant body to the ceiling. The short trip's gravity mismatch left Eric a bit woozy.

Elevators kind of suck now.

Surveillance cameras watched from their wall-mounted perches, so Eric knew better than to think he was sneaking around unnoticed. Still, the emptiness of the corridor he entered gave him the creeps.

"I assumed this would be a restricted area, but not straight-up abandoned."

The curved wall ended. Eric felt as if he stood in the center of an oversized hollow rectangle. Taped posters sporadically covered the yellowish-metal walls. Hand-drawn equations marked each sheet. The floor's oddly patterned tiles were visible between drafting tables, metal crates, and scattered tablets. The strangest sight was his reflection looking back at him.

The wall at the far end was a giant mirror.

This is Dad's lab; I know it! Eric thought. *I remember seeing it from outside through the window.*

Mouth agape, a realization struck him.

It's a big two-way mirror, like an interrogation room on some cop show.

Memories of telling off David while floating outside the giant window flooded Eric's brain.

"He didn't see me," Eric said aloud, softly. "He didn't hear me. He didn't know..."

"A secret multimillion-dollar project means nobody sees anything in here," David said.

His father's image startled Eric.

"Dad!"

"I guess Super Society members get special security clearances."

"I don't even have a superhero I.D. card or anything," Eric said.

He caught himself talking to David's reflection. The real thing looked like he hadn't changed clothes or slept since they both got to the tower.

David picked up a tablet, popped out its stylus, and scribbled some notes. His eyelids sagged like sunken ships.

"You haven't left this room much, huh, Dad?"

"On the contrary," David said before yawning. "This was only the developmental site. My team has begun refitting the rooftop. How about that, eh? The new MegaCore—my invention—is sitting at the top of the Pantheon Solutions building!"

David leaned against the wall as he slid to the floor.

"Oh, I guess you and your super-kiddies will have to find a new hangout."

"Not my awesome locker!"

David sent him a quizzical look. He fought to keep his drowsy eyes open.

"I just mean, uh," Eric said, searching for a way out of the uneasiness. "The spring formal dance is tonight, and I need something nice to wear."

"The junior hero takes time off from fighting crime to go party," David said, chuckling. "The other sidekicks have to stay home or something?"

I wish I could just tell him that Melvin, Tiffany, Jaycee, and Yvette are the other members of the Super Society. It'd be waaaay simpler if I could tell him Mr. Maddox is Truther. As if talking to Dad wasn't awkward enough.

"We got a message earlier saying Truther's on monitor duty tonight, so—"

"I'm glad you're having fun, Eric," David said, not looking up as he tapped away at the tablet.

The anti-grav backpack gleamed under the ceiling lamps. Eric studied how the pack looked strapped onto him in his off-duty attire. It took some getting used to, like everything.

"Do you really not know what I've been up to?" Eric asked. "Wait, you don't still think my flying power is just an act, right?"

"Son, we're moving at warp speed here," David said. "I'm sorry I haven't had much time to check out your superhero stuff. I really am. It's this incredible opportunity for you and... Look, you gotta understand that I'm finally close to seeing my vision become a reality."

"Yeah..." Eric said, eyes cast down. "I get it."

He tugged at the shoulder strap of his pack. Eric exhaled a deep, slow breath, letting his gaze wander.

"I came looking for your advice," Eric said. "About,

um, girls. Well, a girl."

David rubbed his temples.

"Man, this I don't need right now," he said, wincing. "I showed you the educational videos online, remember?"

"Oh, no, no, no, we don't need to go over the biology stuff again! Just... What did you say to mom to get her to like you?"

David's eyes closed. A little smile cracked open his lips.

"We were both students in the same line at this advanced machine learning conference," he said, lost in a dream. "We were there to see some presenter we both forgot the name of. We didn't want to let each other think we didn't know, so we acted like we knew what we were talking about."

David's speech slowed the more he surrendered to what appeared to be a blissful haze.

"We only ended up embarrassing ourselves in front of all the other smart people there..."

Eric knew David drifted due to pure exhaustion, but he liked his dad this way.

"I didn't care," David said, "'cause I was talking to the angel with the strawberry blonde hair..."

Eric had heard the story of how his parents had met a thousand times before. He could stand to listen another thousand times, but Baron's voice cut in.

"Your father's dedication is nothing short of remarkable."

"Mr. Maddox!" Eric said.

The surprise of seeing him popped Eric up in the air. Baron's pearl-colored suit and matching tie entered the mirror's reflection. David covered a yawn but let his eyes show his displeasure.

"Come to make sure I'm not lounging on the job?"

David asked.

"For the record," Baron said, facing Eric, "I didn't order David to work around the clock."

"I wasn't, I mean," Eric blurted. "I was only—!"

"Visiting your father requires no explanation."

"I was just asking if he had advice on..."

Maybe I don't mention how I like Mr. Maddox's daughter, Eric thought.

"I wanted to know if he had something I could wear to the dance tonight. If you saw what's in Dad's shoe collection, you'd think I'm crazy for asking."

David's annoyed frown met Eric's uneasy smile.

"The suit makes the man," Baron said.

Baron glanced over to David, who narrowed his eyes right back at him.

"In your special case, though, Eric," Baron said. "The man makes the suit."

"What do you mean?" Eric asked, tilting his head like a confused animal.

David blew out a heavy, frustrated sigh through his flared nostrils. Baron patted the steel shell backpack and winked at Eric.

"You've already designed the outfit that brings out the real you."

DAVID

He watched his son glide away. Eric's sneakers floating over the floor unsettled David. He had witnessed the anti-grav backpack's capabilities before, but at that moment, the power seemed... He couldn't place the word.

"Freaky, right?" Baron said, also staring as Eric disappeared into the building's halls.

"It looks like something I shouldn't have to get used to."

"David," Baron said, turning to him. "Our world is never static. The earth moves beneath our feet even when we don't notice. Nothing ever stays the same. So, there is nothing to get used to. Intellectuals like ourselves embrace change."

"Spare me the phony philosophy, Barry," David said, crossing out a note on his tablet. "And, intellectual? I'd feel a lot smarter if I got paid for my hard work."

"Compensation will be delivered upon demonstration. I can have Dahlia or Chelsea assist you with reviewing the contract if you would like."

"You know what I'm going to do once I get compensated?" David said, tossing the tablet onto a nearby workbench. "I'm taking Eric and leaving this city. I'll have bigger and better places to go. As you said, the planet doesn't stay still, and I have a lot of catching up to do."

"Our association represents so much more than money," Baron said. "The MegaCore is the catalyst to what will be a paradigm-breaker. So much glory awaits. Don't let your pride kill your potential."

"I'm a one-and-done contractor, but nice try."

"A deal's a deal, David."

"I have work to do," he said, yawning.

"So, so much more."

David turned to inspect a MegaCore power-usage chart on the tablet.

"Now it is your turn to spare me of your phony attempts at playing coy," Baron said, sliding his hands into his pants pockets. "You know the details of our assets arrangement."

"So, what you meant about initializing a developmental partnership—I'm just your employee? A lackey?"

The large mirror on the other end of the room was impossible to ignore. David was fine with not having a view of the Plant Pipeline, but every reflective surface in the lab drove him stir-crazy. He couldn't escape what was happening to him.

Is that what I'll be remembered for? Just one of Pantheon's nameless tech monkeys?

"You must complete your contractual obligations," Baron said. "And moral ones. I don't want to involve, shall we say, a more extreme authoritative presence to ensure your cooperation."

"You can leave the lawyers out of this," David said without looking back at him. "Or were you going to sic Truther on me? I'll finish the job."

"Jobs, David. And the one you have to do now is of the utmost importance."

"You think I'll cut corners or something, Barry?" David said, turning to face him. "You think I don't understand what I have to do? How huge this is? It's the MegaCore. My MegaCore!"

"I want the Ultranaut warsuit."

David's head recoiled as if he'd been splashed in the face with ice-cold water.

"Wait—is this why you want my engine? To power a fleet of armored machines?"

"Among many other things of a particular interest," Baron said. "But let's focus on the unit you already have."

"The prototype hasn't exactly been a hot-seller," David said regretfully.

"You were quite boastful of its reprogramming,"

Baron said.

"It's undergone an overhaul, sure. It's completely operational; not like anybody cares. The only thing the scientific community thinks of when they see it is…"

He failed to look Baron in the eyes.

"Heck, it was in your hangar where… Well, where the incident happened. Why would you, of all people, want it now?"

"I'm in the Boxworth business," Baron said as his eyes sized up the scattered equipment in the room. "Talents get absorbed all the time in big tech; this is not unusual."

"The thing about my business, Barry, is that the name stays with me. I know what the contracts say, but it's my tech, my patents, my legacy."

"Eric is doing remarkably well with the Icarus name."

The words stung David's lungs.

"Your son has such a pivotal role to play," Baron said. "His future is beyond bright. And it will be spent here at Pantheon Solutions. With me."

Gut-clenching rage tightened David's insides. He took slow, deep breaths, calming himself.

"I only want what is best for the boy," Baron said. "His career trajectory could see him ascend beyond just being a member of the Super Society. People love him, but the event at the comic convention was too chaotic. Eric was never meant to be placed in so much danger so soon."

Leaning against the smooth wall, David frowned his lips to one side. The spiel from Baron induced nausea.

"Popularity is a fickle thing," Baron went on. "Much of my profession deals with marketing. Eric will need a new foe to vanquish to boost his appeal, and he needs it soon. All of the Super Society will benefit, yes, but Eric is the one in the spotlight now."

"The mascot, you mean?"

"He needs a controlled enemy. One that will have no issue with, shall we say, a more performative loss. Ultranaut can be piloted remotely, so—"

"Okay, just a minute!" David said, pushing himself from the wall.

"Eric already hates the suit, no?" Baron reminded. "Frankly, anyone who has ever seen it does as well. You said as much yourself."

The truth sunk in David's stomach.

"What are you asking me to do exactly?" David said. "Send my armor to go crash a high school dance?"

"No, let Eric enjoy himself for a night. He deserves it; they all do. He and his classmates will soon face a great change—with summer break looming. They may as well have the dance."

Baron paced in front of David.

"I will arrange the choreographed encounter with Ultranaut. This is not something Eric can know about."

"Why the secrets, Bar'?"

"Eric's mettle is being tested. Your prototype symbolizes the boundaries he must break through. It's safe; it's... catharsis."

David had no response.

Fake a fight with Ultranaut? How has my life come to this?

"I want you to understand what this means for Eric," Baron said, stopping in front of him.

Before David could muster a retort, Baron swiveled and walked away.

"Remember what is expected of you, David," he said as his voice disappeared in the distance.

He waited until Baron stepped out of sight until

he picked up the tablet. The corner-mounted cameras served as reminders that he was not alone. David had to be careful.

The security firewalls I installed should protect me, he thought. *But I could do without a Pantheon surveillance camera recording my passcodes. Baron can't have everything.*

He hunched, hiding his fingers as best he could while inputting a series of commands on the touchscreen. A new window displayed the words "Boxworth Remote Automated Interactive Network."

"BRAIN!" David whispered.

The screen blipped into a sound wave image.

"What can I do for you, Mr. Boxworth?" the automated assistant's voice said, bouncing the sound wave.

"BRAIN, I secretly installed you. No one else can know you're a part of the MegaCore's programming, understand?"

"Understood, Mr. Boxworth. How can I be of assistance?"

"I need you to get something for me..."

He typed in a sequence of numbers. David looked at his reflection in the wide mirror across from him.

"I've already lost so much," he said. "I won't let Eric become some Pantheon lifer."

"Awaiting further commands, sir."

"BRAIN, initiate Double-X protocol—exfiltration and extraction. Let's bring my boy home."

Chapter Nineteen: *DROP*

ERIC

NEWS CREWS CROWDED THE ENTRANCE of the gymnasium. Looking down at them from high above, Eric thought the students arriving in rented limousines must be getting a kick out of the red-carpet treatment. Eric knew, though, that the media was there for him. He flew over the roof and descended by the back, robbing the reporters of a big scoop. He smirked at the thought of some drone following him and how the cameramen would kill to get whatever footage it may have.

The warm early evening air carried cigarette smoke. No rebellious delinquents were visible, so Eric figured he was safe to land undetected next to a dumpster by the backdoor. However, he worried about getting the putrid stench of trash and smoke in his costume.

He knew the backway would be unlocked from his history of sneaking out of P.E. Muffled party music thumped from inside. He stood in the glow of the overhead light, straightening his dark blue gloves. He adjusted his multi-pocketed belt and rubbed smudges off the smooth Super Society double-S insignia belt buckle. He inspected the glossiness of the sky-blue "up" arrow emblem on his chest. The backpack held securely in place. His hair was as good as it was going to get. Donning the superhero uniform made by Baron—based on his design—turned out to be an easy choice.

Eric swung the door open—blaring beats of an up-tempo dance song hit him in the face. It was dark in the narrow space behind the metal bleachers, with enough room for Eric to hide. He overheard Melvin and his fellow gamers above him, deep into a heated fantasy card game. Eric slid down to avoid the light from their phones.

"Gentlemen, tonight's the night we dance and talk to girls!" Melvin said. "After this game, of course."

At least I'm not the only superhero who couldn't find a date, Eric thought.

Peeking through a slit under a silver plank, Eric saw the sparkles from a disco ball flickering over the dancing kids in the middle of the basketball court. Below an enormous "GOLDEN EAGLE PRIDE" painted sign, bashful wallflowers intermixed with clusters of chatting teenagers too cool to boogie, congregating around the punchbowl table. Eric spotted chaperone Valerie standing with her arms crossed next to Yvette, whose thumb scrolled over her phone's screen at the speed of boredom. Everyone else wore cool suits or stylish dresses, looking beautiful and young.

Eric scanned the rest of the gym like he was on a reconnaissance detail. He saw Jaycee standing by a sparkly photo booth near the dance floor's edge. A giggling couple finished their posing in the booth, then moved on, clearing a better view of Jaycee. Nodding with the song, she seemed eager to join the party. The elegance of her pink, blinged-out dress surprised him, but he wasn't sure why. He didn't know much about girls' formal wear, but Jaycee's outfit was a quick favorite. She wore her blonde hair up, and it looked like she had makeup on, which was different. Jaycee smiled, per usual. She was so pretty it made his heart hurt.

Eric slid over, emerging from behind the bleachers with his boots a couple of inches above the wooden floor. He set his course for his teammate, but his classmates spotted him. A burst of cheers exploded, much louder than the boisterous tune playing. The well-dressed mass rushed to him with smartphones held up to document the grand event. The fashionable flock blocked Eric's view of Jaycee.

"Eric Icarus in the house!"

"Hashtag superhero dance party!"

"Who'd you come here with, Eric?!"

"Why are you the only one with a functioning anti-gravity backpack, like, why doesn't the Army have 'em, too?"

Eric held his hands up to calm them, not wanting to say there was enough of him to go around verbally but still getting his message across. Despite being afloat, maintaining a relatively average height did him no favors while scoping for Jaycee. More ecstatic faces obstructed his view, and Eric felt a trickle of worry that he'd experience a repeat of the previous panic attack in the school hallway. Eric made a giant leap, stopping just below the ceiling. The adolescent armada's heads flipped up and applauded at the aerial stunt.

"No need to be alarmed," Eric shouted down at them. "I'm here on official Super Society business to ensure everyone's safety."

Their smiles bent in confusion but held their excitement. From Eric's perspective, he had an open view of the shiny decorations, colorful banners, and streamers adorning the gym directly over center court. He floated higher than the day he climbed the rope in class. Everything looked smaller now. The other teens waited, antsy for a cue of some kind.

"What are you standing around for?" Eric yelled. "Party on!"

Celebratory hollering erupted, followed by energetic dancing. Eric freely eyed the area, satisfied by his quick conjuring of a convincing lie about being on duty. He searched past the hanging disco ball a few feet away in his proximity. He skimmed over the grooving DJ's station under the backboard to his right. A scan of the stands on both sides of the main dance floor saw sporadic kids and a few tired adults sitting out songs, but that was it. Jaycee had vanished.

Pink dress—Eric had a visual. Jaycee had pursued on foot to the punchbowl. Soaring toward the backboard on the other end of the court, Eric positioned himself over the refreshments table and landed. Eric stalled, seeing Kev standing next to her. He stood out as the most dapper guy there by far in his glossy sharkskin blue suit. The color scheme's similarities stressed Eric. It was as if Kev somehow found a cooler, sleeker, more formal version of Eric's crime-fighting costume.

"Eric Icarus! What an entrance!" Kev said, welcoming him to their little circle.

"Yeah, uh, hey," Eric replied, focusing entirely on Jaycee.

"We were supposed to all show up together, flyboy," Jaycee said, then sipped from her plastic cup. "Too busy making an appearance at a flea market or something?"

"Jaycee, for that joke to work, you gotta aim

higher, like, say I was officiating a pro wrestling wedding. You know, something much more upscale and believable."

Eric felt queasy, letting his burgeoning quick-lie-cunning go into hyperdrive, but he was desperate to avoid talking about how he had ghosted her texts—texts that included Kev.

"Would you believe I couldn't decide on what to wear?" Eric said.

"Solid outfit choice," Jaycee said. "You look really 'fly'—get it?!"

Eric let out a courtesy chuckle despite his mental meltdown. Complimenting Jaycee was on the agenda, but he was at a loss for words.

"I like your dress a lot," Eric blurted.

"Isn't it amazing?!" she exclaimed, lifting her arms to twirl. "My mom surprised me with it! I mean, Ms. Cooper, I mean, ah, you know!"

"Yeah, and I have no idea how much dresses cost," Eric said. "But that looks super pricey, and your mom got it on a teacher's salary. That's incredible."

"I... What?"

"Any other Super Society members coming?" Kev butted in, doing something useful for once. "I'd love to meet Powerhouse! It must be awesome to have other young people on the team, huh, Eric?"

Eric and Jaycee exchanged knowing glances. A redhead in a tight, strapless cherry-colored dress led her girl squad to Eric.

"Eric Icarus!" Tiffany called out. "Hey, roomie!"

"Tiffany?" Eric asked in disbelief.

"You remember mi amigas from Spanish class, right?" she said, gesturing to her girls.

"Uh, what's up? I mean, hola?" Eric said.

He thought Tiffany was pretty, but tonight she was

breathtaking—not that Eric would openly admit it. Still, an intensity of Tiffany and her entourage made him uncomfortable. Jaycee's cocked eyebrow and sly smile didn't help. Eric could tell she relished seeing him crumble under pressure.

"It's been a dream of mine to dance with a real-life superhero," Tiffany said. "How about you show me what that jetpack of yours can do?"

He felt hands twisting his esophagus.

"Oh, I, um," Eric said, feeling his face get hot.

The music shifted to a slow dance song.

"This is my jam!" Jaycee shouted.

Tiffany tugged at Eric's arm, leading him to the crowded dance floor.

"Get your phones out, ladies," Tiffany instructed to her backup unit. "This is going to be legendary!"

The girls whipped out their bedazzled devices and snapped pics. Flabbergasted, Eric found himself being dragged deeper into a sea of swaying high schoolers. Before they could get entirely out of Jaycee's earshot, Eric grabbed Tiffany's arms to stop her in her tracks, which she seemed to enjoy.

"Take-charge attitude—I like that in a guy," she said, but he faced away.

Eric winced when he saw Jaycee get closer to Kev.

"You know you're not gonna get away without dancing to at least one song tonight," Eric heard Jaycee tell Kev, then he saw her poking his shoulder.

Kev's bashful laugh was audible over the ballad.

"Are you dating the punchbowl?" Tiffany asked, annoyed.

"Huh?" Eric said, zipping his eyes back to her.

"Smile for the camera, honey," Tiffany ordered.

She pulled Eric so that their backs were to Jaycee and Kev. Eric looked over his shoulder, but a soft hand yanked him by the chin, forcing him to pose. Tiffany grinned wide while Eric looked afraid for his life. The other young ladies toggled between portrait and landscape pictures. They tapped and tapped, capturing this moment in time. Tiffany planted a lingering kiss on Eric's cheek until the photo op was complete. One of the other girls turned her phone over so Eric could see the big crimson lipstick mark on his worried face.

"Dancing's not really my thing," Kev said in the background, much to Eric's relief.

Tiffany placed Eric's hand on her hip, cutting his comfort.

"So, for real, are you seeing anyone?" Tiffany asked as they started a halfhearted waltz. "I'm not just asking because you're, like, famous with connections, but I'm a social media influencer, and I think we'd make a lot of sense together."

"Me and making sense haven't been friends lately, you know?"

He felt the all too familiar nervous sweat spill.

"Our super manager, Baron Maddox—"

"Mr. Maddox?"

"That's the one! Wow, all this and brains, too!" Tiffany said, scoffing. "Anyway, his company offers college scholarships. I waaaas the hot new girl on the team. But then you came along, and now you're his new toy. So, I need you to get me to meet with him—"

Eric spun her, twirling the flowing lower part of her dress.

"Keeping my identity as Extra separate has made it so much more difficult to land licensing contracts for my brand," Tiffany said as they swayed. "Being a publicly known hero is such a genius move. I wish I thought of that!"

He dipped her so he could spy on Jaycee. Kev had

his hands in his pockets, and Jaycee held her cup to her face, taking awkward gulps.

"Mr. Fly Guy, my spine is about to snap in two, so if you wouldn't mind..."

"Oh, jeez! Sorry!"

Eric eased Tiffany upright.

"Alright, just one dance," he overheard Kev say. "Just don't make fun of my two left feet!"

Red alert sirens blasted in Eric's mind.

"Uh, Tiffany?" he said to the irritated girl. "I'm sorry, but I have to, er, secure the... perimeter."

He grimaced, realizing that he'd run out of cunning wit.

"We have enough chaperones," Tiffany said. "So, we gonna get busy, or what?"

"Ex-excuse me?!" Eric stammered, feeling his cheeks go red.

"Get down to business and talk P.R. deals," she clarified. "Don't flatter yourself, hon."

Eric saw Jaycee laughing with Kev from the corner of his eye as they shuffled their way through a clumsy box-formation dance. Eric's heart hurt again, but this time it felt like icicles puncturing his heart.

The music swelled as cheek-to-cheek pairs came of age in real-time, but Eric's eyes followed his friend and her tutor. He silently begged for them to try not to look so happy together. Jaycee threw her head back in a spirited chuckle. A near-slip from Kev landed Jaycee's face on his shoulder. She let her head nestle there far longer than Eric's liking.

"Earth to Eric!"

His attention snapped back to Tiffany. Her glitter-infused eyeshadow somehow twinkled faster the more aggravated she became.

"I'm a busy woman, so I'll cut to the chase,"

she said. "I want the superhero girlfriend life for the summer until I get a scholarship, endorsement deal, and a clothing line, and then we amicably part ways. But I have demands. One: my alter ego, Extra, remains single as far as my followers know. Two: I pick where we go on dates. Three: my ride-or-dies are now your friends, too—this is non-negotiable..."

She prattled on with different prerequisites, but Eric's concentration abandoned her as quickly as it had returned. As he shifted his eyes, Eric saw Jaycee and Kev edging near them. Kev made a cumbersome move to spin Jaycee. Eric seized the opportunity.

Lacking grace entirely, Eric flung Tiffany mid-sentence into a strategically timed twirl, straight toward an unsuspecting Jaycee. The two girls followed through with their pirouettes and tangled into each other.

The collision captured both dancers' and wallflowers' attention, each head turning to watch the chaotic exchange.

Jaycee pushed Tiffany off her, throwing her into Kev's chest, but the action offset Jaycee's balance—before she fell, Eric caught her in his arms.

Jaycee's brow furrowed in anger.

"Hey, watch it, Boxworth!" Jaycee said. "I mean, Icarus! Ugh, never mind!"

"Can I cut in?" Eric said.

"Little late for that."

"I need rescuing. Just go with it!"

Eric took Jaycee's hand into his, placing his other one on her waist, gliding her away from their confused dance partners.

"Tengo que ir al baño," Eric shouted over his shoulder to Tiffany as he danced with Jaycee in the opposite direction.

"What?!" Tiffany yelled back.

"You should really pay more attention in Spanish class!"

"Are you kidding me?!" Tiffany screeched.

"I know Spanish, and I am a tutor..." Kev said.

Eric watched Tiffany form a smile and caress Kev's bicep.

"Thanks for the save, Jaycee," he said after they danced into the center of the gym.

"No sweat. Wasn't exactly my idea. I'm sure dancing with Tiffany must've been terrible."

She nodded, eyeing his kiss-marked cheek.

"That wasn't my idea, either."

"If these people only knew that you're basically the Super Society's mascot."

He scrunched his brow, letting his jaw hang open.

"Low blow."

He feigned offense. They rotated in a lazy sway, ignoring the stares from the other dancers.

"At least you can wear your costume. I haven't been in any action in, like, forevs! If I don't punch a bad guy soon, I'm gonna explode!"

Eric tensed. A sudden dagger of pain impaled his senses. The fiery reminder of being earthbound set every nerve ending ablaze.

"What's wrong?" Jaycee asked as her eyelids fluttered. "You've been grounded too long, haven't you?"

"Yeah, but if I go up right now..."

He hunched over slightly, trying to compose himself. He looked up. Jaycee lowered her head to match his. Eric locked eyes with her.

"...I won't want to come down."

A spike of pain jolted his limbs into motion, and Eric wrapped his arm around Jaycee's waist. Her eyes bulged, and he held her tight against his chest. Before she could respond, Eric lifted them. She hooked her arms under his, and he felt her claw around until she clung to a backpack strap.

"Hope you don't mind," Eric said while they rose above the cheering crowd. "That was getting painful."

"I get it, I get it, but I'm not crazy about having an audience!" Jaycee said, peeking over her arm. "Just don't drop me!"

"I won't, I promise," he said. "But I need this if we're gonna dance."

He tightened his hold and used his left hand to grab onto her right. He gently pulled her slightly off him, and they bent their arms, interlocking fingers. He led her in a slow, makeshift dance, gliding at least ten feet above the other boys and girls. Their fellow students clapped, hollered, and whistled. Eric noticed Yvette and some grownups plying through the group and heard them call for him to get down. Eric smiled. She smiled back.

Jaycee's blue eyes pierced into his. Her hair glistened in the cascading disco ball's flickering reflections. Eric couldn't get enough of whatever hint of perfume she wore. Floating up there made him feel like it was just the two of them dancing on air.

"No offense," Jaycee said. "But no way you're this strong. Not enough to keep this up anyway."

"What can I say? I've been inspired to take more risks."

"I'm such a bad influence on you," Jaycee said.

Now or never, Eric thought.

He leaned in for a kiss.

Jaycee recoiled, whipping her head back. The sudden shudder caught Eric off guard. He felt her slump, slipping from his grip. Desperate to hold onto

Jaycee, Eric spiraled in a haphazard descent. They made a clunky touchdown, Jaycee barely staying upright but somehow stumbling away.

The stunned kids and adults gave them space, but at least fifty cameras pointed at them. Jaycee, red-faced, adjusted her dress as a spatter of jeers and laughter trickled from the onlookers. She looked perplexed, unsure of what to do next. Eric took a step toward her, but the physical torture proved too much, and he sprang back up. Amongst the raucous chorus of hooting and clamoring, he saw Jaycee shake her head and flee the scene.

Even in the dimmed mood lighting, Eric saw all their faces: mouths agape in disbelief or crooked with sniggering. The lights from their smartphones popped up like little stars. Eric's heart pounded, and he couldn't calm his breathing.

The music came to an end.

GOLDEN EAGLE PRIDE
NORTH NEW St CLOUD HIGH
SPRING FORMAL
EXIT

Chapter Twenty: *LEVEL*

ERIC

THE NIGHTTIME AIR COOLED BY only a few degrees, but the special fibers of Eric's temperature-controlled suit left him numb to the elements. Standing on the edge of the main school building roof made the skyscrapers seem so far away. Far away is exactly where he wanted to be. Quitting typically soothed to Eric, but even with wanting for nothing in the illustrious Pantheon Tower, returning there felt like giving up.

He curled his fingers around the dark blue strap connecting to the symbol across his chest, letting his hand hang there. In a relaxed stance unbefitting of a noble guardian, Eric listened for the chatter and activity from whatever media crew would still be left. The reporters and bloggers had flooded the gymnasium after his fall from grace with Jaycee. After zig-zagging his way through the rafters and ceiling ventilation and support structures, Eric was able to sneak away.

Ideas of communication with his dad sparked up in Eric's head, but he didn't see the point. Eric's father was too busy, like always. Same situation, different location.

He felt Baron would heed his call, but Eric didn't want to bother him. He especially didn't want to contact any of the other Super Society members. His teammates were the last people he wanted to see.

"Hey."

The sound of Jaycee's voice-activated tears, but Eric made a quick wipe of his face and fought the urge to bawl. He turned to see Jaycee standing in her pink dress by a boxy storage unit. She looked like the sophisticated grownup, readying to lecture the kid playing superhero dress-up.

"Hey," Eric said back, taking a few steps closer to her. "I panicked. I bailed. I..."

A tidal wave of emotion brewed from his gut, causing Eric to look away, frowning hard as he suppressed the sadness. He exhaled, dispelling the crying fit before it could take over.

"I guess my skin's just not as thick as I thought it was," he admitted.

She leaned against the side of the metal unit.

"You didn't bail. You're still here," Jaycee said. "Easy to find, too. Predictable, Boxworth. I covered for you, though. I said you were called to an emergency Society meeting. Not my best lie, but I tried."

"Thanks."

Eric looked down at his boots.

"I totally misread what was going on. I thought... something was going on."

"Look, I just wasn't expecting—"

"No, no, it's cool. I just found a new way to embarrass myself on a nuclear level even after being a beloved superhero."

"You weren't the only one humiliated, Eric."

"The kiss was a mistake, okay?" he said, raising his head. "I blew it. That's what I do. That's my real superpower."

"This isn't just your cute awkward underdog act, this…"

Jaycee let out a checked breath.

"The whole thing was a mistake!" she said. "I can't believe I let you carry me up there like that in front of everybody! Like, the whole school saw that! And how is Tiffany supposed to feel?"

"I dunno, I just, I guess, to be honest, I thought maybe you'd…"

His mouth suddenly felt very small.

"I thought you'd like that I chose you over some other girl."

"Chose me?" she asked, standing up straight. "Cutting in on Kev and me so you could 'choose' me to be the one you show off like I'm some conquest?"

"Whoa, Jaycee, that is so not what I was doing!"

"Then what was the plan?"

"I was—I mean, look, there were probably a lot of girls who would've loved to, ya know, dance with me, but I—"

"So, you did me this huge favor, is that it?"

She crossed her arms, awaiting an explanation.

"I was jealous, alright?" Eric said, spreading his arms. "You're with Kevin. I get it."

"Are you serious?" Jaycee asked, eyes bulging just enough to show her genuine disbelief—and outrage. "In case you haven't noticed, I don't have a lot of friends, Eric! I'm always away doing Super Society stuff! I start hanging out with someone other than you, and you get all weird!"

"So, you're not dating Kevin…?"

"No, not that it's any business of yours!"

Eric knew that shouldn't have been so comforting to hear, but reluctant relief found him regardless. He turned to look away from her. The night grew darker by the minute, it seemed.

"I didn't think you cared what other people think."

"I wore this dress tonight because I don't care what other people think," Jaycee said with a thick layer of sarcasm. "I wear a costume with metal sleeves and save people, but, yeah, I don't care what they think! I guess it doesn't matter now, anyway. S'not like I'll be getting to do any superhero stuff again."

"I'm sure your dad—"

"My dad gave me away!" Jaycee snapped.

She stomped toward him, but stopped herself from getting too close.

"All he does is spend time with you now!"

"Come on, that's not true," Eric said, facing her, ready to dish out some cynicism of his own. "Why would your dad waste his time with the team mascot?"

"You can legit fly. He's literally obsessed with you."

"Yeah, that's right, I can fly!" Eric said, approaching Jaycee. "I'm, like, a miracle of nature, and, well, I guess I just don't get why you're not obsessed, too! You're the one telling me to be bold all the time, but then you tell me how much of a jerk I am for using my powers!"

"Ego much?!" she shot back, eyes fluttering like crazy. "If my—if Truther didn't order me to spy on you in the first place, then you wouldn't even be here!"

The words traveled through his ears well enough, but they struggled to compute. Creasing his brow, Eric titled his head.

"What do you mean 'spy' on me?"

"I..." Jaycee said, eyebrows raised. "You had to have known, er, I, uh... 'Spy' may not be the best choice of word—"

"Is 'stalking' better?"

His body felt lighter than air, but his heart weighed a ton.

"So-so-so, you reported on me?" Eric asked, unsure of how to speak. "You knew, the Society knew, Truther knew, which obviously means your dad knew…"

"We didn't know anything!" she said, looking frazzled with guilt. "Not at first! I saw you flying after the big fight with Cybertooth at your house, and I was told to keep tabs—"

"Why would—what, you thought I was a bad guy or-or-or—I was gonna hurt people?"

"O-M-G, no!" Jaycee said, taking a step closer.

Eric held up his hand and backed away. A volcanic surge of emotions threatened to carry him away.

"I was just trying to figure out what your deal was, that's all!" she explained.

"You pretended to be my friend."

"No!" Jaycee said before softening her voice. "I mean, initially, sort of, yeah, but—"

"You pretended to like me."

Nausea seeped into Eric's belly. He walked away from Jaycee, alongside the edge of the building.

"Eric, please!"

"Don't bother, Jaycee!" Eric yelled back, unable to take his eyes off the concrete below his feet. "You don't have to lie anymore!"

"For serious, you need to listen—"

"I understand now; I really do!" Eric shouted as he pivoted to face her. "You were just following orders! Keep an eye on the flying freak!"

"Come on—"

"It's lame what your parents are doing!" Eric said, refusing to let her get a word in. "There's no way your mom will let you sneak out to be a superhero, and your dad is just letting it all go. That sucks. That really sucks. But you have a parent who actually does want you! And guess what else? You aren't forced to do any of this crime-fighting stuff like I am! You can live with your mom and choose to ditch all this, and frankly, I hope you do because I don't need you around acting like you care about me!"

"There you are! We got a Super Society trouble alert!" Melvin said, sucking wind as he burst through the access door across the roof.

He tapped at his ear.

"I already sent fer the—" Melvin said between gasps. "—*Pegasus*! It'll have our uniforms in it!"

The shock dulled Eric's senses, slowing the process of forming coherent thoughts.

"What?" Eric asked. "What's going on? Why don't you have your costumes with you? When do I get a comm, anyway?"

"This was supposed to be our night off," Melvin said. "Nobody was thinking they'd need to go back and change."

"Eric is already dressed out—and he can fly on his own, remember?" Tiffany reminded as she pushed Melvin aside to step in front of him. "Ugh! Naturally, this happens just as things were heating up between Kev and me!"

"Whatever, the dance was lame," Melvin said. "Except for Eric's epic fail with Jaycee!"

Jaycee sent Melvin a look that could kill.

"Got here as fast as I could!" Yvette said, jogging through the doorway. "We don't have much intel yet, but something big is headed our way—something dangerous."

"Who's attacking what now?" Eric asked. "A supervillain?"

"Eric, this is gonna be a real fight—you up for it?" Jaycee said. "Look, just go back home and—"

"Home?! You're talking about Pantheon Tower?" Eric interjected. "You still call it home?"

"Fine, you're right," Jaycee said in a huff. "I didn't want to bring this up in front of everyone like this, but I can't go with you. My mom is driving me back to her—our—place tonight. There's no way I'm getting out of it."

The others looked at each other in stunned silence.

"Eric, I know you're a, er, special kind of hero..." Jaycee said. "A rookie, I mean..."

Thankfully, she's not bringing up how I'm totally a fake superhero, Eric thought. *She's still protecting my secret even though I put her personal business on blast. I suck so much! All of this sucks!*

"The team needs us, though," Jaycee said. "They need you."

"Need me to do what?" Eric asked. "Embarrass myself even more? Hold the team back while I'm trying not to get killed by some evil maniac?!"

"C'mon, Eric," Melvin said. "The Society sticks together, no matter what!"

"Melvin's not often right," Tiffany added. "But he's right about that, roomie."

"Don't patronize me!" Eric said. "None of you wanted me to join in the first place!"

I can't be here right now! he thought.

Anxiety clawed at his brain, quickening his pulse.

"We gotta move to the rendezvous point!" Yvette said. "Truther is on his way. Eric, if you wanna go home, we underst—"

"I may stay there for the time being, but that place will never be home!" Eric yelled.

Eric's outstretched hand stilled Melvin and

Tiffany's approach.

"I thought Pantheon Tower was only supposed to be a temporary home for you guys," Eric said. "Melvin and Tiffany will be gone as soon as someone other than Mr. Maddox adopts them, right?"

Yvette opened her lowered palms, surrendering.

"I get that you're mad right now," Yvette said. "But we have work to do."

"Of course, you could be like Go-Go," Eric said, sending a crooked eye Yvette's way. "Going nowhere 'cause nobody ever wanted you!"

Yvette shook her head in disbelief. Jaycee stepped in front of her.

"So uncalled for!" Jaycee said. "You can be pissed at me, but don't drag anyone else into your little 'mantrum!'"

"You know what, Jaycee?" Eric said. "At least Yvette is making an effort to continue being a superhero even with going to college next year! I can't believe you'd give up being Powerhouse so easily!"

Jaycee narrowed her eyes.

"Don't cross a line you can't come back from, Eric."

"You all were never my real friends! I don't even know you!"

"Eric, shut up!"

He shook his head, stunned by Jaycee's outburst. He lifted his finger, preparing to unleash another verbal onslaught.

"Don't you hear that?!" Jaycee asked.

Her worry worried Eric. He listened to the night around him but heard nothing... at first. A distant whirring crept along the air. Eric gave a concerned expression to Jaycee before turning.

A speeding comet of bluish energy headed straight for them.

"Everybody, get back," Eric ordered as if he had an inkling of what to do.

Jaycee stepped toward him.

"I said—" Eric said

The rush of air and the booming sound of engine thrusters pushed against them. Eric whipped his eyes over to see a hulking suit of armor make a heavy landing in front of him. The robotic humanoid frame stood at least four heads above him. Smoke spilled from the chrome casings attached to the thing's thick steel boots. He knew this mechanical monster well.

"Ultranaut..." Eric whispered.

He waved his arm behind him but couldn't feel or see Jaycee. Eric couldn't pry his eyes off Ultranaut's gleaming green glass helmet. The sheen from the surrounding lamps made it difficult to see through the translucent visor. The robot's boxy arms moved, and Eric trembled, taking a weak defensive stance.

"Eric, watch out!" he heard Tiffany warn from behind him.

"Wait, I've seen this thing before!" Jaycee said. "It's, it's—"

"The thing that killed my mom," Eric said in a hushed tone.

Ultranaut spread its huge hands, facing its metal palms at them.

"Eric—you need to—come with me," the robot suit's speakers spat out between bouts of static feedback.

Its rotor gears audibly struggled, and its geometrically shaped limbs fidgeted. Wires coursed in and around the suit's legs—the cords within the plated abdomen section constricted themselves into thick vines. The head wobbled in a frantic fight to regain control of itself, then stopped. It stood straight, arms at its sides. The little blue dots of light across its body blinked rapidly, then abruptly shut off. Eric held his breath.

Flat slats of blue-coated metal extended over the helmet and down over the forehead area. The angular silver steel sheets on the sides of the head curved forward, quickly connecting to form a protective faceplate. The top of the faceguard pointed down like a "V," making it resemble a menacing knight.

"Dreadnaught mode activated," the armor stated in a deep, automated voice.

In a controlled motion, it aimed its wrist-mounted cannons at Eric.

"Target acquired."

Chapter Twenty-One: *DOGFIGHT*

ERIC

"**G**UYS—RUN!" ERIC SHOUTED BEFORE SPRINGING into the air.

Dreadnaught blasted its thrusters, following him up.

"I'm not leaving!" Jaycee yelled from ten feet below.

Levitating higher as Dreadnaught's cannons remained trained on him, Eric quickened his breathing—he strained to yell back. His thumping heart pounded his sternum.

"Go! Now! Get help!"

"Come on; we gotta evacuate everyone; let's go!" Yvette ordered the others, and they followed her.

Eric made quick pats over the dark blue utility pockets lining his belt. Flipping a few lids up, his probing fingers found nothing. The thin cargo pockets on his outer thighs carried only his phone and wallet.

"Uh, 'Dreadnaught?' Wouldja believe I have all these pockets and didn't think to bring anything useful for a supervillain fight?"

White light emitted from inside Dreadnaught's barrels, charging up for a big blast.

"That's not good."

Floating backward, Eric saw Jaycee and the others making a run for it. He secretly wished she stayed, but Eric knew he couldn't risk placing Jaycee in danger, especially when she's not in costume as Powerhouse.

At least she's not alone.

Dreadnaught's lower thrusters flashed with power, and its back-mounted propulsion pack beamed with teal-colored flares.

"Uh oh," Eric mumbled.

He reached for his smartphone to call for help, but Dreadnaught popped up and rocketed toward him. Leaving his phone pocketed, Eric jettisoned himself away. Glancing over his shoulder, Eric spotted a spark—Dreadnaught zapped a laser blast. Eric spiraled to dodge, jumbling his sense of direction.

Eric bumbled down onto the paved walkway between buildings. He tumbled in and out of flying to soften the impact. He pushed himself up to see a horde of teens, staffers, and a handful of lingering media crewmembers pour out of the gymnasium. They swarmed across the grassy terrace toward him, curious to check out the commotion.

"No-no-no-no!" Eric said while throwing his hands up. "Everybody! Back in the gym!"

His running transitioned into a speedy floating motion while waving at them to seek shelter. Alarmed and confused faces met him. The crowd's phones, visors, and cameras lit up, ready to record any action. Desperate, Eric pushed his hands down while soaring toward them, but the people ignored his flailing arms.

Behind him, the armored beast's engine roared. The crowd screamed at the sight of Dreadnaught and fled for the gym with Eric trailing them. Eric faced his armored adversary only to see it burrow through the air, picking up speed. He veered upward, passing

Dreadnaught. He led his pursuer to follow him, but Dreadnaught flew too fast.

Dreadnaught bucked Eric up like a mechanical bull then yanked him back into its clutches. The crushing metal arms of the automated attacker trapped Eric. He imagined this was like being trapped in a trash compactor. Eric couldn't move or see anything past the white-painted steel but felt the forward momentum. A seismic crash shook Eric's bones. The deafening noise rattled his senses.

Eric's insides wiggled as he was flung from the hulk's body. Eric smashed into the prop box by the photobooth set, igniting a small explosion of fake mustaches and oversized novelty sunglasses.

Back in the gym, Eric thought. *Exactly where I told everyone to go.*

Hunched over. Eric peeked at a terrified group of kids huddled on one side of the dance floor.

That's just great.

Pain ached his muscles, but adrenaline triumphed enough for Eric to get to his knees. Dreadnaught stood over him, glimmering in the disco ball's speckled light. Beyond the towering automaton, Eric saw how the main entrance's metal and the concrete foundation had been wrecked—the doors had been knocked clean off. Eric would've been a stain on the hardwood floor if he hadn't been in Dreadnaught's vice.

"You—you protected me?" Eric said. "That wasn't a programming glitch, was it?"

Dreadnaught's wrist cannons pointed at Eric.

"Lethal force has been authorized," it said in its unforgiving, monotone voice.

"Definitely a glitch!" Eric said.

The faculty members directed the students to rush to the back of the court, leaving them in the line of fire.

"Everybody! Out of the gym!" Eric yelled.

A sparse group of teens bolted for the locker rooms, but many of them lined the back wall. With few options of escape and a killer robot blocking the way out, they weren't budging. Glowing white energy radiated from Dreadnaught's cannons. Eric had to act fast.

He shifted his eyes.

The punchbowl!

Afloat, Eric dashed to the table on his left and grabbed the enormous clear plastic rim. He whipped up the bowl, sloshing the bubbly drink, and heaved it at the machine. Sticky-sweet red juice splashed over Dreadnaught's armor, dripping off the slick steel plating and wires. Dreadnaught peered down at its punch-splattered body, lowering its gauntlet.

"Are you serious?" Tiffany shouted.

Eric glanced at the huddled mass, half a basketball court behind him. Tiffany stood in front of her girl pack amongst the other students.

"I thought it would short-circuit him!" Eric said. "Can't someone use one of their many smart devices and call the cops or something?!"

Jaycee, Melvin, and Yvette did what they could to herd the frightened masses, but panic made for a formidable enemy.

Where is that helicopter? Eric thought. *If the team doesn't get their super-suits soon, it's just me, which means we're all in big trouble!*

Dreadnaught snapped its cannons back up, inciting shrieks of terror from the captive audience. Eric propelled himself to the rafters. Energy rays missed him by a fraction of an inch. Arching at full speed, Eric led the blasts away from the civilians. The lasers struck the metal support grating, sparkling upon impact. Severed pylons fell to the floor. As he curved along the upper wall, Eric saw a few kids narrowly avoid getting stabbed by shrapnel.

"Sorry!" he yelled to them while rushing toward Dreadnaught.

Eric flew past his aggressor like a speeding bullet, blurring through the jagged hole and out of the building. The rumble of Dreadnaught's afterburners signaled Eric to boost himself even faster. His pursuer bolted, hot on his heels.

Stay on me! Leave the civilians out of this!

Up, up, up. Eric's instincts pushed him above the school grounds and into the dark clouds.

"Let's see how high you can go!" Eric said through the frenzied wind.

Fists outstretched, he flew higher, using every ounce of willpower to accelerate. His aerial abilities remained a mystery to him still, but desperation was in Eric's DNA.

Dreadnaught gained on him, pushing Eric harder and faster into the unknown.

Come on; you can do this. At the very least, you'll buy yourself some time.

Scared, Eric pressed onward to the stars. The thermal insulation in his suit struggled with the icy air. Keeping his eyes open proved near impossible, and his teeth chattered to the point that he thought they would shatter. Eric had to decide how far he could take this.

Releasing from his rapid ascent, Eric's insides jangled. Giving himself to gravity was easy since he was about to pass out anyway. His lucidity held long enough to see Dreadnaught overshoot him, disappearing into the upper limits of the troposphere.

Hazy hopes that Dreadnaught couldn't function at that extreme height—or that maybe its gears would freeze—were the only coherent thoughts Eric mustered. Fading consciousness hid him from feeling the full force of the dangerous descent. Eric was blacking out in three... two...

Wake up! he commanded himself.

Adrenaline coursed through his veins, allowing him to fight back the sleep and confusion.

You can do this. Slow, steady—you got this.

His errant freefall drifted him over the school's football field. The big, green rectangle below grew bigger with every second. Eric extended his fingers like a wizard summoning a protective spell. With a thought, his body slowed, readying for a cushioned landing on the turf not far below. Turning his head, Eric saw a shimmering blue streak.

"You've gotta be kidding me—"

Dreadnaught sped like a missile aimed right at him. Eric made a complete stop, sliding over as the armored attacker charged past him. Eric watched Dreadnaught's momentum carry itself, unable to pull up in time and—

CRASH!

The merciless machine lay a heap of metal on the five-yard line. Eric touched down on the colored grass of the end zone. From a safe distance, he inspected the unmoving, facedown Dreadnaught. Its little lights deactivated, and smoke plumed from the inactive thrusters. Eric planted his hands on his kneepads, exhaling a deep, relieved breath.

Eric had planned on avoiding stepping onto this field throughout his high school career.

And it sucks even worse than I imagined.

A tidal wave of fatigue overtook him. Eric plopped down on the ground, staring at the lifeless husk. Eric defeated it—the monster that killed his mother. His father's creation lay dead by Eric's hands. Eric's body rebelled against him. He rolled over in exhaustion.

Whrrr! Clank! Whrrr!

The churning of gears prompted Eric to do not only the best sit-up of his life but perhaps his first-ever attempt. Dreadnaught stirred across the goal line, standing itself one section at a time. Eric shuddered. The shock sparked the all-too-familiar anguish of prolonged stretches of non-flying.

"C-c-c'mon!" Eric stammered through the internal torture. "Really bad timing!"

Sequential blue lights blipped up its frame as Dreadnaught powered up its cannons. The looming colossus took a rigid step forward with its weapons locked onto Eric. He knew he should move but fear paralyzed Eric.

"Target acquired," Dreadnaught stated. "Primary directive: terminate with extreme prejudice."

Crackling energy spit from the barrels, followed by a discharge of glowing laser fire. Panting, Eric covered his eyes, readying for the worst.

Bwang! Eric flashed his eyes open to see a barricade of pink-and-orange-colored costumed girls absorbing the blast.

"If there's no off-switch, can we at least find the mute button on this robo-hobo?" a collective of cynical voices said in unison.

Tiffany, appearing in costume as Extra, fizzled her duplicates into nothingness. The wall dissipated, leaving the lone authentic redhead standing in the way of Dreadnaught.

The armored destroyer marched for the unimpressed superhero. A flurry of hyperactive strikes clouded around Dreadnaught, stopping it in its tracks. It convulsed with each supersonic hit. Dreadnaught keeled over, fidgeting as it rolled onto its back. Yvette, dressed as Go-Go, materialized next to Extra. The two heroines crossed their arms, satisfied with the takedown.

"Man, great timing on getting the uniforms!" Eric said to the ladies. "I thought I was a goner for sure!"

Still pulling up the trousers of his outfit, Melvin arrived as Supercut, huffing and puffing from the sideline.

"Let's—less—les' cut to the chase!" he sputtered while catching his breath.

Fikt! Supercut popped a long finger-claw while propping his yellow boot onto Dreadnaught's chest plate. He sliced the meshy neck area of Dreadnaught. Sparks spat from the severed cords.

"Lessee who we're dealin' with here," Supercut said, retracting his blade.

He placed his gloved hands onto the sides of Dreadnaught's helmet.

"What in the—" Eric blurted, levitating off the grass.

Jaycee sprinted into Eric's periphery, joining Supercut. Eric nearly called out for Powerhouse but remembered Jaycee was not—and could not be—in costume. Supercut hoisted the chartreuse casing off Dreadnaught, but Eric couldn't see. Extra and Go-Go crowded around Supercut, further obstructing the view.

"David Boxworth?!" Go-Go exclaimed.

"Eric!" David cried out. "Where's my son?!"

Eric hurried to his teammates and pried his way through. His father's frantic face stared back at him.

"BRAIN got the suit! I was going to take us away from Pantheon!" David babbled. "I lost control; something forced a full system reset! Dreadnaught took over! You have to—!"

Supercut pointed his clenched fist at David's mouth.

"Shut yer—" he said, sucking wind. "—trap!"

"Hey!" Eric said, pushing Supercut.

The husky boy snarled at him.

"We'll take it from here, Eric," Go-Go said, placing a firm hand on his shoulder.

The *whupping* of the *Pegasus'* rotary wings chopping the wind entered Eric's ears. Downfield, the squad's sleek, silver, aquatic-like helicopter landed on its long struts. Its loud engine dominated all surrounding noise. The rear access hatch lowered, and inside, Truther stood. He pointed, and three large white orb-shaped drones flew out.

The cyber-balls hovered over David, releasing bright-orange coils that ensnared his bulky outer armor.

"Wait-wait-wait!" Eric shouted, attempting to follow, but Go-Go and Extra blocked his path.

"We'll get down to the bottom of this, I promise," Go-Go assured.

Eric watched in disbelief as the drones struggled to haul his dad away—the suit must've been heavier than a bus. David fell silent; Eric wondered if he'd been tranquilized.

Eric's Super Society compatriots hightailed it to their ride. Jaycee hesitated, slow to approach Eric. The forceful winds had ruffled her pink dress. Their last exchange hung between them like a dense fog. He drifted to her. Jaycee's eyes opened like wide saucers.

"Eric, I—"

"Don't!" he snapped. "Just... don't."

Eric flew to the *Pegasus*, unsure if he'd be allowed to see his father or if he wanted to.

Chapter Twenty-Two: *FLOAT*

ERIC

THE SPRAWLING FOOD COURT'S NEVER-ENDING racks of gourmet cuisine lost their luster. Over the weekend, Eric's trips to the cafeteria had reached double-digits, but not even the tastiest treat satiated his true craving—peace of mind.

"Maybe Mr. Maddox summoned me here for a last meal," he said to himself. "Dad strapping on the Ultranaut armor was too crazy. There's no way Mr. Maddox will trust me to be on the team now. Not that I blame him."

Eric strolled by a display case packed with decadent cheesecakes then entered the lonely lunch line.

"My father, my problem, I guess," Eric said softly. "I have to settle this somehow."

He slid a flat, dark green plastic tray across the three metal rods adjoined to the long row of food selection cabinets.

"I can't believe the stupid robot dog was right about responsibility," Eric said aloud. "This would be a lot easier if even thinking about Dad didn't make me wanna puke."

He peered at the deserted sea of circular tables. "It's not even three yet. Where is everybody?"

Farther along the serving track, sealed steel lids rested behind glass cases. Eric guided his empty tray down the line with two fingers dipped below the rack. He made a little game of hurdling his digits between the metal support bars placed intermittently on the rods' underside. Blank mustard-colored walls stood beyond the row where Eric thought a lunch lady should be. He stopped at the site of a powered-down ice cream dispenser and sighed. Behind it, a solitary stainless-steel refrigerator waited for the following day's rush.

"One would assume that a company with the slogan 'Think Infinitely' would have a headquarters that operated twenty-four hours a day."

He recognized Valerie Cooper's voice, but not her defrosted cadence.

"Or at least a fully staffed cafeteria during peak business hours," she said.

Valerie strolled by a few empty cushioned red chairs, with Jaycee trailing not far behind. Valerie's shoulder-length hair swayed as she strutted across the tiled floor. She brushed the dust from her sharp light blue button-collar top with black slacks, finished off with matching sensible flats on her feet. It was her usual boring teacher outfit, but Valerie's smirk made her far livelier than any time Eric had seen her in class.

Jaycee, however, looked like she was being led to a firing squad.

I know the feeling, Eric thought.

Across the spacious room, Baron emerged from around a corner. Dressed to impress, Baron entered wearing a sophisticated dark gray suit. His face, though, stayed solemn and stiff as he approached them.

"Delighted as I am to see you," Baron said,

greeting his ex-wife and daughter, "pulling Jaycee out of school wasn't necessary."

"No need to worry. It's an excused absence," Valerie said. "This is the only time you said you could carve out for a meeting. So, I made it work."

"Business never sleeps," Baron said. "Ongoing developments in several projects require my constant supervision."

Eric lingered by a cash register a few yards from them. He felt unsure if they had noticed him.

Ummm... Should I just leave?

"Regrettably," Baron said, "this is the only chance I've had to check up on Eric."

A tablet attached to the register by Eric awoke with a soft white light. Unassuming as it was, Eric thought it might as well have been a spotlight. Nevertheless, he resisted the urge to fly out of there.

"I hope you are not opposed to his presence here," Baron said, nodding at Eric.

Jaycee momentarily looked away from the floor. Her eyes fluttered at the sight of Eric. She glanced back down, but her grinning mother was happy to call out to him.

"Missed you in class this morning, Eric," Valerie said.

Eric's lips twisted at the awkwardness. Something commanded him to check his white shirt for stains or crumbs from previous snack scarfing sessions.

The good news—at least I'm not naked like in a bad dream, he thought. *Bad news—I'm not dreaming, and this is really happening.*

"Hey, Ms. Cooper," Eric said with a jerky nod. "I was, uh, sick today."

She replied with a slow, confused nod. Jaycee curved her, walking up to Eric. Baron and Valerie resumed talking about signing documents and other legal mumbo jumbo, but Eric focused on the sour girl approaching him.

"I copied notes for you," Jaycee said. "Well, Melvin did, but he gave me a copy."

"Oh, cool, thanks."

She looked down at the purple zigzag pattern on her t-shirt.

"Hey, so," Eric said, sheepish. "I wanted to talk to you."

"Something wrong with your phone?"

The remark hurt Eric nearly as much as the tiny biting sensation in his feet—the mysterious force punished him for going too long without flying.

"...Just need to make some final reviews, and we're done with the paperwork," he overheard Valerie say to Baron.

I can't risk using my power in front of everyone—stupid me forgetting the backpack.

"Gonna have to make this fast," Eric said, grimacing at the stabbing ache. "I'm an idiot. A big, dumb baby who overreacted. I'm..."

He made his best *oof* face, wincing at the spiky tingling up his legs.

"Is that your weakness acting up?" Jaycee asked. "Or does it hurt that much to say you're sorry?"

Wisps of letters struggled to form the words Eric wanted to say. Constricting discomfort split his brain in disjointed directions.

"You said you don't have a lot of friends, remember?" Eric said, squinting. "Well, I don't have much experience in that department, either."

A few yards beyond Baron and Valerie, a pair of blonde women wearing similar pantsuits exited an elevator. Eric would've thought they were hot if it weren't for the anguish.

Jaycee peeked over to see what had grabbed his attention.

"Ah, Chelsea and Dahlia," she said. "The airhead twins."

"What's up with the whole 'model' employee thing?"

"Pantheon won't outright say it," Jaycee said, "but their philosophy is everything about them should be beautiful, from the hardware to the assistants."

Eric puckered his face, leaning against the cash register station. Valerie looked over. Eric took deep breaths, attempting to act casual. She resumed her dull discussion with Baron.

"Believe me, Dad's wandering eyes were brought up in the divorce," Jaycee said. "Speaking of hating your dad's guts... have you talked to Mr. B—?"

"I don't want anything to do with him."

The mere image of David stung Eric's mind's eye. Then a different ache struck him. Eric gritted his teeth, grunting as he suppressed a cough.

Jaycee shook her head.

"Eric, if you need to go float or something, just—"

"No, no, I want to say this," Eric pleaded. "My powers and why it hurts when I don't use them—it's something I don't understand and maybe never will. When I first flew, I thought I was cursed or something."

Raised eyebrows accented Jaycee's wide eyes. Her thin frown looked anything but hopeful.

"But you, more than anybody," Eric said, "more than your dad even—you showed me how amazing my power is. How amazing I am."

The corner of her mouth perked up a bit, almost smiling, but not quite yet.

"I dunno how to fix a relationship because I've had

zero practice in it," Eric admitted. "Pardon the pun, but I'm winging it here."

"That was funny," she said with a soft chuckle. "That's the best feeling, isn't it? To finally have the right opportunity to say this awesome thing you've been holding in."

Eric caught a glimpse of strawberry blonde hair disappearing into the elevator.

Wait, that wasn't an airhead twin...

Chelsea and Dahlia stood at the other end of the food court, waiting by a coffee brewer. Eric blinked half a dozen times, trying to confirm his unreliable vision.

Am I seeing things?

"Uh, flyboy," Jaycee said, noticeably irked at his inattention. "This is that opportunity to say something awesome."

Brushing past her, Eric nearly fell over a chair as he stumbled over to the elevators.

"That's pretty flushed, Eric!" he heard Jaycee call from behind. "Be that way, then! See if I even care!"

Eric's determined dash blurred Baron's and Valerie's confused faces. Moving past a mural of the Pantheon lightning bolt logo, Eric approached the elevator and rammed his thumb onto the "up" button. He had no way of knowing what direction the mystery woman could have gone, but he'd scour the entire tower if he had to.

It couldn't have been her... he thought, grimacing with each painful step. *I'm going loopy with pain. S'gotta be it.*

The silver doors opened, and he stepped inside the mirrored interior. The twenty-seventh-floor marker was lit on the upper paneling, which Eric took to indicate the woman's location.

"Of course, it's one of the many mystery levels I

haven't been to."

He drummed his thumb on the button. Pulleys yanked the car upward; he let his body follow by going weightless. Eric's eyes rolled back in euphoric relief.

The doors retracted, taking him by surprise. His reflections turned with him as he charged into an overwhelming shock to his system—total darkness. Faint auxiliary lanterns lit one by one, brightening small portions of the reddish-brown walls. The space was not much larger than any of the building's other hallways. The high-mounted lamps emitted a low light but shined enough for Eric not to feel like he was in a horror movie.

"How does anybody know where to go in this labyrinth?"

A sliver of white light sparked from what could've been miles down the long corridor. Flying, Eric picked up the pace. The thin glowing rectangle grew closer now, only mere feet away.

When Eric finally reached the end, which came far sooner than he had anticipated, he found himself on one side of a large steel door. It denied him the easy, automated access every other area offered. His fingers sifted through the dim light but couldn't feel any buttons, dials, or sensors.

"Authorized personnel only," a mechanical voice said. "Access denied."

"Robot Door, this is gonna sound crazy, but hear me out," Eric said. "I dunno if I'm even in the right place, but I could've sworn I saw—"

"Super Society member voice recognition successful. Access granted."

Guess Dad wasn't kidding about superheroes getting special treatment.

The doorway slid open, revealing an intense light

bombarding his eyes. Eric raised an arm, shielding himself from the glare. His vision eventually adjusted; a swirl of colors morphed into shapeless objects, taking form. Eric blinked, bringing the image better into focus.

Clothing racks?

Eric entered on foot, brushing his hand along a row of multicolored leather tunics with patterned textures imprinted up and down the sleeves. Dull gray winged helmets lay on a cart next to an arrangement of blue and green bracelets and yellow utility belts with baggy pockets. Just ahead of Eric, a glass container encased various padded pieces of body armor. A bank of translucent storage containers sat unattended on the other side of the hanging rack, from shoebox-size to large crates. Inside them appeared to be masks, gloves, and folded-up capes.

I'm in the superhero sewing room? Eric thought. *I'm insane. This is what being insane is like.*

"You look lost. This building can be a maze, huh?"

It was a voice he'd recognize anywhere. He looked behind him, and there she was, beautiful and vibrant. Eric's body felt nimble and hollow, ready to be filled with nothing but her energy. Impossible as it seemed, sound crept out of Eric's mouth.

"Mom?"

Chapter Twenty-Three: *DESCENT*

ERIC

"**F**IVE REEEALLLLLY LONG HUGS IS maybe enough for right now, huh, Eric?"

Releasing his arms from Eliza was like leaving his warm bed on a chilly morning to go to school. The unmistakable strawberry blonde hair flowed just a tad below her shoulders. She was just like Eric remembered her. This woman was no memory, though—his mother, Eliza, stood before him, a warm presence in a violet blouse. Every word was gospel.

"Anyway, like I was saying," Eliza said, "the most challenging thing I had to make was when Extra requested a sequined tactical vest."

Go-Go, Supercut, and Extra's costumes hung on a rack above a storage cabinet.

Their gear is still attached to their uniforms, Eric thought. *That could mean they'd be ready for action at a moment's notice—or somebody rushed the uniforms to storage.*

Either way, it was of no concern to Eric. He hopped onto the bin, utterly enchanted. He followed Eliza's every slight movement with starry eyes.

She's here, Eric thought through a dreamy fog.

It was as if his brain was out of breath.

I don't know how it's possible, but she's here!

"Utility belts and those kinds of things aren't hard," Eliza continued. "But Extra had specific design demands with glitter and diamonds—the mock-up looked amazing, but Truther nixed the whole thing. Shame, too; I was proud of that gaudy mess."

Eric could've sat there all day and through the night, repeatedly hearing Eliza's soft chuckle.

"For one of Mr. Maddox's super-dupers, you've got a real interest in crime-fighter garments. I never get visits from members of the team here."

"I love designing outfits and stuff!" Eric said, perking his head up like an excited toddler. "Mr. Maddox even let me sketch out my own costume!"

"How fun!"

Flashbacks of hearing about his mother's untimely demise haunted the back of Eric's skull. The ghosts of the past were not strong enough to cloud this moment, however.

Don't wake up, Eric, he ordered himself. *If this is a hallucination, just let it be.*

"Does it ruin a bit of the mystique?" Eliza asked. "Knowing that the paragons of truth and justice all have to get measured and fitted?"

"I guess I never thought about it, but someone has to sew up these costumes, right?"

She took a small tape measure roll and extended it across an oversized yellow tunic spread over a wide craft table. It resembled the look and size of what Supercut would wear.

"I suppose I never put much thought into who or what programs all the gizmos around here," she said while pushing a needle onto the collar to pin down the textured top. "Making sure all the gadgets work must have Mr. Maddox working 'round the clock."

Eric's gaze lingered on her, but her head lowered, focused on marking where she planned to make alterations. Eliza gave a gentle smirk, oblivious to the awestruck boy sitting five feet from her.

Nobody must know about her, Eric deduced. *Do I really want to find out what's going on here?*

"So, uh, how long have you been a superhero seamstress?"

You got her back. That's all that matters.

"Oh, I began here... What has it been?" she said. "Three years now."

He took a deep breath. An urgency was building in Eric's belly, making him sick with guilt. Eric slid off the countertop and onto his feet. His heart threatened to beat through his chest. His breathing grew labored, like sucking a milkshake through a thin straw.

"Listen, I don't know how or why this is happening, but this is my chance... I need to tell you I'm sorry," Eric said as tears welled.

He approached the table, standing across from her as she worked. His spilled guts went unnoticed.

"I hate Dad right now, but please, you know you can talk to him, right? Don't be angry with him. Take everything out on me. I'm the one who deserves it."

After swiping a pair of scissors, Eliza started with tiny cuts on the extra-large shirt sleeve.

"The day you di—Ultranaut, er, Dreadnaught malfunctioning... You wouldn't have been there if I didn't beg you to go! You left, and it's my fault! Everything is my fault!"

Eliza ceased her scissoring, placing the cutters down with the same ease one would lay down a newborn. Then, carefully, she rose to meet Eric's anxious eyes.

"I can't believe I'm just now putting this together," Eliza said.

Eric held his breath.

"Your real name is Eric Boxworth, right? That means David Boxworth must be your father! I heard he was working here now. He must be so proud to have a superhero son!"

Eric's insides hollowed as his soul melted from his body. Whether she was a hallucination, a ghost, or an afterimage of his truest desires, this wasn't who he remembered. Eliza had been far more intelligent than he ever could've hoped to be. The person in front of him was an ethereal goddess, but she wasn't his mother.

Eric wondered if he cared.

Theories of amnesia or some traumatic brain injury bubbled up in his thoughts. He forced syllables to reach his tongue.

"Mom—er, Eliza?" Eric said, unsure of how to even breathe at this point. "My flying... It's not from the backpack I wear like everyone thinks... I can fly. Really fly."

"All these automated whatevers keep advancing. It's maddening trying to keep up with modern technology."

She nonchalantly rummaged through a junk drawer in the cabinet behind her.

"I lost another holo-imager. Third one this week!" Eliza said. "Great, now I have to go get another camera."

Eliza walked around the table, brushing past Eric on her way to the door. Desperate for some form of reciprocation, he followed her out.

"Mr. Maddox likes seeing three-dee pictures of the

new uniforms," she said. "Isn't that neat?"

She walked at a brisk pace down the dim corridor. Eric kept a short, habitual distance as if he didn't want to bother her. As they passed one faceless door after another, Eric felt that Eliza had forgotten he was there.

Finally, she stopped at a seemingly random doorway. Without the need for any command from Eliza, the hatch slid open. Eric snuck in behind her seconds before the door re-shut itself. He found himself in an elevator, smaller than any other lifts he'd been in. Eliza pressed a numberless white button on the panel, and they went up. The steel walls' distorted reflections messed with Eric's senses.

"Do you need something from this storage level as well?" Eliza asked. "Can't imagine why you'd need anything for your super team from there. It's mostly old junk."

"Dad's made a living off junk these past few years."

With a disorientating shift, the elevator stopped, then the doors opened. A darkened crypt-like area waited on the other side, similar to the other secretive hallways but far vaster. Eric trailed Eliza as she strolled by several aisles of tall, cylindrical pods. The overhead lamps' limited proximity hid the total number of vertical coffin-like hunks of metal.

"The prototype weapons and doodads are back around here," Eliza mentioned with a casualness that betrayed the eeriness of the dungeon.

Eric held back, careful to let her walk ahead. Looking at the pods, he spotted the horizontal metal plates sealed over where someone's face might be.

"Are you also some type of... prototype?"

The words tasted like poison, but Eric's curiosity forced the question.

"I remember the explosion the most, funny as that

sounds," she said, much to Eric's shock. "Not really the robot going crazy and shooting everything. No, it was when its laser-thingy hit a generator, I believe it was. The brightness, the heat. I still see it like it was yesterday."

The sharp words stung like a slap to his face. Eric froze in his tracks while Eliza continued ahead of him.

She's describing the day of her death, Eric thought, shivering as if a ghost passed through him.

"I have memories of seeing everything from up high, like an angel," Eliza went on.

Eric stalled, slow to keep up.

"Then I awoke," Eliza said. "And I'm here, up to my neck in leather and spandex."

She halted at a shadowed space untouched by the lights.

"I think this is where I'm supposed to be," she said.

Eric walked like he was moving through quicksand, hesitant to join her.

"Isn't it so fun that you're a superhero?" she said. "Such a perfect way to keep a close eye on your progress, right?"

"Who brought you here?" Eric asked in a near whisper.

He felt as if the slick tombs on either side of him were closing in. The farther they walked, the darker the room got. Eliza disappeared into a dark space, deeper into the vast room. The shadowy spot seemed to repel light.

"Mr. Maddox, of course!" she answered, fully submerged in the abyss.

The quietness between her words danced up Eric's spine.

"I hope he finds what he's looking for soon," Eliza said. "He's spent so many years searching for another one like me. There are so many fakers out there; isn't that sad?"

"What do you mean, others like you? Aren't you, you know... an android?"

A single overhead lamp burst to life, shining blinding light directly over where Eliza stood. Eric fought to keep his eyes open, and he could see the pod standing next to Eliza through his fingers. She faced the large shell, but this one was different. There was a clear window panel the size of a large computer monitor near the top. The lamp's glare made it difficult to see who or what was inside.

"I hate, hate, hate it when people refer to them as androids or robots."

The familiar voice bellowed from the surrounding blackness.

"More accurately stated, they are synthetic, made of artificially produced living tissue."

Baron stepped into the light, bearing a warm smile for Eliza. Standing tall in his charcoal suit and slick black shoes, Baron blocked Eric's view of the pod.

"Some models are more advanced than others," Baron said, welcoming the delightful grin she had for him.

"Mr. Maddox? What's going on?!"

"I place a high value on the truth, but the timing of its revelation is something I carefully calculate," he said. "This is, admittedly, premature."

Squinting as his eyes struggled to adjust, Eric stretched his arms out wide, open to receiving an explanation for this absurdity.

"Um, is this your secret mancave, Mr. Maddox?" Eric asked, nervous about the answer he could receive. "You chill here with your weird petri-dish-people?"

A knowing grin spread under Baron's mustache.

"We're beyond playful rhetoric, Eric. Ask what you really want to ask."

"Okay, then," Eric said, unsheathing his angry confusion. "Mind explaining why you have a-a-a clone?! Of my mom?!"

"Eliza is my most successful attempt, but still, sadly, a failure."

Her cheery smile held tight. Eliza's eyes remained full of hope in a soulless way. Baron looked over at her, opening his palm to her head.

"Don't touch her!" Eric yelled, though his bravery did not extend to his feet.

"Eliza is far more advanced than, say, Chelsea or Dahlia," Baron said. "Her memory replication is, in itself, remarkable but falls drastically short of the ultimate goal."

Baron cupped the air around her cheek but did not touch her skin.

"She remembers Dreadnaught's disastrous weapons demonstration. The sensation of ascending. Even dying, to an extent."

Baron sent his calm eyes to Eric's distressed face.

"But, as I said, her memory is incomplete."

Eliza stayed put, brainlessly beaming, while Baron approached Eric.

"Certain imperfections are by design," Baron revealed.

Eric took a step back into a defensive stance.

"I found it simpler to block out me retrieving her right after the power generator explosion," Baron said. "In the chaos, it was no challenge to arrange for a drone to transport her here quickly. It was my hangar, after all. Loaning one of my facilities to host your father's career-defining moment was something David never thanked me for, by the way."

"You tried to save her? This is crazy..."

Get a grip, Eric! he thought, desperate to put the pieces of reality back together. *This has got to be all some big mistake.*

"Look, Mr. Maddox," Eric said, holding up a hand in surrender. "I know everybody said it was a freak accident, but... You're not the one I blame for it."

Baron placed a hand on Eric's shoulder. What he lacked in fatherly reassurance, he made up for in deathly dismay.

"You're a very bright young man, Eric," Baron said. "You possess an aspect of intellect your father does not share."

The overhead lamp poured over Baron's face, making his eyes look like shadowy pits.

"David is prideful and passionate, two qualities that have hindered him for years."

His darkened gaze drifted back to Eliza.

"You're no doubt piecing together that I abducted your mother and left you to think the faulty machine killed her."

"You killed my mom?!" Eric said, sliding out from Baron's grip.

"If I may correct you, it was your father who killed her love, who killed her spirit, and killed her future by refusing to let go of his foolish ambitious obsessions."

Eric levitated a few inches, forgetting gravity.

"The linear deduction is you would've pursued what Eliza told you, then you'd tell your father, causing a distraction from him completing the new MegaCore," Baron said. "I'm finally on the cusp of being able to stop withholding truths anyway. The world will find out soon enough, so I may as well inform you now so you can focus on posing as a superhero."

"I'm telling my dad, and we're getting as far away

from here as possible!"

Baron stroked his mustache.

"I would never condone breaking up a family."

Rattled, Eric forced his shaky legs to push him higher.

"I should've never let Jaycee take me anywhere near this place!" Eric said. "I always knew you were one of these wealthy eccentric types, but not straight-up demented!"

"You'd deprive yourself of being with your mother?"

"That-that thing?!" Eric shouted, pointing at the mindlessly smiling woman. "That perversion from your sick—sick!—mind isn't my mom!"

"No, she is not," Baron agreed. "This is."

Baron moved aside, providing a full view of the pod. Eric approached it to see past the polished glass's sheen.

"Oh my..."

"She sustained a near-fatal injury from a piece of shrapnel from the explosion," Baron said. "I've preserved her here. She's known only dreams since."

Eric trembled, and the tears he'd been holding back broke free and streamed down his face. Behind the clear pane stood his mother, the real Eliza, held in place by black restraints clamped onto her shoulders. Even suspended in time, age had lined her lovely face. Her hair retained its youthful vibrancy, and her eyes were closed, deep in slumber.

Eric pressed his fingertips onto the cool glass. He rose, pressing his forehead onto the bottom portion of the pane. Beneath Eric's arm, Baron reached and slid his hand over a bare area of the pod's surface. The outline of a square with rounded edges formed, revealing a tablet-sized panel that retracted into itself.

It uncovered a sleek screen and a small assembly of buttons below. Baron depressed a circular, flat knob. The monitor displayed her vitals.

"I've maintained her health," Baron said. "All the tests and procedures did nothing to revive her from her coma, but I harbor hope for her eventual recovery."

With his forehead resting on the steel below the window frame, Eric felt Baron's words sink into his ears and ooze down to his stomach.

"What tests?" Eric muttered more than asked.

It wasn't just the thought of poking and prodding Eliza that sickened him.

He's gonna do the same to me, Eric thought. *He was always going to.*

"I confess to weak moments of doubting what I had witnessed," Baron said. "Too many times, I had to renew my dedication. My obsession, it turned out, was discovering the root of how your mother evaded those initial blasts from Dreadnaught."

Eric watched a tear drop to the tiled floor.

"What..." he said in a defeated breath. "What are you talking about?"

"Her ability to fly, of course."

Eric's head snapped up, his wide eyes staring at his static mother.

"It happened so quickly," Baron said. "There, at the weapons demonstration, I saw what no one was meant to see. I postulate Eliza reacted on pure instinct to levitate as she did, unaware she possessed such power. In a fleeting instant of primal survival, she hovered and flew a short distance across the room to dodge Dreadnaught's barrage. I deleted all digital traces of this, but the sole video copy I kept is something I've studied every frame of."

Eric's blood rushed with a mixture of rage and

confusion. He backed away from the stasis pod, away from Baron.

"She passed on her gift to you, Eric."

Mom could fly like me?! Did Dad know?

Sinking to the floor, Eric stumbled backward. A fluster of terror surged through him, igniting his nerves.

"Don't you see? It's genetic!" Baron shouted, followed by a euphoric laugh. "My theory of the existence of superior humans is true!"

Eric turned, bolting down the aisle, bumping into a pod as he made his escape.

"After creating so many synthetics, I resorted to cybernetic means," Baron continued. "But no drone could ever replicate Eliza's natural ability."

Eric burrowed toward the elevator. He slammed his hands on the door, stopping himself. Patting down the walls around the hatch, he felt no buttons or switches.

"Come on! Door open!" Eric ordered, desperate for a verbal command to do the trick.

"The Super Society was supposed to be my way of publicly seeking out others like Eliza."

Baron's voice moved in the shadows.

"Time and time again, those so bold to show off their powers were all dependent on a suit or some other mechanical assistance. Such asinine frauds."

"Pot and kettle, Mr. Maddox!" Eric yelled back.

He slammed a frustrated fist onto the unmoving metal elevator door.

"Gotta get help," Eric whispered. "Gotta get Mom out of here!"

He flew in the opposite direction of Baron's voice, speeding through gaps of darkness the dim lights produced.

"Kismet guided you to me," Baron said, still unseen but sounding dangerously close. "With you under my control as Eric Icarus, I can observe your development until my ultimate agenda is primed for execution. And, honestly, it was hardly a challenge to convince you to live out a fantasy—a life—your father could never provide!"

Eric halted, nearly crashing into a wall.

"Your mere existence vindicates my efforts!" Baron yelled. "Powered people are real, and soon, I'll join your elite race!"

Can't think about all this super-people stuff, Eric thought, pushing his mind through Baron's onslaught of unearthed secret horrors. *Just find a way out of here!*

He propelled himself off the wall, only to get lost deeper into the maze of tombs.

"I've been gracious, Eric. I've freely provided you— as well as David and Jaycee's mother while we're on the topic of handouts—with everything you desire. None of that will matter once I transcend. Even the other members of the Super Society will no longer serve my purpose."

"The MegaCore is just something to keep my dad busy until you carry out your nefarious plan, huh?"

Eric felt his way through the obscurity but touched only more steel chambers.

"Will he still get paid after your little master race thing or whatever it is you're doing?"

Eric prayed his cocksure comment would throw off Baron, buying him time to think of an escape plan. Eric turned, startled to see Baron standing before him.

"David's invention is the most important factor. I need a strong enough battery capable of powering the transference process. Eliza's gifts will live on in me."

"What're you gonna do with that power anyway, huh?" Eric said, fighting not to look away.

Keep him talking!

Baron cocked a half-smile.

"Take over the world, of course."

"Y-you think just being able to fly will do that?" Eric said, trembling. "Look at where it got me!"

"You have such a narrow scope of your abilities."

Eric's brain scrambled for exit strategies but came up blank. Baron stepped forward, and Eric backed up, shuffling his feet and dipping as if tripping over air.

"Command over world leaders," Baron said. "Limitless wealth. Influence over society. With proper use of your power, so much is possible.'

Baron's hand closed around Eric's throat. Eric heaved, desperate for air.

"Before you choose to defy me, think of how much I'm hurting you now—and how much I could hurt your father."

"Leave... my dad..." Eric coughed out.

"David's safety is up to you. You'll join me willingly anyway because let's face it. I've been more of a mentor to you than your father could've ever been."

He tossed Eric down by a nearby pod. Wheezing, Eric rolled onto his back. He looked up at the tomb, erected like an ominous monolith. He tilted his head to see into the window panel. A plaque displayed a name, but Eric didn't need it to recognize the prisoner inside.

Time Thief's lifeless husk hung within the tomb. The deadened villain served as a grim omen of Baron's true nature. Next in the series of pods were similar units, each with nameplates just below their sealed window panels. Enough light made the codenames legible: Blowhard, Demono, and Anomalita. Eric had a hunch that these super-criminals didn't get so much as even a trial.

"Have I satisfied your curiosity?" Baron said, speaking in a low, menacing tone.

Eric watched Baron's shiny shoes step closer to him through squinted eyes. In the ailing light, Eric saw his frightened face reflected in Baron's slick shoes.

"I've kept Jaycee and her mother waiting long enough."

"What're you gonna do to Jaycee—?!"

Baron's hands shot outward, gripping Eric's arms like steel vices. He hoisted Eric with ease. Instinct sparked action to fly, but Eric could only yelp in pain. Even without the Truther power suit, the man bore formidable strength—Eric wasn't going anywhere.

The pod next to him opened like a casket. Eric reached for the door, but Baron shoved him inside. The otherwise featureless outer shell of the vertical pod contrasted with the open door's intricate details. Eric likened the side facing inward to something like an upright cockpit.

"Mr. Maddox, please—!"

The door shut, *clicking* with each lock. With Eric's arms stuck at his sides, he wiggled but had no room to move in the cramped space. His breaths came out in short, frantic bursts. He felt himself become afloat—the tall tube wasn't meant for a short teenager. Eric had enough room to rise, high enough to look through the viewing panel, but that was the extent of his freedom.

Baron approached, getting too close for comfort in front of Eric's face. The thick glass between them did little to put Eric at ease.

"Reserve your energy, young Mr. Icarus," Baron said through a speaker. "The stronger you are, the more useful you are to me. You'll see this in time."

"If I'm so powerful, then just use me!" Eric

shouted with quivering lips. "Leave my mom alone!"

"Eliza remains the primary source of power for my transformation. However, my intentions for you, Eric, are far more expansive."

Eric's darting eyes spotted an operations panel mounted at mid-chest level. Its console was complete with an ergonomic keyboard, touchpad, and a multitude of small monitors.

"This is the same model of piloting chamber your father will operate when the MegaCore is complete," Baron said, his breath fogging the glass. "What beautiful symmetry. It's like poetry."

Baron turned, tapping the panel on the large cylindrical pod across from Eric's. Baron slid a thin lever to the left, and a plate retracted, exposing the window underneath. Locked inside the steel tomb, Cybertooth writhed in fury, but his restraints held him in place.

"I'm gonna bust out of here and tear you to pieces!" Cybertooth screamed from within his pod—his crackling voice pumped in via Eric's pod's speakers.

Trapped, the sound bounced off the metal walls mere inches from Eric's sore ears. Panic seized Eric's muscles, but he forced his eyes open.

Baron stood to the side, so Eric peered through. He watched the villain behind the other pod's window. Thick steel clamps wrapped around Cybertooth's ashen neck and metallic arms, holding him steady as he wriggled like a savage animal refusing to be tamed.

"Computer, display info," Baron commanded.

Holographic statistics and data projected on the glass in front of Cybertooth's fuming face.

"Hmm. All test results came back negative," Baron said. "I'm still uncertain where you received your power enhancements, but you're still just a cyborg."

Cybertooth's squirming persisted.

"How disappointing," Baron admitted. "I spent too many fruitless nights studying these villainous nuisances, desperate to find a link to something greater. My patience has been rewarded, however, and soon enough, none of this will matter."

His eyes met Eric's through the glass.

"Thanks to you. Do you see this, Eric?"

"Big mistake showing yourself to me!" Cybertooth shouted from behind the window. "I'm gonna find everyone you love and rip 'em apart! I'll remember that face!"

"The truth is, Cybertooth," Baron said as he tapped a button on the panel below the window. "You won't remember much of anything."

White gas hissed into the pod's interior. Cybertooth shifted his eyes, angry and confused.

Oh no! Eric silently screamed. *Mr. Maddox is insane! There's gotta be a way to warn Jaycee! To warn everyone!*

A thick, sharp needle plunged into Cybertooth's temple. Eric gasped while watching him jitter in agony, vibrating until his eyes went dead. The needle removed itself from the half man-half machine, and his head dropped as far as the restraints allowed. Cybertooth's metal faceplate slid down, then fully fell off his head. The exposed orifice spewed out wires and vomited cords.

The data projection reappeared with Cybertooth's vital signs. The monitor showed his heart rate as a fidgeting line that spiked with every slow beat. The brain activity displayed an uninterrupted flat line.

"What did you do?!" Eric shouted.

"Removed an undesirable."

"So, anybody you deem unworthy, you'll lock up

and lobotomize, is that it?!"

"If they're lucky."

Baron stepped away from the windowpane.

"You've caused quite the deviation from my plan," Baron said. "While I realign my path, you should rest, Eric. You're going to need all your strength for what's coming next."

The faux-Eliza emerged from the shadows—her empty smile etched across her false face. Baron nodded at her as he tapped his smartwatch.

"Ah!" he said, pleased with himself. "Today is just full of fortuitous variables."

"Let me out of here!" Eric screamed.

"Calm yourself. If you're worried about DNA testing, all the scary needle stuff will come later."

"Somebody help me!" Eric bellowed.

"Don't you want to hear my good news?" Baron asked. "The MegaCore is operational! David can go above and beyond when properly motivated. I hope this runs in the family."

The strange impostor stepped up to Eric's window.

"Good night, sweetie," Eliza said.

Gas poured in from dispensers above Eric's head. The cloudy fumes fogged up the glass. With no choice but to breathe in, his eyes glazed over. Eric slid, so his feet floated above the pod's floorboard. He bobbed like an aimless bubble trapped in the tight confines of the tube.

"I'll get you out of here, Mom," Eric said, the slow words oozing from his drooping lips. "I'll save you..."

His head slumped onto his shoulder, joining his mother in sleep.

Chapter Twenty-Four: *DEPARTURE*

JAYCEE

"THIS IS OUTRAGEOUS, UNFAIR, AND just so typical," Valerie huffed as she approached the cash register tablet where Jaycee waited. "Of course, something comes up just as we are about to finalize everything."

Jaycee leaned on the serving track's three metal rods next to her mother. She let out a frustrated sigh of her own.

And typical Eric, bailing instead of just talking to me, Jaycee thought.

"Coffee. Iced. Black," Valerie said to the unmanned register.

The screen awoke with soft white light. The kitchen hummed to life. Jaycee watched Valerie take a seat at a nearby table.

"And to have one of his airhead assistants tell me he's needed in a meeting that can't wait, well, that's just insulting."

"I'm not on Team Airhead," Jaycee said. "But, I mean, Dad needed assisting, and that's kind of their job."

"If Baron thinks he can wait me out," Valerie said, "then all of his intellectual accolades need to be revoked because that's just plain dumb."

A floating white orb whisked by Jaycee, triggering her into a fighting stance. She lowered a fist when she realized it carried a chilled glass in its steel clamp. The beach ball-sized drone presented Valerie with her coffee. She took her drink, and the server-bot coasted back to the kitchen.

Jaycee spiked her lips into an annoyed smirk as Valerie browsed her phone, sipping away.

"Have fun with your cold brew battle of wits, Mom," Jaycee whispered. "Meanwhile, I'm gonna go find Dad and Eric and get some answers."

Her mother didn't raise her eyes from her phone as Jaycee strode by.

Just keep looking at your phone as I sneak away, easy-peasy.

"Just where are you going, young lady?"

"Bathroom," Jaycee answered while her mind scrambled for lies. "Is that still allowed?"

She picked up the pace en route to the elevator.

"There are restrooms by the cafeteria, you know," Valerie called out.

Jaycee tapped at the button to open the silver doors.

"Ew, the one Eric has been using for the past two days?" she said as she hurried into the car. "I'll take my chances on another floor."

The doors shut, and Jaycee breathed a sigh of relief.

"Seeing how Mom still hasn't figured out I'm Powerhouse, chances are good she'll buy that."

She pressed the button and felt the car lift. In less than a minute, the doors reopened.

Dad could be anywhere. I'll probably have better luck finding Eric first.

Jaycee sprinted through the labyrinthine halls. A door slid open as she approached it. Jaycee rushed in but abruptly halted. Yvette, Melvin, and Tiffany sat at the center table, digging into a spread of extra-large pizzas inside the break room. Dressed in their school clothes, they appeared casual and chatting. Delicious as the pies smelled, Jaycee sniffed something odd in the air. The large windows were tinted black, indicating this was a private party.

"Didn't think you'd be here," Yvette said, glancing up as she sprinkled red pepper from a small packet. "We would've invited you to the last supper."

"I was looking for Eric; I thought he might have stopped by here," Jaycee said, stepping to the edge of the table. "What do you mean, 'last supper?'"

"We figured Ms. Cooper, er, yer mom was keepin' ya outta the loop," Melvin said, piling another slice onto his already stacked plate. "We thought you wouldn't, like, be allowed back into Pantheon Tower— or we woulda totally told you about this at school today."

Melvin slid a piece of pizza from his stack to an empty plate next to his. He shoved it toward Jaycee. Across from Melvin, Tiffany squirmed on her bench in disgust.

"My mom only brought me here because my dad summoned us," Jaycee explained. "He wanted to fast-track whatever official documents are needed to..."

Her eyes drifted into an empty gaze over the open pizza boxes.

"...Give up custody of me. Maybe I won't ever get to come back here after all. Or maybe even see Dad again."

Yvette sent her a woeful look.

"He's keeping you guys," Jaycee said. "But he can't keep his real daughter. I'm sorry, I shouldn't have said anything—"

"No, it's okay," Yvette said. "We're still going to be a team no matter what happens."

"Eric's been off the grid, so his loss," Tiffany said, taking a bite. "He's got the right idea, though. No one can make you sign an NDA if they can't find you."

"An N-D-what's it?" Melvin asked with a mouthful of crust.

"A non-disclosure agreement," Tiffany said, rolling her eyes. "You know, that thing you signed, saying you don't know anything about anything? We always knew you were clueless, Melvin, but I guess it's good to have it in writing."

Jaycee tilted her head, utterly confused.

"Wait, why would you have to sign anything like that?"

"Guess you have been in the dark since the dance," Yvette said. "We all got notices from Truther saying that soon—real soon—we'll have to turn in all of our superhero gear. Dunno where, though—our HQ is off-limits now."

Jaycee stroked her ponytail, trying to compute what they were telling her.

"Wait, so that means—"

"It means we're SOL," Melvin said.

"S-O-what?" Tiffany asked.

"Sh—" Melvin started, then coughed, course-correcting his comment. "...Er, we're out of luck. It means the Super Society is done."

"Mr. Maddox is purging us," Yvette said. "I don't know when we'll have our final mission, but when we do... It'll be as if we never put on the masks."

"No way," Jaycee said, stunned. "He'd never do that!"

"I don't know if you've met your—I mean, 'our' dad," Tiffany said. "But the guy pretty much does whatever he wants."

"It's gonna suck not being Supercut!" Melvin exclaimed, snarling. "What am I gonna do all summer?"

"Mr. Maddox will make you get jobs," Yvette said.

Tiffany and Melvin groaned at that.

"It's not that terrible, you guys," Yvette said. "It's part of a college credit program thing. S'what I did a couple of summers ago."

Jaycee backed away, gutted by the news.

No more Super Society?! I can't believe it. How can they talk about summer break as if this isn't flushing Armageddon?

"Pfft," Melvin scoffed. "I bet Truther won't have to get a regular job."

"Oh, please," Tiffany said. "Truther is just one of the 'himbos' that works for Mr. Maddox."

They still don't even know Dad is Truther, Jaycee thought. *Guess he kept that classified for a reason. Oh man, was Dad planning this all along?*

"Look," Yvette said. "We love being heroes, but it had to end sometime, right? Maybe not risking our necks every other day will be a little better for our health, huh?"

They looked at Yvette, absorbing her authority. Jaycee always admired Go-Go as the team's field commander in combat, but she gained a new level of respect for Yvette Wallace.

"I start Dawson U in the fall," Yvette continued. "Tiffany, you're already a social media influencer without anyone knowing you're Extra. And, Melvin, tell me you wouldn't like getting to spend more time as a dungeon master."

Melvin and Tiffany raised their eyebrows, pursing their lips as they reconsidered their situations. They each nodded, acquiescing that life wouldn't be so awful. Jaycee did not share the sentiment. She frowned, envisioning a dull life at home with her mother.

"And, Jaycee," Yvette said. "We all heard what Eric said at the dance. And... we all saw what happened. But he's had a rough time of it, ya know? You and Eric are still gonna be tight. He'll come around."

"I hope so," Jaycee said, sighing.

DAVID

David caught his haggard reflection in the black mirror of his smartphone's lifeless screen. He hadn't changed clothes since he arrived at Pantheon Tower—unless piloting the Ultranaut suit counted.

I can't let the armor be known as Dreadnaught, he thought. *That can't be my legacy.*

David winced, recalling his fight with Eric. It had been two days since the Dreadnaught disaster, and his son had made no effort to see him.

If I could just somehow make him understand.

David shook the thought away and activated the device in his hand. Reviewing his screen, he directed his eyes to the power level (low), the news alert notification amount (high), as well as the network connectivity status (through the roof). His second-natured reflexes nearly sent the phone back into his pocket—belt clips were terribly uncool—but he decided to keep it out just in case Eric called or texted. The statistical improbability of that happening saddened him, but David still wanted to be prepared for an instant connection.

It's not like I have anything else to do.

The yellowish-metal walls of the workshop seemed so much farther apart now that drafting tables, three-dimensional printers, and generators were seized. David stood in the center of an oversized hollow rectangle—an emptied toy box. The oddly patterned tiles of the walls were more visible, and the ceiling seemed much higher. Even stranger was the sight of Jaycee approaching him.

"Mr. B, I don't know if I'm supposed to be here—in fact, I know I'm not," the girl said before huffing out a frustrated sigh. "This is a long shot, but... I'm looking for Eric, and... Well, I'm worried about him."

"Eric is a very troubled boy," David said. "He won't talk to me, and, frankly, I don't blame him. Eric just needs time to process. But he's being well looked after. In the meantime, he wants space, and I'm respecting that."

Her head moved from right to left, taking in the emptiness of the lab.

"Space, huh?" she said. "What've you been doing in here, anyway? Is this what 'genius jail' looks like?"

The bags under David's eyes felt like saggy anchors.

"If you're referring to... the dance..." he said, carefully choosing his language. "Pantheon likes to handle things internally."

"Terrorizing my friends and me in your exo-suit seemed pretty external to me."

"That was a malfunction!" David snapped.

Jaycee didn't flinch. Her steely stare troubled

him. This girl was used to facing erratic outbursts—he wondered how much worse she's had to handle in her young life.

"That wasn't my fault," David said after collecting himself.

"Yeah, well, while you were glitched out, that robot tried to execute Eric."

"I know," David said, forcing the grim words from his mouth. "I may not have been in control of the armor, but the optic and audio sensors were working just fine. I... I saw and heard everything."

Jaycee eased up—but not too much.

"You don't need to fret, Ms. Maddox; I won't be going anywhere anytime soon. Pantheon Tower is my gilded cage for the time being."

"Poor you," Jaycee said, crossing her arms. "Do most prisoners get paid as much as you are?"

"I'll let you know once I finally get a check."

"Oh, I'm sure it's just sooo awful for you here," Jaycee mocked. "I'd do anything to stay here, but I've pretty much been evicted."

She threw her head back, releasing her arms as if giving up entirely.

"Ugh! Things are all so messed up! Everything has gotten so weird lately. Outta the blue, Dad wants to ditch me, Eric ghosts me, and I'm the only one who seems to realize how flushing horrible all this is!"

A flat frown formed on Jaycee's face.

"What's gonna happen to Eric?" Jaycee asked, quieting her voice as if discussing a forbidden subject. "I'll see him at school, right?"

That steel outer shell of hers had thinned a bit. David pitied her as much as he could anyone.

"From what I was told, he'll complete his studies here with tutors."

The weight of the unwelcome news slunk her shoulders.

"Ms. Maddox—Jaycee," he said to her.

Her head sunk, looking at the floor.

"Things are pretty messed up right now," David continued. "Heck, I'm the mayor of Messed-Upville."

Jaycee looked up just enough to squint and scrunch her nose, souring at the bad joke. But, in a way, it comforted David.

"When he's ready, Eric will make a move. That goes for your dad, too. Until then, it's best if you leave things be."

"You don't know me that well, do you?" Jaycee said.

She walked away. David watched her turn a corner and vanish. He rested his face on the cool metal wall. Eyes closed, he considered dozing off in hopes of dreamless sleep.

"Subterfuge suits you," Baron said as he emerged from behind him. "Sprinkling truths into crafted lies. Very natural."

Baron stood before David. The man's sleek gray suit looked too perfectly tailored and clean. Something then commanded David to check his black shirt for stains or crumbs.

"You have my wife," David said. "There's nothing natural about any of this."

The words felt heavy and tasted foul.

"Did you come to tell me it's done?" David asked, almost afraid of the answer.

"It was not as exactly as I envisioned," Baron said. "But Eric is detained. For the time being—for his own safety. Throwing a monkey wrench in my well-laid plans seems to be a family trait with you Boxworths."

"Learning you kept Eliza here all this time…"

David said. "That wasn't really on the agenda, either. I still can't believe it. But you did save her, or what could be saved."

"The efforts to keep Eliza maintained are not without consequences."

"It's best that Eric is in a pod," David said, brushing his hair back. "He's too delicate to handle seeing her this way. Jeez, I can't even bring myself to see her."

Rubbing his eyes left hazy twinkling spots clouding his vision.

"Eliza could fly. And my engine will fuel the transference of her abilities to you. You! Baron Maddox—with superpowers!"

David placed his hands on his knees. His chest heaved, taking a deep breath.

"If I threw up, would a little drone come and clean it up?"

"I know this is a lot to take in," Baron said, putting a hand on David's shoulder.

David batted it away.

"If I asked how you're going to do it—specifically," David said, standing straight. "Using the MegaCore's power generation, I mean. Would you tell me?"

"Divert your focus on what's truly important."

"You're right," David said, relenting. "Eric is safe; that's all that matters."

"He is. And my daughter is safe as well, thanks to your cooperation. Jaycee may never forgive me, but she will be removed from any danger."

"It's still unforgivable what you did," David said, sneering. "You hacked into Ultranaut! Then, you reset the system back to its original programming. You reactivated Dreadnaught!"

"You went rogue," Baron said, shrugging. "You

deviated, so I inhibited you. But it led to an opportunity to further include you in what will reshape humankind. To cement your destiny."

"You mean it's easier to keep me in line this way."

David scoffed, shaking his head.

"You went so far as to dress up in your Truther costume," David said. "Which is still just unreal to think about. The little twerps all look the same to me. I get why I couldn't figure out that Eric's classmates were the other Super Society members. But you? I should've spotted you, Barry."

David raised an eyebrow, sizing up Baron.

"You were there, ready to whisk me away in that helicopter of yours. You let it all play out; the fight between me, in the armor, versus Eric—the whole dance disaster. How long were you going to let that go on? You really expect Eric to go along with your little power trip once he wakes up?"

"You have much to learn about loyalty," Baron said. "I wasn't specifically steering the boy's allegiance away from you, but rather, it was all to navigate his trust toward me."

Angered, David stepped closer to Baron, face-to-face. Baron's dark, deep mustache hung over an unmoving and unimpressed frown.

"You can make him a fancy costume and parade him around as your toy superhero," David said, eyes narrowed. "You can have all the stolen powers you want, but my son will never willingly follow you, especially not now. You've been lying to him from the start so you can get what you want."

"You had no qualms about dishonesty when speaking to Jaycee."

"The part about wanting to get paid was true," David said.

"Oh, David," Baron said, backing away. "What more incentive could you possibly need?"

He gestured for someone to enter.

"Eliza," Baron said, leading the young woman in from the hallway. "I believe you and your husband have much catching up to do."

She was as beautiful as the first time David ever laid eyes on her. Her deep brown eyes shined like they did the day at the advanced machine learning conference. David flashed back to how they met, standing in the same line to see some presenter they'd both forgotten the name of. Those full lips spreading that hopeful smile he'd tattooed on his brain had also been preserved somehow. The unmistakable strawberry blonde hair that flowed just a tad below her shoulders still stirred him. Her violet blouse hung loosely on her, slightly hiding the stunning form David so vividly remembered. She was young again.

"How fun; I never get to talk to any of Mr. Maddox's eggheads," she said. "I'm gonna pick your brain clean! Just how in the world does your machine work...?"

David's unrested mind quieted the doubt of this being real and simply watched his wife talk. Eliza's voice sounded just as playful (an overbearingly cute trait that David always smiled at, which infuriated her during arguments), but his drowsy reverie muffled the words. The memories of his spouse's untimely demise during the ill-fated weapons demonstration haunted the back of his skull. The ghosts of the past were not strong enough to cloud this moment. At that minute, that second, David was no longer a widow and once more just a fool in love.

"I have kept Valerie waiting in the cafeteria long enough," Baron said. "Her wrath is not something I look forward to."

Baron made his way out. Before disappearing into the corridor, he looked back.

"You'll be protected from what's to come."

Baron walked out of sight, but his voice carried a parting message.

"Enjoy this second chance, David," he said. "But the next time you feel roguish, remember who gave you this new future."

"It's so sad about that other Eliza, right?" she said into David's smiling eyes. "Warming in that oven of hers, but only half-cooked."

She sounded nothing like the woman he married, but that person was an empty shell now—a husk being mined for scientific data... and power.

"There's nothing left of her. Not for me," David said, grabbing Eliza's hand with a soft touch. "I'm not reopening that wound."

Her smooth skin sent shivers up David's body.

"We can do it over now," he said.

David's rough hands didn't feel worthy.

"I'll get us the means to leave here. We'll do anything we want, free from everything!"

"You just might be the most peculiar man I've ever met," she said, smiling wide with blank eyes. "Can we bring that flying boy of yours? He's got a wild streak in him! It's not good for one so young to be alone."

"Eric will, in time, understand," David said, drawing her closer. "This is our chance to be a family again."

He kissed her. Still stretched in a grin, Eliza's lips slowly pressed against his. He pulled away and held up their hands, entwined as one.

"This is our chance to go home."

ABOUT THE AUTHOR

As an author drawn to superhero sci-fi aimed at young adult readers, Jon McBrine adds a unique spin on coming-of-age stories - by adding superpowers, snarky villains, and big robot fights. Focused on pure fun and adventure, Jon also showcases the people under the mask (and spandex).

Jon works in the Dallas area as an author, graphic designer, illustrator, and comic book aficionado. He combines these different fields of work to build interesting projects that capture humor, intrigue, and authentic emotion. His ever-evolving career trajectory keeps his sense of wonder alive—and his coffee cup full.